Randa Abdel-Fattah is an aw
bestselling author of *Does My He*
author of eight novels for young adults, Randa is also a
litigation lawyer and human rights activist. *No Sex in the City*
is her first adult novel. She lives in Sydney, Australia, with her
husband and two children.

www.randaabdelfattah.com
@RandaAFattah

Also by Randa Abdel-Fattah

Does My Head Look Big in This?
Ten Things I Hate About Me
Where the Streets Had a Name
The Friendship Matchmaker
The Friendship Matchmaker Goes Undercover
Noah's Law
Buzz Off

RANDA ABDEL-FATTAH

No Sex
in the City

SAQI

Published 2013 by Saqi Books

1

© Randa Abdel-Fattah 2013

ISBN 978 0 86356 711 7
eISBN 978 0 86356 716 2

A full CIP record for this book is available from the British Library.

Printed and bound by CPI Group (UK) Ltd, Croydon, CR0 4YY

Saqi Books
26 Westbourne Grove, London W2 5RH
www.saqibooks.com

It's only fitting that I dedicate this book to my loving husband, Ibrahim El-Kadomi, who thankfully swept me off my feet from the moment we met (in the family-lounge-room-first-date-arranged-set-up style), early enough to save me from too many matchmaking disasters.

One

It is a truth universally acknowledged that a single man in possession of a student visa must be in want of an Australian wife.

This truth is so well fixed in the minds of single girls who hold Australian citizenship that any such young man, whatever his feelings, is instantly suspected of being more interested in obtaining permanent residence than genuinely falling in love with them.

Hassan from Turkey, who is at this moment sitting in my lounge room eating crème caramel, confirms this truth. Hassan has been in Australia for a little over five months. He has an IT degree under one arm, student visa under the other, and barely speaks a word of English. Well, apart from his recitation of the lyrics of *Titanic*'s theme song, 'My Heart Will Go On'.

Poor Hassan. It's so obvious to me that he's interested in me because a) I'm single and the matchmaking busybody aunties in my local Turkish network know I'm 'available'; and b) I'm an Australian citizen and so would be Hassan's ticket to permanent residence.

Hassan has brought along his equally visaless roommate, Salih, for support. Salih's in the family room, making small talk with my parents (no doubt trying to ascertain the marital status of any other female members of the family), while I sit in the formal lounge room with Hassan, trying to have a conversation with somebody who has an English vocabulary range of about forty words, and who expends most of them on asking me if I know 'how to speak the Turkish'.

'No,' I lie.

'You no speak the Turkish?' he presses.

'No, I no speak the Turkish,' I repeat in a droll voice.

I'm a pretty reasonable person. But if there's one rule I'm going to insist on it's that The One has to speak English. Although I can understand Turkish, I don't speak it fluently enough to express myself as well as I'd like (in fact, my parents speak to me in Turkish and I reply in English). As far as I'm concerned, you can't communicate effectively with somebody when you're too busy concentrating on the grammatical composition of your sentences.

Hassan looks crushed. I smile weakly at him and take a sip of my tea. I look around the room. I must remind Mum that the chair in the corner needs to be reupholstered. If I'm going to put up with this lounge room on such a frequent basis, we may as well redecorate in my favourite colours.

When Salih telephoned my dad out of the blue, explaining he'd obtained our number from Aunty Sevil, who'd obtained our number from Aunty Arzu (both of

8

whom were complete strangers to our family), he reassured my dad that Hassan knew English. My father took the usual biodata: age, education, family, visa status and English proficiency. I agreed to invite him to our home because I'm still optimistic enough to believe that your destiny can spring up when you least expect it.

I'm willing to compromise on visa status if sparks fly and it's Mr Right walking through the door. There are plenty of Aussie-born dropkicks, so I don't automatically discriminate and assume every overseas student or visitor is an undercover visa hunter.

But English proficiency is another matter altogether. The chances of sparks flying with a guy who knows forty English words (most of them exhausted on a Celine Dion song) are pretty low. Either Salih was embellishing, or he has a different understanding of what it means to *know* a language.

'So what do you think about the current state of federal politics?' I ask. 'Do you think there's a lack of policy conviction?'

Yes, okay, I'm cruel.

Hassan gives me a blank look, takes a gulp of his tea and then says, 'I love cooking and the bitch.'

'The beach?'

'Yes, the bitch.'

He grins at me. So far he has about ten variations of smiling. The 'I have no clue what you just said' smile. The 'maybe if I flash my teeth like so, she will forget we can't communicate to save our life' smile, and so on.

I smile. Queasily. I need to put the poor guy out of his misery. Only he doesn't seem too miserable. For God's sake, what if he thinks this is actually working? Well, his commitment to memory of a Celine Dion song is just not turning me on. So I sit up straight, fix my eyes on his and say, 'Ah, Hassan, I'm sorry but I don't see this going anywhere. You're obviously a very sweet guy but I think it's important that people in a relationship can actually have a conversation. I'm sure there are more suitable girls out there who paid attention during Turkish weekend school. I was too busy sticking chewing gum under the desks to learn much. Unfortunately we can't get by in Turkish *or* English and I don't know sign language. I also suck at Pictionary, so I can't exactly draw you a representational diagram every time I want to communicate with you. So goodbye and good luck.'

Okay, so I don't say that. While I can be cruel, I'm not *that* cruel. I endure another ten minutes of Hassan's extensive repertoire of smiles, interspersed with him quizzing me again on how much of 'the Turkish' I know, whether I like *Titanic* and how often I swim in the bitch. Finally, when I consider it polite to end our formal-lounge-room first date, I stand up and invite him back into the family room.

Salih and Hassan leave a short while later, Hassan managing to actually look hopeful when we say our goodbyes.

When Mum closes the door I throw up my hands in frustration. 'No way!'

'So much for being fluent in English, hey?' my dad says

gruffly, shaking his head.

'He had nice eyes and was very polite,' Mum says.

'You don't have to be so kind, Mum,' I groan. 'He's not your son.'

'Didn't I tell you time and time again to pay attention at Saturday school?' she says.

'Oh Mum, don't even go there.' I turn to my dad. 'When he calls, tell him I didn't feel *the click*. But go easy on the poor guy. He's emotionally fragile ... a Celine Dion fan, for God's sake.'

I stomp upstairs to my bedroom, ignoring my mum's rant to my dad about my obsession with 'clicking', and throw myself face down on my bed.

I've had enough.

I'm twenty-eight.

I'm attractive (according to my friends and family who never, *ever* lie about these things).

I've got a master's in human resource management, I volunteer every month at the Sydney Refugee Centre, I'm well travelled, I have excellent taste in music, I watch the ABC news, I have the *Guardian* saved as an application on my iPhone, I'm very good at getting maximum points out of two-letter words in Scrabble, I never jump queues, I pay my bills on time, I never order 'just a salad', I'm great with kids, I don't freak out at the sight of a spider, I turn off the tap when I'm brushing my teeth – Goddammit! I DESERVE TO BE SWEPT OFF MY FEET!

Calm down.

Take deep breaths.

But how can I calm down when my checklist means that the pool from which I'll pluck out Mr Right is pretty small? That is:

1. He has to be Muslim. (I don't care what ethnicity. If he's Turkish it's just a bonus as it means the in-laws will have more in common.)

2. Even though I want to be with a Muslim, I'm not exactly observant. Spiritual? Yes. Rituals? Quite lazy. Sure, I don't drink, I've never had a boyfriend (in fact, most primary-aged children would have more experience than me) and I'm inconsistent about keeping up with the five daily prayers. As for fasting in Ramadan, I try to get through most of the month, but there are days when I cave in to the temptation and end up going to McDonald's. Notwithstanding, it would be nice to meet someone on the same religious level, or even a bit more observant than me. Not a totally clueless guy, or a fanatic either.

3. Mr Right has to be educated and employed and care about social justice.

4. He doesn't have to be super good-looking by any objective *Cleo* or *Cosmo* measure. Just attractive to me.

5. Oh! And he has to exist outside my fantasies.

I'm well and truly fed up with meeting guys who barely make it past dot point one. I need to vent, but I can't exactly talk about this to my colleagues, who think I make Mormons look wild given that I'm a twenty-eight-year-old non-drinking virgin who is open to the idea of a blind date organised by family. (I'm happy to meet a guy at a party or through friends too, but, really, who am I kidding? With my kind of checklist, what are the chances?)

Sample scene one:

'So you're twenty-eight. And you've never had sex? Never even kissed a guy?'

'Nope.'

(Cue bodies thudding to the ground and ambulance sirens blaring.)

Sample scene two:

'You don't date?'

'Nope.'

'So how do you get to know a guy *before* you get married? You need to try before you buy.'

Honestly, you'd think I was going to meet my future husband on my wedding day – quick introduction in the car park and on with the nuptials. It's a bit hard to explain that I've got to know guys without being their girlfriend. I'm like a character in an old Doris Day movie: all old-fashioned courtship and pent-up sexual tension. Well, maybe not. Those movies are nauseatingly sexist. Okay, so it's probably better explained as two people getting to know each other with a mutual understanding that their 'dating' is limited to their search for a marriage partner. Now I sound like Wikipedia. Needless to say, none of the explanations tend to go down too well.

Eg: 'But that's so backward! How can you marry a guy you've never even kissed? Haven't Samantha and Carrie taught you anything?'

'Yeah, how to match my accessories with my outfit.'

I'm twenty-eight, armed with a personalised checklist, ready for a love life and most definitely *not* having sex in the city.

I sit up against my headboard, perching my MacBook on my lap. I log on to my email account and send an email to my best friends, Lisa, Ruby and Nirvana.

There are many things that unite us, not least that we're active in the community, passionate about politics and human rights, single, living at home and time poor.

Lisa Roth works half the week as a caseworker at the Sydney Refugee Centre and the other half in a women's refuge. One word sums her up: dedicated. Working in the community sector is never a nine-to-five job, and Lisa often works long hours or takes her work home. I know this because I volunteer after-hours at the refugee centre and Lisa's always there past five o'clock. She usually stays back so that we leave together.

Ruby Georgiou is a lawyer in one of Sydney's top-tier firms. It goes without saying that she has insane working hours. Given that she's one of the youngest lawyers on a fast-track path to partnership, it's little wonder. Add to that her pro bono work at a legal centre in Redfern and you can understand why she's rarely home. As for Nirvana Ajmera, she's a midwife and does shift work, including regular graveyard shifts, which is when most babies choose to announce their arrival. Nirvana also teaches Sindhi to preschoolers at Saturday morning classes at her local temple.

The four of us met at a protest at Sydney University, which is where we all studied. I think it was about student union fees, or the wars in Iraq and Afghanistan, or overpriced food on campus. I can't remember exactly because we seemed to be protesting about something every month. There were some guys standing near us who weren't taking it seriously, talking throughout the speeches. When one of them made a comment about the speaker's breasts, we simultaneously blasted them. They didn't know what had hit them, being ripped to shreds by four girls from different directions. The four of us had a laugh afterwards, introduced ourselves to each other, and quickly became the best of friends.

So it's only natural they're the ones I email. It's been a while since we've all been free at the same time for a catch-up.

Oi! Lisa, Ruby and Nirvana,

Okay, so we're all on the 'Where is The One hiding out?' quest. (Don't deny it, Lisa. I know you must be too.) Are they lost in Ikea, desperately trying to find the exit? Are they being questioned at Sydney Airport while being filmed for *Border Security*? Have they fallen into a manhole? Are they delayed on a Tiger Airways flight?

I'm out of answers!

Are you finding it increasingly hard not to self-combust after yet another failed matchmaking experience, either of the traditional kind (Nirvana and me), or the setting up by friends/eyes locking across a crowded room/etc kind (all of us)? And I bet my life that, like me, you're all sick to death of hearing people call you 'old-fashioned', 'prude', 'frigid', 'picky', 'fussy' (the list goes on).

As you can tell, I need to vent. So I hereby declare the

official and virtual inauguration of the No Sex in the City Club.

Our first meeting is on Friday, 8 p.m., Chocolate Spice in Newtown. Come along with your emotional baggage, horror stories, impossible checklists, twenty-something angst and an appetite for a high-calorie emotional-eating pig-out session. If you're dieting (that means you, Nirvana – no points calculators or carb-to-protein ratios allowed), positive, optimistic or in love, don't bother showing up. Only those who can truly indulge in a proper dose of self-pity (and comfort eating) are invited.

Love Esma

PS. I miss you guys. It's been two weeks. What's that about?

Two

I work at a recruitment agency finding potential employees for various clients, predominantly in the pharmaceutical industry. It's Friday and I'm on my way to my last appointment for the day, at a pharmacy in Bondi. It's two in the afternoon and the traffic is killing me. I turn up the music in my car (a bomb of a Honda Civic that is the bane of my mum's existence as she can't understand why I'm nearly thirty and still haven't managed to save up for a 'nice-looking' car). Pearl Jam blares out of the speakers and I instantly feel calm. Until a truck veers onto my side of the road. I swerve out of the way and slam my hand down hard on the horn. The truckie sticks his head out of his window and yells, 'Ah get ova ya PMS willya!'

'Learn how to drive!' I yell back.

The traffic light changes and the truckie blows me a kiss and continues in the opposite direction, leaving me fuming.

I just want to get the appointment over and done with so I can get back on the road before the real traffic jam begins. I live about an hour's drive away from Bondi – when there's no traffic. If I get trapped on the motorway in peak hour I'll never make it home in time to get ready for tonight and drive to Newtown to meet the girls.

When I finally arrive at the pharmacy I take the liberty of parking in a staff car space. I quickly apply some lip gloss, get my file in order, smooth out my hair and hurry in through the front door to meet Mrs Goldman, who ushers me to the back room for our meeting.

'Like I told you on the phone,' she says as she pours me a glass of chilled water, 'I want someone hard-working and honest.'

'Of course,' I respond, smiling broadly at her. 'That's the least an employer can expect. I've short-listed four résumés for you to review. As you specified, they are all recent graduates with excellent qualifications.'

'And Jewish,' she adds.

I blink at her.

'Jewish only,' she repeats, holding out her hand for the résumés.

'Er ... well ... that isn't really appropriate,' I say.

'What do you mean?' she snaps. 'Is being Jewish inappropriate?'

'No, I didn't mean it that way! I mean it's, well, it's unlawful to discriminate on the grounds of—'

She waves her hands at me and cuts me off. 'Don't talk to me about the law,' she says. 'People do this all the time. You go to Cabramatta and everyone working there is Vietnamese. Are you telling me that's pure coincidence? You go to Lakemba and they're all Muslim. Work with the rules of life, Esma, not against them. Find me a Jewish graduate. Most of my customers are Jewish and I want somebody who understands their needs.' She snatches the résumés from me and looks at the one on top.

'Huh!' she exclaims. 'You think an old Jewish bachelor is going to ask *Indira Singh* for Viagra? He wants to ask Naomi Kreutner, who can then go spread the word and *bang*, he's back in the dating scene again.'

The way I see it, asking Indira Singh would protect the old fellow's anonymity. Wouldn't he prefer that to having his local community knowing he was throwing back Viagra?

Oh well, who am I to argue? I've been a virgin for twenty-eight years. I'm not exactly an expert on Viagra.

Mrs Goldman flips through the résumés and hands them back to me. 'Not one Jewish name,' she says with a sigh. 'Back to the drawing board, Esma.'

'I can't advertise in a way that discriminates against non-Jews,' I say.

She flashes me a condescending smile. 'My dear, nobody is asking you to break the law. I pay you to be creative in the screening process. Ask the right questions and you will work it out. And don't feel bad. People do this all the time.'

'Really?' I mutter, knowing full well that she's right.

'Of course! It was only yesterday that I was talking to a friend who's started a waxing business. Most of her clients are of a Mediterranean background, so she needs an assistant who knows how to rip off that kind of hair. Most of the Anglos, well, you couldn't make a tiny plait out of their leg hair. And still they complain!' She stands up abruptly. 'Don't disappoint me, okay?'

I smile warily and collect my things. 'I won't,' I say, conscious that my boss will kill me if I lose this contract, given that the Goldmans own five pharmacies across the eastern suburbs and have only just come on board as a new client.

The traffic on the way home is bad but not shocking. I call my boss, Danny Blagojevic, and give him a blast about Mrs Goldman.

'You're overreacting,' he scolds. 'She's the client and it's up to her to hire whoever she wants. It happens all the time.'

'I'm going to pretend I didn't hear that,' I mumble.

'Like she said, it all comes back to the screening process. Just specify that speaking Hebrew is a bonus. Advertise in the *Jewish News*. Use your imagination ... So how'd your family date go the other night?'

I almost hit the car in front of me.

'*Excuse me?* How on earth do you know about that? And it wasn't a *family date*.'

'I heard you on the phone. So the guy was fresh off the boat, hey?'

'I'm really not sure what you mean by that, Danny,' I say. 'Are you referring to European settlers?'

He chuckles. 'If you want to hook up with an asylum seeker, that's your call. But how's he going to afford a ring or house when he's locked up in a detention centre?'

'That's offensive, Danny.'

'When are you going to realise it's not the eighteen hundreds?' he presses. 'They had the sexual liberation movement in the sixties for a reason, you know.'

'Oh, give it up,' I say mildly.

What I really want to say is, *Shut the F up, Danny!* But self-preservation wins out.

Let me explain. Danny's a forty-year-old spoilt rich boy in an unhappy relationship ('My wife married me, put on ten kilos and has been a bitch to me ever since'), who opened the recruitment firm when he was twenty-three and has since refused several offers to buy it for over a million dollars. He likes his expensive clothes, expensive watches, expensive cars. He's a pretentious prick who can turn on the charm one moment and viciously cut you down the next.

The thing is, I've never been in his bad books. In fact, for reasons that elude me, I'm his favourite. And it makes our relationship excruciating.

'I told you, you're crazy to want to settle down,' he says. 'Marco's a top bloke. I'll set you up with him – you can have some fun, and Jesus, if it works out and you're that desperate for commitment, he might even call himself your boyfriend. But trust me: you don't want to get married. Only masochists choose that path.'

'Not everybody is unhappily married,' I say. 'So don't go projecting your failures onto the rest of us.'

'Ooh, see, that's why I want to set you up with Marco. You two are never lost for words.'

'Have a great weekend, Danny,' I say.

'Yeah, that's frigging unlikely given Mary's forcing me to go furniture shopping with her.'

I want to tell Danny where he can stick his furniture shopping, but he's my boss. There's only so much I can say without crossing the line. And as annoyed as I am by his constant remarks about my way of life (not drinking, making up excuses to get out of after-work partying sessions at the local club, wanting to settle down with a Muslim, volunteering to help 'queue jumpers'), I've never taken him on about any of it. I need this job too badly.

Because I have a secret.

About two years ago, my dad's 'gambling for fun' turned into a serious addiction. He hasn't been near a fruit machine since, and is slowly trying to get his life back on track. The thing is this: I'm part of the 'back on track' plan. And nobody, including my mum or my sister, Senem, knows about it.

I only know because I came home from work early one day to find Dad alone, sobbing in the lounge room. Before then I'd only ever seen my dad cry when his mother and, later, his father passed away.

'Dad?' I said, shocked. 'What's wrong?'

'Our house,' he said. 'Our house.'

That's when I noticed the letter in his hand. I walked over to him. It was from the bank, advising of the arrears on a loan. Our house had been used as security against the loan. The letter warned that the last two monthly repayments had to be paid within seven days or enforcement steps would be taken. I almost cried out when I saw the outstanding balance: just under one hundred thousand dollars. I remember the burning sensation that came over my face, as though I'd stuck my head in the doors of a furnace.

'What's going on?' I asked, desperately trying to remain calm as I sat down next to him.

'Your mother doesn't know,' he choked out. 'Neither does your sister. Nobody knows. This is between you and me only.'

My mum, who defies most of the usual stereotypes about migrants, housewives and Muslims (the trifecta), has nonetheless always been happy to leave Dad with the responsibility of managing the finances. Since migrating from Turkey, she hasn't done a single day's paid work, preferring instead to be a housewife. She's happy to let Dad be responsible for paying the bills and mortgage. Dad has had lots of jobs but for the past ten years he's mainly worked as a cleaner at a hospital. I always thought that this must work for them, because I'd never known them to fight about money.

I nodded and he took a deep breath, wiping his eyes with the back of his sleeve. I'd never seen him so vulnerable; he seemed defeated and helpless. Then and there the dynamics between us shifted for good. I was still his daughter, of course, but suddenly I was also his confidante.

I'd grown up to believe that my parents were infallible; I was their daughter and respected them as wiser and more experienced. That didn't mean I wouldn't argue and fight and attempt to shift the power balance when it suited me, but there was always a line – drawn out of respect, deference and gratitude – that I would never dare cross.

Every word Dad uttered that day threatened to erase that line.

'I never meant for this to happen,' he said, speaking to me in Turkish. His voice was thick with shame. 'It was just for fun at first. When I was with my friends at the club I was happy. One thing led to another and we tried the fruit machine. You win once and you think, *Why can't I win again?* I couldn't stop. Like my smoking.' He let out a small, cheerless laugh. 'The cigarette burns down to a stub and I look at it, surprised by how quickly it's gone. So I reach for another cigarette, thinking I'll savour this one, but then in another second I forget I'm smoking. It's become so natural to me that I hardly know I'm doing it. That's how the gambling was.'

I sucked in my breath. 'Are you still gambling?' I eventually asked.

'No, thank God I quit. I met somebody at the mosque ... he'd gone through the same thing and he's helped me. And I haven't gone near a machine for two years.'

'Two *years* ... How have you kept this from us – from Mum – for so long?'

He stared down at the carpet. He hadn't looked me in the eye since he'd started speaking. 'There are many things that even the closest of people can hide from each other. Being deceitful is easier than being honest, especially when the other person has such trust in you.'

I tried not to cry as he spoke.

'I took out a loan against the house, but I've missed a couple of payments. That's why the bank is now chasing me. And this is why, Esma ...' He turned to face me then, grabbing my hands and holding on tight. 'I *need* you, darling. I have no one but you to depend on. I *can't* lose this house. Your mother would never forgive me. It would destroy her – the betrayal, the shame.' He squeezed my hands. 'I need to ask you to please help me pay the loan.'

Dad went on to explain how he'd taken extra shifts at work but that it was getting very hard to meet the monthly repayments. He needed my help. He also needed me to keep his secret, even from my sister, Senem. He didn't want Senem's husband, Farouk, to know. It would mean losing face in front of his son-in-law.

'I've begged God's forgiveness,' he continued. 'And I beg yours too. But I don't wish to beg forgiveness from your mother. We have to spare her that.'

I couldn't sleep much that night. I thought long and hard. Cried. Wallowed in self-pity, anger and hurt. I remember I woke up numb. I left the house for work before Mum was up, glad I didn't have to look her in the eye and pretend that the security she took for granted rested squarely on my shoulders. Dad had already left. He was working longer hours now.

When I arrived at work I sent an email to the accounts department instructing them to direct debit more than a third of my wages to my dad's loan account.

So that explains why I'm tied to a job I love but a boss I hate. Every time Danny edges into sleaze territory I have to bite my tongue, because my parents' house, and maybe their marriage, depends on me keeping this job.

Three

My sister, Senem, is one year younger than me and is so happily married it's sickening. Of course, I love her to bits and I wish her all the happiness in the world. Hers is one of those 'you wouldn't believe it ...' stories.

It started like this. When Senem finished her beauty therapy course at TAFE, she worked at a salon that shared the same floor as a Chinese massage parlour in a shop along a prominent road in the eastern suburbs. There was nothing dodgy about it, and yet the fact that the salon was next to a remedial massage parlour meant that a lot of men would arrive for a spray tan or back wax and expect to be offered something more as part of the price. Senem got sick and tired of having to call security. It turned her off the whole industry altogether. Well, that and the Brazilian waxes.

After Senem quit her job, she got a job with Virgin Blue, working at the check-in counter at Sydney Airport's domestic terminal. She was lucky enough to get a long break before starting and went on a holiday to Turkey with Mum. Within four days of arriving, Senem met her soulmate, The One, at our grandmother's house.

Our grandmother was hosting a massive feast for all the family and friends in honour of Mum and Senem visiting. Farouk, the son of my grandmother's cousin's friend's brother's daughter (or something like that), was invited. It was all arranged. We know this because my grandmother has never shied away from reminding us that the only reason she's hanging onto life is because she wants to see us married.

It was arranged that Senem and Farouk would be seated next to each other at the table. Apparently one of our younger second (or was it third?) cousins attempted to sit next to Senem and my grandmother rapped her knuckles with her walking stick. She's a charmer, my grandmother.

Senem called me later that night to announce she'd fallen in love. I told her she was an idiot and should stop watching movies starring Drew Barrymore. She insisted she'd experienced love at first family-get-together sight. This was inconceivable to me as Senem has always been the rebel of the family and, unlike me, had absolutely no tolerance for family set-ups.

I demanded proof. She explained that she'd been so mesmerised by Farouk that she'd drunk a glass of Coke.

Enough said.

Senem is gorgeous and works hard to maintain her beautiful hair, beautiful skin and beautiful white teeth. She is scrupulous about what she eats (organic mainly), sips on herbal tea and warm water between meals, and even now still maintains her Friday-night ritual of a face mask, nail kit and rom-com DVD. So basically she would rather touch a used syringe than drink Coke. She practically uses gloves when she plays her 'look at the coin in the Coke' party trick.

Within three weeks of Senem drinking Coke, Farouk's family and my extended family got together to celebrate at my grandmother's house. My dad and I were still in Australia and attended the prayer ceremony via Skype. Everybody recited a prayer and Senem and Farouk's intention to marry was officially recognised by the family. One month later, Dad and I flew to Turkey to attend a lavish engagement party. I rejected every guy my grandmother tried to set me up with (because of her myopia she had no clue that she was, for the most part, recommending balding, overweight, cross-eyed guys) and spent most of my free time sightseeing and having the time of my single life, much to my grandmother's consternation.

A year later and Senem and Farouk were married. Which means my grandmother's very life, as she constantly reminds me, now depends on me finding Mr Right.

When I arrive home from Mrs Goldman's pharmacy at six-thirty I find Senem sitting on the kitchen bench helping Farouk with the cooking. I completely forgot they were coming over for dinner tonight.

'I've got to love you and leave you,' I say apologetically, giving Senem a kiss hello.

'Why?' Senem pouts. 'I haven't seen you all week.'

'Yeah, I know, I'm sorry but I've got plans.'

'I'm making my famous lasagne,' Farouk says, dangling a lasagne sheet in front of my face. 'Tempting?'

I laugh. 'Is it that wholemeal crap Senem used to make Mum buy?'

He grins. 'No. Senem insists on having only a salad tonight.' He pulls a face. Senem takes a sip of her water.

I punch my fist in the air and cheer. 'Save me a piece.'

'Why can't you stay?' Senem moans. 'You're so mean. I've got so much to tell you.'

'Yes, but I can't get out of this. It's ... er ... kind of a business meeting.'

'On a Friday night?' Senem isn't convinced.

'Come upstairs and help me pick out an outfit and I'll tell you.'

She hops off the bench and gives Farouk a peck on the cheek. 'See you soon!'

'I'll miss you, hon!'

I stick my finger in my mouth and make barfing noises.

Upstairs in my room I take out two tops and lay them on the bed. I kick off my work pants and put on my jeans.

Senem inspects the tops, chooses the black one and passes it to me. 'So?' she says. 'What meeting are you going to? Amnesty? Human rights lecture? Peace protest?'

'Prefer it if I spent my free time shopping and getting my hair done?' I ask cheerily.

'You do get your hair done and you love to shop.'

I smile ironically. 'Yes, I'm the activist with good hair and style.'

'I wish I could be like you,' she says with a sigh. 'But work is so draining. Not to mention life is *so* much busier since I got married.'

'Oh Senem, that's pathetic. I'll take *any* excuse but that.'

I pick up my eyeliner and apply a thin line. Senem flops down onto my bed and examines her nails.

'Do you remember how we used to talk about finding Mr Right?' I say.

'How could I forget? What he'd look like. His job. How we'd know if he was The One. Whether people's teeth bump when they kiss.'

I burst out laughing. 'Oh my God, yes, I remember that. Anyway, you went and betrayed me by finding Farouk and leaving me at the mercy of matchmakers who'll throw any Turk my way so long as he's single and wants to get married.'

'You have a point. Thank God I never went through that.'

'Yes, you've always been spared a lot of things ...' The words hang in the air but she's flipping through one of my magazines and is oblivious to my meaning.

Senem and I have very different personalities. I'm the dependable one. The one my parents can rely on. The one to cover up for Senem, who always bent the rules more than I did.

'I'm over it,' I say, pulling on the black top. 'Since Seyf, I haven't met a guy who's shared my obsession with Pearl Jam and Tool.'

'No more contact with the scumbag, hey?'

'Nope.'

I've never told her about the last time I saw him. It was at Big Day Out in 2006. I've been listening to Tool for fifteen years, so when they started playing I couldn't help but go a tiny bit mental and run into the mosh pit. The crowd was going nuts and it was so packed that I was being lifted off the ground. The crowd moved and swayed, and before I knew it I was in an empty area, shouting out, 'Yay! Dance space!' I looked around and realised I'd actually been sucked into the fight circle. I panicked, and was knocked around a bit before I managed to get out of there (I lasted four songs, though, and was quite proud of myself). And as I walked away, rubbing my sore arms, a big goofy smile on my face, I saw Seyf standing in the crowd, staring at me, jaw almost to the floor, his wife hanging off his arm.

That knocked the smile off my face.

'How's work?' Senem asks. 'Is your boss still a pig?'

'Yes, unfortunately I'm still working for a Neanderthal who wants to flirt with me *and* set me up with his best friend.'

'No cute single guys who are just as intent as you on saving the world?'

I groan. 'There is nobody eligible at work. Or around work. Or through work. I'm *not* bitter, though,' I say, laughing bitterly.

Senem starts prattling on about how she and Farouk have found their dream apartment and are a couple of months away from saving enough for the deposit.

I'd love to tell her about the predicament I'm in. To tell her that I don't know how I'm ever going to be able to buy a place of my own when I'm managing Dad's debt. I want to vent about the fact that all the pressure is on me to save our parents' marriage. Dad seems to think I have less to lose because I'm single.

But I hold back. I won't betray my dad.

'I want my own place,' I say when she's done talking. 'What if I'm thirty-five and still living at home? That's just tragic. If you've got any suggestions, help me out, because the other night was the last straw.'

'You mean Hassan?'

'Mum told you, huh?'

'She's spewing about your bad Turkish. I told her to get over it, so don't stress.'

'That's easy for you to say.'

'Hey, don't take it out on me. This is my *kismet* – your destiny will come when you least expect it.'

'I swear to God, Senem, if I hear that statement one more time I'm going to stab myself with my nail file.'

'Okay, okay.' She flips over onto her stomach and rests on her elbows. 'So what does all this have to do with your meeting?'

'I've created an excuse to get together with my girl-friends, to vent about the drought of eligible men. The No Sex in the City Club.'

She bursts out laughing. 'Oh come on, it can't be that bad.'

I sit down next to her. 'Don't be so smug. I just want to wallow in some self-pity without being judged, okay?'

She smiles. 'Okay.'

Four

We squeal for five minutes.

'It's been ages!'

'Your hair looks gorgeous red!'

'You've lost weight!'

'I love your shoes!'

When the waiter is fed up waiting for us to move out of the entrance of the restaurant, he takes a step into our huddle and politely but firmly asks us to move to our seats.

'I've been doing step classes all week in preparation for tonight,' Nirvana boasts, 'and I'm hanging for a skim iced chocolate. Apparently the colder the drink, the more calories your body expends trying to heat the liquid.'

'Nirvana,' I groan, 'I said no *skim*. And a drink is *not* emotional eating.'

'Oh, for crying out loud, Esma,' Lisa says, 'there's nothing to be emotional *about*.'

We pore over the menu, the waiter standing over us, daring us to lose the plot again. We place our orders, proudly totalling about five million calories between us. In the end we succeed in convincing Nirvana to break her diet because it's Friday and she's always vulnerable on a Friday. It's Monday to Thursday when you can't prise her jaws open for anything with an energy value higher than a carrot.

Nirvana's of Indian background, Gujarati to be precise. We call her Miss Bollywood because she has typically beautiful Indian hair (silky black and flowing down her back), luminous hazel eyes and layers of lashes. She's the most mild-mannered in our group, all class and refinement and measured words (there's no swearing or outbursts of irrational name-calling for her). She's a size twelve to fourteen (manufacturers can be so evil that way) and is always on a different fad diet because she's under the illusion that she resembles a heifer. But Nirvana's tall, and even though we're always trying to convince her that she's a head-turner, she still insists that she won't be content until her thighs stop rubbing.

Out of the four of us, Nirvana and I come from the more conservative backgrounds. We're both still virgins, and although Nirvana had a couple of boyfriends during university and was in a long-term relationship for three years, it's always been behind her parents' back. She's ready to settle down, and in the past couple of years has, out of desperation, agreed to be more open to traditional matchmaking attempts. Like me, she's had her fair share of over-my-dead-body 'suitors'. Only last week she met somebody who insisted that he was a 'very modern Indian boy'. Here's how the scene went:

Guy: I was born in Australia, I've got properties, earn good money and I'm very independent. Don't worry, I won't be following the old ways.

Nirvana: Great, that's how I was brought up too. So where do you live?

Guy: At home.

Nirvana: Didn't you say you have properties?

Guy: Yes, investment properties.

Nirvana: So will you move into one when you get married?

Guy: Of course not. My parents have extended the house for when my wife moves in. It's fully equipped with plasma TV and surround sound. But no kitchen, obviously. Dinner is always with the family.

Ruby is Greek Orthodox, and I only introduce her by her religious and ethnic background because it means a lot to her. She's fiercely proud of her Greek heritage, speaks the language fluently, observes all the traditions and has always been an active member of her local Greek youth organisations. Throughout university, she made sure she was on every executive committee and generally bossed everybody around, whether it came to organising the annual Greek Ball (which we all went along to) or running youth camps. She's since relinquished control to the younger crowd but still helps out with the occasional community event. Ruby comes from a very educated and successful family. Her dad is an aeronautical research scientist, her mother is a psychologist, one brother is a doctor and the other is a pharmacist. Lisa, Nirvana and I refer to Ruby's family as 'the Nobel Laureates'.

Ruby has wild curly hair that refuses to be styled and looks different every time I see her. One day her curls are loose and bouncy, the next they're tight and frizzy. She's got an unforgettable face: strong jawline, thick, beautifully arched eyebrows, and massive dark eyes framed by funky glasses which aren't prescription but which she insists on wearing a couple of days a week because she's a Gemini and gets bored with her look every five seconds.

Ruby is an astrology fanatic. In her own words: 'I'd rather die single than fall for a Taurus, Cancer or Pisces.' So Ruby's Mr Right checklist is therefore just as unviable (some might say screwed-up) as mine. Despite being into astrology, Ruby is exceptionally bright (she was made an associate at her law firm within a year of starting there) and pretty much fits the profile of the 'CC' lawyer (confident and cocky – again her words, not mine). She was in a relationship with another law student throughout university and a couple of years afterwards broke it off. She's now also ready to fall in love again, but has experienced absolutely zero success so far. Thankfully Ruby, like Nirvana and me, thinks that finding Mr Right adds to your life rather than defines it.

Lisa, on the other hand, takes a completely different view.

Lisa has sky-blue eyes, freckles and a mop of long dark hair. She's intolerant of anybody she views as politically conservative, and when it comes to issues such as climate change, asylum seekers, women's rights and the Israel-Palestine conflict, her convictions are absolute and non-negotiable.

Although Lisa's Jewish and identifies herself as such, she's not religious. In fact, she's agnostic. That's not for lack of effort on her mother's part. Ever since Lisa was little, her mum has been dragging her to Hebrew classes and Jewish functions. Her parents keep kosher and observe the high holy days, although they're not so religious as to observe Shabbat. When Lisa finished high school, her mum took her to Israel. She thought it would help Lisa embrace her Jewish identity, but the plan backfired. Lisa got involved with a human rights group and ended up spending her time in front of bulldozers in the West Bank.

So Lisa's the odd one out in her family, disagreeing with them on Israel, religion and, most importantly for her mother, marrying a Jewish guy. Lisa has no interest whatsoever in finding Mr Right, Jewish (as her mother so desperately hopes) or otherwise. She thinks marriage is stifling.

While Nirvana and I are definitely not having sex in the city, Lisa and Ruby are no longer virgins. However, they're still quite conservative by today's standards and have only been with one guy each. I know this because this is the stuff best friends know, up there with menstrual cycles, embarrassing fantasies and family problems (well, okay, maybe not all problems, given the skeleton in Dad's closet).

'So are you going to call this meeting to order?' Lisa asks.

'The No Sex in the City Club idea was really just an excuse to catch up,' I say, smiling. 'I needed something to entice us out of our crazy work schedules.'

'Speaking of crazy work schedules, how's work going for you?' Nirvana asks Lisa.

Lisa scrunches up her face and lets out a sigh. 'You know what it's like. See a kid you've known since she was on the streets graduate from high school one day, help out a woman whose husband's used a cricket bat on her the next. The good, the bad and the ugly.'

Ruby pulls a face. 'Did the bastard get charged?'

'Yes. Sentencing won't be for a while though. Unfortunately, the woman isn't pressing charges. The good news is that the DPP has decided to prosecute him anyway.'

Ruby's eyes narrow. 'Lisa, do you ever meet guys who redeem your view of men?'

Lisa lets out an exasperated laugh. 'Of course I do. I'm not so cynical that I walk down the street suspecting every male of being a sex offender or wife beater. But I'm not going to start waving the banner for the marriage institution.'

'You're quite sure that nobody could persuade you?' I ask.

'The idea of marriage makes me feel claustrophobic.' Lisa squirms in her seat. 'I'm moving out of home next year. That's the plan anyway. It's bad enough living with my parents; I don't want to live with someone else who's going to be asking where I'm going and what I'm doing. When I move out of home next year I want to be free to make my own decisions.'

I regard her with wry amusement. 'Your mum is going to flip out.'

'That's why it's taken me this long – if I had my choice I would have moved years ago. But she needs to come to terms with the fact that I'm not going to stay at home until I marry one of her hand-picked Jewish bachelors.'

Ruby cocks her head. 'Are you a self-hating Jew?' she says, wagging her finger.

'No, you idiot. I couldn't care less what a guy's background is. If he's the right person and Jewish, fine. It'll satisfy my mum. But unlike you lot, it's not part of my obligatory selection criteria.'

Ruby knocks the end of a sugar sachet against her chin and then, in a tone that suggests she's reading a list aloud, says, 'I want Greek Orthodox background, family from the same island if possible. A Sydney Uni graduate, although UNSW will do. Eastern suburbs.' She pauses. 'I like things to be complicated, as you can tell.'

I snort. 'No, complicated is the wrong word. You're just a snob.'

Ruby pokes her tongue out at me.

'I want a Gujarati and a Hindu,' Nirvana says, 'because culture and religion are big parts of my life. Especially when it comes to raising children.'

'Oh well, that's easy because I don't want children,' Lisa says, taking a sip of her juice and then setting down her glass.

'You don't mean that,' Nirvana says.

'Yes I do,' Lisa says. 'I have no desire to marry or be a mother. I might entertain the idea of a serious relationship if I met someone special enough to accept that the thing I'm most passionate about in life is my work, but I have no intention of having children.'

'You can't be serious,' Ruby says. 'The marrying thing I understand. You've always been against it. But you're fantastic with kids. I've seen you in action.'

'You're a natural,' I add.

'So what?' Lisa says. 'Why can't I be a natural with other people's kids? Why does the fact that I have no desire to have children mean I'm somehow going to fail to fulfil my *real* destiny?'

'It doesn't,' I say. 'It's just surprising.'

'I totally respect where you're coming from,' Ruby says. 'It's your choice. I just hope you don't regret it one day.'

'I think I can be the judge of what I might or might not regret,' Lisa says.

'My uterus practically contracts every time I see a baby,' Nirvana says with a laugh.

'That would be a bit of an occupational hazard in your line of work, wouldn't it?' Lisa says.

'How is your work?' I ask Nirvana.

'Wonderful, actually,' Nirvana says. 'But I don't want to talk about work. I want to vent about home.'

'Vent!' I cry. 'That's why we're here.'

'You know how my dad's sister and her husband have been staying with us from India for the last four months? Well, I'm slowly losing my mind. My dad wants to appear all strict and in control in front of them. Thank God they're leaving in a week.'

'Your dad's always been strict, though,' Ruby says.

'Yeah, but he's going overboard. And what makes it so frustrating is that my aunt and uncle left my cousin, who's a year younger than me, back home in India, where I know for a fact she's partying hard and having the time of her life while my dad's imposing curfews on me simply because my aunt and uncle are here.'

I pat her hand in solidarity. 'Don't worry, Nirvana. You're not the only one old enough to own her own property and conceive a baby but who still has to argue with her parents about late nights out.'

'Your parents have mellowed a lot,' Nirvana says. 'Remember uni?'

Lisa grins. 'She had to be home before midnight.'

'Ahh, yes. The Cinderella rule.' I laugh. 'Please don't remind me. Although, when I think about it now, Dad was such a softie. I'll always be in pigtails with plasters on my knees as far as he's concerned. If I ever do get married and have kids, he'll put it down to an immaculate conception. Do you know he came along with me to orientation day because he was so worried I'd get lost on campus?'

'I'll make enquiries into a counsellor for you tomorrow,' Lisa quips.

'Excuse me,' Ruby cries, animated. 'I have a horror story of my own!'

We turn our attention to Ruby.

'Two weeks ago I'm at church, dressed to kill of course, and sure enough I catch the attention of a guy whose looks can only be described as close to perfect. He gets my number through the usual grapevine and gives me a call. Given the horrors of my past blind-date experiences, I invite my cousin and her husband and make it a double date.'

I squeeze my eyes shut. 'This is going to end badly, right?'

'In flames,' she says. 'So we agree to meet at a café in the Rocks. Balmy night, postcard Sydney, with the Harbour

Bridge and Opera House close by. Sets the mood nicely. Of course, Kat being Kat insists on leaving two hours early because she can't handle the stress of parallel parking and wants to find a spot in the car park. So we get to the restaurant early. At about five minutes to eight, the time we agreed to meet, Kat suggests I wait in the toilets: that way when he arrives I can walk in.'

Nirvana interrupts then to summarise what is obvious to all of us given our collective expertise in blind dates. 'Walking in' serves the dual purpose of a) showing off one's figure, and b) avoiding the uncool situation of a girl waiting for a guy. There are some things the feminist movement just can't change.

Ruby becomes more animated as she speaks. 'So Kat sends me a text message at five past eight. It says: *They're here. Jesus Christ.* Now what the hell am I supposed to think about that? I'm standing in the middle of the bathroom wondering who *they* are and why Kat is cursing. Is it *Jesus Christ he's hot?* or *Jesus Christ he's wearing suspenders and lipstick?*'

'So what happened?' Lisa cries.

'Married?'

'With children?'

'Gay?'

'With puppies?'

'Mum,' she answers.

'Huh?'

'He brought his mum along.'

We look at her blankly and then collectively scream.

The people at the surrounding tables look at us as though we're uncivilised toddlers.

Ruby sits back and flashes us a triumphant look. 'Can anybody beat that? I don't think so.'

'He brought his mum?' I repeat.

'Yes. Hot Stuff's mum had fluffed her short curly hair out and was clearly wearing her best outfit. She ordered a herbal tea, as it was too late for caffeine, and a banana and walnut crêpe which she shared with her son. She asked me all sorts of highly relevant questions such as what law I practised, whether I liked children, what car I drove and how often I attended church. Then she patted Hot Stuff on the arm and invited Kat and John outside for some air so "the couple could get to know each other without the oldies", which was an interesting twist on things given she's in her early sixties and Kat and John are twenty-seven.'

We all exhale loudly, exchanging incredulous glances.

'Look on the bright side,' Lisa says. 'Any guy who can't eat an entire pancake by himself is better off single.'

Our waiter suddenly descends on us, delivering our coffees and dessert orders. When he leaves we raise our drinks to a toast.

'To No Sex in the City,' I say. 'May you be a temporary phase in our lives.'

Five

'You're looking particularly good today,' Danny remarks as he pops his head into my office on Monday morning.

'The appointment at CV Chemist in Chatswood got cancelled,' I say, ignoring his compliment.

The thing that annoys me most about Danny's flirting is that it comes across as him just being good-natured, not sleazy. Danny is one of those guys who is overfriendly with all women, edging into flirting territory all too often. 'What a beautiful outfit you've got on today, Mrs Kennedy!' 'Love that perfume, Veronica!' So if I kick up a fuss about his random compliments on my looks, as I've done in the past, he turns it back on me and acts like I'm paranoid and oversensitive. It's not that I can't handle him. It's the fact that I have to. I just want to come in, do my work and enjoy a pleasant but professional relationship with my boss. I don't want to get dressed wondering whether he's going to have an opinion about my outfit accentuating my eye colour.

'The furniture shopping didn't go too badly, after all,' Danny says, entering my office and sitting on the chair in front of my desk. 'Did I tell you Mary and I are starting counselling next week?'

Here we go again. This is another thing that totally freaks me out. The incessant D&Ms about his marriage. *Dial a friend*, I want to scream. The last time I checked, the employer/employee handbook didn't include a chapter on how bosses should seek marriage advice from their employees. But I can't exactly tell him to piss off. I have to put on an act.

'It's great you're going to work through your issues,' I say, trying to muster a sympathetic tone while I continue typing, hoping he'll get the message and leave me to do my work.

'The pharmacy out in Burwood Road called,' he says, stretching his hands up and crossing them behind his head. 'They're really happy with the pharmacist you placed there. She's flown through probation. Well done.'

I'm relieved. It was a difficult placement. I wasn't confident that the girl I recommended would last, as she had to travel for about two hours to get there.

'We're having Kristy's farewell drinks at the Ivy on Friday night,' Danny says. 'You got my email, didn't you? Because I didn't get your RSVP.'

'Er, yeah, sorry, I forgot to reply.'

Bars really aren't my thing. I have never touched alcohol and, according to Danny, I'm a 'nerd' and a 'prude'. Danny, of course, can't remember enlightening me with this piece of information as he said it when he was completely tanked at last year's Christmas party, of which he has no memory after the lucky door prize.

I rarely go to bars and I've come up with a zillion excuses every time we have a work function at one. Why Danny thinks I'd be interested in a night at the Ivy (especially considering I've already shouted Kristy to a farewell lunch) is beyond me.

'Marco will be there.'

Ah, so that's why.

I lean back in my chair and tap my pen against my desk. '*Danny*,' I say in a low growl, 'would you please quit the Marco and Esma campaign? It's not going to happen. Find yourself another project.'

He laughs. 'Look, if you want to continue with this ancient arranged-marriage stuff, it's your life.'

'Really? It's my life. What a revelation.'

'I'm just trying to help out.'

'By *arranging* a set-up with a guy who I have absolutely no interest in?'

He shrugs his shoulders. 'Okay, forget Marco. I'll let him know he's off limits to you. He's not Muslim, therefore he's out of the question.'

'Would you please just drop the subject?' I say, turning back to face the computer as a signal that the conversation is over.

'Fine,' he says, standing up. He switches to the tone he uses when he decides to ditch the nice-guy act and play the part of boss. 'I'd appreciate it if you tried to make an appearance on Friday. You're one of my senior staff. It says a lot to have you there.'

Oh boy.

'Yeah, okay, I'll make an appearance,' I mumble.

Needless to say, contrary to Danny's reassurances all week, Friday night is most definitely all about setting me up with Marco. It makes my skin crawl to think of Danny trying to hook me up with his friend. Marco's thirty-five and works in IT. He doesn't even work with us. His 'What brings you here?' is about as plausible as the toupee on the old guy standing to my right, who is quite clearly suffering a late midlife crisis judging by the barely pubescent girl hanging off his arm.

I've been here half an hour and I'm sitting at a table with Danny; needs-to-go-easy-on-the-gel Marco; Kristy (in la-la land given it's her last day and she's leaving to backpack across America for six months); Veronica, our care of the elderly recruiter (oozes coolness); Kylie, another pharmacy recruiter (also cool); Dora, our accounts payable (torturous silences in the lifts); and Simon, our IT guy (the office gossip). The rest of the team is at the bar.

We're all having a laugh with Kristy, making fun of her plan to find herself an American boyfriend and settle down in the US.

'So will *any* American male do?' Danny asks.

'Well,' she replies, 'he can't have a criminal conviction, he can't be a bum and he can't be a Republican.'

'So you're not picky then?' Veronica says.

Kristy smiles. 'As an illegal immigrant I've got fat chance of hooking up with a Republican, don't I? I'll take my chances with a Democrat. But for what it's worth, I'm a donkey voter anyway, so ideology has nothing to do with it.'

'You're a donkey voter too!' cries Simon and they give each other a high five.

'Marco's been to the States, haven't you, Marco?' Danny says.

'Yeah, I travelled there in my gap year and I go there for work every now and then.' Marco smiles at me. 'It's a great place.'

'Marco's been to Turkey too, haven't you?' Danny adds as he takes a handful of peanuts and shoves them into his mouth.

I want to burst out laughing. Even the busybody match-making aunties I know are more suave than this.

'Yeah, I have,' Marco answers enthusiastically. 'Turkey's probably my all-time favourite country. The people are so friendly and the food was awesome!'

I actually feel sorry for him. It isn't his fault. Danny probably told him I have the hots for him. Why else would he consent to torturing himself by coming along to the farewell drinks of his friend's employee?

Danny and Marco are looking at me. There's an obvious expectation I'll respond with something like, 'Oh wow, you've been to Turkey! What a coincidence. My parents were born in Turkey! That means we have so much in common and the foundation for a lasting relationship! That you found the people there friendly only serves to reinforce that we were made for each other, seeing as a) I'm of Turkish origin *and* b) I'm friendly! And to make things even more serendipitous, you loved the food! Well, guess what? I can cook! So, will you have my babies?'

It's tempting. But I don't. Instead, I say, 'I got gastro when I was in Turkey.'

Veronica squeezes my thigh under the table, fighting back laughter. Danny coughs but I get a short, unsure laugh out of Marco.

'You know something, Kristy,' Danny says, turning to face her, 'I reckon you probably will find your perfect American match. And you know why?'

Veronica whispers in my ear, 'Here we go. Danny's feeling philosophical and oh so Oprah again.'

'It's because Kristy's flexible,' Danny says, winking at Kristy and then taking a swig of his beer. 'She's open to meeting anybody. She doesn't set herself up for failure by putting up a wall of restrictions.'

Enter Danny in one of his 'let's focus on Esma' moods.

I sit up tall in my chair and cross my arms. 'Oh, come on, Danny. Just get it out before you burst.'

'Everybody, I've been unfair on our Esma here,' he says. 'I've been on her back to open herself up to life, loosen the shackles of her stone-age faith. But that's only because I feel she's missing out. And as an equal opportunity employer, it pains me to see Esma missing out on all the opportunities for fun and excitement that people like us enjoy.'

I roll my eyes. 'Hang on, don't say another word. I just want to remember this moment in my life, 7p.m., Friday 12 March. Danny is pitying me.'

Danny wags his finger at me. 'Well, Esma, someone as gorgeous and fun-loving as you shouldn't be dragged down by archaic rules.'

'Lay off her,' Dora says, hitting Danny on the arm.

Although it's always been obvious that I'm uncomfortable with Danny giving me a hard time about my faith, I've never actually engaged with him on the subject. I've tried to shut it down as soon as he raises it. But I figure now is probably a good time to put an end to the subject once and for all.

'Thanks, Dora,' I say, 'but I'd like to have this out.'

'Ooh,' Simon teases. 'This should be good.'

Danny looks amused and leans back in his chair, waiting for me to speak.

'Danny,' I start, 'you think my lifestyle choices are backward and that you're liberated and I'm repressed.'

'Those are your words, not mine.'

'Okay, let's examine your theory. First, what am I missing out on?'

'A relationship with no strings attached. Just for the fun of it. You don't have to be a genius to know what kind of fun I mean. Having a drink at the end of a long day at work and loosening up and unwinding.'

'Hear, hear,' Simon says. 'No offence, Esma,' he says with a wink.

Danny continues, on a roll now. 'Flirting with a stranger – anybody, not just somebody who matches your religious and cultural stats – wondering if there's something between you. And other stuff that's R-rated for you given you're a vir … given your moral code.'

I flinch but I'm not going to let him get away with it. 'Okay, forget the drinking thing,' I say. 'Lots of people who aren't Muslim don't drink. But let's look at the fact that I won't have a relationship outside of marriage.'

'Thank God for those relationships,' Simon shouts with a laugh.

'Okay,' I continue, 'so let's put aside the fact that I want to marry a Muslim, that my faith is important to me and I want to be able to share it with my partner. Let's say that's negotiable and I meet somebody at a work function, or party, or maybe through a mutual friend.'

'Mmm,' Danny says.

'Well, I have no idea if he's in it for the long-term. I don't know his intentions. The majority of people eventually want to get married.'

'Not really,' Danny says.

'Oh, come on, Danny,' I argue. 'Don't pretend marriage isn't the norm and that those who want it are weird. Are you telling me being in a de facto relationship is the aspiration of *most* people? There are zillions of wedding magazines. I still haven't seen any editions of *De Facto*.'

'Nothing wrong with being in a de facto relationship, though,' Kylie says.

'You couldn't have *The Farmer Wants a De Facto*,' Dora contemplates aloud. 'It wouldn't work.'

'I never said there was anything wrong with it,' I say. 'If that's what you want, go for it! But I'm upfront about the fact that I'm interested in marriage – not cohabitation, not a boyfriend, *marriage*. I put it out there from the beginning and it just takes out the complication. You cut out the uncertainty, the relentless interpreting of every text message, every conversation.'

Marco, at this point, looks like he's about to puke. Really, I feel sorry for him. He would have had no idea what he was in for when Danny asked him along.

'But—' Danny tries to interrupt but I cut him off.

'Wait! Let me finish first,' I say.

'Fine, on with the speech!' he cries boisterously.

'Just ignore the religious stuff, yeah?' He shrugs and I continue. 'You have to admit that the way I approach relationships has a good chance of getting certainty and clarification. That's what people want. Aren't the endless D&Ms with your circle of friends about whether he's ready to commit all about trying to obtain clarity? About trying to align your understanding of the rules of the game of love with his? Well, if you come to the relationship with the same understanding of the rules of the game, then the only thing that's left is applying those rules.'

At this point Veronica's nodding her head, Simon is trying to spoon a floating peanut out of his beer, Dora's focusing intently on me, Marco's struggling not to pass out and Danny's giving me a cocky and totally unconvinced grin. I ignore them because I'm having my rant once and for all, whether they like it or not.

'But if you're playing the game with the rules of soccer and he's playing with the rules of league, then that's a lot of mess to clean up before you even start to work out if you're both going to end up on the same team. I'm not saying that knowing the rules means both people are going to stick to them, but it sure cuts out a lot of bullshit.'

Veronica lets out a whopping cheer. Dora nods slowly

but looks like she's trying to process what I've said. She's not into sport, so I'm guessing my metaphor flew straight over her head.

Marco stands up, rubs his hands together, gives us all a quick smile and says goodbye, rushing out of the bar as quickly as it takes for Danny to down the last of his beer.

'And that's how it's done,' I whisper to Veronica, who bursts out laughing.

Six

Every month I volunteer at the Sydney Refugee Centre in Surry Hills in a programme called Teenzone. Some of the teenagers I work with are in community detention, waiting for a decision about their refugee status. Others have already been granted refugee status. When I first started volunteering (Lisa helped me get the position), I was helping out with ESL classes for teenagers and adults.

I know it's a stereotype but most of the refugees who attended ESL classes were motivated and focused on learning English. At the same time they were struggling with accessing housing, social services and health care. Some of the students were under eighteen. A couple of them had sought asylum alone, leaving their family behind. And while the adults in my class got on with the business of trying to find housing and work, the teenagers were just boys and girls trapped in a cage of adult problems.

So I approached a digital arts and cultural organisation to run workshops and seminars with the teenagers. The change in the kids has been amazing. We've had volunteers come into the centre to offer training in hip-hop music.

We've had student actors run acting classes. The Refugee Council received a donation of computers and we've had some IT training too.

I try to mix up the classes. Sometimes it's just help with homework; other times we've written plays, songs, speeches and blogs. I'm trying to get a digital storytelling workshop happening, but I basically need to find someone who will do it for nothing because our resources are so limited.

I feel energised as soon as I walk through the doors, and today I can see Lisa through the large windows in the interview room sitting at a table across from a young man and woman, deep in conversation.

My class is waiting for me in one of the rooms. We're a small group of six. There's Sonny, a seventeen-year-old refugee from Sri Lanka, who was moved from Christmas Island to community detention several months ago. He arrived in Australia by boat, leaving his parents and the rest of his family in a camp in the north of Sri Lanka as they couldn't afford to pay the people smugglers the money needed for them all to come at once. There's Christina, also seventeen, who's from Iraq and has been granted refugee status. Faraj, also from Iraq, is the youngest in the group, at fourteen. His family arrived by plane two years ago and are still waiting for a decision on their refugee status. Then there's Miriam and Ahmed, sixteen-year-old twins who arrived by boat from Afghanistan and have since been granted refugee status.

'Okay,' I say, clapping my hands together. 'Today we're going to continue our five-minute stories. I'm still trying to organise the digital movie-making workshops.' A collective sigh of disappointment. 'It's okay,' I say, 'we'll get there eventually. We can still work on our scripts and storyboards.'

Miriam raises her hand. 'I have started mine.'

'That's great! Are you comfortable sharing it with the class?'

She laughs, her large brown eyes holding my gaze. 'Yes, of course.' She takes out a piece of paper from her bag, tucking a strand of hair behind her ear, and clears her throat. I remember the first time I met Miriam. She was fourteen years old, but she looked older then, her face lined with anxiety and fear. She barely knew any English. And now she's trying so hard to write poems and short stories.

'My story in five minutes,' she reads, her voice strong and confident. 'I come to Australia from Afghanistan with my brother, Ahmed, and my mother and father. We left behind my grandparents and much family. We know my uncle was killed by the Taliban and another uncle is hiding in Pakistan. In Australia we are un-un—' She pauses, smiles self-consciously at the class, then ploughs on. 'We are unlearning how to live in war. We must learn how to live in a peaceful country. When we walk in the street, we must unlearn being scared. We must unlearn looking over our shoulder. We must unlearn being quiet. We must unlearn not trusting the police officer.' She stops and looks up at me. 'That is all I have done. Still more.'

'That was brilliant, Miriam,' I say and she beams at me. I turn to the others. 'Anybody else?'

For the next hour I help the others work on their scripts.

It's mainly about helping them find the right words; words that mean something to them, rather than me speaking for them.

When we're done we hang out for a bit, drinking tea and eating some biscuits. As usual, Sonny is making us all laugh. He lives in a small flat in Auburn with five other refugees and always has a story to share.

'There is one man in the flat who loves the farting!' he says gleefully, his sharp eyes bright and alive. 'He is *loving* to fart.' We burst into hysterics. 'Yesterday I am screaming at him that the smoke alarm will be complaining soon.'

When it's time to go home, I hover in the main office area, waiting for Lisa, who's still in the interview room. She notices me and quickly ducks her head out the door. 'Hiya,' she says breezily. 'I need another hour. Don't wait for me. Call me tomorrow, yeah?'

'Okay, sure.'

I drive home exhilarated, humbled and overwhelmed by a sense that it's here, at the centre, that I am really starting to find my own identity and place in the world. My parents have always told me how lucky I am to have grown up in Australia, but it wasn't until I started working at the centre that I really understood my blessings. Not in any material sense, but simply because I enjoy the freedom and dignities living in peace brings. I never appreciated that properly until I met people like Sonny and Faraj and Miriam and Ahmed and Christina, who have had the most basic human rights denied them. And so, each time I meet them, they refocus the lens through which I view my life.

Seven

I'm not one of those girls who needs a man to complete her. If that was the case I would have settled for the first, fifth or tenth guy I've met or been set up with.

I want to settle down. But I don't want to settle. Ha! I should get that made up into a bumper sticker. That way, at every family event, when the aunties and uncles interrogate me about why I'm not married yet, I won't have to squirm in my seat any more. I'll just say, 'Let's take this discussion to the garage. Meet my bumper bar.'

I'm not bitter about the fact that I attend more engagement parties and baby showers than girls' nights out, and that most of my friends and relatives are either recently married or having their first babies (I know all there is to know about pelvic floor exercises and midwives with farmers' hands). In fact, I am genuinely happy for my friends, and the interior decorator in me secretly loves seeing coordinated crockery and linen strewn around a room filled with wrapping paper and the sound of friends laughing. As for baby showers: who doesn't love a newborn's singlet or a pretty basket of baby shampoo and rattles?

And I can even handle the married girls – the ones who used to moan and groan about never finding Mr Right – jostling me and joking about how they miss the days when they were 'free of responsibility' and how they're jealous of my single status – wink, nudge, giggle.

I can definitely handle all that with grace and good humour. But for the love of God, I can't handle these three things:

1. being forced to watch the unedited version of a wedding

2. being subjected to endless hours of baby talk (eg: he pooped five times today; she got out of bed at one, then two, then two-twelve, then three, then three-fifteen, then four; I mashed the potato, pumpkin and peas and added organic stock, and then I forgot myself and added salt and so I started all over again, because according to page twelve of *How to Cook Organic Food for Your Baby*, if you add salt you might as well add gin, that's how bad it is)

3. being told I haven't found love because I'm too fussy

So you can imagine the torture I'm enduring tonight. My parents and I are visiting old family friends. One daughter, Sevil, has just returned from her honeymoon, and another, Arzu, has just had a baby. We've been invited to watch the wedding video (three hours long, plus the highlights DVD).

It's been forty minutes, although we're only thirty minutes into it because Sevil's father insists on rewinding any scenes we appear in and then pausing so that we can relive the moment and drink in a shot of ourselves yawning or taking a massive bite out of the entrée, sauce dribbling down our chin.

'Penang and Langkawi were perfect,' Sevil gushes.

'Did you do any water sports?' I ask.

'Esma, look at Sevil in this scene!' Sevil's dad cries. 'Look at how well she dances!'

'Yes, she looks great!' I cry, then turn back to Sevil. 'I heard the jetskiing is awesome there.'

'It was fantastic, although there were jellyfish and—'

'I'm not sure if I should be demand feeding or feeding every three hours,' Arzu interrupts as she burps her baby. 'But my nipples are seriously aching,' she whispers, leaning closer to Sevil and me. 'They're all cracked, and honestly, when she latches on it's like a million knives being stabbed into the tips of my—'

'Esma! You're not watching,' Sevil's mum says. 'You have to watch this part. You remember when they lifted Sevil up onto the chair and she nearly slipped?'

'Satin dress on the satin chair covers,' my mum says, clucking her tongue in disapproval.

'You're right, Ozlem,' Sevil's mum says. 'She nearly slipped!'

'So you were saying about the jellyfish?' I try again.

'Oh yeah, there were jellyfish in Penang, so we were warned not to go in the water, but the jetskis looked so tempting and then—'

'Did everybody hear that burp?' Arzu exclaims.

Sevil's mum claps her hands and my mum beams.

Arzu, sounding like a cross between a character from *Sesame Street* and a recovering alcoholic, says, 'Did my baby princess do a burpy burp? Did she now? Did she do a fuzzy wozzy burpy burp and vomit all her milky milk onto her mummy's new Prada top? We don't care now, do we, baby?'

Vomit? Did somebody say vomit?

Sevil leaps up to get the tool kit (wash cloth, baby wipes and air freshener); Sevil's mum goes into the kitchen to get a tea and coffee refill – ordering Sevil's dad to pause the DVD so she doesn't miss a minute – and I resign myself to the fact that I have no choice but to endure the next three hours. So I sink back into the couch and do what everybody does when they have a spare moment: play with my smartphone.

I notice a text message from Ruby: *Call me! Help!*

I look at the time. It's only seven-thirty. We'd agreed she'd message me at eight-thirty.

Ruby is on a date with a guy she met at a thirtieth. We'd agreed that she'd text me if she needed to get out of the date. That would be my cue to call her and provide an exit strategy.

The only problem is that she texted me at seven-thirty and the date started at seven.

I get up, excuse myself and lock myself in the bathroom.

Ruby answers on the first ring. 'Hi, Esma, how are you?'

'Are you on your way?' I say, reciting our script.

'On my way where, hon?' she answers, feigning cheerfulness. 'I'm out at the moment.'

'You've got a dress fitting and you're an hour late!'

'Oh my goodness! I'm so sorry, Esma. Could we re-schedule?'

'No. If we don't do the bridesmaids' fitting today, I'm going to call off the wedding, kill the bridal party and hold you responsible. How bad is it?'

'Terrible! That's absolutely terrible. I'm so sorry, Esma, I'll be there as quickly as I can.'

She hangs up. I wait five minutes, during which time my mum knocks on the door to ask if I'm okay as they're waiting for me before putting on the DVD.

'Bad kebab for lunch,' I groan from behind the door. 'I'm sorry from the *bottom* of my heart, but they'll just have to continue without me. Nature calls.'

'Okay,' she says. 'I'll have a lemon tea waiting for you when you get out.'

'Sure thing, Mum.'

Ruby calls and I answer.

'What is wrong with me that I attract these idiots?' she wails. 'I've gone out and bought nicotine gum because I'm honestly close to smoking again.'

'Don't you dare!' I scold.

She pops her gum. 'I've already thrown four into my mouth. I'm going to kill somebody! It starts out normal. We order coffee, enjoy some general chitchat. Then he suddenly says, "I have a series of questions I'm going to ask you so I can determine your personality."'

'*What?*' I sit on the edge of the bath.

'Then the nob asks me whether I'm a climate change

62

sceptic, whether I believe marijuana should be legalised and my opinion on the privatisation of prisons.'

'He sounds like a repressed *Q&A* audience member.'

'I tell him I believe carbon should be taxed and he has a tantrum, throws down his napkin and asks me why I feel the need to send Australia back to the Dark Ages. Then suddenly he stops and says, "You have greedy eyes."'

'Has he escaped a mental institution?'

'*Then* he asks me to confess to the most I've ever paid for a pair of shoes and I say I don't want to, but then I tell him just for a laugh and he pushes his coffee cup into the middle of the table and says, "That is ridiculous and superficial."'

'He said all this with a straight face?'

'He didn't smile once. And then when you called and saved me and I got up to leave, he was genuinely disappointed because, according to him, "it was going so well and he felt such a connection". Then he tried to kiss me goodbye and arrange another time to meet!'

'What did you say?'

'I told him I'd check my calendar but I had a colonoscopy scheduled next week.'

'Yeah right.'

'He said he'd call the week after and wished me luck as he'd developed haemorrhoids after his last colonoscopy.'

'Do we have signs painted on our foreheads, Ruby?'

'Yes. *Only Losers May Apply*.'

Although it's true that I love my married friends, and their babies are the sweetest things (even if they can turn their mothers' brains to mush), it's Ruby, Lisa and Nirvana that I can really be open and honest with and know they'll understand.

We're meeting up for another No Sex in the City get-together. Tonight it's Thai in Surry Hills. The food is fantastic, the atmosphere infectiously buoyant, and we're all celebrating because Nirvana has met somebody who:

1. has, thus far, displayed no psychotic tendencies
2. owns his own business (financial independence: always on the list)
3. is also Gujarati
4. is good-looking and very funny
5. matches Nirvana's star sign (important in Hindu tradition)
6. is into her (evidence: called her the day after they met and spoke for an hour)

'I have it on good authority that Anil's family's not into joint families,' Nirvana says happily. 'His sister's married and she doesn't live with her in-laws.'

Nirvana's father's mother has lived with Nirvana's parents since they first married. For Nirvana's mother, that's thirty-six years with a full-time mother-in-law. Nirvana's seen first-hand how challenging such domestic arrangements can be and is consequently paranoid about the joint family thing. She tends to throw the question into her standard first-date conversation opener: 'So have you travelled much? Do you like your job? Do you plan on living with your parents when you get married? Are you into sports?'

'So how did you meet?' Ruby demands. 'Rewind a bit.'

'At Sunita's wedding last Saturday. We were at the token singles' table. I'm sure Sunita and her family set the whole thing up.'

We quizzed Nirvana, throwing a hundred questions at her.

'We clicked, the conversation flowed, there were no awkward silences. We were laughing and joking and it was very relaxed. Obviously we were both putting forward the best versions of ourselves – that's what everybody does, right? – but at the same time I didn't feel it was one big con job. And he was normal.' She sighs hopefully. 'Such a welcome change. Remember Arshpreet?'

We all screech with laughter. Arshpreet was Nirvana's most recent failed arranged meeting. He had a habit of referring to himself in the third person, for example: 'Arshpreet has to make a decision about whether he's going to open his own business or remain an employee. And Arshpreet is finding it very difficult to decide.'

Funnily enough, Nirvana had no problem deciding Arshpreet was not the guy for her.

'Anil asked for my number,' Nirvana goes on, 'and he called me the next day. We spoke for an hour. And we've been talking or texting all week. He's taking me out for dinner tomorrow.'

'You're gushing!' Lisa says with a laugh.

'And glowing,' Ruby adds.

'And a little gaunt?' I tease. 'Have you been too busy on the phone to fit a meal in?'

'Gushing, glowing, gaunt,' says Lisa, popping a cashew into her mouth. 'Ah, the signs of love.'

'I've been eating fine,' Nirvana says defensively.

I snort. 'South Beach, Dukan or North Korean prison rations today?'

'Dukan,' she says.

'Animals only?' Lisa asks.

Nirvana nods. 'It doesn't give you very nice breath,' she says, scrunching up her nose. 'I'm always chewing gum. But it's worth it.'

I give her a dubious look. 'Whatever you say, Nirvana.'

'Don't you want to know what he does?' she says, ignoring me.

'Of course.'

'Fire away.'

'He used to be a financial planner. Now he runs his own business. Two petrol stations!'

'So he's Indian and he owns petrol stations,' I say with a loud laugh. 'Not at all a cliché.'

Nirvana giggles. 'I've been running from clichés for so long, but they always track me down.'

Eight

My parents were deadset against me getting married before I graduated from university because they wanted me to focus on my studies. Engaged was fine. Married would have to wait. I agreed. I didn't want to settle down before I graduated. I wanted to start working, enjoy financial independence, travel. Work out who I was and what I wanted in life.

I had no objection to meeting someone and getting engaged. I had it all planned out: fall hopelessly in love with someone at university – maybe through the Islamic or Turkish Society, or with somebody in the same faculty as me – and then enjoy a couple of years of engaged bliss (everybody I know who's married says engagement is like an extended honeymoon). In other words, I'd have a fiancé who took me out, spoilt me rotten with chocolates and flowers (I had fantasies of flowers being delivered to me during class on Valentine's Day) and with whom I could build a collection of memories to share as we grew old together.

Romantic comedies have a lot to answer for.

It didn't happen. Well, I did fall for a guy, Seyf, and he wanted to take things to the next level, but it didn't work out. I met plenty of guys after Seyf, but I soon realised we had little in common, or that they were really interested in my friend, or that they wanted me to be more traditional (like Kamil, who admired the fact that I was studying but thought it was ultimately unnecessary, given my place was in the home), or less religious (like Mohamad, aka 'Alan', who preferred it if I drank, went nightclubbing and sneaked away with him to the Central Coast for a long weekend). Other guys I met through the traditional channels. They'd visit me at home and we'd enjoy a formal-lounge-room date (or garden-pergola date, depending on the time of year). If I felt a click, a connection, and the guy did too, we'd go out for a coffee or dinner.

That's when my dad invented the Rule of Six.

When Yusuf (who was the only Brad Pitt lookalike I have been blessed to meet) invited me out for a coffee in Leichhardt (I was eighteen), my father sat me down and introduced me to his new policy on public 'meetings' (he refused to use the word 'date').

'You must have a minimum of six people at any meeting with a boy. If it is only you and the boy, and somebody sees you, it looks like a date. That is no good for your reputation. If there is another couple with you, it looks like a double date. That is doubly no good for your reputation. But if it is six people, you, the boy and four other people, it is acceptable because six is a group.'

There were many obvious problems with the Rule of Six. The boy would usually be bewildered by the fact that he was effectively taking five people out on a date. Those five people would very often be my sister and friends, because my father did not approve of the boy bringing somebody for support.

'He is the boy,' my father would say. 'He doesn't need support. Let him feel uncomfortable. You are the girl. It is all about your needs and your comfort.'

So the boy would usually end up having to get to know me in the presence of five strangers (and shout them all coffee too). If the five chaperones used their brains and left us alone (which almost always happened, not that I told my father that), the damage had usually already been done. Either my chaperones would hang around during the awkward introductions and be so nice that they appeared to have stronger feelings for the guy than I did, or some of them would think they were doing me a kindness by jokingly reminding the guy that they'd arrange a painful death for him if he upset me. This served to scare most of the guys off because it made me look as though I came from a family with connections to Sydney's underworld – never a good matchmaking look.

My father eventually mellowed and the Rule of Six was, thankfully, forgotten.

Which is why, when Yasir telephones the house on Saturday to ask me out for coffee, my father simply hands the phone to me and leaves me to sort out the details. The Rule of Six has finally given way to the Rule of Two and it's about bloody time.

Mind you, I have no idea who Yasir is. But the community connection network has led him to me nonetheless. Here's how it worked:

My dad
↓
Deniz (met my father in the seventies when they were flatmates; works as a teacher at St Clements)
↓
Havin (also works as a teacher at St Clements; is also Yasir's aunt; spoke to Deniz as follows: 'Deniz, my sister's son wants to settle down but can't find the right girl. Do you know anybody?')
↓
Deniz ('Yes. My old friend's daughter.')
↓
Havin speaks to Zeynap, Deniz's wife, and gives her a number for Betul, Yasir's mum.
↓
Zeynap calls Betul and vouches that I'm a *wonderful* catch.
↓
Havin calls my mum to let her know Betul will call her and that Yasir is a *wonderful* catch.
↓
Betul calls my mum.
↓
My mum gives Betul my mobile telephone number and the house number, just in case.
↓
Yasir calls my mobile. I'm in the shower at the time and don't pick up and don't bother returning the call because I don't recognise the number. Everybody I want to speak to has their number saved in my phone, and anybody not in my contacts

is either a telemarketer or our local Blockbuster store chasing the last season of *The Wire* (I swear I can't find it).

↓

Yasir calls the house phone. My father picks up. He hands me the phone and ...

↓

... we arrange to meet at a café in the Strand on Pitt Street Mall after work next Monday.

We've added each other as friends on Facebook so at least I know what he looks like. Yasir's profile picture is nice. He's not drop-dead gorgeous or butt ugly. There's a big spectrum between those two ends and he's sitting about halfway.

I'm wearing one of my most flattering suits and stunning high heels that have already given me blisters. Senem came over last night to do my hair, giving me some soft curls, which, she insists, suit me more than the dead-straight look. I didn't bother arguing with her, although today's been really hot and the roots of my hair are a little frizzy from the humidity, undoing much of her hard work.

My make-up is minimal. Unlike Senem, I'm into natural tones and pale glosses. My skin tone is olive, my eyes and lashes dark brown, like my dad's, and so I suit earthy colours. Senem, by contrast, takes after my mum and is pale with green eyes, loving to experiment with bright and bold tones. I wouldn't be caught dead wearing red lipstick, whereas Senem looks gorgeous in it.

I enter the Strand, trying to remember all the magazine articles I've read about the most flattering and slimming way to walk. Keep my thighs close together, one foot crossing over the other, try to walk sideways (reducing frontal view of body mass), stick boobs out (don't have much to stick out), keep shoulders back and head up to avoid any double chin ... Those poor models. They really do deserve their million-dollar salaries.

I spot Yasir leaning against the window of the café.

The blisters are worth it.

His profile pic doesn't do him justice. He's a trendy dresser (tick!) and has a real presence about him (tick!). Some guys exude confidence and he's one of them (two ticks!). Our eyes meet as I approach. We smile at each other. Then he invites me to sit down at a table he's reserved at the back of the café.

'Have you hurt yourself?' he asks once we've sat down.

'Pardon?'

'Just now, you were walking like you'd had a fall or something. Are you okay?'

I stare blankly at him. 'Um ... yeah, twisted my ankle at the photocopier today.'

'Apply some Deep Heat tonight. Works wonders.'

'Ah, yes, sure.' I'm mortified. 'Good advice.'

'Are you hungry?' he asks as he rolls up the sleeves of his shirt. 'It's a scorcher today, isn't it?' He pours me a glass of water from the jug the waitress brought over to our table as soon as we sat down.

'I know. I've been in the office all day, so I didn't notice until I made my way here. Thank God for air conditioning.'

'I'm with you on that,' he says with a grin. 'I was planning on wearing my suit jacket and tie. A friend told me I'd look more impressive. But when I left the house I just couldn't do it. I mean, how much influence is a tie and jacket going to have? Not to mention that I would have arrived here hot and sweaty. Not exactly appealing, right?'

I give him a cheeky smile. 'Sorry to have to tell you – the tie and jacket would have made a world of difference.'

'Really?' He sighs. 'Is there any way I can redeem myself?' He has a real sparkle in his eye.

'I'll think about it.'

We order some food and spend the next hour talking and flirting easily. There are no rules for first dates, but I've been on enough to know there's a standard repertoire of safe topics: travel, personal interests, friends, taste in music, film and books, and a bit of current affairs (we're Muslim, so the whole 'no religion or politics at the dinner table' is just not going to happen). Then the conversation turns to work and I ask him what he does.

'I've been a builder for about two years,' he says. 'Before that I was an accountant.'

'Ahh,' I murmur knowingly.

He chuckles.

'What's so funny?' I ask, although I'm smiling too.

'I think accountancy, up there with law or auditing, is one of those professions you can leave and people don't even bother to pretend to be surprised. They just give you a sympathetic look.'

I laugh. 'You're right. In fact, they don't wait to hear why, they wait to hear why you didn't do it sooner.'

'See, you get it.'

'Well, some people would argue building is like throwing money into a fire, so it would make sense to have a builder who actually understands that most people don't have a blank chequebook when they're building their house.'

Yasir feigns a look of horror. 'You don't trust builders?' I shake my head. 'Who would have thought? We enjoy such popularity.'

I let out an exaggerated laugh.

'Burnt, huh?' he says and I nod.

'My parents renovated our kitchen and bathroom some years back.' I shudder. 'It's still a painful topic in our family.' He laughs. 'Seriously. It was a disaster. The tiler laid the bathroom tiles on a slant. You go cross-eyed looking at them. And then he had the audacity to try to convince us that we needed to get our eyes checked.'

'Ouch,' he says, drawing in his breath. 'Did you take it further?'

'I wrote a bunch of letters and he came back and supposedly fixed it. But we're still not very happy with it.'

'You should have gone straight to the Department of Fair Trading.'

'I know, I know,' I say with a shrug. 'But – this is going to sound silly – I felt sorry for him. He'd just split up with his wife and it was obvious he was distracted and going through a crisis. In the end I thought it just wasn't worth the fight. Not in the larger scheme of things. There are worse things in life than a less-than-perfect tiling job in your bathroom.'

'I would have fought it all the way,' he says. 'I can't stand being taken advantage of.'

This is true for me too, partly. I'm not a pushover. I do stand up for myself. Just not all the time. And when I don't it's not as simple as a lack of courage. With the tiler I felt crippled by my pity for him. With Danny, I'm crippled by my sense of duty to my parents.

'So tell me more about the career change,' I say.

'I was unhappy working in an office. I know that sounds really pretentious. I mean, there are many people who don't like working in an office but never get the opportunity to try something else. I lasted six years. While I was working I helped a cousin build his house. I got a taste for building work and loved it. I figured that if I was ever going to make a change, it had to be when I was young. So I did. And now I buy rundown homes, renovate or detonate, and then sell.'

'That's really inspiring,' I say, and then I laugh. 'That sounded so dorky. But seriously, you walked away from a career you studied hard for, to do what you're passionate about. Not many people have the courage to do that.'

'My dad has a different view. He flipped out when I came home and announced I'd quit my job. Me being an accountant was something that gave him immense pride. He's still struggling to accept my decision to turn my back on it.'

'Why?'

Yasir pauses before answering. 'Many reasons,' he says. 'He had a lot to do with me getting in to accountancy. So it was a bit of a slap in the face, at least from his point of view.'

'What do you mean?'

'When I was in high school, Year Ten, I mucked around a lot. Got really bad marks. My sister had just been accepted into pharmacy and my dad was constantly fighting with me to follow her example. One day, before the Year Ten certificate exam, he sat me down and, for the first time in his life, spoke to me man to man. He's been driving a taxi for years. He told me that if I wanted to get my Year Ten certificate and then leave school to drive a taxi, he'd support my decision. He said it was a good job, steady income, pick up a client from the airport, drop them off at their destination. He said I had two choices. I could either drive a taxi and pick up the businessman from the airport, or I could *be* that businessman and get picked up by a taxi driver. He didn't care which path I decided on, so long as I made a decision and stuck with it. Then and there I decided I wanted to be that businessman. A professional. So I studied like mad, did really well in the HSC, and went on to do accountancy.'

'I guess that explains your dad's lack of enthusiasm for your career change.'

'My dad complains that it's like I was driving a Porsche and now I've downgraded to a bicycle. He can't see that this is what makes me happy.' Yasir smiles. 'But he'll get there,' he says optimistically. 'When I build him a house, and the business becomes more successful, he'll realise life's too short not to follow your passions.'

It's seven o'clock when I call an end to the date, ascribing to my 'leave them wanting more' rule. It's the only rule

I've agreed with in the relationship books Senem read obsessively before meeting Farouk. Having flipped through one or two, I have to say the bestselling 'love gurus' lost me after advising that on the first date a woman shouldn't overwhelm a man with her career triumphs but instead let him shine.

When we say goodbye Yasir says three of the most beautiful words in the English language: 'I'll call you.'

When I check my phone on my way home I see that Lisa, Ruby and Nirvana have all sent me text messages.

Was it fate at first sight? lol (Lisa)

Well???? (Ruby)

Hey babe, how did it go? (Nirvana)

I send them all the same reply: *I don't want to get my hopes up but ARGHHHHHHHH!*

Nine

Here are some vital stats.

Days since I met Yasir: 4.

Telephone conversations that have lasted over one hour: 7.

Text messages: 1 million.

Butterflies in the stomach: rapidly breeding.

Number of times I have stared into the distance when I should have been conscientiously attending to work demands: countless.

'Er, sorry, what did you say your work experience was?' I repeat during a telephone conversation with a candidate applying for a pharmacist manager role.

'I had two weeks at Target.'

I wonder what Yasir is doing now. *Focus*.

'Target? What do you mean? Does Target have a pharmacy?'

'No. I was working in Layby.'

I take a deep breath and unlock my phone, checking if there's a message. Nope. I sent the last one. The ball's in his court. Get your hands on that ball, Yasir! Oh God, I'm turning into one of those psychos who want to be stalked on their phone, Facebook wall and email 24/7.

'But I got an awesome chance to build on my skills.'

Ah, yes, I have a job. 'How old are you?'

'Sixteen.'

Good Lord. 'And you don't think that's an issue?'

'No.'

I take a deep breath. 'Do you realise that you need a Bachelor of Pharmacy and a minimum of five years' experience as a practising pharmacist to get this job?'

'Okay ... but that's what I want to do when I go to uni, so can't you still consider me? Trust me, Layby can get pretty busy.'

My phone beeps. A text from Yasir. *Dinner tonight?*

'Of course!' I cry.

'Really? You're the bomb! That's awesome!'

'No, sorry!' I splutter. 'I didn't mean you. Call me in fifteen years and we'll talk then.'

I hang up.

I've got it bad.

My mother is hovering at my bedroom door, watching me get ready.

'How is it going with Yasir?' she asks hesitantly.

'So far, so good,' I say, putting on my earrings.

She takes a step in. I know she doesn't want to appear to be pressuring me, but as much as she wants to be subtle, she can't help interfering. My mum's bright, serious-minded and fiercely dogmatic about the things and people she believes in. Sometimes the force of her convictions is too strong and she can't let go enough to give us the room to make our own mistakes and choices.

'Is he serious?' she asks me. 'Sometimes parents think their children are ready to settle down but they're not. Have you asked him?'

I've had guys come for the formal-lounge-room date, only to find out that they're there under pressure from their parents; one guy, Ali, already had a girlfriend he had every intention of marrying.

'Mum, it's been a week,' I say, rolling my eyes. 'Relax!'

She raises an eyebrow. 'I'm just warning you.'

'Remember that I've done this a zillion times. I don't need the warnings any more.'

She shrugs. 'No need to get upset. I'm just trying to have a conversation.'

'You're trying to force a helmet on me when I'm already in protective gear.'

She clucks her tongue at me. 'I'll leave you then, seeing as you know everything.' She's about to turn on her heel and walk out when I stop her.

'Mum, sorry,' I say, giving her a tight squeeze. 'I'm just nervous.' I'm also terrified that if I leave the house with my mum upset with me, I'll be struck dead on the way home. But I don't tell her that.

'I just want you to be as happy as I've been with your father,' she says, giving me a warm smile. A smile filled to the brim with self-sacrifice and love and tenderness and trust. Knowing all I do, it makes me ache.

Dad pulls me aside on my way out and thrusts a hundred

dollars into my hand. 'I want you to buy yourself a present,' he says softly. 'I know it's not much, but you deserve something, darling.'

Just then Mum walks in. 'Deserves what?' she asks. Her eyes fall on the money in my hand. 'Oh, that's sweet, Mehmet,' she gushes, giving him a warm smile. 'Always so generous with your family.'

Dad mutters something under his breath and quickly leaves us alone.

I play heavy metal in my car all the way to the restaurant. But as loud as the music pounds in my ears, I can't drown out the voice that warns me that my parents' marriage will be buried forever if my mum ever finds out about my dad's guilty secret.

I meet Yasir at an Italian restaurant in Drummoyne. When I see him I get that funny feeling in my stomach. I walk over to him and his smile is so genuine, so warm, it makes me melt.

We don't hug or kiss (although I'm obviously thinking about what it would feel like), just shake hands and take our seats. Granted, I'm far from being the world's most religious person, but if there's one thing I won't compromise on, it's my 'no touching before the ink dries on the marriage certificate' rule (except for shaking hands – ooh, how positively scandalous!).

We order our entrées and I can't help but wonder what's going on in Yasir's mind. I wish I could just come out and ask him whether we're on the same page: whether our getting to know each other is for the long-term. But I'm not suicidal. I'm not going to bring up the C word with a guy I've known for seven days.

Yasir's phone vibrates on the table, jolting me out of my nervous thoughts.

'Sorry,' he says, checking his phone. 'It's work. Just give me a sec.'

'Problems at work?' I ask when he's put his phone away.

'A bit of a disaster, actually. I'm scared to tell you. Given your low opinion of builders.'

'You're changing that, so don't worry.'

'Am I now?'

'Slowly. *Very* slowly.' We grin at each other. 'So what's the problem?'

'I arrived at the house we're building today to find that the painters have painted the walls in the wrong colour. Electric blue. Throughout the entire house, mind you. Not just one feature wall. You would think they'd have realised something had gone amiss in the paint delivery. I mean, I don't think I've ever come across an electric-blue house before.'

'What a nightmare.'

'It's our mistake, so we have to wear the cost.'

'That's terrible.'

'It could be worse. I had a job once where a contractor I hired to do the plasterboard did such a dodgy job that I refused to pay him. He got me back by putting a carton of milk in the cavity of one of the walls and sealing it up.'

I burst out laughing.

'Of course, the milk went off pretty quickly and the stench was overpowering. We had no idea where the smell was coming from. It was only when we had the plaster-board removed by the new contractor that we found the carton of rotten milk!'

'You're supposed to be redeeming the construction industry's image, remember, not validating my low opinion of it.'

'Hey, short of mopping the floors with Chanel No. 5, I did everything I could to get rid of the smell. I went the extra mile. See what a nice builder I am?'

'Very nice,' I admit. 'And at least your job has its moments.'

'And what moments do you savour in your work?'

'Ah, now that's a tough one.' I tap my fingers on the table as I think. 'Strangely enough, pharmacy recruitment does have its fair share of amusing anecdotes. A couple of weeks ago I reviewed an application for the position of pharmacy assistant from a guy who put down as his reference a female escort who had apparently been a male pharmacist for ten years before an operation and career change.'

We go on like this for the rest of the evening, laughing and swapping stories. If you can laugh with a guy for a couple of hours, I reckon it's a safe bet that you're onto a good thing.

Ten

It was Brooke Shields who once said, 'Smoking kills. If you're killed, you've lost a very important part of your life.'

There are some statements you simply can't take back. And that's the way it is tonight.

I'm standing beside Ruby and Lisa at Anil's thirtieth. Nirvana's brought us along as support, and because Anil wants to meet her friends (a big step in any relationship).

It's a barbecue lunch at Anil's family's mansion in West Pennant Hills. Nirvana has filled us in on the family background. Anil's parents divorced when Anil and his sister were young. It was apparently quite a scandalous split, with Anil's dad running off with a friend of the family. Anil's mother struggled on her own until she struck gold, marrying a very wealthy man, and was effectively able to throw that in the face of everybody who'd whispered and gossiped behind her back.

For a family of four, the house is gigantic. I'm talking seven bedrooms, three studies, four rumpus rooms *and* a glass lift.

'This kind of wealth is obscene,' I say to Ruby and Lisa

as we stand in our huddle, holding onto our drinks (fruit cocktail for me) in the enormous alfresco area surrounded by manicured hedges and lawns and overlooking a stunning lap pool. 'I mean, who really needs this much space? And a lift? How excessive is that?'

'The lift is for my grandmother,' a voice behind me says. 'She can't walk.'

I turn to face Anil. 'Um, sorry ... that was so rude of me ... I didn't mean to—'

'—insult your friend's boyfriend's paralysed grand-mother?' Anil says, a severe expression on his face. 'Don't worry about it! It's *so* cool.'

I look down at my shoes, trying to avoid his eyes. Then Anil laughs loudly. 'Gotcha!'

Relief washes over me.

'The house *is* pretty over the top,' he says.

I don't dare nod in agreement or smile too enthusiastically. 'No, no, I was just joking,' I say, trying to sound as sincere as possible. 'It's an amazing home. It should be on one of those television shows. Your family obviously has beautiful taste.'

Nirvana joins us at that moment and Anil puts an arm around her.

'We have expensive taste,' Anil boasts. 'If you work hard you deserve the best of everything your money can buy. That's the philosophy my stepdad and mum raised me on: excellence in everything.' He proudly puffs out his chest as he glances at Nirvana. Then he squeezes her towards him and she grins up at him. 'This house cost one and a half million dollars to build,' he continues. 'The interior decorating cost another million. Come into the family room and I'll show you ...' Anil takes Nirvana's hand in his and starts to lead us back into the house where we're ambushed by a young couple.

'Anil, is this Nirvana?' the girl squeals.

Anil smiles proudly. 'Nirvana, this is my sister, Neela, and her husband, Sunil.'

Sunil has the typical look of a guy being dragged to a party. He looks Nirvana up and down, grunts a hello and stands to the side, giving off a very strong wake-me-when-this-is-over vibe. What he lacks in social graces, Neela makes up for in over-the-top enthusiasm.

'You're gorgeous!' Neela cries, grabbing Nirvana's arm. 'Come and let me introduce you to the rest of the family. Anil's told me so much about you. My mother and stepdad won't be here until later. We've kicked them out until cake time.' She drags Nirvana away, Anil and Sunil following. Lisa, Ruby and I are forgotten.

The three of us turn to face each other. We're silent for a moment, although I can almost read their thoughts. Sure enough, Ruby, as direct as usual, is the first to voice them.

'We're in trouble.'

I give them a look and nod slowly.

'How do we pretend to like him?' Lisa moans.

'What does she see in him?' I whisper. I know it's a harsh assessment and first impressions are often deceiving, but how do we look past the bragging and vanity, especially when Nirvana is so humble and modest?

Ruby thinks for a moment and then says with a sigh, 'Look, everybody has their redeeming qualities. So he's a bit of a show-off. From what we've seen so far, and all Nirvana's told us, he's put her on a pedestal, and we couldn't want more for a friend. He's romantic and she's head over heels. And maybe he's a great cook. Well read. Champions women's rights.'

'Feeds the poor and needy and donates blood every week,' I add.

Lisa laughs and then says, 'We've got to like him for Nirvana's sake. Focus on his good points.'

Nirvana comes rushing up to us a while later, while we're standing over the buffet table helping ourselves from the countless varieties of Indian cuisine on offer. In the middle of the long table is a dazzling feature: a massive chocolate fondue fountain. No expense has been spared.

'He has good taste,' I whisper to Lisa.

'Well, he likes Nirvana, doesn't he?' she whispers back.

I smile as I help myself to fresh naan bread.

'Having fun?' Nirvana asks us in a chirpy voice. She looks radiant, her eyes all sparkly, her cheeks dewy, her long hair loosely curled and hanging down her back. 'Anil's family's great! And they like me!'

Ruby snorts. 'Don't act so surprised.'

I place my hand on Nirvana's arm. 'Ruby's right,' I say. 'Liking you was never in any doubt. When do his parents arrive?'

'They should be here soon.' She lets out a nervous giggle. 'I'm so worried!'

'Don't be!' Lisa reassures her as we walk over to an empty outdoor table. 'You're the girlfriend every parent dreams about for their son.'

Anil's parents arrive shortly afterwards. Lisa leans in close to Ruby and me and says, 'His stepdad is the spitting image of Master Splinter from *Teenage Mutant Ninja Turtles*.'

Anil's mother, on the other hand, is regal. High cheekbones, bright hazel-green eyes and a stylish bob.

We watch them sweep down on Anil, smothering him with kisses and hugs. They take a step back and Anil grabs Nirvana's hand. He looks at her with tenderness and affection, unable to wipe the goofy grin off his face as he introduces her to his parents.

All night we watch Anil dote on Nirvana, refilling her glass, offering her food. Neela hovers close by, grinning at them both, and seems genuinely welcoming of Nirvana. Sunil has slunk off to the games room and is watching TV (I know because I saw him there when I went to the bathroom).

After we've sung happy birthday and Anil's cut the cake, Anil leads his parents over to us.

'Mum and Papa, these are Nirvana's best friends,' he announces proudly.

Master Splinter and Anil's mother smile warmly at us.

'Welcome to our home,' Master Splinter says. 'Ever since Anil met Nirvana he hasn't stopped talking about her. We're delighted that he's so happy and has found such a lovely lady.'

We all give the obligatory 'Ohhh' in unison, and Nirvana and Anil beam.

'Yes,' Anil's mother adds. 'Any friends of Nirvana's are now our friends too. You're welcome here any time. Come over for a swim. There's a jacuzzi and sauna too. Pamper yourselves, especially in these hot days.'

'How about tomorrow at eleven?' Ruby jokes, looking at the lap pool.

'Of course, of course,' Master Splinter says in a booming voice.

Suddenly Anil's mother engulfs Anil in another big hug. 'I can't believe my baby is thirty! I know mothers should never play favourites,' she says conspiratorially, leaning in closer to our huddle but looking at Nirvana, 'but Anil has always been such a wonderful son!'

Anil laughs and Nirvana smiles at them, although I can tell she's a little overwhelmed. Neela, who has walked up to our group with Sunil dragging his heels behind her, laughs and says, 'It's okay, Nirvana. I'm from the same womb but even I can't compete with Anil.'

'Christ,' Ruby mutters under her breath.

'Oh, Neela,' her mother coos, pinching Neela's cheek. 'You've always said that, but you're my daughter. I love you just as much as I love Anil.'

'Oh, come on, Mum,' Neela says playfully. 'Anil is Mr Perfect and always has been.'

I study Nirvana's face. She's trying her best to smile, but I can tell she's wondering how much truth lies under the banter.

'Anyway,' Anil's mother says, turning to Nirvana, 'Neela's with her in-laws now, as it should be. She's such a good daughter-in-law. I'm so proud of her. Isn't that right, Sunil?'

Sunil hasn't been listening to a word of the conversation. He's been standing silently cradling his drink as he looks around, examining the guests.

'Sunil?'

'Hmm?'

'Neela's been a wonderful daughter-in-law to your parents, hasn't she?'

'If you say so.'

Anil's mother is oblivious to his tone and flashes him a triumphant smile, as though she should be rewarded for all her daughter's redeeming qualities.

Neela looks uncomfortable now. 'I'm just going to get myself a drink.'

'I'll come with you,' Sunil mumbles, clearly desperate to escape. 'I need another one.'

'Anil's always been dependable, caring and *so* sweet,' Anil's mother continues, oblivious. 'Do you know what he did for my birthday? Sent me and Papa on a holiday to Hawaii!'

Nirvana's face muscles tense for the slightest moment. Anil's arm is around her and he's grinning at his mother and rolling his eyes, although he's not being rude. I get the impression he's used to his mother talking about him like this but that he doesn't really take it very seriously.

We, on the other hand, don't have the luxury of expressing our true feelings and are forced, for the next ten minutes, to listen to Anil's mother gush about how Anil has always been the perfect son and how the girl who steals his heart should count herself as the luckiest girl in the world.

Maybe I'm overreacting, but if there was a panic button handy and I was in Nirvana's shoes, I would be pressing it.

Eleven

'Question,' Ruby says in a commanding voice. 'You're talking to a guy on the phone. The conversation is going really well, in fact beautifully, until you hear the flush of a toilet.'

'Ew!' Nirvana and I cry in chorus. Lisa chuckles quietly.

No Sex in the City is at a café in Leichhardt tonight.

'He keeps on talking as though nothing has happened,' Ruby continues. 'So I ask him if he's on the toilet and he denies it. I say, "But I just heard a flush," and he says, "Yeah, that was my brother." So I ask him if he normally joins his brother in the toilet and he laughs and admits that, yes, he was in the toilet. So I tell him I can't be with someone with such a different sense of hygiene to me. I mean, even though I'm a Gemini, I have some Virgo characteristics. I just can't handle the thought that this guy is talking to me about how much he loves my curly hair while on the toilet! So I hang up on him and delete his number, just in case I'm tempted to call him back in a moment of weakness.'

Lisa groans. 'Ruby, you are *such* an idiot. Tons of people talk while they're in the toilet.'

'Do *you*?'

'No!'

'There you go. Because it's disgusting.'

'Of course it's disgusting,' I add. 'Nobody's disputing that. But I think Lisa's point is that you turned away a guy who you were otherwise getting along with, who you were attracted to, who was ticking all your boxes—'

'But who lacked basic hygiene.'

'Would somebody please inform Ruby that most guys lack basic hygiene?' says Nirvana.

'Generalisation!' I cry.

'Of course it is,' Nirvana answers, 'but it's also the truth.'

Ruby cocks an eyebrow at Lisa. 'My dad and brothers are *very* clean, thank you very much.'

Nirvana leans in close to Ruby and, in a mock-sympathetic tone, says, 'I hate to break it to you, sweetie, but if that's true, your dad and brothers are freaks of nature.'

'The point is, Ruby,' Lisa says, 'you turned away a guy over something that's pretty small in the scheme of things.'

Ruby nurses her mug and shrugs. 'That's me. I can't change who I am.'

'No,' Nirvana says excitedly, 'but you can change *him*! That's what we do, isn't it? Meet a guy, fall hard and then work out what habits Prince Charming is going to have to give up and what habits he can keep!' She laughs. 'I'm slowly working on Anil's makeover. He can go on about money and designer brands a bit too much sometimes.'

'Oh, really?' I say innocently. 'We hadn't noticed.'

Lisa kicks me under the table.

Ruby says, 'What terrifies me is getting into a relationship thinking you can change all the bad habits, and then failing hopelessly.'

'Which is why you don't go in with that kind of attitude,' Lisa says.

'You can't change people, Ruby,' I say. 'People spend their entire marriages trying to change each other, but it doesn't work. Since when do people change? Ruby, you've got a case of OCD, dumping a guy for taking a leak.'

'Oh, I doubt it was only a leak!'

'Okay, information overload. Nirvana,' I continue, 'you're falling for a guy while thinking of all the ways you can change him.'

Lisa shrugs. 'So what you're really saying, Ruby and Nirvana, is that we could replace the word "marriage" with "makeover". To love, honour and change – is that how it goes?'

'I'm not saying that you should change core values and qualities,' Nirvana says defensively. 'Just bad habits.'

'And it's a two-way street,' Ruby says. 'Although clearly men have worse habits than women.'

'Good luck with that,' I say. 'You're both fighting an up-hill battle if you think you can change lifelong habits.'

Oh My God. Yasir seriously has a bad habit of leaving it to the last minute to sort out plans to see each other. For example, the other night we were speaking on the telephone before we went to bed and agreed we'd have dinner the following night. The next morning I waited for him to contact me to make arrangements. By two o'clock I still hadn't heard from him. I called but he didn't answer. So I left a text message. He called me at six, as casual as ever, asking me where I wanted to go and what time.

I was annoyed but tried to contain myself. 'What took you so long to let me know we're still on for tonight?' I asked, trying to disguise the tension in my voice.

'I was busy at work.'

'It takes less than a minute to send a text. I wasn't sure if I should catch the train home or wait for you in the city.'

'Where are you now?'

'On the train home.'

'Oh. It would have been easier to meet up and then I could have dropped you off at home.'

YOU THINK?????

'Exactly,' I said, calmly and sweetly as ever.

And so the conversation went. I kept my cool but I was a bit pissed off. It's been three weeks since we met. We talk almost every day. We catch up about twice a week. And I've noticed Yasir's very carefree, easy-going and tardy.

The excesses of his character – nonchalant, unreliable, calm – clash with the excesses of my character – super-organised, a bit highly strung and over-punctual. It's not that I'm neurotic or that he's an irresponsible bum, it's just that I don't think he's responsible enough and he doesn't think I'm relaxed enough. We haven't fought about it or anything. So far it's only jokes (more on his side when he sees me clearly trying to curb my anger at the fact that he's showed up forty-five minutes late to a dinner date).

So I take back all my indignation at Ruby and Nirvana. Yasir's tardiness, lack of consideration and nonchalance MUST BE REFORMED.

Let the training begin.

'Yes, sir, I understand. You want a pharmacy assistant who is either twenty or over thirty ... Oh, sorry, what was that? ... Thirty-two? ... Okay, so twenty or over forty, but nothing in between because you don't want anybody going on maternity leave.'

I take down further instructions and then hang up the phone with a heavy sigh. Sometimes I hate dealing with clients. Some of them seriously think they're above the law. When I explain the law to them, they laugh dismissively, seriously believing they're not bound by any equal opportunity rules because they're trying to run a business.

I put the file to one side and head to the kitchen to make myself a much-needed coffee. I pass Danny's office on the way. He sees me, jumps out of his chair and follows me.

'Coffee break?' he asks.

'Yep.'

'I could do with one too. I've been on the phone with my wife since I got in. She's convinced that having a baby will bring us closer together and solve all our problems.'

Ew, ew, ew! I do NOT want baby-making and Danny to figure simultaneously in my imagination.

'She's monitoring her ovulation cycle now. You know what that means? Oh well, at least I'll be getting more—'

'Danny!' I shriek, almost dropping the milk. 'There are some things I don't want to know about! Get a counsellor or a best friend, but spare me the details, okay?'

For a moment he looks hurt. I turn my back to him and quickly make my coffee. My head tells me I don't need to put up with this. But he's the boss in a small company. We don't even have a human resources officer. I'd have to take my complaint to him. Fat lot of good that's going to be in getting the problem resolved.

I go back to my office, fuming.

Twelve

It's seven-thirty on a Friday night. I've just finished my jog around the block and am driving to the DVD store to hire a movie when the phone rings. It's Yasir and my insides go all funny again, as they do whenever I think of him. We haven't spoken since Wednesday. He was in Newcastle for a conference all day yesterday.

'Hi!' I say happily, exercise endorphins rushing through my system. I'm not even bothering to disguise my pleasure at hearing his voice. 'I've just burnt four hundred calories! And I'm about to hire a movie and get some popcorn and a jumbo bag of Maltesers to cancel out all my hard work. What are you doing?'

'Not much,' he says, his tone uncharacteristically subdued. 'I'm at home actually ... Um, can we talk?'

'Yeah, sure, just let me pull over.' I park in the closest side street. I start to panic. Has a family member died? Has he lost his job? Nothing prepares me for his next words.

'Yesterday I took some time to think things through. I don't want to hurt you by dragging this on any longer. It's just ... I don't see us together. I think you're wonderful.

You're sweet and smart and beautiful and you make me laugh. But I think it's best if we just stay friends. I'm really sorry.'

I'm gutted.

'I–I don't understand,' I stammer. 'I thought things were going really well. You said so yourself at dinner on Wednesday.'

There's a long pause. Has he died on the phone?

'Are you still there?'

He coughs.

I should be so lucky. Death would spare me the humiliation of rejection.

'Like I said,' he says uncomfortably, 'I took some time out yesterday to think it all through. I can't help the way I feel. I just don't feel that spark ... It's got nothing to do with you or anything you've done. I guess we weren't meant for each other.'

I'm angry now. I feel like I've been led on. How can he have talked to me only two days ago about the future and said how much he loved my personality and flirted with me and now suddenly realise I'm wrong for him?

'But I'd love to stay friends,' he adds hopefully.

There are two ways to respond. With dignity. Or without.

Stay friends? Listen here, you moron, I'm almost thirty, I have all the friends I want in my life.

Why, oh why, did my parents have to bring me up to be so conscious of *self-respect* and *dignity* and *integrity*? How on earth do those virtues give you any sense of satisfaction?

'I respect your feelings, Yasir,' I say quietly. 'If you don't feel a spark, that's fine.' (I hope you develop a nasty rash all over your body.) 'I wish you all the best.' (And lose all your teeth, and ...)

'Wow, you're so ... mature about this,' he says. Is that frigging doubt in his tone now? 'I expected you'd freak—'

Oh shut up. I cut him off. 'Bye!' I cry, then I hang up and burst into tears.

It's a tough night. It's hard to tell myself that this is a lesson to learn from, an experience to make me stronger. That Yasir wasn't my destiny. It's all meaningless in the face of the emptiness inside me, the hollowness of feeling so utterly happy one moment, filled with hope and big dreams and gorgeous, joyful optimism, then feeling empty, numb and confused in the next.

I want to run myself down, wallow in self-pity. Why is this happening to me? Aren't I smart enough, interesting enough, good-looking enough? I spend most of the night feeling sorry for myself, then finally fall asleep, exhausted.

Thankfully I wake up angry. Nothing like anger to extinguish self-pity.

I'm a strong person. I've been burned before, in some cruel and rude ways, too – like the guy who told me that he couldn't be with me because he had an ideal image of what his future wife's physique would be and mine didn't match up to it. I know I can get through this. I've always had an endless capacity for optimism. I might whine and vent with my girlfriends, but deep down I know that love is waiting for me somewhere.

What upsets me most is not the rejection but the fact that I was happy getting to know Yasir. And I believed he felt the same way. Now I'm left doubting my own intuition and judgement.

In the morning I message Senem with the news. She insists on coming over for a debrief, but I tell her not to bother. I'm not going to sit down and analyse every text message, email and conversation. Doing the 'he said this', 'he said that', and driving myself crazy in the process. So I go for a run around the park, hammering my feet onto the footpath, trying to sweat out the pain, searching hard for some endorphins.

When I return, I find my mother sitting in the lounge room, feet up on the coffee table, a mug of tea in one hand and a book in the other. I collapse next to her, drawing in some deep breaths. She glances up at me, smiles and then continues reading. We sit in easy silence for several moments, Mum reading, me staring at the swirls of colour on the rug, until I say, 'Yasir's not interested. It's over. Whatever *it* was.'

She looks at me and frowns. 'What happened?'

'He called me last night. He just wants to be friends. Apparently he doesn't feel that spark.'

'Like *the click*?'

'Mum, don't even go there,' I snap. 'There's a difference between not feeling anything towards a guy who can barely string together a few words of English, and Yasir, who has spent three weeks leading me to believe there was something between us.'

'Did he explain himself?'

'No.' I wrap my arms around a cushion, hugging it close to my chest. 'What annoys me is there's no proper closure. I just have to accept the decision and move on.'

She suddenly utters a spectacularly taboo Turkish expletive, surprising herself and me in the process. We exchange glances and laugh. 'You're better off without him. Don't we always say it's best for these sorts of things to happen before you're engaged? Look at Nuray – engaged for a year and then she ends up breaking it off because the guy's a miser. All that heartache. All those wedding plans in a mess. And still we say she's better off this way than marrying him and finding out too late. So you got hurt after three weeks? You're one of the lucky ones.'

We both know she's just as upset as I am and that she's trying to make me feel better. I know that inside she's probably wondering why I seem to attract such 'bad *kismet*'. I know she's thinking this even as she scoffs at Yasir's idiocy and congratulates me for avoiding getting further involved with him.

I go and have a shower. When I later return downstairs to make myself some lunch, I overhear my parents talking. My mum is blowing her nose. Great. As if my own disappointment isn't enough to deal with, I now have to cope with the fact that my parents are upset too. I hover at the kitchen door, drawn to listen even though I know it's only going to make me feel worse.

'She's better off without him,' my father says. 'Who does he think he is, rejecting her? What's there not to like about her? He's an idiot!'

'He told her he doesn't feel a spark.'

'Sparks and clicks and lightning bolts! What to do with this stupid generation? They want to go into cardiac arrest just to feel a sign that they've made the right decision. It's because they're gutless. The men nowadays are gutless! They want to have their fun, but when it comes to deciding about marriage, they're like kids in a toy shop. They want everything and when you ask them to pick one, they can't. They're either greedy or too stupid to know what's best for them.'

Wonderful. I've been reduced to a catalogue item at Toys R Us.

'Esma is from a good family,' he cries loudly, no doubt assuming I'm still in the shower and can't hear his tirade. 'She's educated! She's beautiful! She's smart! Funny! Successful! Sincere!' Not that he's biased or anything. 'And that gutless idiot rejects *her*!'

My mother sighs. 'What can we do? This is her *kismet*.'

'I'm going to mow the lawn.'

'Okay. But don't make a big issue with Esma. Just act normal. She doesn't need to hear us talk like this.'

My dad knocks quietly on my door later that night.

'Esma,' he whispers. 'Can I come in?'

'Yes,' I call out. I'm sprawled on my bed, preparing for some interviews at work tomorrow.

He takes a step into my bedroom and looks around shyly. 'Are you busy?' he asks nervously.

'Just doing some work.' I smile.

'That's nice ...' His voice falters. 'My shift was cut today. But don't worry, I've got a double shift tomorrow.' He pauses, scratching his chin. Then, as an afterthought, he says, 'They're a good hospital.'

Dad has always worked long hours, in low-paid jobs. Without any formal qualifications, he's been a bit of a jack-of-all-trades. But he's taken pride in what he does. For most of my life I can remember him working erratic hours. He worked in a chocolate factory (Senem and I gorging ourselves sick on all the free bars of chocolate he was allowed to bring home). For a short time he worked in a furniture factory, sanding and assembling timber furniture, until the place went broke and he took up cleaning.

Mum and Dad pushed Senem and me to excel at school and obtain the education they never received. Because it was apparent that I was the studious type and Senem wasn't, they encouraged me to attend university, and were overjoyed when I did. My degree is framed and hangs in the formal lounge room. Corny, but still sweet, I guess.

He clears his throat. 'The other day your mum mentioned to me that she'd like to see you save to buy a property ...' He speaks in a low, hesitant voice.

I sit up and cross my legs. 'That's just Mum talking. We both know that's not possible.'

He looks crushed and it suddenly strikes me how much he's aged. He's lost weight and there's far more white in his hair now.

'Every minute of the day I think about how I'm affecting your future.' He falls silent again and then adds, 'This business with that stupid boy ... I had hoped so much ...'

'The thing is, Dad, that even if it had worked out with Yasir, it wouldn't have solved *your* problem. You'd still need me. Me getting married would probably only complicate things. I can't keep something this big from the person I marry.' My voice is strained and I can feel anger pounding in my ears.

He winces at my words. 'I've tied myself into a million knots ... you along with me ...'

I stare at him, suffocated by my sense of duty and respect and love and pity.

'What would you have me do? Tell your mother?' He says this solicitously, genuinely seeking my opinion rather than asking a rhetorical question.

But how can you tell your wife that you've gambled away her house? I think of all the nights my father must have returned from the club to an evening of deceit and festering secrets. How many times did he greet her with a forced smile after he'd fed their money into the fruit machines? Why wasn't the image of my mother's face powerful enough to help him resist the temptation?

They could never afford to buy back into this suburb, even with the balance of the equity in their home after repossession. House prices here are just stupid compared to when they moved here twenty years ago.

And what would happen to my parents' marriage if Dad confessed? Would it survive his betrayal? Would Mum forgive him? What choice would she have? How could she support herself? Would she stay with him because she had no choice, and end what was once a happy marriage in bitterness, hurt and pain?

I'm suddenly furious with my mother for placing all her trust and reliance in my father. How naive she must be to think that life is so safe and predictable that you can survive without some level of independence and autonomy.

I go round and round the loop of questions and scenarios as my father waits for my response.

But I don't need to respond. My silence is enough of an answer.

Thirteen

'I *hate* this case I'm working on,' Ruby says while I'm multi-tasking, talking to her on the phone, typing up a report and scanning my emails. 'It never gets any easier.'

'If it's any consolation, the fact that you haven't been desensitised is probably a good thing.'

'Misdiagnosis of cancer in a teenager. They cut out most of her stomach and then, oops, discovered that actually she had reflux, not cancer.'

I wince. 'Is the insurer denying the claim?'

'No. I've advised them to pay up. It's not a question of liability. We're just negotiating the settlement.' She sighs. 'Anyway, I don't want to think about it now. How are you holding up?'

'It's a little hard for me to feel self-pity in the face of that kind of suffering.'

'Stop being a saint. If I judged my life against my medical negligence practice, I'd be a basket case. But I don't. Because I'm human, and while relativity is great for the soul, too much of it is paralysing. We all have to function and cope with the life we've been given. So for God's sake, enjoy a good rant about that spineless dropkick, will you?'

'You know what kills me the most?'

'The "it's not you, it's me" line? That line should attract a jail term.'

'Well, yes, there's that. But really, what's killing me is that there's no closure. I don't even know why he thinks there was no spark when it was going so well.'

'I know,' she says, her tone suddenly gentle. 'That's the worst part of it. He gave you a pathetic reason and you just have to accept it. I know it's a cliché, Esma, but you're better off without him.'

'That's what makes it all so hard. I'm not moping around, focusing every last atom of energy into finding a man, but I'm so ready for romance ... I hate to admit it, but I have this secret fear that I'll be *that girl* ... the girl nobody falls in love with.'

'Maybe the answer is online dating.'

The lack of irony in her voice makes me laugh.

'Trust me,' she says. 'I've heard great stories.'

'They're in the minority.'

'Have you tried it before?'

'No! I have my dignity.'

'Don't be such a snob.'

'I'll try it when I'm really, really, *really* desperate.'

'Don't be an imbecile. Taliah and Jaydin met online. And what about Julian and Carol? They're madly in love, thanks to the web. So get over it, will you? I'm creating a profile and logging on tonight. It can't hurt. In the meantime, do you want to start boot camp with me?'

'Why? I've got a gym membership.'

'Last visit was when?'

'Hmm ... I had highlights in my hair – I remember because I drove to the gym after my hair appointment then drove back out of the car park because I didn't want to waste a good blow-dry.'

'You had highlights last year.'

'Yeah ... I really need to go in to cancel my membership.'

'Jesus, Esma, you need to get fit again.'

'I run all the time. You know I do. And since when do you like exercising? I can barely get you to take a flight of stairs in the shops.'

'Okay, okay,' she laughs. 'This is boot camp with a difference. The trainer is Greek and, I'm told on good authority, dazzling. Lots of the Greek crowd from our local church go there. It's become a social thing too. Well, at least according to Pina, who's been doing it for the last year. So I'm going to sign us up. Maybe we'll meet someone.'

'How can we meet someone when we're puffy and red-faced? I don't care how hot your body is, nobody looks attractive doing star jumps.'

'Good point. But I'm sure it's not *that* intense. We'll just take it easy. We're not there to actually get fit or anything. You've got to learn to be strategic, Esma. Slot yourself into groups and scenes where you're more likely to meet some-one who meets your criteria.'

'That sounds so sad and pathetic.'

'No, it's about having a proactive attitude. All those movies we've seen have given us a warped view of reality.

We're waiting for our destiny to bump into us at Coles, probably in the tampon aisle knowing my bad luck.'

'It'll be the herbal tea section for me. We'll both be reaching up for the orange-flavoured laxative tea. Our hands will brush, we'll gaze into each other's eyes, and we'll click over a conversation about which tea produces the best results ... Are they all from your church?'

'Nah. There's a mix. I'm sure you can meet a Muslim there.'

'Wonderful. So he'll be Muslim and enjoy a good work-out too. We were meant for each other.'

'I'm booking us in, okay? Mondays, six in the morning in Ryde, starting in a fortnight. I'm changing my shift at the legal centre, so you can't bail on me. Deal?'

I say yes. Because sometimes you've got to seize fate rather than wait for it to seize you.

'How's the online scene going?' I ask Ruby the following week.

'An infinite source of laughs. Which is, I know, unfair to those who do meet with success. But clearly my online profile is attracting the nutters.'

'I told you so.'

She whips out her phone and scrolls through her messages. 'The other day I got this one,' she says, and starts to read aloud: '*I am a healthy, prosperous engineer in the USA for thirty-two years from Greece, sixty years old. I am healthy like a thirty-year-old man. I jog two kilometres a day. I am better than others because a) older men don't cheat, b) older men have more time and money, and c) I'm fun-loving with still a lot of hair.'*

'What a turn-on.'

I enjoy teasing Ruby about her online disaster, but as adamant as I've been about never veering into online dating territory, I'm starting to reconsider. That's what happens when the offline scene is so woeful – you change strategy and become more flexible. Even if the thought of meeting in person a stranger I first met in cyberspace freaks me out.

When Dad quit gambling he started to pray the five daily prayers. It was new to us, as we hadn't grown up with him or Mum praying. Even now Mum only prays on special occasions.

It wasn't an overnight conversion for Dad. At first he started praying at the mosque on Fridays, when he could make it. Then he started waking up for the pre-dawn prayer, going straight to work after that. Then, before I knew it, he was maintaining all five prayers. He hasn't become a zealot. I've never heard him ask Mum to join him and he's never bothered me about it. He just withdraws at prayer times – quietly, humbly. It seems to give him solace and peace.

I understand prayer before dawn. When I do manage to get my lazy butt out of bed and pray, I get it.

But humanity is not meant to wake up before sunrise to exercise.

It's Monday morning and I wake before dawn (I pray, seeing as I'm up anyway and I'd really appreciate God's help with push-ups and jumping jacks) and then leave the house. I actually drive as the sun is rising on a MONDAY MORNING! It is not remotely transcendental or inspiring. The drive to the park where boot camp will be held is a struggle. The voice in my head does not relent: *Go back*, it whispers over and over again. I actually have to put the radio on full volume to drown it out.

When I arrive at the oval I get butterflies in my stomach. There are about forty people warming up and stretching on the basketball court. Some of them are huddled in groups, laughing and joking as though it were the middle of the day instead of the crack of dawn. I love exercise. But I'm not, and never will be, a morning person.

I catch sight of Ruby, who looks stunning in her hot-pink and black Nike Lycra outfit. She's wearing make-up and her curly hair is pulled up in a complicated style more suited to a cocktail function. She's the perfect example of somebody who has never exercised seriously in their life, labouring under the delusion that what you look like at the start of a session is what you'll look like afterwards.

Ruby sees me and waves. 'Esma! Over here!' she cries.

I jog over, hoping her enthusiasm is infectious. She's standing beside two girls, whom she introduces as Theresa and Pina. They're both stretching and look almost as eager as Ruby.

'Isn't this great?' Ruby exclaims and then leans in closer to me. 'Did you see the guy over there with the blue hoodie?' She closes her eyes for a moment and sighs. 'To die for.'

'Don't go dying on me this morning,' I threaten. 'I wouldn't trust myself to save my own mother, let alone you.'

Ruby flings an arm across my shoulders. 'Well hello, Miss Grumpy!'

I manage a laugh. 'I really hate exercising when even the birds are still asleep.'

'You'll get used to it,' Theresa says as she raises her leg straight up, doing a vertical split. Ruby and I stare at her in awe.

'Are you a dancer?' I ask.

Theresa bursts out laughing. 'I was a size eighteen three years ago.'

We are both momentarily deprived of speech.

'Alex, the trainer, changed my life.'

'Eight o'clock, eight o'clock,' Ruby interrupts. 'Stunner. Oh and five o'clock. Perfect face. And ... wait ... yep! He's not wearing a ring.'

Theresa and Pina grin.

'How can you tell from so far away?' I ask.

Ruby smiles slyly. 'Practice. Plenty of practice.'

'Well, don't bother,' Pina says. 'He's going out with the size-six hottie over there.'

Ruby frowns. 'She'd better have a bad personality.'

'She's actually one of the nicest people we train with,' Theresa says.

Ruby shakes her head. 'You can't have looks *and* personality.' She pouts. 'That's so unfair.'

I glance around at the group, taking a closer look. There's no doubt there are some good-looking guys here. So now I just need to figure out their religion, then their level of religious observance, moving on to education, career prospects, temperament, capacity to engage in quality conversation, ability to make me laugh, travel experience and, just for the fun of it, interest in commitment.

Alex rounds us all up and we gather around him in a semicircle. He's lean, buff and, well, okay, has a perfect body. There's a tattoo of a cross on his right arm and some elaborate calligraphy on his left.

He waits for silence. Some people jog on the spot, waiting for him to start. I join in, trying to warm up my muscles. I try to persuade Ruby to do it too, but she refuses. 'Are you nuts?' she chides. 'One hour of training is enough.'

'Youse are machines,' Alex starts when we've all quietened down. 'Youse have to believe in yourself.' Ruby and I immediately exchange amused glances, educated snobs that we are. 'Don't let your mind talk to youse. Don't give in to the pain. Everybody feels pain! Love the pain! Don't think you're alone. Fight it! Get through it! Push yourself. Give me everything youse got. That's all I expect. I don't care if youse can only do two push-ups. If two is the best youse got to offer and you've pushed yourself to the max, then I'm happy. Don't get to the end of the session thinking youse could have given me more. Get to the end of the session thinking you're gonna die.'

Ruby shoots me a look of alarm. It's the first indication she's given that she realises what we're in for.

'If you get to the end thinking you're about to die, then you'll know you did your best and I'll be happy.' He glances down at his clipboard. 'Some of youse haven't filled out the forms. I gotta get all the details on here. Cos of the lawyers and stuff. Bill, where are ya, man?'

An overweight guy calls out, 'Here.'

'You need to fill out your emergency contact details. You've put down triple zero.' Some people laugh. 'That's not what the form means. I'll put down your wife, yeah?'

'What the hell is my wife gonna do for me if I pass out? Man, this is my first time exercising. I'm overweight, unfit and I smoke. If I'm in an emergency you call triple zero, cos the only people I'm gonna need are the kind you find in an ambulance.'

We all burst out laughing.

'Okay, okay,' Alex says after he's finished taking down some details for two more people. 'It's six on the dot now. We gonna get things started and have an awesome session! Come on!'

In the next hour I want to cry out for my mother at least fifty times. We do squats with heavy medicine balls, skipping (I'm sure I could skip as a child, but now it seems that colonic irrigation would be more pleasant), boxing and kickboxing rounds and lots of running. Lots. I thought I was a runner, but my jogging sessions around the block are nothing to what we do. Twenty one-hundred-metre sprints with thirty seconds 'recovery' in between. At number three, Ruby looks like she's about to pass out. 'It's okay,' I tell her during our 'break'.

'I can't do it!' she shrieks. 'He's a madman!'

'I HATE YOU!' a girl cries out to him.

'Excellent!' Alex cries back. 'Hate me! Think about how much youse hate me while you're running. I've got pensioners who have had hip replacements doing this! YOUSE CAN DO IT! GO!'

We take off. Ruby and I are panting like ex-smokers (which we are) and asthmatics (which we are not). We make it to the finishing line and Alex blows the whistle twice, indicating that the session is over. With no thought for how we look, Ruby and I collapse onto the dewy grass, our lungs dangling at our feet, our faces bright red. When I finally catch my breath, I look around. There are others on the ground too, or hobbling back to the basketball courts. Pina and Theresa come over to us and offer us each a hand, pulling us up.

Ruby's curls have come undone and are cascading down her back. Not, I'm afraid, in some BBC-period-romance way but rather in an I-need-defrizz-serum-and-a-stylist way.

As for me, I'm euphoric.

'That was *so* not what I expected,' Ruby gasps as we limp back to collect our bags.

'It was better!' I cry maniacally.

'We told you you'd love it!' Theresa says, patting me on the back.

'I feel fantastic!'

Ruby looks at me aghast. 'We *look* shocking!' she complains. 'That was *not* exercise, it was torture. And even though we're surrounded by eligible bachelors, I only caught the fat guys perving at me. There has to be more of an incentive than getting fit!'

'You've already paid for the six weeks,' Pina says, 'so don't quit now. We all start like that, but we end up addicted.'

Ruby stops dead in her tracks and casts an evil look at Pina. 'Addicted? You are not normal. And neither is Alex. He's a sadist.'

'Well, not really,' says a voice from behind us. It's Alex. He grins at Ruby and she laughs nervously, clearly embarrassed. 'What's your name?' he asks her.

'Ruby.'

'I know you want to quit,' he says.

She stands up straight and looks him in the eye. 'Yeah, that's right,' she says boldly. 'Haven't you heard that the "no pain no gain" mantra is outdated?'

'Well,' he says, taking a step towards her and grinning, 'maybe that argument works to sell gym memberships, but it doesn't work for me. Sure you're gonna feel pain today, and believe me, when you wake up tomorrow you're gonna be cursing me even more than you are now.' Ruby holds his gaze defiantly. 'But if you stick with me, the pain'll get better and you'll learn to love it.'

Ruby laughs cynically. 'I almost passed out! I wanted to vomit!'

'So vomit!' he says cheerfully. 'Happens in most first classes. Go over to that bush over there, let it out, then get right back into it. Don't be weak, Ruby. Don't let your mind play games with you.'

'What star sign are you?' Ruby suddenly asks.

He looks perplexed but answers, 'Aries. Why?'

A smile spreads slowly up to her eyes. 'Figures,' she says smugly.

He half-laughs. 'What are you on about?'

'Aries are naturally active and energetic people,' Ruby says authoritatively. 'Me? I'm a Gemini. I party. Not exercise.'

'Oh, Ruby,' I chide. 'Enough with the astrology.'

Alex grins at her. 'Ruby, you're gonna go home tonight and your mind's gonna tell you this isn't for you. You'll start thinking of the Ariel and planet stuff. It's gonna tell you that you're better off doing some aerobics class. That's fine. But just remember, nobody started here as an athlete. Everybody felt just the way you did. See Theresa here? She called me the day after her first class crying cos it hurt so bad. Look at her now. She's lost weight but I don't care about the weight. That's the easy part. She's fit now. She's healthy and happy. Trust me. Stick with me for the next six weeks and I can guarantee you'll be craving these sessions.'

I watch Ruby as she stares at Alex. Being her best friend I can see the subtle shift in her stance, the loosening of her facial muscles, the widening of her eyes. I can just see her assessing Gemini/Aries compatibility.

'Like all of us who've been here for a while, you're gonna be into training,' Alex says.

Actually, no, Alex. She's going to be into you.

Fourteen

Sara Lopez emerges from the lift with the latest pram (all sparkly and spaceship-looking), matching baby bag (designer, of course) and tiny, adorable nine-week-old baby fast asleep in the spacecraft, snug in an Oroton wrap. Sara (formerly Zumba fanatic and herbal-appetite-suppressant addict) has that first-mother look. A mix of glowing, delusional, exhausted and overjoyed, with a dash of the paramilitary about her (I'm a little scared when I place my hand on little Delilah's chest and Sara, who is talking to Veronica, snaps her head back to look at me and then takes a step closer to the pram, like a bodyguard averting an act of terrorism).

'She's not due to wake up for another fifteen minutes,' she says, her voice high-pitched and, well, bordering on hysterical. '*Puhlease* don't touch her!' She sniffs the air dramatically. 'Is somebody smoking?' she cries.

Veronica and I exchange wary but puzzled looks.

'Impossible,' I say, careful to tread delicately. 'The smoke detectors would have been activated.'

'Well, I know the smell of smoke,' she says breathlessly.

Then she laughs nervously. 'Maybe it's coming up through the vents. Honestly, people are so selfish. Don't they realise the effects of passive smoking?'

I resist, reminding her that a) we're on level five; b) like all modern buildings, the windows are unable to be opened as a precaution against mass suicides (I don't really know anybody who likes their job); and c) the selfish people smoking are huddled in the alley adjacent to our building, about a five-minute walk away, and would probably be under the sensible impression that cigarette smoke won't affect a baby snug in its pram five floors up in the nearby building.

'I don't allow smokers to even hold my child,' Sara says self-righteously. 'A disgusting habit.'

She's clearly forgotten that she is an ex-smoker who formerly backstabbed an asthmatic client who complained of her smoking at a function.

Suddenly Delilah wakes up and lets out a piercing cry. It hurts to hear it.

Sara leaps at the pram. 'She's awake! Time for a feed!'

The cries continue and I feel like stripping Sara down and throwing the baby at her boob. Delilah's cries draw Danny out of his office.

'Oh, Sara,' he says pleasantly. 'Welcome back.'

'Just a visit, Danny,' Sara says cheerfully.

Then she sits down at the lunch table, whips her boob out of her bra and starts to unwrap the screaming Delilah (confusing the more appropriate order). Danny's jaw hits the ground. Veronica smirks at me. Danny keeps staring until Sara finally starts feeding Delilah.

Danny takes a step towards me as Sara talks to Veronica, filling her in on all her stories of new motherhood.

'Mary got her period yesterday,' he says wistfully.

Ew ew ew ew!

'Danny,' I say firmly, 'I don't need to know that.'

'She's devastated.' He leans in close to me and whispers, 'She says I'm shooting blanks.'

I put my hands to my ears. 'Danny,' I say through gritted teeth, 'there is a line. Professional and personal. You're crossing it.'

He pouts, pretending to be wounded. 'I thought we were friends.'

'You're my boss.'

'You're such a prude,' he jokes, as he stares at Sara's breast.

'And you're a jerk,' I snap.

'Hey,' he says, suddenly serious, a flash of anger in his eyes. 'If I'm your boss, then that would be out of line. You can't have it both ways.'

I hold his gaze for a moment, defiant, but nonetheless trapped by the unstable dynamics of our relationship. I turn to Sara, wish her luck and storm to my office.

At the staff meeting later that week Veronica and I are laughing about a candidate who applies for every job we advertise (whether it's pharmacy, care of the elderly or legal), changing his qualifications depending on the job. Danny interrupts, announcing that Sara won't be returning to work after all. We're all shocked. She was one of the best staff, always over budget, with a killer rapport with clients.

'Apparently she doesn't want to be a working mum. She's too much in love with motherhood,' he says sarcastically. 'After all the time and money I invested in building her career, she throws it away to spend her days breastfeeding and changing nappies!'

'Oh, come on,' Veronica says. 'Not everybody wants a career. Some women prefer full-time motherhood.'

Danny smiles insincerely. 'You're right, Veronica. Which is why you can't have it both ways. I stand to lose too much. Thank God your relationship is on the rocks. I can't see you popping out a baby any time soon. As for Esma here, she's so fussy she's unlikely to find anyone who meets her high standards. My star employees! Don't either of you even think about having a baby in the next five years if you want to see yourselves moving up in this place.'

'That's outrageous,' Veronica cries.

Danny laughs. 'Veronica, we're recruiters. We all know that's how the world works. And I'm the boss, remember. It's my way or the highway.'

He looks at me then. I avert my gaze. I think of rusty nails and eyeballs. It is strangely calming.

Nirvana calls me a couple of hours before we're due to meet for our next No Sex in the City get-together to tell me that she can't make it.

'Why not?' I exclaim.

'Anil's booked dinner and a movie,' she says apologetically. 'A double date with his sister and brother-in-law. I'm sorry,

Esma, but I can't cancel when he went to all the trouble.'

'I went to trouble too,' I whine.

'Oh ... Did you book already?'

I clear my throat. 'Well, no, but I went to the trouble of suggesting it.'

'Sorry,' she says, sounding less apologetic this time. 'You understand, though, don't you?'

'Of course,' I mutter. Then I feel a pang of guilt. The last thing I want is to play the role of the jealous friend. That's so high school. 'I'm just being silly,' I add quickly. 'Have a great night out together.'

Her voice switches instantly and she's her enthusiastic, bubbly self again as we discuss what she's going to wear and how she's going to do her hair.

When I meet the girls at Darlinghurst that evening and explain to them that Nirvana can't make it because she's on a date with Anil, Ruby can't disguise her displeasure.

'*Any* other night,' she declares, 'any other night would be acceptable, but not a No Sex in the City night! That's just wrong.'

'Oh, Ruby, give her a break,' Lisa scolds, taking a sip of her soda. 'You guys go on and on about meeting The One and when he bloody well arrives you whine about his timing.'

I burst out laughing. Ruby shoots me a look.

'You complained first.'

'Okay, okay,' I say, backing down. 'Let's just order.'

When we're done ordering, Ruby places her hands on the table, stares intently at us and says, 'Would you think I'm an idiot if I told you that I've got a crush on Alex?'

I burst out laughing again.

'Wow, thanks!' Ruby jokes. 'Make me feel good, why don't you?'

'Who's Alex?' Lisa demands.

'Our boot-camp instructor,' I explain.

Lisa laughs hysterically.

'What's so funny?' Ruby asks.

'The idea of you at boot camp.'

'Yes, I know,' Ruby says. 'But apparently Alex is worth the agony of sit-ups because I'm actually looking forward to the next session.'

Lisa gives Ruby a wry smile.

'We're polar opposites. I'm sure of that. But he's ...' Ruby looks upwards, searching for the right word.

'Irresistible?' I offer.

Ruby grins. 'That will do.'

Lisa smiles. 'It's been a long time since I've met somebody who's had that effect on me.'

Ruby isn't buying. 'Come on. I don't believe you. No intense animal magnetism?'

Lisa thinks for a moment. 'Nope. Not since uni.'

'Christ, it must be a side effect of working with women who only experience the worst in men.'

'Give me some credit. I'm intelligent enough to distinguish between scumbags and decent guys.'

'So basically the last guy you took any interest in was Jerry at uni?' Ruby asks.

Lisa, who is finding the whole conversation amusing, nods.

Ruby studies Lisa's face. 'I thought the whole celibacy

thing was because deep down your mum's nagging was working and you hadn't truly turned your back on your religion.'

Lisa laughs loudly. '*Celibacy?* You make me sound so ...'

'So *me*!' I say and we all laugh.

'If my soulmate came along and I actually had the time to notice, sure I'd be interested. But in the meantime I'm not interested in the occasional fling or casual relationship. That's not because I'm religious. It's because I'm just not a *casual* person. I don't fling anything or anybody to the side. I'm never going to be a short-term loan. I need full-term, and exorbitant rates of interest.'

'That is so lame,' Ruby says, hitting Lisa playfully on the shoulder.

'I know,' Lisa says, grinning. 'But it's true. I'm intense and I need meaning and connection, and casual sex just isn't going to deliver that to me.'

'Would you be with Alex if you had the chance?' I ask Ruby.

'Maybe. I don't know ... Well, no, not if it was just casual, although God knows I'd love to. But that's not me either. I know this confident exterior is deceiving, but deep down I'm old-fashioned too. Not as prehistoric as *you*, Esma. The sky won't fall on me if I'm not married first.'

'Thanks for putting it that way,' I say dryly.

She winks. 'But I need commitment, and given it's becoming increasingly difficult to find a guy who doesn't expect sex after one or two dates, I'm beginning to think I might die a virgin.'

'But you're not a virgin,' I say.

Ruby sighs. 'It's been so long, my hymen has probably grafted back together.'

Fifteen

Monday morning

'I have issues,' Nirvana says flatly as soon as I answer her call. 'Not with Anil, or his stepdad. With his mum. She's clearly suffering from mummy's boy syndrome.' (You don't say!) 'She gets up in the morning as he's leaving for work to iron his work shirts for him. He laughs it off. He thinks it's sweet. This is not good.'

Wednesday morning

'At dinner last night she asked me if I could cook Indian food. I told her the truth. I don't particularly like cooking. She coughed into her vindaloo. Anil laughed and gave me a hug. I could have sworn she muttered a prayer under her breath.'

Sunday evening

'I think she's stingy. She doesn't look that way when you meet her with the two-carat ring and Mercedes-Benz, but I caught her washing *used* foil. It was all greasy from the butter chicken. Esma, I think this is going to be a problem.'

At today's Teenzone session we're working on a new project. Using donated suitcases, the class are painting their personal stories into the suitcases. When they've finished, we're going to take photographs of the painted suitcases and create an exhibition space at our next fundraising event.

Sonny and Faraj are mucking around with the paintbrushes, while Miriam and Ahmed, who hate being separated and are working beside one another, are bent low over the table, mixing colours. I walk over to Christina, who's tracing the image of a church onto her suitcase, and ask her what it means.

'It is the church we used to visiting in Iraq,' she says without looking up. She's focused on the pattern, and her features – small blue eyes, ginger eyelashes, thin light eyebrows and a dusting of freckles on her nose – are all scrunched up in concentration. 'It was burnt down. I do not remembering every detail of it. But I remembering there was one window. My parents liking to sit in the chairs near this window. Hanging next to this window was a picture of Jesus. He was bending and holding the cross. I wanting to painting that on my suitcase.'

'Why?' I ask gently, crouching down beside her.

She shrugs. 'I do not know. I just remembering that picture. Staring at it when I was more little. Sometimes I feeling I left Jesus behind in my country,' she says matter-of-factly.

'But don't you take faith with you wherever you are?'

She smiles. 'Yes. We going to the Iraqi church here. But

it is not being the same for me. I have many more things in my mind and I forgetting faith sometimes. Maybe if I paint it, I will not forget.'

'I met an extraordinary woman today,' Lisa declares as we drive home together in my car. 'Twenty-one, from Somalia. She lost a lot of her family in the famine.' She shakes her head slowly. 'Do you think some people are just born with a bigger capacity to cope with death and grief? I mean, how the hell do you live day in and day out watching loved ones die of starvation?'

I shrug. 'I don't know. But how can we know? We've never really been challenged in life. Sometimes I feel embarrassed in class. Like I should be apologising for having it so good.'

She throws me a sidelong glance. 'You know what bugs me? Sometimes I catch myself feeling good about my work. Congratulating myself for being so caring.' She rolls her eyes. 'Then I go home and do my best to forget about all the tragic stories I've heard.'

'Yeah, I know. It reminds me about what that guy, I can't remember his name, wrote: *We're victims of weapons of mass distraction.*'

'I like that,' she says, nodding thoughtfully.

I know I'm not a superficial person – I care and I do a bit more than the average person on the street – but I also know that I'm capable of switching off. When I think about the students I work with, my worries seem meaningless in comparison. But does that mean I'm supposed to accept everything that happens to me – Dad's debt, being unhappy at work – just because I'm grateful that I don't live in a war zone, or that there's always food on our table? Do I sit back and accept that I don't need to strive for things to be better because, when measured against those less fortunate, I've been blessed with the best out of life?

When I talk to Lisa about this, she tells me not to beat myself up because I'm fortunate enough to have been born in a peaceful, affluent country. 'Sometimes that kind of guilt can stop us acting, and that's no good to anyone. At least you're doing something, and all you can do is hope that it makes a small difference to people's lives.'

I nod slowly, musing over her words, and then say, 'To be honest, sometimes I also feel that my focus on finding Mr Bloody Right feels trivial in comparison to the things we struggle with at the centre. At the same time, I guess that while finding a partner might not be as essential to life as being safe and secure, it's at the heart of life.'

'Of course it is,' Lisa says. 'It's not at the heart of mine, I have to say, but for most people it is – including people who've been on leaky boats and locked up in detention! We've seen some happy endings here, haven't we? Mohamed and Fariha met through the centre last year and ended up getting married. There's nothing selfish or frivolous about wanting to find love.'

'I wonder if I'll meet a guy who feels the same way as we do.' I laugh. 'I just need to meet the male equivalent of you. Somebody who's interested in ideas and life and social justice – all the complicated, messy stuff.'

She giggles. 'Did I tell you what happened with my mum last night? She suggested I go to a Jewish singles party with my cousin. You pay the lady organising it and then you attend a dinner party with about fifteen other single Jews. I refused.'

'I'm sure you did better than that.'

'Okay, so I told her I'd rather kill myself than go. Figuratively speaking of course. So in true form she carried on and vowed to kill herself first if I don't go. Trust my mum to match me on a suicide vow. You can't win with that woman.'

Sixteen

My fingers hover over the keyboard as I stare at my computer screen. I hesitate before pressing enter, then squeeze my eyes shut and let out a yelp. I toss my MacBook to the side and lie on my bed, staring up at the ceiling fan as it turns round and round.

I've
created
an
online
dating
profile.

The gravity, the sheer enormity of this decision, strikes me when I consider that I've boycotted the entire online dating scene for the past ten years. At university it was very popular among my Turkish friends to meet guys in Turkey through ICQ. Some of them even met up with the guys when they visited on family holidays. Most of the guys turned out to be total losers and the complete opposite of their profiles ('uni student' was actually a middle-aged kebab-stand owner; 'entrepreneur' in fact sold cheap trinkets to tourists in the bazaar; 'good-looking guy' was fat and balding). Two friends did find their husband through the net, though. One of them now lives in Turkey and the other brought her man here. They are both, as far as I am aware, very happy, and therefore form part of the fairy-tale circle one pretends to disdain but secretly hopes to join one day.

On this site I can 'purchase' contacts (presumably the payment requirement filters out people who aren't serious), and 'kisses' are for free.

I have lost all dignity and have made myself available on the open market. I am commercial merchandise now, selling my heart through the online shopping mall, albeit with certain conditions (my usual checklist).

I call Lisa and confess the loss of my RSVP virginity to her.

'You're an idiot,' she happily chides me. 'There's nothing wrong with it.'

Ruby is delighted. 'It's about bloody time.'

There is a flurry of activity overnight. A new product on the market. Instant interest.

Dear Esma
I'd like to catch up for a coffee to discuss my résumé. It needs work and seeing as you're in the industry, it'd be great to get some insider feedback.

Damn. I shouldn't have put my job as part of my profile.

Hi, I'm interested in getting to know you better. I'm also a Muslim. I've tried the Muslim online dating site but didn't have much luck there, so I bit the bullet and gave this site a try. Look forward to you contacting me.

Hmm. I'm not sure. Why should I pay for the contact when *he's* initiating? Ruby warned me about this. Lots of tight-arses out there, she said, who will expect you to pay for the first contact (an email). I send a message back:

Hi, it'd be nice to get in touch. Send me an email telling me more about yourself ☺

I thought I'd be inundated by contacts through RSVP. But I haven't heard back from the guy who was interested in getting to know me more. I can only assume one thing: just like Ruby warned me, he's a tight-arse. Asking me to make the contact (and therefore pay) and giving me the flick when I didn't.

I've had some other messages, the combined effect of which has convinced me that the majority of guys are pathetic, sad, idiotic losers who are socially dysfunctional.

Sample of evidence to support my sweeping generalisation:

Are you attractive? You MUST be attractive. Intelligence is a bonus but not a necessity. Look forward to your reply.

Me: Intelligence is a MUST for me. So goodbye.

So when you say you're a Muslim, do you wear that tea towel on your head? Cos I really hate that. It's oppressive. Have you assimilated since you moved here?

Me: I occasionally wear a tea towel on my head. I've been known to wear a tablecloth and nappy too. I am very oppressed and degraded and in need of rescue. I would say I am assimilated given I was born here.

Hi.

Me: Have you developed early-onset arthritis in your fingers? Even so, two letters masquerading as a message is inexcusable. Not to mention you can still hold a pen in your mouth and type with that.

Seventeen

Senem and Farouk are at our place for dinner tonight. Dad's shift has changed again and it's a rare treat for us all to have dinner together. Mum is cheerful and upbeat, hovering around us like a flight attendant in first class, serving more food onto our plates, refilling our glasses and ignoring our appeals to stop fussing and just sit down. But Mum's never really known how to sit still. If the house is her workplace, then hosting dinner is where she earns her KPIs, and this is one woman who won't accept anything less than a glowing performance appraisal.

Dad's just as excited to be home having dinner with us and is also fussing, in his own way. Tugging at Mum's sleeve every time she nears him and pleading with her to sit down beside him, coaxing Senem to eat more ('You're too thin'), edging the plates of food closer to Farouk (who is, of course, the 'son he never had', but still the Son-In-Law and must therefore be pampered and impressed, even though Farouk is so easy-going that he wouldn't care if Mum and Dad served him a TV dinner) and periodically patting me on the hand and smiling at me with sadness and affection.

We're listening to Senem tell us another one of her funny work stories. Working at a check-in counter for a domestic airline provides a never-ending supply of anecdotes. Tonight it's about a woman who went a teeny weeny bit crazy because Senem refused to allow her to bring her kitten on board. We're laughing along with Senem (who at this point is standing up and mimicking the woman) when my phone beeps, notifying me of a message on one of the Muslim online dating sites I joined in a fit of insanity. I open the message and giggle.

We live in a time when oceans are turbulent and tsunamis are very frequent due to global warming and plate tectonics. So it's unsafe to sail (in ships). But the sky is clearer and safer than the seas. That's why I offer you a friendplane, instead of friendship. So be my friend. I guarantee, you'll find me SAFER than expected.

'What's so funny?' everybody asks.

'Oh nothing. It's just that I think I've found the man of my dreams.'

I hand my phone over to Senem and show her the message. She explodes into a fit of laughter.

Farouk leans over to look and I snatch the phone from Senem.

'I don't think so, Farouk!' I tease. 'There are some things for sisters' eyes only.'

He grins. 'Don't worry, I'll get it out of Senem on our way home.'

Senem snorts. 'Keep dreaming.'

'Ah, Farouk,' I say, 'don't make the mistake of thinking Senem would ever betray me. You may be her husband, but you just can't compete with me. We're from the same womb, remember? That trumps a marriage certificate any day.'

One of the things I've always admired about Farouk is his geniality. Rather than taking offence, he's clearly enjoying the banter and plays along. I think his good nature has made his transition from Turkey to Australia smoother than normal – although that's not to say it hasn't been a challenge. Farouk secured a job at an IT company towards the end of his first year in Australia. Senem confided in me that there were moments during his year of job-hunting when he felt disillusioned and bored, and he spoke about them possibly moving to Turkey, where he owned an apartment in the coastal city of Antalya. The job rejections seemed to compound his homesickness, and Farouk often lamented that life in Australia was so quiet and boring compared to Antalya, with its long summers and bustling Mediterranean lifestyle. It took Farouk some time to adjust to the reality that life here was pretty much focused around long work days. He never tired of singing Turkey's praises, pulling out the old 'we work to live rather than live to work' line.

He was right, of course. Having spent most of my summer holidays in Turkey during university, I'd recognised the difference in lifestyles, at least among my family and their friends, who were relatively affluent and lived in the heart of Antalya, fitting work around their social life rather than the other way around. I sympathised with Farouk's culture shock, especially once he started working long hours. But rather than get depressed about it all, he proved to have the capacity to enjoy life irrespective of where he is. And so despite the long hours, Farouk and Senem have a vibrant and busy social life and treat weekdays like the weekend – in comparison to the rest of us who often just eat dinner, watch some television, set the alarm clock and collapse into bed.

After dinner we take advantage of the balmy weather and sit under the pergola. Dad's smoking and absorbed in deep conversation with Farouk about the latest events in Turkish politics – their mutual pet topic. Mum's nursing a hot cup of Turkish coffee, while I sip on instant coffee and Senem drinks a herbal tea. Senem begins to share another funny work anecdote with Mum. I watch them all interacting so easily and happily, and feel a pang of love for my family. It's in these simple moments that I understand the virtue in helping Dad to pay off the loan, because to refuse to do so would probably mean these moments would be forever lost.

And as long as I can help it, I won't allow anything to threaten my family.

Eighteen

'Anil proposed!' Nirvana screams into the phone.

'OH MY GOD!' I cry.

We meet at a local café within half an hour.

'Okay, details! When, where, how?'

'He told me he'd booked dinner but when he picked me up he said he needed to stop by his place to get something. I went in to say hi to his parents. He led me to the lounge room and—'

'Nirvana!' I holler. 'Backtrack, backtrack! We cannot have this conversation without the set-up!'

'The set-up? Oh yes, of course. Emerald-green Charlie Brown dress. Jimmy Choo heels – best eBay purchase of the year. Make-up: got it done at a MAC counter because I needed to buy some products anyway and it was redeemable.'

'Ooh! I love makeovers!'

'Hair: half pinned back, kicked out. Enough detail?'

'Yep.' I nod once firmly. 'Bollywood starlet.'

'Oh yes, *very*,' she jokes.

'So tell me about the proposal.'

'Our parents were there, which was a surprise. Neela

and Sunil too.'

'A group affair, *naturally*.'

'Oh, and a group of his mum's friends too, which, now that I think about it, is a little weird but anyway! He led me to the front of the room, and I was giggling and blushing – thank God for Studio Fix Extra Coverage – and then—'

'Were you nervous?'

'Very! All those grinning faces looking at me, clearly in on it.'

'Lucky you said yes.' The words come out before I can stop myself.

Luckily Nirvana takes the joke and, laughing, says, 'Yes, lucky I did.'

'Did he get down on one knee?'

Nodding, she bursts out laughing. 'The thing is, he knocked one of the ornaments off the table when he did!'

'Oh no! Don't tell me it was a religious statue?' My eyes widen with the possibilities. 'An urn containing the ashes of a family member?'

She clutches her stomach, laughing. 'No. It was a large, hideous statue of a koala. But with the fuss his mum made, you would have thought it *was* the ashes of her ancestors. She leapt out of her chair and quickly swept up the pieces. Then, all flustered, she reassured everybody this *wasn't* a sign and that nobody should *dare* think it was a bad omen.'

I half-laugh, not believing what I'm hearing.

Nirvana snorts. 'It was fine. Really. Anil made a joke and everybody laughed it off. What can I say? Indians can be very superstitious. Like Anil said, she was pre-empting the gossipers. Want to see the ring?'

'Yes!'

She proudly extends her arm and shows off her ring. I grab her hand and hold it closer to me.

'WOW! It's enormous! I'm so happy for you.'

Her voice wobbles. 'I'm so happy for me too!'

We laugh loudly and the owner of the café comes around to see if we want to order another coffee. He's an old Armenian man and has had the café ever since we started coming here in our university days.

'Ooh,' he says, spotting the rock weighing down Nirvana's hand. 'What a beautiful ring for a beautiful girl!' Nirvana smiles shyly back at him. 'Just engaged?'

She nods and he congratulates her and insists on a free coffee to celebrate.

It's funny how weddings almost always make people gush and go all warm and fuzzy. No matter your background, almost everybody seems to get it: the idealism, the joyous optimism, the wholehearted belief that your love is indestructible.

The next day Ruby, Lisa and I pay Nirvana a quick visit after work. Ruby's still got to head off to Redfern Legal Centre for her monthly roster, and Lisa needs to go home to pack for a trip to the coast to give a three-day workshop on domestic violence awareness as part of a regional campaign she's involved in.

Ruby and Lisa gush and squeal over Nirvana's ring; having already seen it, I stand proudly to the side, adding in my own comments and details ('It's three carat, white gold!'). When

Nirvana gets to the koala part, Lisa and Ruby guffaw loudly.

'I'm under no illusions that Anil's mother is going to be anything but hard work,' Nirvana groans.

'What about Anil's dad?' I ask. 'You hardly ever mention him. Has he had any involvement in Anil's life since the divorce?'

'No, not really. He lives in Brisbane. He remarried years ago and has his own family now. That's why Anil's mother is so gossip-conscious, I think. He remarried within a year of the divorce. It took her ages to get over the stigma. She was a single mum for about eight years before Anil's step-dad came along. It was a fairy-tale ending for her, anyway.'

'Depends on your definition of fairy-tale,' I say under my breath.

'What's going on between Neela and Anil?' Lisa asks. 'There seemed to be some tension at the birthday party.'

Nirvana shrugs. 'Not between Anil and Neela. They're great with each other, *when* I've seen them together, despite the mum's obvious favouritism. I think the issues are between Neela and her mum. There's a lot of baggage from the divorce, I think. We don't see Neela that much anyway. She lives an hour away from her mother's place and she's almost never there whenever I've been visiting. She lives near her in-laws and apparently she's always hanging out with them.'

'Voluntarily?' Ruby scoffs.

Nirvana makes a face. 'Not sure. Anil doesn't know much about Neela's life. I've asked him but he says Neela doesn't say much. There's something going on between her and Sunil. I don't think they're very happy. I've never seen the slightest bit of affection between them. Never a kiss or hug. But you never really know what's going on inside a marriage, do you?'

'Anyway,' Ruby says, quickly losing interest in the topic of Neela's marriage, 'we're thrilled for you! There's plenty of time later for you to dissect your in-laws. For now let's focus on *you* and your engagement plans. What kind of party do you have in mind? Obscenely lavish and therefore perfect? Or boring and intimate?'

'No prizes for guessing which you'd prefer, Ruby,' I say.

Ruby grins. 'Well?' she demands, turning to Nirvana. 'If you need a project manager, I'm up to the task!'

Nirvana laughs. 'Thanks, but I'll pass. I've seen enough of your project management skills from our birthday parties.'

'What do you mean?' Ruby says, batting her eyelashes as she feigns surprise.

'Oh come on, Ruby,' Lisa says. 'You're a born dictator. I'm sure there are committee members from your Greek Club university days who are still in therapy after organising events with you.'

Ruby laughs loudly, demonstrating that she is taking all of this as a compliment, and we all laugh along with her.

We spend the rest of the visit discussing Nirvana's ideas for the engagement party. It seems, from the little time she's had so far to discuss such details with Anil, that she's more interested in something classy and intimate: just close family and friends in a small reception or garden party. Nirvana prefers to leave the extravagant celebrations for the wedding, where she has every intention of celebrating her Indian culture to its fullest.

The four of us are excited and animated and lively, intoxicated by Nirvana's happiness. Yet on the drive home later that evening I wonder if things will change between us now that Nirvana's engaged. You often hear about friends drifting apart when a guy steps into the picture, how people can forget their friends as they 'move on with their life'. The thought that this might happen terrifies me. But something deep within me knows our friendship isn't just filling up a temporary space, waiting to be replaced by our respective Mr Rights. None of us thinks that we're living some kind of transient existence before love and marriage come along and our so-called 'real life' begins.

My grandmother has often said to me, 'Hurry up and get married and start your life!'

Really? So my existence until now has been a figment of my imagination, has it? I'll take my first *real* breath, laugh my first *real* laugh, cry my first *real* tear when there's a man at my side?

My God, I need a bucket.

The life I'm living now is real and enriching and full, and my friendships form a part of it, whether we're in relationships or not. I'm not naive. I know life can take people in different directions, but the closest of friends can remain so despite the tyranny of distance. Anyway, as far as I'm concerned, if a friendship is threatened when you start to share your heart with somebody else, it was never anything special in the first place.

And what the four of us have is special. That much I know.

Nineteen

Nirvana, Lisa, Ruby and I are holding our No Sex in the City get-together at a nail salon, where we're getting pedicures thanks to the vouchers Ruby won at a work raffle.

Nirvana's telling us the latest labour horror story from work (we're all suckers for stories about episiotomies and crazy birth plans) when her phone rings. We instantly know it's Anil because her voice becomes all fluttery and sweet. Since the engagement she's upgraded (or downgraded, depending on your perspective) Anil to 'baby', 'sweetie' or 'honey'. As the rest of us are not in the throes of new love, we have no tolerance for these gushing displays of affection. We make gagging noises and she waves her hands at us to shut up.

'Ohh, baby, I miss you too,' she coos. 'Sure, we'll talk tonight. Yep, I'm out with my girls. They say hi too. Pardon? Oh, yes, sure, say hi back to your mum ... Okay, honey, bye ...' She hangs up and turns to us and, her voice back to its normal, less nauseating tone, says with a sigh, 'Oh God, Anil's mum is *killing* me.'

It becomes apparent very quickly that Nirvana is

living a Bollywood movie and that a producer would snap up the rights to her story in a second. This would be the pitch:

Nirvana, the beautiful heroine, has finally met The One. Anil is suave, kind, educated and successful. He dotes on Nirvana and is not even afraid to use the C word. There have been weekend trips 'just for fun' to furniture and white-goods stores, and the couple have found, to their delight, that they both share a preference for neutral shades and agree that leather is a more sensible choice than fabric (leather being far more suited to a home with children, which, of course, is part of 'their future'). And when the subject of children is raised in aisle five, near the black leather ensemble with matching chaise, they giggle like schoolkids, their minds filled with images of a baby that will represent a fifty per cent contribution from each of them (with the sum total constituting only the best parts of their looks and personalities).

However, despite their perfect relationship (they only argue about Anil's unfortunate habit of forgetting to apply the handbrake, which has, so far, not resulted in any loss or injury to life or property), a dark force hovers at the edge of it, threatening to send them plunging into relationship oblivion.

Anil's mother.

Cue theme music to *Jaws*.

(Description: regal and menacing looks, albeit with a tyre of fat around her stomach that sits proudly above her sari.)

Anil's mother, Preedi, has nothing personal against Nirvana. It's just that she has something against any girl who is going to take her son away from her. The eldest and only son, Anil, is the golden child, who stood beside her in her dark days as a single mother. Preedi has struggled to accept any girl Anil has brought home. And now Anil is engaged to be married, and Preedi must pretend to be happy when really all she wants to do is banish Nirvana from their lives. Because now she will lose her firstborn forever. Not to mention that Nirvana doesn't seem to want a big traditional engagement party. She wants something 'intimate' and 'classy'. Fifty people! Not the two hundred people that should be there. What would the community think??? This formerly struggling divorced mother is now the proud wife of a rich man and more than capable of sending off her son in STYLE, thank you very much!

'She's a witch!' I cry, scaring the girl who is buffing my toenails (she doesn't speak much English, so she can only smile and nod at me).

'Your mother-in-law is just *such* a cliché,' Ruby says.

'Can't she do the whole evil mother-in-law thing with a bit more of a twist?' I say. 'I mean, it's so *old*.'

'Playing devil's advocate for just a moment,' Lisa says calmly, 'try to see things from her point of view. It might help you work out how to deal with her. If she feels she was ostracised because of the divorce, then that clearly affected her relationship with her kids. And she seems to want to get back at everybody in the community who gave her a hard time.'

'I know,' Nirvana says ruefully. 'But it would be so much easier to appreciate her point of view if she wasn't so manipulative. For example, at dinner the other night, Anil and

I were talking with his stepdad—'

'Master Splinter,' we simultaneously correct her.

Nirvana giggles. 'Oh, that is so mean. He's the *nicest* guy.'

'We know,' I say matter-of-factly. 'But he's a dead ringer for Master Splinter.'

She pauses, thinks for a second, and then grins. 'You're right. So, Anil and I were talking with Master Splinter,' she looks at us and we nod approval, 'about the engagement plans, and Anil's mum was quiet. When Master Splinter left the room she looked at us sadly and said, "I'm so happy for you both."'

'Well, that's good,' Lisa says.

'*Wait!* Then she said, in this *pitiful* voice, "But it's hard for me ... " She patted Anil on the hand. "You will always be the best man in my life, darling. Husbands come and go, but not sons. As happy as I am for you, I'm sad to lose you."'

Ruby, who has just taken a sip of soft drink, coughs. The Coke comes out through her nose, sending us into a hysterical fit.

'I couldn't help myself,' Nirvana continues once we've calmed down. 'I told her I felt hurt by her comment and shouldn't she feel instead that she was gaining a daughter? And Anil, who by then had given his mum a big reassuring hug – BARF – laughs and says, "That's right, Mum, I'm not going anywhere. You're not losing me. You're gaining Nirvana."'

'How did you not puke on all the clichés?' Lisa cries.

Nirvana bristles. 'Believe me, it took all my self-control. She was supposedly fighting back tears and forced herself to reassure us she was very happy and not to worry, she'd be *fine*.'

I suddenly let out a giggle. My pedicurist has started with the pumice on the balls of my feet. This is not a good thing – I am ticklish and I wriggle around in my seat. I can't exclude the possibility that I might kick her in the mouth. She is looking at me and smiling while she scrubs my feet raw.

'Can't Anil see through it all?' I ask when the torture session has finished and we're on to the more soothing task of applying nail polish.

'Of course not,' Nirvana says wearily. 'I love him to bits, but he's a mummy's boy through and through.' She puts her face in her hands. 'It's going to take all my fortitude not to commit a homicide before the engagement party.' She looks up sharply. 'Not to mention she is so intolerant of my dieting.'

'What do you mean?' I ask.

'You know how I always carry a small cooler around? For my ice cubes. She thinks I'm mad.'

A couple of months ago Nirvana read that eating cold food burns calories as the body has to heat up the food to body temperature for it to be absorbed into the bloodstream. Ever since then, she's insisted on the majority of her meals being served cold (it always throws waiters). Then she came across the bright idea of munching on ice cubes all day. So it's not unusual to see her carrying a small cooler in her oversized handbag and popping ice cubes like chewing gum.

'Nirvana!' I thunder. 'I'm on your mother-in-law's side with this one.'

Nirvana opens her handbag, takes out the cooler, lifts the lid and throws an ice cube into her mouth.

'You're mental,' I mutter at her.

'I'm burning calories just sitting here getting a pedicure. That's not mental. It's smart.'

Lisa rolls her eyes. 'Please extend my sympathies to Anil.'

When we finish and I'm at the counter paying, my pedicurist hands me a receipt and says, 'If mother-in-law dog, give her bone.'

'Oh,' I say, startled. Then I flash a charming smile. 'Is that a Thai saying?'

'No,' she says gruffly. 'Experience.'

Senem sends me an instant message at work.

> Senem: Guess what? Me and Farouk might be moving in with you guys for six months while we save for the deposit!!!! It'll be like old times!!!
>
> My jaw drops.
>
> Me: Really? When?
>
> Senem: The lease ends in five months. But we can't afford to renew it *and* save. We'll only be staying for six months. I know it's a burden on Mum and Dad but Farouk and I will insist we help with the bills.
>
> Me: You know Mum and Dad will have a fit if you suggest paying the bills. They've never taken a cent from us.

It's not a lie. Before the debt, Dad had refused any offer from us to contribute to the shopping or bills. If I wanted to help out, I bought groceries without asking anybody and just put them in the cupboard. But to actually give my parents money would send them, especially my dad, into a fit of anger. Which is why I'm sure that asking me for financial help has deeply wounded Dad's pride.

Senem: Well, Farouk will try anyway. And I promise I won't hog the bathroom. And you and Farouk get along so well, so it won't be like all those other horror stories you hear about. Mum's so excited. Are you?

Me: OF COURSE.

My use of capital letters is the equivalent of a forced smile. There are many words I can use to express my feelings, and excited is not one of them. If the situation were different – if I wasn't basically spending most of my salary trying to save Mum and Dad's house from being repossessed – then I would have welcomed Senem and Farouk back home. But the fact is that they're moving back to Mum and Dad's so that they can save to buy their own place. And I can't save to buy my own place because I'm paying off a loan that I never asked for. The cruel irony of the situation isn't lost on me. Nor is it lost on my dad, who calls me within the hour, Senem presumably having spoken to him about the plan.

'Esma, have you heard?'

'Yes,' I mutter.

'I don't know what to do. Your mother is so excited.

There's no question of refusing. She's my daughter, of course we can't refuse.'

And what about me, Dad? I want to scream.

'I'm sorry, Esma. I really am. It will only be six months. They've promised that. And I have good news. I'm getting a pay rise. That will be forty more dollars a week into the loan. Everything makes a difference, yes?'

'Yeah, of course ...' My voice falters.

'I'm taking on an extra shift at work, too. With Senem and Farouk moving in, the bills will be higher, and I don't want that to affect you.'

'Okay, Dad.'

'God will reward you for being so kind to your parents,' he says. 'He won't ignore that I don't have an atom's weight of disappointment in you, Esma. Only pride and love.'

I bite down on my lip to stop myself from crying.

Twenty

Danny pops his head into my office as I'm about to leave for the day.

'Any plans this weekend?' he asks.

'Not that I'm aware of so far,' I say cautiously.

His face breaks into a grin. I have no idea what's going on with him. Ever since Sara's visit, and the subsequent tense work meeting in which he basically took it upon himself to exercise control of our reproductive rights, he's been relaxed, pleasant, jovial even. The random compliments have even returned (apparently I'm 'dressed to kill' today; this was offered at the same time as Danny complimented Shae on her new bag, so I couldn't exactly take offence).

It's as though our little spat never happened. Once again, I'm left confused. Every instinct in my body tells me that Danny has crossed the professional line one too many times and that his antics are unacceptable.

Maybe the best thing is to try to find another job. I'd probably have a case for constructive dismissal, but to sue Danny would mean witness statements and rallying staff to stand by me. It would all be so messy and stressful that

I don't think it would be worth it.

I tell myself to take each day as it comes, and try to ignore the voice in my head that says that's just a cop-out.

Eleven-forty-five. Snug in bed. Coaxing myself into sleep with a fantasy involving Colin Firth (who, in my fantasy, has converted to Islam after meeting a Muslim extra on the set of *Pride and Prejudice* and therefore now ticks every conceivable box in my checklist), his proposal of marriage to me (during an Oscar acceptance speech), Turkey consequently being accepted into the European Union (even the EU has a thing for Mr Darcy), and Colin and me becoming national heroes (in Turkey, the UK and Australia) and a text message ... Huh?

Who'd be texting at this time? I roll over to face my bedside table and check my phone. It's from Ruby.

Can you bring your Mink headband to boot camp tomorrow? I want to wear it. See you then!

I try to recall my fantasy but the moment has gone. I'm left thinking about push-ups and sprints and fall asleep exhausted.

'GIVE ME AS MANY SQUATS AS YOUSE CAN IN THIRTY SECONDS, STARTING NOW!'

My legs are burning from the half-hour of kickboxing we've just done but I throw myself into my squats, trying to lower my butt as far down to the ground as I can. If my muscles could talk they'd be shouting filthy curses at me right now. I look over at Ruby. The mink headband is a bit lopsided now and she's struggling with the squats, stopping every time Alex turns his back. As soon as he turns around and is looking in our direction, she's trying her best, scrunching up her face in a look of intense concentration. I'm too tired to laugh.

Later that day I'm on my way to an appointment with a client when Ruby calls me.

'What would you say if I told you that Alex went to the same Greek weekend school as me when we were kids?'

'I'd say, "Wow, what a coincidence, and did he do push-ups for fun during recess?"'

'I wouldn't have a clue. Probably. But he was two years above me. So while we may have crossed paths, I can't remember him and he can't remember me.'

'You've got it bad, haven't you?' I say with a laugh.

'I stayed back after you left class and talked to him,' she tells me. 'Then a few of us went for a coffee. His – how can I say this ... his *vocabulary*, is deceiving.'

'What do you mean? Did *youse* have fun?'

She laughs, but not as heartily as she would have done a few weeks ago. 'He's not some dumb-arse. I know the way he speaks is unpolished and, dare I say it, a little *westie*—'

'Not everybody can – or *wants* to – live in the eastern suburbs or over the bridge, you snob.'

'Yes, yes, I know, which is why I'm qualifying what I'm saying. I had my preconceptions. I've been fed a diet of them growing up.'

I pretend to yawn and she yells at me.

'You know what I mean!' she barks. 'Give me a break.'

'Luckily you're my best friend, otherwise I'd suspect you actually thought the *educated classes* only lived in your suburb.'

Ruby, being Ruby, ignores me and goes on. 'Alex is a high school drop-out. Okay, I accept that. But he's turned himself into a businessman. He's running these classes all over Sydney and doing corporate sessions too. His dad didn't have much of an education either, but he's built up an investment property portfolio. Apparently his dad isn't happy with his decision to build a personal training business as opposed to taking on the family business. Alex says it's been a struggle to get his family to approve, but now that he's doing so well, they're starting to accept his decision.'

'Sounds to me like you're struggling to come to terms with the fact that you're interested in a guy who comes from a completely different background to you.'

She lets out a short laugh. 'I'm attracted to him. And there's chemistry. Lots of science-lab, Bunsen-burners-exploding chemistry.'

'Okay. That's good.'

'The problem is that, like it or not, I've been raised to believe the only kind of relationship that will work for me – and for my family – is one in which the guy is Greek, educated, successful and moves in the same social class as we do. My family defines itself by its status in the community. Alex's family might be from the same island in Greece, but they move in a different crowd, attend a different church ...' Her voice trails off.

'In a nutshell, you move in different socio-economic circles?'

'Yes.'

'And you're worried about how he'll fit into your family and with your colleagues and church community?'

'Yes ...'

'Ruby, has Alex asked you out?'

'No.'

'Then quit being a lawyer who has to conduct a hypothetical risk assessment about everything and just see what happens! You do this *all* the time. Leave the analytical Ruby at work and let your love life take its course naturally. Okay?'

She agrees. She'll restrain herself. Boot camp will be about getting fit. And if something develops with Alex, it will be a bonus and she can worry about snobby parents and compatibility then. This is what she promises me.

Not for a second do I believe her.

Twenty-One

It's survival of the fittest. There are tears and blood and soft-tissue injuries. There's rivalry, bullying and misappropriation of goods. The adults have weary, haggard faces, as though they've been in battle and are waiting for their sleep and food rations. I've never experienced anything like it.

Arzu has persuaded me to join her at her local play centre. We haven't had a chance to catch up properly since she became a mother, and she called me this morning and suggested I join her at Lollipop Land. Naively, I agreed, assuming we'd be able to enjoy a coffee and a long chat while adorable cooing babies sat quietly and contentedly in their prams or crawled in the baby corner.

Except it's half-price Saturday and every baby, toddler and child in the north-western region seems to be here, fighting for control of every toy and inch of territory. This place is probably the best form of contraception around, I think to myself.

Arzu and I are trying to talk, but Malek has just started crawling and is not stupid enough to restrict herself to the baby corner when there are rides and toys in enticing primary colours across the room. So I'm walking around with Arzu, coffee mug in my hand, trying to have a conversation.

'We never used to argue,' Arzu says. 'Before we had Malek we were the perfect couple – that's for the big kids, sweetie – but now we're both so exhausted that we're almost always at each other's throats. Yasin is just such an involved dad.'

'Isn't that a good thing? I mean, lots of women complain that they do everything.'

'Look, he's great with helping out in the house, and honestly, with Malek, I'd be lucky to have the time to boil an egg – over here, sweetie. What I mean is, he fusses over how I feed her and wrap her and how I put her to sleep and what brand of dummy to use. She came out of me. You'd think I'd know how to heat a bottle! DON'T eat food off the floor!'

My phone rings. It's Mum.

'What's all that noise in the background? Where are you?'

'A children's play centre with Arzu.'

'I can't really hear you.'

I walk to the toilets where it's relatively quiet. 'Can you hear me now?'

'Yes, that's better. I got a call today from Aunt Gulcin.'

I know where this is going.

'There's a Turkish guy, originally from Germany. He's been in Australia for seven years. He speaks fluent English. He's tall.'

I burst out laughing. Mum always does this. She knows I have a thing for tall guys and thinks just mentioning height will be enough to hook me.

'So what does this *tall* guy do?' I ask.

'He's a doctor!' she answers breathlessly.

'Hmm ... What else do you know about him?'

'He's thirty-three. According to Gulcin he's very socia-ble and handsome. And tall.'

I never, ever take the aunties' word for it when it comes to looks and personality. I'm sure they heard 'doctor' and blanked out everything else.

'Does he live here with his family?'

'No, his family is in Germany. He was born there. His parents are here on holiday for a couple of months.'

My imagination immediately plunges into a ridiculous fantasy: stunningly good-looking (and tall) doctor with wonderful sense of humour sets up a local practice in suburb with harbour views. I have no in-law issues given my in-laws live on the other side of the world. Yearly visits to Germany, with detours to Turkey, Paris, London, Rome and Spain. I'm spoilt rotten by my in-laws who, seeing me once a year, are only exposed to my charming side.

My fantasy is interrupted by a little boy who walks in, opens the door to the cubicle, stands next to the toilet, looks intently at me and then says, 'I'm doing a poop.'

'Invite him over,' I say to my mum. And then I silently remind myself to be careful what I wish for.

I open my email account at work, take a sip of my cap-puccino and follow it with a bite of my peanut butter on toast. I'm scanning through my inbox, deleting all the junk industry news and notifications ('How to Tell a Candidate

Their Résumé is Rubbish without Lowering Their Self-Esteem' etc), when I nearly choke on my toast. There's an email from Marco.

> Hi Esma,
> It's good to hear from you. I've got tickets to the Latin-American Film Festival this Saturday if you're interested?

It's good to hear from you ...
I repeat the phrase over and over in my head. What is he on about? Have I accidentally sent him a text message? I reach for my phone but then stop. That's impossible. I don't even have his number. I drum my fingernails on the desk. *It's good to hear from you ...*
I scroll down Marco's email. To my horror he's *replying* to an email. From me.

> Hi Marco,
> How are you? I've got no plans this weekend if you're free?
> Esma

I feel physically sick. Somebody has obviously hacked into my account. It takes less than a second for me to realise it must have been Danny.

I'm livid. I storm through the corridor and throw his office door open. 'How dare you?'

He's sitting at his desk and looks up, a bewildered expression on his face. 'Excuse me?'

It takes all my willpower to contain myself. 'Danny,' I say calmly, 'did you use my computer to send Marco an email from me?'

'No.' What a hopeless liar. An infuriating grin erupts on his stupid face. He stands and throws up his hands as if to apologise. 'Okay, yeah, I did. I'm sorry.' He giggles. 'No, look,' he says, noticing I am unmoved, 'it was a little joke. You hadn't locked your computer. It was completely harmless. Marco knows it was me. Almost as soon as I sent it I told him.'

'A joke?' I say furiously. I pause, and take a deep breath. 'You used my computer. You sent a guy an email from me basically asking him out on a date.'

'Yeah, but he knows it was me. I told him.'

'But that's besides the point. And if you told him, why has he just sent me an email inviting me out on Saturday?'

Danny puts his hand to his mouth to stifle a laugh. He's behaving like a schoolkid, not the director of a company. There is no remorse. He's actually acting like it's the funniest prank he's ever played.

The stony expression on my face must make him realise I'm not impressed by his apology. So he tries again.

'I'm really, *really* sorry. You have no idea. I've just been under so much stress at home and things between us were so tense. I just wanted it to go back to normal. Fun and games, mucking around.'

Good Lord, he thinks there's an 'us'. And what fun and games is he on about? So we've cracked some jokes. I do that with everybody in the office.

'That wasn't mucking around,' I say through clenched teeth. 'That was an invasion of my privacy.'

He sits back down at his desk. 'I suppose this isn't the best time to tell you that you're up for a promotion in June? I'm making you team leader.'

Of all the scheming, manipulative things he could do! Deflect attention away from his atrocious behaviour with this news. How am I supposed to believe it's even true, not just some decoy he's thought of on the spur of the moment to calm me down?

'A promotion with a pay rise,' he says carefully, clearly measuring my reaction with each word.

'How about we talk about it tomorrow?' I say curtly. 'I need to go clean up this mess you made with Marco.'

I spin on my heels, not daring to stay another minute longer.

Twenty-Two

Nirvana is in panic mode. It's ten-thirty at night and she's driving home from her future in-laws'.

'Mum and Dad are organising and paying for the engagement party. That's the tradition: the girl's side pays. But his mum is insisting on preparing all the food. She won't accept Mum doing anything.'

'Why?'

'Isn't it obvious? She wants all the credit to go to her! Plus she's a control freak. Anil's side of the family is bigger than ours, so her argument is that she knows what kind of food will appeal to her family. It's like our family doesn't exist. It's like my mum's going to serve up dog food! For fuck's sake!'

Nirvana is usually pretty mild-mannered and not prone to outbursts. Her use of the F word tells me things are bad.

'What does Anil think?' I ask.

'When it comes to his mum, he doesn't think. He can't see anything negative. According to him, she's trying to ease the load for Mum. But tell that to my mum. She's so angry. She feels like Anil's mum doesn't trust her judgement. She doesn't feel it's a burden. She wants to do it! – Yes, I'll have a Whopper with fries, thanks. – Oh, and check this out—'

'Did you just order a Whopper and fries?'

'Yes.'

'My God, there will be world peace yet. Are you feeling okay?'

'Of course I'm not feeling okay! Anil and I agreed we wanted something classy and intimate. A small reception. But the next thing I hear, Anil's mum wants to invite practically the entire community, which means we have to hire a big hall.'

'Did Anil talk to her?'

'He thinks that because he's her only son, she just wants to celebrate with everybody and show me off. He says she's trying hard to prove herself in front of all her friends and family. I get that, but it's not fair on my parents. They're not as wealthy as Anil's family – my God, these fries taste unbelievable! I miss salt!'

'Yes, hon, it's hard to find in frozen water.'

'What can I say to him? "Anil, your mum's a control freak"? "She's too selfish to think about how my parents are supposed to afford putting on a show just for the sake of *her* image"?' She's on a roll now. 'Sure, I'll just tell Anil that my parents now have to pay for a massive engagement party just because his mum wants to impress Sydney's Indian community using somebody else's money!'

I try to calm Nirvana down, but it's futile. It seems her parents made the foolish decision to invite Anil's mother along to the reception centre as a courtesy when they were booking the place. But Anil's mum promptly took over, putting a higher tab on the bar, ordering the biggest cake and demanding Nirvana only order designer saris from the most expensive shops in India. Of course, Nirvana's parents couldn't exactly refuse or they'd look cheap. So now the engagement party is going to cost them a fortune.

'What did Anil's parents do for his sister's engagement party?' I ask. 'They would have paid for it, wouldn't they? Did she organise the food? ... Nirvana? You there?'

'Yeah, sorry, just had a bite of a Whopper. I've died and gone to heaven.' She groans loudly. 'Can you imagine Neela's mother-in-law taking charge? Like that could happen! There are so many double standards,' she says angrily. 'She treats Neela's husband like a king. I don't know why when he's so moody. You can barely get a word out of him. He just grunts hello and watches TV. Sunil and Neela had a fight the other day and Neela's staying at her parents' for a couple of nights. Not that I saw much of her. She excused herself and went to bed early. But I overheard Anil's mum arguing with Neela – she wants Neela to go back to her own house. She thinks it's wrong for her to leave her husband over a misunderstanding.'

'She took her son-in-law's side?'

'She thinks Neela should save face in front of her in-laws and sort out her problems quietly. She thinks that because Sunil's out of work, Neela needs to be more patient with him.'

'That's bullshit.'

'I know. I'm sure she's just scared of what people would

say if Neela's marriage broke up too … But can you see how frustrating it is for me? Am I being self-centred and spoilt, Esma? I just feel that she bends over backwards to make Sunil feel adored, as though she's glad Sunil married her daughter so she can tick that burden off, but with me I sense it's forced. Because I'm *stealing* Anil.'

I wonder about Anil's mother's motivations. Is she just a control freak who's trying to sabotage the engagement? Or does she genuinely want the biggest and best for Anil and Nirvana, no matter how much she's going to resent Anil getting married?

I ask Nirvana if Anil's mum treats her badly, but she says she doesn't. She's always overly sweet to her, especially in front of Anil. Insists on serving her food first at meals, refuses to let her wash the dishes or clean up. Even the control-freak act with the engagement party was delivered in such a way that it made Anil's mum look like she was just the overexcited mother of the groom.

According to Nirvana, what's going on between them is subtle and manipulative. Like Anil's mum commenting that girls nowadays don't have time to be proper wives, not bothering to learn how to cook the traditional foods. Apparently she said this as a playful jab at Neela, but Nirvana insists it was meant for her because everybody knows Neela's an excellent cook and Nirvana's samosas make a Happy Meal look like a fine dining experience.

'Why don't you talk to Anil about it?' I say, although as soon as I make the suggestion I realise how stupid this advice is. If Anil defends his mum, he'll inflame Nirvana even more. If he concedes there's a problem but doesn't want to confront his mum, Nirvana will flip out too. If he does agree to confronting his mum, what exactly is he going to say without causing a problem between the two women?

'It will just make matters worse,' she says, and I know she's right. 'Okay, we'll talk later,' she says with a sigh. 'I need to go buy a kilo of Cadbury now.'

Twenty-Three

Senem is having a girls' night at her house and has invited me over to hang out with some of her closest girlfriends. There are five of them, all married: Hatice, Zuleyha, Sue, Betul and Lana. Sue, Zuleyha and Lana have children, and Hatice is a newlywed.

'So I'm the token single woman in this group, am I?' I joke as I walk into the lounge room, the last to arrive.

'Esma!' they squeal, and they jump up and smother me with hugs.

I immediately lunge at the baby closest to me, Lana's six-month-old baby boy, Erdel, who is gurgling and being utterly adorable. I scoop him up in my arms and carry him against my chest, stroking his soft fine hair as he peers over my shoulder and chews on my top. The girls settle back in their chairs and we cover the usual ground: how our jobs are going, any holiday plans on the horizon, latest movies we've seen. Then, when I get a chance, I ask Hatice about her honeymoon.

'It was incredible,' she says. 'We spent a week in the Maldives and then two days in Bangkok on our way home.

It's so hard to be back. I'm exhausted.'

Zuleyha, who moved to Australia from Cyprus nine years ago when she married Betul's brother, laughs. 'Of course you're exhausted,' she says cheekily. 'You're a newlywed.' She nudges Betul in the side and they both giggle. 'And your hair is curly again,' Zuleyha adds. 'No point straightening it, huh?'

They all laugh, except for Macedonian Sue, who's the only non-Turk in the room and therefore doesn't get the joke. 'What's so funny?' she demands.

'In our tradition you have to wash your whole body, including your hair, after sex,' Lana explains. 'Both the man and the woman. So you can pray.'

'I still don't get it,' Sue says.

'Well, when you get a blow-dry, what's the last thing you're going to do afterwards? Wet it, right? So you can always pick a newlywed girl because their hair's never done – what's the point when they're showering all the time?'

'Ahh!' Sue cries, the joke dawning on her, and she joins in with the laughter.

I can't help but turn my head away to hide the blush creeping over my face. Even though I'm the oldest in the group, I'm the only virgin and I never fail to feel embarrassed by how open and candid these women are about their sex lives, throwing out all the strict religious rules about keeping your relationship with your husband a private matter.

'Don't worry,' Zuleyha says mischievously, winking at the girls as she directs her advice to Hatice, 'it's just the newlywed phase. Wait until you're married for nine years, with three children, working full-time, juggling a zillion responsibilities. There's more time for blow-dried hair, let's put it that way.'

'Why wait for three children?' Lana cries. 'Just one will do the trick. Out the baby pops and then the only thing you think about when you see a bed is sleeping! It's all you think about, day and night.'

Sue jumps in. 'I know exactly what you mean. Sometimes I race to get into bed first, close my eyes and pretend to snore so Steven thinks I'm asleep and won't bother me!'

They all cackle wickedly and I drop to the ground and offer Erdel a rattle, propping him up on my lap as I listen intently.

'Steven had the gall to come home the other day all excited that he'd bought me some herbal tablets,' Sue moans. 'He thinks it will help with my low libido.'

That gets them going again.

'They don't work,' Betul says when she's got her breath back. 'Trust me, I've tried them.'

Sue sits up straight on the couch, her face animated. 'I said to him, "Honey, you know what's going to turn me on the most?" You should have seen his face – it was like offering him a winning lottery number. So I told him, "Helping around the house, washing the dishes, picking up your dirty laundry. The less I have to do, the more energy I will have." So simple. How'd you think he took it?'

They laugh.

'Exactly,' she says. 'He doesn't get it. It's not that I'm

rejecting him. I adore him. I'm just tired *all the time*. I'm juggling being a mum with my job at the bank. It's full-on.' She looks at me then and says, 'Listen up, Esma. Absorb all this precious advice. I bet you only think about how romantic and passionate marriage will be because, I tell you, movies have a lot to answer for. But this is the real world here.'

Senem groans. 'Oh, give it a break, will you?' she says. 'It's not that bad.'

My ears perk up. Although Senem and I are close, we've never discussed anything personal or intimate between her and Farouk, and I've always respected her privacy. The only time the issue came up was the night before her wedding.

My mum, aunt and I were helping Senem pack her bags. We've always been like that, in each other's lives down to the last detail. Senem and Mum were ticking off items on a list they'd prepared the week before (we're all neurotically organised) while my aunt was folding clothes. I was sitting on Senem's bed holding back tears as the whole I'm-losing-my-sister thing started to hit me. Then, out of the blue, while Mum was counting out how many T-shirts Senem had packed, she suddenly launched into what must have been a rehearsed birds-and-the-bees speech. Senem and I simultaneously cried out at Mum to stop because it was so painfully embarrassing watching her colour code T-shirts while trying to explain what both of us had picked up years ago via *Cosmo*, the school playground and our religion teacher at Turkish weekend school, who had answered all our questions about sex and periods, and taught us sex wasn't something to be ashamed about so long as we experienced it only through marriage. Mum looked relieved that she didn't need to continue. Senem and I exchanged looks that managed to convey both mortification and amusement and we all just went on doing what we were doing as though Mum hadn't, twenty seconds earlier, actually referred to the vagina as a 'lulu' (the cutesy word she'd used when we were kids).

'Well, now we know who out of this group takes a different view on the matter,' Betul says, grinning at Senem. 'Farouk obviously has special talents!'

'Oh, don't be so crude,' Senem says with a laugh. 'It's not that at all. It's just that you're making marriage seem like some kind of scorecard or tit for tat. I suffer here, you have to suffer there. I'm tired so you don't get sex, so it evens out. But everybody's emotions get ignored in the process.'

'Honey,' Lana says in a practical, no-nonsense tone, 'like it or not, it does become a scorecard, it's just a matter of survival. My husband and I keep tabs on who's been babysitting the most, who put the kids to bed last, who slept in last on a weekend. It's a credit-debit system. Obviously I'm almost always in credit, except for when I had a girls' weekend in Queensland and he got ahead of me, but as soon as I got back the tables turned again.'

'It's not like that for me and Farouk,' Senem says. 'We share the chores. He does all the cooking, doesn't he, Esma?'

'Well, yes, and thank God because your cooking is terrible.'

'See!' Senem says, nodding in agreement. 'It doesn't have to be an unfair division.'

'Stop rubbing it in,' Betul says, throwing a cushion at Senem, who dodges it so that it lands on Sue's head.

'Hey!' Sue cries.

'Not all guys are slack around the house, and not all women get turned off sex,' Senem says.

Sue, Betul, Lana and Zuleyha all burst into hysterics. Then Zuleyha turns to me and says, 'Sweetie, Senem's talking about the minority, and don't go thinking this is only to do with Turks. Sue here is Macedonian and she'll tell you herself that background has nothing to do with it. Men are just born lazier and hornier than women. So don't get into any relationship with false expectations. And train them when you first get married, like your sister here has, or you'll end up doing the bulk of the chores for the rest of your life. But don't get us wrong, we're all happily married and love our hubbies, don't we, girls?'

They cry out a chorus of agreement and I shake my head and smile. 'Listening to you all, I think I'd rather take a vow of chastity than get married,' I joke. 'I mean, the positivity and optimism has been overwhelming.'

'Just don't say we didn't warn you,' Sue says in a sing-song voice.

Twenty-Four

A random guy, recommended by a family friend, is visiting my house so we can discover, by engaging in a random choice of conversation topics, whether there is a mutual spark that might potentially lead to love and marriage.

I mean, nothing to it, right?

I throw most of the contents of my wardrobe onto my bed. Then I systematically discard anything I think is ugly (these arranged dates usually result in mass wardrobe clean-outs).

I end up deciding on jeans (because casual is best) with a khaki shirt-dress and ballet flats. I know Mum would prefer I wear heels (because height gives you confidence, etc), but there is no way I'm wearing heels in my own house. Not after last time.

Mum had bought me a beautiful pair of black pumps and I'd agreed to wear them only because they were a gift. But they were new and therefore a torture chamber for my heels and toes. So I was hobbling rather than walking. This would have been bad enough, but then Mum mopped the floor right before the guy and his family arrived. So when they rang the bell, I walked downstairs into the hallway, timing my entrance as they were welcomed into the house by my parents. I took a step off the stairs and slid, landing on my backside right at their feet. Suffice to say, this did not work in my favour. Nobody can really recover their dignity after that kind of introduction.

I woke up this morning before dawn to pray. Whenever I need something I suddenly become devoted to my prayers. I begged God for the following:

> To send me Mr Right.
> To give me the intelligence to judge fairly and wisely.
> To let me fall for the *right* Mr Right (I know plenty of girls who thought they'd met Mr Right only to discover he was Mr Wrong).
> If he is The One, let him be The One who makes me happy, not The One who ends up being a loser who treats me badly/picks his toenails/can't hold down a job/hates kids/tries to make money by selling McDonald's Happy Meal toys on eBay/etc (I think it's sensible for one's prayers to address all possible contingencies).

I also asked for forgiveness (that went on for quite a while), guidance, world peace, health and Australia hosting a World Cup (I was up at dawn, I figured I had nothing to lose).

Then, for good measure, I jumped onto a charity website and donated some money to a well being built at an Indonesian orphanage.

I'm ready.

Good deeds? *Check* (assuming the credit card isn't maxed out and the money goes through).

Make-up? *Check.*

Good outfit? *Check.*

Frizz-free hair? *Check.*

The doorbell rings. I run to my bedroom window, which has a view down to the front porch. My stomach plunges – in a good way. Although the guy's face is obscured by the security door, what I can see is promising. A very *tall* guy (yippee!) is standing on the porch, next to a couple I assume are his parents. He has dark hair which is styled really nicely (the correlation between a comb-over and lack of a spark is statistically proven, in my experience) and he's wearing jeans and a shirt. From this view, he has passed the superficial 'looks' threshold. Having met one too many guys who think a bottle-green polyester suit and mustard tie is attractive, I have a particular appreciation for guys with a dress sense.

When they walk in moments later and I'm standing face to face with him, I go weak at the knees. Some people are just made perfect. They're like hand-crafted furniture. It's a little like walking through Ikea and seeing an antique masterpiece sitting among the Billy bookcases.

Which is why it devastates me to realise by the end of the evening that I can never be with him.

Don't get me wrong. I'm trying *so* hard to look past his personality and accept him purely for his looks.

And yes, he's a doctor, the in-laws would be safely tucked away in another country (conveniently in Europe, thereby giving us excuses to travel there), and he's the most unbelievably good-looking male I have ever met in my entire life. And I've been to Italy, so that's saying a lot.

But there's just one problem. Metin is completely self-absorbed. He's not arrogant or boastful, going on about money or peeking a look at his reflection in his fork (Mum polishes everything before these visits). It's just that he seems to have no interest in asking me anything about my life.

In these kinds of situations, questions usually drive the conversation. When you have no history in common, you have to probe, find out about the other person, take an interest in who they are, what they've been up to, you know, for the past twenty-odd years. I'm not interviewing Metin, subjecting him to a personality test or anything weird like that. I'm just trying to make conversation.

When we've settled down in the pergola and Mum's served us a drink, I ask him, 'So have you travelled much?'

For the first fifteen minutes, I'm excited. Finally! A guy (who happens to be drop-dead gorgeous) who can talk. It's not like I've only met mutes before, but there have been a few it's-like-pulling-teeth interactions (Q: So what do you like doing on weekends? A: Stuff. Q: Such as? A: Depends).

After fifteen minutes it occurs to me that, actually, I'm not having a conversation with Metin. My question about his travel experience has propelled him into a long monologue about his trips all around Europe. He goes on and on. So I try to butt in.

'Oh, that reminds me of the time I was in Sicily and got robbed at a café.'

'I was almost robbed once, back home in Germany. But I saw the guy hanging around me and was suspicious, so when he reached for my wallet I was quicker than him and caught him in the act.'

Then he launches into more travel stories, and my near-death encounter in Sicily (it wasn't, but how will he know that unless he bloody well asks?) is completely ignored.

I wait for him to ask me where else I've travelled in Europe. But when he stops talking, he well and truly stops. Red light. Nothing else. No turning the question back onto the questioner. So I say, 'I've been to Paris, Italy and Amsterdam.'

His response? 'I love Italy. If I could live anywhere it would be Rome.' He spends the next five minutes talking about *his* experiences in Italy, Paris and Amsterdam, not once bothering to check whether I share his opinions about each country.

I'm getting frustrated, to say the least, because it has now been forty-five minutes and he hasn't asked me a single question about myself. For crying out loud, he still has no idea what I do for a living. Naturally, I've asked him about his job as a doctor, the usual banal questions to cover an initially awkward silence. That keeps him going for a long while too. And when he gets to the stop sign, the point at which you'd ask the other person about their job, he takes a sip of his drink and stops, like he's developed some kind of verbal constipation and is waiting on me to administer a laxative with another question about *him*.

So I hook him some bait. Because maybe he's just socially inept and needs a little nudge in the manners department (which begs the question why I'm bothering, but I banish the question from my mind).

'Growing up, I couldn't stand the ads on TV. If I saw one more commercial associating a woman's happiness with a clean tabletop, I thought I'd go crazy! So I did a marketing degree. I had to take human resources as part of the course. I loved it and decided to go into recruitment. So that's what I do now. My clients are mainly pharmacies.'

'I always knew I wanted to be a doctor. Ever since I was a child ...'

Cue another monologue. And cue me zoning out, offering the occasional nod or 'hmm' while I look around our garden and make a mental note to remind Dad that his flowers need watering.

Twenty-Five

'We have been accepted!' Faraj announces when he walks into class.

We all know exactly what he means and instantly jump up to congratulate him. Sonny lets out a whoop and the others cheer loudly.

I quickly whip out my phone and hold it up in front of him. 'Let's record,' I say with a laugh. 'Actually, here, Christina, you can be the interviewer.' I pass her the phone and she grabs it, giggling. She immediately falls into character.

'Okay, everybody, please be sitting down for the interview,' she commands and the others sit down on the tables.

Faraj pretends to fix up his collar and spikes up his hair with his fingers. He clears his throat and then tries to give Christina a solemn, distinguished look, failing miserably. We all laugh at him.

'Okay,' Christina starts, holding up the phone and pressing record. 'Faraj, welcoming you to television and please be telling us the news you have today.'

Faraj clears his throat again. 'We be accepted in Australia and now having a new home.'

'And please be telling us where you are born?'

'I born Iraq.'

'Can you telling us about Iraq?'

Faraj gives her a cheeky grin. 'Since the war, Iraq is being full of ice cream and parks.' He becomes animated, throwing his hands about and walking around so that Christina has to follow him. '*Every day* is visiting the beach!'

'Oh yes, I knowing all about that!' she exclaims. 'Cinema ... and parties in the street!'

I look at Sonny, Miriam and Ahmed, who are watching with delight. Christina turns the phone to them. 'What about your countries? What can be telling us? Is it being the same?'

Miriam and Ahmed giggle. 'Too much peace and quiet,' Ahmed declares with a fake pout. He folds his arms dramatically and stares at the phone. 'We getting bored with so much peace and quiet.' He pretends to yawn, then buckles with laughter.

Christina laughs and turns to Sonny. 'And you, Sonny? Tell us what's so special about Australia to you?'

Sonny grins at her. 'Nothing special. There is no war. Is that not being enough?'

'My brother's way younger than me, right? And my dad wants him in the family business. He's grown up working weekends for Dad, just like I used to, but I've told him he's not allowed to quit school.'

Alex, Ruby and I are having a coffee at the café around the corner from the oval before class starts. Alex is offering an extra Saturday morning session and it starts later than the Monday classes.

To Ruby's delight, we walked into the café to order and found Alex sitting at a table, bent over some paperwork. We went up to him and started chatting; one thing led to another and he pulled out two seats and asked us to join him.

'Does he want to quit school?' Ruby asks.

'He thinks he'll make more money if he starts young. But I've told him he'll have to answer to me if he drops out. I don't want him to make the same mistakes I made, you know?

'Anyway, enough about me and my boring family story. I need you guys awake before class.' He grins at us. The waiter comes and takes our order and Alex insists that coffee's on him.

Ruby's lips are curled in a smile. When Alex finishes ordering he turns to face us. I can tell from his body language that something is going on with him too. As we talk, I notice the way he steals a glance at her and then quickly turns his gaze onto something else; the way he pays her special attention until he remembers I'm there too; the way his eyes seek out her approval.

His phone beeps and he checks his text messages.

'Some people are so persistent, hey?' One leg keeps jiggling as he talks. Full of energy, he can't sit still. The enthusiasm and vibrancy he brings to his workouts is evident when he talks as well. 'This real estate agent keeps hassling me about an apartment he showed me in Parramatta. It's a shithole, yeah? You can't even imagine how bad it is.'

'Try us,' Ruby says with a grin.

Alex holds her gaze, grinning back. 'Okay, they've got a small balcony,' he says. 'They covered it with fake plastic grass.' We burst out laughing. 'Wait,' he says, holding his hand up to stop us, 'there's more. I called one room the "tetanus room". I told the agent I was probably gonna need to get a shot on my way home, that's how bad it was. Nails sticking out of the floor and walls. Just randomly. The kitchen is so small that if the microwave door's open you can't open the fridge. The taps were installed back to front but they never bothered to change them over, so you're basically gonna be scalded at least once a day.'

'Oh come on,' Ruby teases. 'It's about having a little vision. Some imagination.'

'Hey, I got plenty of imagination,' he says. 'You don't get into the fitness industry without seeing people's potential. I can work with fat. I can work with the skinny guy who's got the body mass of a toddler. But I can't work with plastic grass. Come on, Ruby, cut me some slack. There was so much floral wallpaper in the place, I felt like I was gonna get hayfever.'

Ruby's eyes sparkle. She keeps on teasing him and they flirt and banter naturally, forgetting I'm there, which is fine with me.

Despite the obvious chemistry between Ruby and Alex, I can't help but wonder if things would work out between them, mainly because I know Ruby's family and I just can't see them accepting somebody with Alex's background.

Ruby has always had it drilled into her that education and social status are non-negotiable qualities in a partner. And try as she might to defy her parents, until now she has conveniently fallen for guys who ticked all the right boxes. Her two boyfriends at university were both law students; one of them was a member of the Greek Club too. And so Ruby's parents have never had their expectations challenged, because Ruby's never liked anybody who's fallen short. Nor has she tried to rewrite the rules. And that's what she would need to do if she were to have any hope of Alex ever being accepted by her family.

Of course, I'm jumping the gun here, and if either Alex or Ruby knew what was going through my mind they'd probably think I was an idiot. But there's no denying the electric charge in the atmosphere, and that I'm witnessing two people beginning to fall for each other.

Nothing like starting the morning screening résumés to put a smile on my face. Into the slosh pile go all the résumés for 'farmacist positions'. I'm also not persuaded by candidates who 'have conviction this job was made just for me and I will fit into it like a hand into a glove'.

Veronica and I have a habit of sending each other 'the worst offender' emails (she receives applications from people 'who believe that no matter how disgusting a job is cleaning up an old person they deserve to be treated with less harm than young people').

Veronica sends me an email:

A candidate just called – Carla Wayne – and when I asked her to spell her surname she said, 'W for wrist ...' I'm not sure if she's very clever, or very stupid. Beat that?

I'm in the process of sending Veronica back a line with my contender ('I was born to dispense pills'), when I receive an email from Danny, who isn't in the office as yet.

Esma, I need your advice. I'm at the shops now. You're always telling me I'm not nice enough to my wife. I want to get her something to make her feel sexy again. You know how she's been since she put on weight. What kind of lingerie do women like? Bra and undies set, or a corset type? I don't trust this sales lady (she wants to sell me everything). Black or red? Please help!

I'm tempted to forward his email to Veronica, but I've never spoken openly about my problems with Danny to anybody in the office. You just never know whether others will turn the situation around and blame it all on you. If Veronica or anybody else thinks that Danny pays particular attention to me, then any time I get credit for something they'll assume it's because he's playing favourites.

I feel sick. I couldn't care less what Danny gets up to with his wife. I don't reply.

I'm in my office at lunch. The door is closed and I'm eating a sushi roll as I read the newspaper. But I'm too distracted to concentrate. I take a bite of my roll and instantly feel nausea in the pit of my stomach.

This mess with Danny can't go on. It's affecting my mood, my sleep, my appetite.

I receive another email from Danny. The subject line? *Promotion Documents.*

Dear Esma,

Please find attached documentation and self-assessment forms for completion. I confirm you are a candidate for a promotion and pay rise as of the end of this financial year and these documents will be used to assess your suitability for this senior role. As we discussed, I am more than happy with your work, and feedback from our clients certainly justifies your progression to a more senior role in the agency, with a pay rise of $20,000 per annum plus bonuses. Please endeavour to return the documents to me within two weeks and we will then start the process.

I look forward to working more closely with you and to developing the agency to its full potential.

Kind regards, Danny BlagojevicDirectorRecruitRight

A twenty-thousand-dollar pay rise.

Twenty thousand dollars?! What the hell is going on?

My mind is in overdrive. Is he trying to buy me off by dangling a career carrot in front of me? And how much will I compromise if I take the carrot? Is he going to think I'm excusing his behaviour? Giving him permission to continue because I'm not kicking up a fuss?

I decide to play it safe.

Thanks, Danny. I'll start working on the paperwork asap.

I press send. Short and not sweet enough. I'm sure I've blown it. But almost immediately I get an email back.

My pleasure, Esma.
So what colour, black or red?

Black, I reply. I press the send button and lose the moral high ground for good.

Twenty-Six

My mum calls me, adopting her breezy 'I'm so happy and you'd better be too' tone of voice as she informs me that Metin is interested in meeting up with me again. I know from her opening line ('The tall doctor wants to get to know you better!') that she's desperately hoping I'm going to squeal with joy. She knows it didn't go too well last time, but if her forced excited tone is anything to go by, she's pretending to have no idea.

So I make it easier for her.

'I'm not interested,' I say bluntly.

She switches instantly. 'What do you mean you're not interested?' she demands in a shrill voice. 'You complain that you haven't met anybody and then this guy arrives and he's a doctor, tall, educated, successful, very nice-looking, talkative, polite, and you don't want him? What is wrong with you?'

'Mum, if I thought he was suitable I'd give him a chance. But he's totally self-absorbed. He didn't ask a single question about *me*.'

'Esma!' she shouts. 'You need to stop this ridiculous

fussiness. You can't tell someone's personality from one meeting. You're being unfair on yourself, rejecting people after meeting them once. What can you tell after two hours? He didn't repulse you, he was nice enough, he deserves a chance.'

He didn't repulse me. Wonderful. A new threshold for eligibility.

'You're wrong, Mum,' I say angrily. 'He had two hours to show some remote interest in me as a human being, let alone someone he might potentially want to spend the rest of his life with, and he failed!'

'Sometimes people get nervous on their first meeting. Maybe he's insecure and felt he had to talk a lot about himself to try and win you over.'

I let out a laugh. 'Oh, come on, Mum! I'm not an idiot. I can tell the difference. This guy just wanted an audience.'

'Esma, you can't judge a person after two hours.'

'Why not? Whatever happened to first impressions counting?'

'Not when you're almost thirty! You can't afford for first impressions to count!'

Ah. So that's it.

'Thanks a lot, Mum,' I say, my voice suddenly thickening with tears. 'My own mother is basically telling me I'm approaching a use-by date. Is that what I am to you? A can of tomatoes?'

'Esma,' she pleads. 'That's not what I meant.'

'Well, I'm not a can of tomatoes, I'm a vintage cheese, and I'm only going to get better with age!'

'Cheese? What on earth are you talking about? What do tomatoes and cheese have to do with giving this guy a chance?'

'I won't force myself to settle just to satisfy some arbitrary time limit. I'd rather die single than be unhappily married!'

'Oh, stop being so dramatic, Esma,' she sighs.

I try very hard not to burst into tears. The pressure feels so intense; there is no hope on the horizon and now I feel like cheese all right – not vintage but a low-calorie cottage cheese with fuzzy mould on the top.

The online attempt has been a total failure, just as I'd expected. Every match to date has been a disaster. So should I be accepting the possibility that my destiny is to be single? To die a virgin? (What a chilling thought!) Childless? Loveless? To watch my younger sister grow old with her husband and attend *their* children's first day at kindergarten, *their* children's graduation?

I start conjuring up more horrid details in my self-pitying projection. I'll be fat – because nobody will be seeing me naked so I may as well have a cottage-cheese arse. And I'll probably be hairy – I mean, really, there'll be nobody to complain about spiky legs. The more I imagine, the more ridiculous and irrational my projection becomes. In reality, I'm one of those people who genuinely believe in looking after yourself *for yourself*, so deep down I know I won't really gorge on chocolate Hob Nobs for the next fifty years just because I don't have a man beside me, but right now I'm too upset to acknowledge that. I can feel the onset of a major hysterical sob-fest. Pathetic.

'Esma ... ? Esma!'

Oh. Mum's still on the line. 'Mmm,' I manage.

'Please calm down,' she pleads.

'Mmm,' I manage again and hiccup.

'Let's talk when you get home.'

Oh no. No more talking. I'd rather rip off my nails one by one with pliers than talk about this topic again. I take a deep breath and mumble, 'Okay, one more chance. Give him my number then.'

Ruby texts me while she's at a wedding.

Alex is here! ARGHHHHH

Here where?

Effie's wedding!

How does he know Effie?

Greek community degrees-of-separation thing.

Have you spoken to him?

No answer.

When I text her again later that night to ask how things are going she doesn't respond. It's only the following night at our No Sex in the City dinner that she fills me and the girls in.

'It could just be a classic case of opposites attracting,' Lisa muses as we sit around a sushi train.

'I think the whole opposites-attract thing is dangerous in the long-term,' Nirvana says.

Ruby has just described her evening at the wedding. She spent almost the entire night dancing with Alex. If Ruby was in any doubt that there was something between them, being thrown together (in a situation where, Ruby reminds us, she was not in sweaty sports gear but dressed up and looking hot!) eliminated any such doubts.

Whenever one of us goes through the 'girl meets boy' experience, the first part of the mandatory quizzing session covers the superficial – and, given our No Sex in the City lifestyle, G-rated details: what was he wearing? What were you wearing? What were his friends like? Is he a good dancer? What did you talk about?

We've moved on from that and are now in the 'I like him, what's the next step?' PG-rated phase. Nirvana is playing the role of devil's advocate. Being in a relationship sometimes makes people think they're suddenly an authority on love. It's not that Nirvana's being supercilious or self-righteous. She's just jumped ship.

'You need some common interests or you'll just grow apart once the lust factor and the initial euphoria is over. I see Neela and Sunil and they're living on parallel train tracks. It's sad, really. I don't think they have anything in common.'

'Having common interests is overrated,' Ruby scoffs. 'I know plenty of couples who get a kick out of the same movies but who have completely different views on life. I'd rather compatibility where it matters: values, goals, sex.'

'Politics.' Lisa is emphatic. 'That's a must. I couldn't be with a climate change sceptic or an anti-feminist.' She shudders.

'It's all one big gamble anyway,' I say cynically, poking my tempura prawn with the end of my chopstick. 'Some things you won't know about until you actually get into the relationship. Like sexual compatibility.'

'With your whole no-touching-before-marriage policy,' Ruby says, 'you won't find out until it's too late.'

I shrug, grinning at her. 'One of my mum's friends told me marriage is like a watermelon. You don't know if it's a bad one until you look inside.'

That sends us all into a fit of giggles.

'Oh my God, I hate fruit proverbs,' Lisa says breathlessly. 'I'll never forget my mum telling me about the virtues of virginity: *Nobody wants a peach that's been bitten into.*'

That sends us into another round of hysterics.

'Back to Alex,' Nirvana says when we've finally calmed down. 'I kind of agree with you, Ruby. But intellectual compatibility is important. I've never met Alex so I can't judge, but don't let your attraction to him make you forget that. Especially somebody like you. I'm not saying you need the same IQ. But what will you and Alex talk about? How will he get along with your family?'

'Nirvana!' Ruby groans. 'I couldn't care less if Alex is able to maintain a conversation with my dad about aeronautical engineering or with my brothers about the dispensation of pills! That's their problem. Ambition isn't the property of the middle class only.'

Lisa grins. 'Wow, Ruby, if I didn't know better I'd say you've changed for the better.'

'There's a tenderness to him,' Ruby says. 'A genuine passion for helping people. Not just because it's good for his business, but because he wants to help people transform themselves. And he's down to earth and funny and completely unpretentious. I know my parents are cerebral snobs and they'll have a fit if I bring home a high school drop-out. Never mind that he's built himself a successful business. He doesn't have a HECS debt so he isn't good enough. But I like him. A lot.'

'So are you a couple?' Nirvana asks.

Ruby's face flushes. 'Well, er ... no. I've gone out for coffee with him a couple of times. And we've spoken on the phone. I've stayed behind after class and spoken to him for ages too.' She quickly pops a piece of sushi into her mouth.

'Ruby, this is a teeny weeny bit crazy,' Lisa says.

'What is?'

'You and Alex aren't going out. And yet you're locked in some kind of pre-emptive-strike mindset – you're expecting trouble and conflict before anything's happened. If you have to work this hard to figure out if somebody is the right person for you when there's nothing even between you yet, that should be ringing alarm bells for you.'

'I'm just trying to be as upfront with myself as possible. I read a self-help book by a trade practices lawyer who said that you should never go into a relationship guilty of misleading and deceptive conduct.'

The three of us groan but Ruby's unperturbed. 'You have to be honest – completely honest – and get it all out there from the start.'

'Love is a commercial transaction, is it?' I say. 'On sale?'

'You have to let each other know exactly what you're getting into.'

'How romantic,' I groan.

'Even if that's true,' Lisa says, 'you're not getting into anything yet. You said so yourself. You're not a couple.'

Ruby throws down her napkin, leans back in her chair and folds her hands behind her head. 'Okay. We had a moment. At least I think we did ... I'm sure we did.'

'When?'

'Where?'

'What happened?'

Ruby raises her hand to silence us, giving a calm-down-before-you-burst-a-blood-vessel shake of her head. She then goes on to explain that at the wedding they went outside for some fresh air. They sat alone together and talked and talked.

'I don't know how to explain it,' she says with a smile. 'I didn't have to pretend to be somebody else. I felt uninhibited, real. With some guys it's all an act. You're both on your best behaviour, like you're auditioning, playing a role that you'll tweak once you get the part. Before the wedding I thought the differences between us might have been insurmountable, but that all fell away because we clicked in so many other ways.'

'Did he kiss you?' Lisa asks.

'No. But we were *so* close. He wanted to. I could sense it. And I wanted to kiss him too, but I wasn't going to make the first move. When the moment came I felt something was holding him back. I don't know what it was. Maybe nerves, although he's one of the most confident guys I know, so I'm not sure it was that ... I don't know ...'

'You should see a psychic,' Nirvana says.

I burst out laughing. 'Nirvana! That is so random. And so – so – nuts!'

Ruby's face breaks into a wide grin. 'I wouldn't mind that actually. It's been a while.'

'I've got an appointment tomorrow at eleven,' Nirvana says. 'I need advice on my mother-in-law. Let's all go together!'

Lisa shakes her head. 'I'm *crushed* not to be able to join you, given my *high* opinion of psychics, but I've got a presentation tomorrow.'

Nirvana turns to me. 'What about you, Esma?'

'Surely after all these years you know me better than that?'

'Yes, I know, I know. You're a nonbeliever. I get it. You don't have to actually get her advice. I just want you there.'

'You'll have Ruby.'

'Oh, come on,' she pouts. 'Come along to support your misguided best friends.'

'It'll be fun,' Ruby says.

I fix my eyes on Ruby. 'I cannot understand how you of all people can believe in these things.'

'Oh, Esma, don't be such a cynic.'

'Ruby,' I cry, 'you're the biggest cynic out of the four of us. You're just not the type to see a psychic.'

Ruby groans and throws a look at Lisa. 'Please shoot me if I ever become predictable enough to be a *type*.'

'So you'll come?' Nirvana presses.

'I mean, give me your hands,' I say. 'I'll read your palms. I'll know as much as any psychic would.'

'Tomorrow? Eleven o'clock. I'll pick you both up?'

'Not to mention most of the time they state the bloody obvious. "I'm sensing you have a mother and a father. I'm sensing the presence of a male in your life. Once upon a time you were a child ... "'

'Esma!' Nirvana snaps.

I raise my hands in the air in mock submission. 'Okay, fine.' Their faces light up. 'But I'm not talking to her. I'm just going along to make sure she doesn't take advantage of my two idiotic friends.'

'Such a sweetie, you are.'

I get home late. The house is eerily silent. The kitchen is spotless, as usual. Mum's cardinal rule is to never go to bed without the dishes done and the worktops smelling pine fresh. I'm about to go upstairs when I hear movement in the lounge room.

'Is that you, Dad?' I whisper.

'Yes, darling.'

I hover at the lounge-room door. Dad's sitting in his armchair, smoking in the dark.

'Do you want the light on?'

'No. Thank you.'

'Okay ...'

'Fun night?'

'Yep.'

'Are your friends well?'

'Yes. They're all good, Dad. Are you sure you don't want the light on?'

'Yes, I'm sure. I like it like this.'

'How was work?'

'Good. I'm just going to have one last smoke then I'll go to bed. Goodnight, darling.'

I walk over to him and kiss him on the head. He pats my hand.

I trudge upstairs, my heart heavy. It's not the first time I've found Dad awake in the middle of the night, just sitting, smoking and staring into the darkness. The cigarette butts are heaped up, falling out of the ashtray. They're always gone in the morning. The lounge room has been aired and there's no trace of him.

Twenty-Seven

'Okay, Esma, suspension of disbelief,' Nirvana says.

'She'd better suspend her disbelief,' Ruby threatens in a low growl, 'or her negative vibes are going to affect the reading.'

We're waiting in the reception of a small terrace in Newtown. Apart from the overpowering scent of burning incense, the place seems pretty normal, not dark and creepy as I expected. On a small pine table to my left is a flyer. Printed in bold letters is the name *Patricia Whiting*, underneath a photograph of a woman with grey eyes and a splendid smile. I read the words at the bottom of the flyer: *Can you handle the truth? I'm a psychic who will tell you what you need to hear!*

I roll my eyes. Nirvana and Ruby chatter excitedly. I wish Lisa were here. I'm going to be ganged up on, I just know it.

'So how much are you paying Patricia Whiting to tell you what you *need* to hear?' I ask in a droll tone.

'One hundred dollars an hour.' The voice comes from my right and I turn my head to see that it belongs to

Patricia Whiting. She's very overweight, much bigger than in her photograph (wonder if she saw that coming?), almost unrecognisable save for those grey eyes that fix on me. She smiles briefly.

'We have a nonbeliever,' she says. There's no hint of rebuke in it. Just a statement of fact.

'Yep,' I say, unapologetically. 'I'm just here as support.'

'Are you still willing to see the two of us for a discount?' Nirvana pipes up, hopeful.

'Yes, for an hour,' Patricia replies. She nods in my direction. 'And will your friend be sitting in?'

I shrug lightly. 'I'm happy to wait out here.' I pick up a magazine and flip through it, opening it at a random page. 'I'll just catch up on my Sidereal Astrology,' I say, reading a headline aloud. Ruby frowns but Nirvana lets out a light laugh.

'If your friends don't mind, you're welcome to accompany them,' Patricia offers.

'Of course she's joining us,' Ruby says breezily, jumping up and grabbing my arm. 'I didn't haul you along so you could look at magazines. Come on.'

I don't bother resisting. Anyway, it will be an interesting exercise, listening to Patricia pretend to know the future.

We're ushered into a small front room. Patricia takes a seat behind a table draped with purple crushed velvet and whips out her wallet. 'I'll just take payment from you now if you don't mind,' she says.

I raise an eyebrow. I'm tempted to ask her if she has a refund policy, but I'm pretty sure Ruby and Nirvana will kill me if I do. Anyway, they're paying and I don't want to interfere with their experience. They believe in this stuff and I should respect that (even if I think they're stark raving mad). I try my best not to give off any bad vibes in case Patricia confuses my energy with theirs and predicts they're going to be hit by a bus on the way home.

After Ruby and Nirvana have paid, Patricia flicks on a desk lamp and takes Ruby's hands, turning them upwards to examine her palms.

'The distance between your pinky and its neighbour indicates you're not lonely. You might, however, become senile later in life, so you need to work on keeping those friends, having a network of support.'

It takes all my willpower not to burst out laughing. I fix my eyes on the scratches and blotches on the floorboards.

'You have a very messy love line. I'm sensing there is a male Scorpio in your life. And there will be a male Aries or Aquarius.' She scrunches up her nose. 'I'm getting a strong feeling about a star sign that starts with the letter A.'

Oh boy. The harder I try not to laugh, the harder it is to remain composed. 'Oh my God!' Ruby exclaims. 'Alex is an Aries!'

I clear my throat.

'Is he an accountant or financial planner?' Patricia asks solemnly. 'I have a strong feeling he deals with money and numbers.'

I bite the inside of my mouth.

'He's a personal trainer.'

'Successful?'

'Yes, very.'

'There you go then.'

'I'm sorry?' I interrupt before I can stop myself. 'I'm not making the connection between personal training and accountancy.'

Ruby rolls her eyes at me as though I'm hopelessly infantile and too dim to understand. 'He makes heaps of money as a successful personal trainer,' she explains.

'Oh,' I say and shut my mouth.

'I sense you're confused about something,' Patricia goes on. 'That you're preoccupied and that it has something to do with this man Alex.'

I'm tempted to remind her that she didn't know about Alex until Ruby mentioned him, but who am I to tell her how to do her job.

'Are you confused?' Patricia asks.

'Well, yes. I'm not sure if I'm reading him correctly ... if he has feelings for me ... Also, if he does, I'm wondering if we're a good match, given we have very different jobs ... are in two different worlds really.'

'The man you're destined to marry is ruled by Venus, and so he has a soft, creative element, but he may not be as committed and motivated as you,' Patricia says soberly. 'He's also very inflexible. Where you have a capacity for broad-mindedness, the man you will marry does not.'

'Is that man Alex?'

'I'm sorry, I can't answer that. I can tell you that you have a very long lifeline. And I see daughters in your future, but no sons.'

When it's Nirvana's turn, Ruby moves her chair to the side and sits quietly, lost in her own thoughts. Patricia takes Nirvana's hands.

'Is there a wedding on the horizon?' she asks.

'OH MY GOD!' Nirvana and Ruby simultaneously exclaim.

I don't bother reminding them that Nirvana's wearing her engagement ring.

'Yes!' Nirvana says breathlessly. 'We haven't set a date yet, though. We're planning the engagement party.'

'You're marrying the man of your destiny.'

Nirvana is positively beaming.

'He is a good man. But I see conflict. I can't see where it is coming from and who is responsible, but there will be challenges.'

Really? What a revelation. Marriage will be challenging.

'Well, there is conflict at the moment.'

'Is it with a female?'

'Yes!'

She had a fifty per cent chance of getting that one right.

'I don't see the conflict resolving any time soon.'

Oh my God, get me out of here.

'Should I confront this woman?'

Nirvana's not revealing who it is. She explained to me on the way here that she prefers to give away as little as possible so that she doesn't lead the psychic. Ruby's too impatient and open to be constrained in the same way.

'Before you confront her you need to assess how that will impact on your relationship with your fiancé. Is it going to resolve the conflict? And if confrontation resolves the conflict between you and the woman, will it create new conflict between you and your fiancé? These are the kinds of questions you need to keep in your mind.'

Nirvana could have paid me instead. I've been telling her the same thing all along.

When Patricia has finished reading Nirvana's palms and moved on to tarot cards, she turns to me.

'Would you like a quick reading?' she asks.

I smile at her. 'No thanks.'

'That's okay. Can I just ask you: have you had a lot of bad luck lately?'

'No.'

'Hmm ...'

'What's that supposed to mean?' I say tersely.

'Well, it's just that I have a sense that somebody may have used some negative occult practices on you.'

'*Excuse me?*'

'You mean black magic?' Ruby cries with a shudder.

Patricia just arches an eyebrow. 'I could offer you some protective charms,' she says.

I laugh. 'No offence, but save the psychic spiel for people who believe in it.'

'Are you always this sceptical? Because I'm sensing a lot of negativity in your life.'

'Actually, I'm an extremely optimistic person and I don't need to be analysed by somebody who makes a living out of stating the obvious and passing it off as psychic inspiration.' I grab my bag off the floor. 'Ready, girls?' I say with affected cheeriness.

Ruby and Nirvana jump up and follow me.

'I'm sorry about that,' Ruby says as we walk towards the car. 'I'm *really* sorry. That whole black magic thing was totally out of line.'

'Yeah, she had no right to say that,' Nirvana adds. 'Cheerful optimism, that's your trademark. How else can you explain your positive attitude even after you've gone on dates with guys who have worn bumbags?'

'Vinyl pants.'

'Gold chains.'

'Exactly,' Ruby says, with a decisive nod. 'Don't pay any attention to her.'

'I'm not,' I assure them. We walk silently to the car. Ruby's driving and I climb into the back seat, leaving the passenger seat for Nirvana.

'Do you think I give off negative vibes?' I ask.

'No!' they both respond.

'She doesn't know what she's talking about,' Nirvana says with exaggerated conviction. 'I mean, come to think of it, I'm wearing my engagement ring. Of course there's a wedding on the horizon!'

We all laugh and I try to banish Patricia Whiting from my mind.

Twenty-Eight

I've resolved to give Metin another try. Ha! It's as though he's a pair of jeans that didn't fit last week and I'm going to try squeezing into them today.

As much as I think Patricia Whiting was an opportunistic phoney, what she said is nonetheless bugging me. A lot. Not because I secretly think I'm a negative person – I know I'm not. I really do approach every new meeting with a guy with honest-to-God optimism that this time *could be it*. Why else would I have agreed to meeting so many guys? I've got cousins and friends who have long since given up on the arranged dates. I'm a trooper, thank you very much.

But what Patricia said got me thinking. Not only about how two people as intelligent as Nirvana and Ruby could fall for that kind of crap, but how maybe, despite how optimistic I feel on the inside, I'm somehow not projecting my positive feelings. She certainly read me completely wrong.

So it's all very well for me to go into a date feeling hopeful that I'm about to meet the man of my dreams, but what if I don't realise that I've got a wall up? That what I feel on the inside isn't translating to the outside?

Maybe ... it hurts to admit this ... my mum IS RIGHT.

Maybe I'm being unfair to myself.

Maybe I'm being unfair to others.

So tonight, as I'm driving to Leichhardt to meet Metin for coffee, I resolve to forget our last meeting. I'm going to give Metin the benefit of the doubt and well and truly open my heart and mind to the experience.

I see him standing on Norton Street in front of the restaurant. Once again my respiratory function is compromised. I notice some girls pass him and look back and giggle to themselves. *That's right, girls*, I think, as I walk up to him, *he's the stuff of dreams (on the outside), and he's my date tonight*. Sure, he'll probably spend two hours talking about himself, but at least he'll be eye candy.

'Hi, Esma.' He smiles and I notice he still has his dimple. Not that there was any danger of it disappearing. Oh my. This is what must happen if you date people for their looks. Rapidly Declining Brain Cell Activity.

He looks me up and down with those big probing hazel eyes – stop it! I must remember I have a brain and it is incumbent on me to use it – and says, in a deep, masculine, sexy – SHUT UP – voice, 'You look great.'

'Thanks,' I say, and giggle like a schoolkid.

'It's good to see you again,' he says when we're sitting down.

'How's your week been?' I ask.

'Oh, not too bad,' he says, pouring me a glass of water. 'Removed a couple of toe warts and looked down the barrel of a lot of sore throats. A pretty average week, actually.'

I laugh. 'All in a day's work for you, hey?'

'That's right. How's your week been?'

Yay!!! He has spontaneously asked me a question.

'Pretty interesting actually. My friends dragged me along to see a psychic. Then one of my clients caught a graduate I'd placed at his pharmacy stealing prescription drugs from behind the counter so her brother could sell them at school.'

'Hmm, that is an interesting week. Even beats toe warts ... So, are you hungry?'

'I'm okay, thanks. A coffee is fine.'

'Oh, come on. We can have coffee later. How about we get a pizza?'

'But I just had dinner.'

'We can go halves if you like.'

I give in and he opens the menu and rubs his hands together, grinning at me. 'You know this is a critical moment.'

I look at him coyly. 'How so?'

'People can be very particular about their choice of pizza toppings. I've known friendships to hang in the balance over a disagreement about pineapples and anchovies.'

'No anchovies,' I say. 'And pineapples are a must.'

'And what are your feelings on the subject of mushrooms and chilli peppers?'

'What's a pizza without them?'

'Seafood or chicken?'

I tap a finger on the corner of my mouth. 'Now let's see,' I say in a voice that suggests I am pondering some important spiritual proposition. 'I like both,' I eventually declare.

He nods slowly, his face serious and contemplative as he pretends to be deep in thought. Then he flashes me a smile. 'You've passed the test. Thank God you're not an anchovy person.'

We order a chicken pizza with extra pineapple and Metin talks to me about his first impressions of Australia when he moved here from Germany. Unfortunately, he wasn't immune to stereotypes about deadly spiders and cuddly koalas.

'Please don't tell me you expected to see kangaroos waiting at traffic lights and koalas on every street corner?'

'No, I wasn't that bad,' he insists.

He laughs. There's a bit of a silence then. I'm resisting asking him another question to keep the conversation going. I can't keep rescuing us, especially when he still hasn't asked me anything about my life. I feel like I know him quite well. I know about where he went to school in Germany, his relationship with his family, his travel experience, his motivation for studying medicine. But I'm still a closed book to him. So I just take the plunge. There is absolutely no point in being shy or disingenuous.

'Metin, don't you want to know about me?'

He looks up from his cup, surprise crossing his face. 'What do you mean?'

I clear my throat, speak kindly. 'It's just that you haven't asked me anything about my life. That's why we're here, isn't it? To get to know each other?'

'Yes, of course,' he fumbles. 'So tell me about yourself.'

I bite my lip. 'How about you ask me what you want to know and I'll answer.'

He looks bewildered. I wonder if I've blown it. Am I being completely high maintenance? Overanalytical? Have I turned him off?

My panicked thoughts are interrupted by the waiter delivering our pizza. The smell of basil makes my stomach rumble, which is evidence that I'm being plain greedy given that I ate a bowl of pasta only two hours ago.

'Yum.' Metin cuts me a large slice and puts it on my plate. 'So what do you do?' he asks. He takes a bite, cheese dangling down his chin until he realises and breaks it off.

I cut him some slack. When I resolved to start afresh, I meant it. So I'm going to pretend I haven't already told him what I do and explain all over again.

'That's interesting ... Oh, is that what you meant when you said a girl was stealing from the pharmacy? You'd recruited her?'

So he had no idea what I meant before and didn't bother to ask me to clarify? I take a bite of my pizza to delay responding. I'm a bit annoyed. But, in the spirit of BEING POSITIVE, I'm going to let that go too.

'Yes,' I say after I've finished chewing. 'I'd recruited her for one of my clients and then she ended up being a thief. Needless to say, the client wasn't too happy. Nor was my boss.'

'I once hired a receptionist I thought was honest and conscientious. Until I found out she'd been stealing patients' credit card details to buy things online.'

'Mmm,' I say, my voice tapering off as I fix my eyes on

the couple at the table next to us.

He puts down his glass. 'Did I say something wrong?' he asks warily.

I lock eyes with him and smile gently. 'I just get a sense ...'

'Yeah?'

'I feel that when I talk, you're not interested.'

'But I am!'

How, then, do I tell him that he's clearly hopeless at the rules of conversation? 'I don't know how to explain myself ...'

'Try me,' he says. There's genuine concern in his eyes, a boyish willingness to make it right. Maybe he really just doesn't get it.

'Okay, so I'm telling you I basically had a bad day with my client and boss. Instead of asking me what happened, you cut through with your own story. Either you don't care what happened to me or you weren't paying attention. It's just that a conversation ... well, it's give and take. You talk, I ask you questions. I talk, you ask me questions. With you it's feeling ... kind of one-sided.' I sit back in my chair. There, I've said it. Let's get the bill and get out of here. The night is clearly over.

'I was paying attention,' he declares. 'I was telling you that story because I didn't want you to feel bad.'

'What do you mean?'

'Bad about your judgement. See, I hired somebody who turned out to be a lying thief too!' He grins at me. 'I was trying to reassure you that everybody makes mistakes.'

A smile slowly spreads to my eyes. 'Maybe we need some basic guidelines about communication, then,' I say.

He folds his arms across his broad chest. I notice the ripple of muscle against shirt, the contours of his forearms. Not allowing myself to get too distracted, I say, 'Okay, Metin, some basic rules! Ask me questions. What's my job? Where did I grow up? Where have I travelled? Have I ever been arrested? What's my highest score on Tetris? What's the weirdest food I've ever eaten? Do I believe in conspiracy theories? Anything, I don't care. Hit me with your most ridiculous question, but at least ask me *something*!'

He laughs, fixing his eyes on me.

'What's so funny?' I say, although I'm laughing too.

'You know, you're quite cute when you're crazy,' he says and my heart kind of explodes. Then he leans in closer to me. 'Now do you believe that I'm interested in you?'

Twenty-Nine

Senem is over at our place tonight. She's started packing up her things in preparation for moving back home and arrived with some boxes and bags for storage. Dad's in the garage trying to find space for them.

Mum, Senem and I are hanging around in the family room when Mum starts to quiz me about Metin. Once again, she's trying to assuage her own anxiety by reminding me of what I should be looking out for.

'Esma, you need to think about whether he can provide for you. Whether he's trustworthy and dependable. Isn't that right, Senem?' she says in Turkish, turning to my sister for a show of solidarity. Senem gives me a sympathetic look.

'Mum,' I say calmly, 'I don't need to be provided *for*, and I can depend on myself.'

'I know you're a hard worker, Esma. I raised you and Senem to be educated and to stand on your own feet. I've been so lucky with your father – he has never denied me anything. But not all men are so good or so responsible.'

I cringe. Is it really possible to share a lifetime with someone and still not know them, understand what they're capable of? The idea frightens me. How am I supposed to know whether a man I've met twice is trustworthy when my mother's trust in my father is so misplaced?

I don't say anything. I've always appeased my parents, protected them from the truth of my feelings. I can't bear to shatter my mother's good faith in my father, so I listen obediently. Senem, happily married and oblivious to the burden Dad's placed on my shoulders, is off the hook, blissfully immune to Mum's lectures. So I continue the pretence, continue to keep the peace, even though a war rages within me.

Today's boot-camp session is torturous. I'm close to exhausted tears at one point. But when Alex blows the whistle, a feeling of euphoria floods through me. I did it! I finished. I feel fantastic and we all clap (well, those of us who have enough energy left to clap) and limp back to our bags.

Ruby and I hover around, chatting to Pina and Theresa. We're waiting for everybody to disperse so that Ruby can have some time with Alex when he's not distracted by people asking him for diet plans and exercise advice.

It's not as though Ruby and I are hidden from view. And yet, as the crowd gets thinner, Alex appears to be avoiding us. He's not looking our way and is focused on packing up while talking to Mikey, the trainer who helps him out.

'Let's leave,' I eventually say through gritted teeth. 'We look desperate.'

'Gotcha,' Ruby says.

I can tell she's hurt but she doesn't say anything until we get in the car.

'That's the first time we've seen each other since the

wedding,' she says, looking puzzled. Then she half-laughs. 'He probably wants to keep things professional here.' Her cheerful tone is forced. 'It's understandable. This *is* his workplace. I forget that sometimes.'

'You're right,' I say, although I can't shake the uncomfortable feeling in the pit of my stomach.

'I wasn't imagining what happened that night,' she says firmly.

'I believe you, Ruby.'

Somehow, though, I don't think I'm the one she's trying to convince.

Nirvana and I are at the fish market in Pyrmont for Sunday lunch. We've ordered a big platter of mixed seafood and are sitting outside, trying to avoid eye contact with the seagulls or making any gesture that could be interpreted as an offer of food. The seagulls are bold enough to glide onto the table, snatch an oyster or mussel, and soar off. We're trying to eat quickly because the sky is grey and the clouds that have been forming all morning are threatening to burst.

Nirvana's phone rings. It's Anil. She takes the call, leaving me to defend our lunch against the marauding seagulls.

I'm in a stand-off with a one-legged seagull that seems to have staked a claim on my food. It's watching me. I'm watching it. I am perfectly aware of how insane I must look, but I swear to God it's taunting me, moving its wing to make me think it's about to launch, and then standing still, watching me wrap my arms around the food in a panic.

I notice Nirvana's voice is going all tense and wobbly.

When she ends the call I ask her what's wrong.

She runs her fingers through her hair and closes her eyes for a moment. When she opens them, she frowns. 'This is getting so frustrating.'

'What happened?'

'My uncle has invited us for dinner tonight. He's doing our engagement invitations for free, so I can't exactly say no. And tomorrow night is my dad's birthday, so we're going to my parents' for dinner. It's a crazy weekend but it's just worked out that way. Anil's mum is upset that we're not seeing them this weekend and that we're spending the whole weekend with my family. So to keep the peace, I suggested to Anil that we have breakfast with his family tomorrow morning. But he said his parents have something on tomorrow morning and wanted us over for dinner. So I asked him if he seriously expects us not to do something for Dad's birthday. And he asked if we could have breakfast with my parents instead. I said no because Mum's gone to a lot of effort to organise a big dinner party. Anil said he doesn't mind, but he senses his mum is feeling jealous.'

'So he's admitting to it at least?'

She nods. 'But he's also defending her. He thinks that she's feeling left out, and apparently his sister told him she's worried my family is drawing him closer to them when it should be the other way round. His sister told him his mum is worried he'll end up looking after my parents instead of her, *the way sons should*.'

'He actually admitted this to you?'

'He admitted it because he thinks it's all a big joke. He

just laughs and brushes the whole thing off. He thinks that's the best way to deal with her. But if it gets out of hand, then it's going to be like this all the time. A competition between the families, with her constantly keeping tabs on how many times we see my family compared to Anil's. I don't want things to be like that.'

Suddenly there's a crack of thunder, and before we have time to gather our food and bags the rain starts in big drops, getting faster and more intense with each passing moment. We jump up and race in the direction of the car park, laughing as we run.

It's pouring down so hard, and we're parked so far away, that I call out to Nirvana to run for cover. We head for the main entrance of the market and duck under the shelter, negotiating our way through the crowd of people who have the same idea. That's when I see him. Standing a metre away from me, with his arms wrapped around a tall brunette – long giraffe legs, big green eyes. Before I can turn round and pretend not to have noticed him, he looks up. It's too late. First surprise crosses his face, then unease, then resignation that we're going to have to acknowledge each other in this awkward moment.

'Hi, Yasir,' I say as casually as possible.

Nirvana looks up sharply and takes a step closer to me.

Yasir mumbles a 'Hi' back. The woman in his arms is staring at us. She doesn't look threatened or insecure. She smiles and then just looks away, uninterested.

There's nothing to say, really. The thought does cross my mind that I could open with a line like, *So Yasir, how soon after you rejected me did you hook up with Miss Universe here?* But there's no way I'm going to appear bitter, so I laugh, do a subtle hair toss (my strong point) and say (rather perceptively), 'What a downpour, hey?'

'Shocking!' Nirvana agrees, with affected enthusiasm.

Yasir, who looks as uncomfortable as I feel, nods. 'We're just waiting undercover.'

Thank God I'm not the only one making banally obvious comments.

'We're going to take our chances,' I say, grabbing Nirvana's hand. 'Take care! Bye!'

I drag Nirvana behind me through the downpour. When we're finally inside the car, panting, water dripping from our hair into our eyes, we look at each other and double over in hysterics.

'Screw them all!' Nirvana yells, stamping her feet on the floor of the car like a child.

'Nirvana!' I cry, shocked. 'What's come over you?'

'Screw them all!' she repeats with a maniacal laugh. 'Do you think Elizabeth Bennet didn't swear into her pillow when Mr Darcy pissed her off?'

I laugh louder.

'I hope she treats him badly,' she says.

'Nirvana!' I scold. 'That's an awful thing to say ... He's actually a great guy. Objectively speaking. I mean, clearly I hate his guts.'

'There's only one thing for it then. How about some retail therapy?' she asks.

'I'm in.'

Thirty

When I first started working at RecruitRight I made the stupid mistake of accepting Danny's invitation to be his friend on Facebook. For someone in recruitment – who knows all about the problems that can blow up when the line between work and personal life blurs – it was a monumentally dumb thing to do. Looking back now, I can only explain my lapse of judgement by the fact that Danny seemed like such a nice, normal guy, with no airs or pretensions about him. He seemed to consciously make an effort not to act like the boss. At the time I thought this was a sign of a progressive workplace that didn't insist on outdated hierarchies and power structures. There could be no glass ceiling in a place where the boss was so determined to be 'one of us'. He ate lunch with us in the boardroom and forwarded us funny emails.

I'm not a diehard Facebook user, posting every thought that enters my mind, but I regularly check in and post my photos. Danny's occasionally made some comments on my photos, but nothing to make me think twice.

Which is why, when I open my Facebook account this

Sunday evening, I'm alarmed to find that Danny has posted a message on my wall.

> I'm really sorry, Esma. I accept I betrayed your trust and I hope you can forgive me and our relationship can go back to the way it was before.

My stomach sinks. Four stupid comments have been posted in response, one from somebody I can't even remember adding. The other three are from old friends I haven't seen for ages.

As for my inbox, I've got five messages, all asking who Danny is.

One thing's for sure. He knows what he's doing.

Fury floods through me. And a niggling feeling that maybe I'm somehow to blame. Good Lord, even though I'm an OHS guru (I run seminars on this sort of thing, for goodness' sake!), I'm still stupid enough to wonder if maybe I failed to maintain a strict professional relationship. Whether it's my fault for allowing the lines to blur.

Here I am in a situation that is spiralling out of control, feeling utterly disempowered. How do I respond without opening a Pandora's box?

Reading Danny's message has brought on a headache and I pop two aspirin. I go to bed but spend all night tossing and turning. I'm not sure whether to deliver a withering line back to Danny on my Facebook wall to put an end to any speculation. But if I do that, won't I effectively be taking Danny on?

You bastard, I think as I get into work on Monday. I can't afford to lose this job, but how can I ignore what's happening?

Okay, here's the plan: confront Danny calmly and rationally. Try to resolve, not attack. Find a solution, not a machete.

I log on to my computer, put my bag away, try to muster up nerves of steel, take a deep breath and walk into his office. Danny is sitting at his desk, drinking a coffee while he types. He looks up and smiles brightly.

'Hey, there,' he says cheerfully. 'How's it all going?'

My eyes search his. What game is he playing?

'Good ...' I say warily. I'm about to sit down on the chair in front of his desk but change my mind. I'll feel more confident if I'm standing, looking down at him.

'Well, actually,' I say, treading carefully, 'I wanted to talk to you about your Facebook message ... and about that email you sent to Marco and just, things in general, between us, some of the comments you make ...'

He presses a hand to his forehead and looks flustered. 'Like I said, I'm really sorry. Emailing Marco was a dumb thing to do. Totally out of line.'

'Putting aside the fact that you sent that email, the message you posted on my Facebook wall was ...' For a moment, I waver, knowing that I'm about to cross a threshold. 'The way it was worded was suggestive. I've had people contacting me thinking there's something between us.'

'Isn't there?' he asks blankly.

'*What?*'

'We're friends. That's nothing to be ashamed about.'

Is he for real?

'That wasn't what your message implied,' I say tersely.

'Well, it's what I meant. I'm married, for God's sake.'

I can't believe he's turning this around. Pulling out the 'I'm married' line when all he does is bag out his wife and whine about how unhappy he is.

'The comments you make ... Sometimes I feel you can overstep the line.'

'What kind of comments?'

I fiddle with the zipper on my jacket. 'Like the way you talk about my personal life, meeting a guy and all that.'

'Really?' He looks flabbergasted. 'You really get offended by that?' He shakes his head as though he's trying to work out some calculus equation. 'Hmm, okay, my lips are sealed. It's just ...'

I look up sharply. 'Yeah?'

'It's just that you were the one who wanted to talk about it, that night we all went for drinks. You wanted to have it out, get your theory on love all out in the open for debate.'

That's just so twisted. I don't even know how to respond. It's as though I'm the one who made it an agenda item.

'But I appreciate your concern and you can consider the topic closed. As for the comments I make, well, people will read into things what they want to. It just suits them not to own up to it.' He pauses, swivelling on his chair.

There's that dark undertone again. You see a flash of it and then suddenly it's gone, leaving you doubting it was there in the first place.

'Your friends on Facebook got it wrong,' he says, resuming his cheerful tone. 'I'm sorry if it caused a problem, but my intentions were completely innocent, I assure you!'

I'm horrified. Is he implying that somehow I'm misinterpreting his comments and behaviour because I secretly fancy him? This is not going to plan.

'How about we put it all behind us, hey?' he says, cocking his head to the side. 'Start anew? You're one of the best people here. I don't want there to be any bad blood between us.' He pats a manilla folder on his desk. 'I've got your promotion paperwork here. Thanks for all the effort you put into it. We're going to be working even more closely together. We have to learn to understand each other.'

Even though I don't trust him, I nod in agreement. I walk out of his office, feeling sick.

Thirty-One

It's ten past six in the morning and we're boxing. Not a friendly hit of the boxing pad, but intense, crazy think-of-Danny's-face kind of boxing. I'm partnered with Ruby, who is holding the boxing pads as I hit them with all the force and energy I can muster. She's struggling to hold the pads firmly, and once or twice I've nearly hit her face because she hasn't been able to give me enough resistance. Finally she lets out a strangled cry, throws the pads on the floor and says, 'Esma! I didn't come here to have my nose broken!'

'I'm sorry,' I cry back, 'but you need to give me more resistance.'

That would usually be a cue for Alex to rush over, pick up the pads and demonstrate the correct technique to us. Except this morning he sends Mikey over instead.

When class is over, Alex announces that he's hosting a party. A chance for everybody to get to know each other outside of class and to celebrate all our hard work.

Ruby turns to me and grins. Then she heads over to Alex, who notices her and gives her an awkward smile before making a beeline for a huddle of guys.

'What was that all about?' she asks me later, throwing her hands in the air in frustration. 'He's avoiding me! I mean, am I going mental? Am I imagining it?'

'No,' I admit reluctantly.

We sit in silence for some moments. Then she unleashes her fury.

'When will guys get we are not idiots? It's one thing to pretend something hasn't happened. It's another to act as though we're the delusional ones. Making up moments from thin air! I'm not a fuckwit! WE HAD A SPECIAL NIGHT! He can't just—' She stops herself, takes a deep calming breath. Puts her hands out as though balancing herself. 'No. I *won't* do this. Fuck him.'

When it rains, it pours. I am living proof that there is climate change. A complete drought of eligible guys and then suddenly a downpour. Well, two anyway.

First there's Metin. And then, only a couple of weeks later, a guy called Aydin, who's also of Turkish background. His parents are good friends with a mutual family friend – aka backstage matchmaker – who suggested Aydin and his family visit us.

When Mum mentions this to me, I go ballistic. How can she possibly expect me to give Metin a proper chance if I'm meeting other people at the same time?

'But, darling,' she says over breakfast, 'that's life. Things don't turn out how we plan. You just never know. What if Aydin is the right guy? Or what if meeting Aydin will convince you Metin is the right guy? None of us knows what *kismet* waits for us.'

'Mum,' I groan, 'it's just too confusing. Why does Aydin have to arrive now? Can't you delay it?'

'I can't exactly tell them to come back another time because you're trying out somebody else first.'

She refills my cup of tea and adds a heaped teaspoon of sugar. My dad is out in the garden, tending to his precious plants. I catch a glimpse of him out the window. He's wearing a baseball cap that has a picture of some Disney character on it. Must be an old one that belonged to me or Senem. He looks cute, watering his birds of paradise with a Mickey Mouse cap on, oblivious to the conversation Mum and I are having inside.

I can see Mum's logic. Unfortunately, if I say no to meeting Aydin, I might never know if I turned away the right guy. So, I agree, and a smile spreads across Mum's face.

Aydin and his parents visit the next night. They're punctual, thank goodness. I remember one guy who arrived an hour and a half late and didn't even bother calling or providing any explanation when he eventually did arrive. I couldn't help it, but his rudeness turned me off completely, and so I spent the night talking about how I was hanging out for marriage so I could let myself go and never worry about my figure again. Oddly enough, we never heard back from him.

My parents open the door and Aydin's parents walk in first. They're the kind of people who smile with their eyes and are pleased with everything they see ('Ooh, what a lovely house! Your garden is so beautiful!').

They're followed by Aydin.

He's not what you would call a looker, not like Metin. Rephrase that: he doesn't have the making-me-melt-give-me-a-cold-shower effect that Metin does. But Aydin *is* attractive (his head is shaved – a look I love on guys who can carry it off, which he can) and he oozes charm, with that affable smile and laidback vibe. Within about fifty seconds of meeting him I like him enough to be thankful I agreed to him coming over.

We all head to the family room and throw ourselves into the usual small talk. At first we play it safe, both talking directly to each other's parents, going with the obvious topics for Sydney residents (weather, traffic congestion and property prices). After what seems like a lifetime (but is about fifteen minutes), Aydin's dad asks if he can go outside for a cigarette, which is the perfect cue for the parents to withdraw to the garden and leave Aydin and me alone.

'Dad doesn't normally smoke,' Aydin says with a grin.

And what a grin.

I must be the unluckiest girl in the world. I meet two guys at the same time who both have irresistible grins. Had one looked like Mr Bean, I might have been safe, but Metin makes my heart race, and Aydin's already making me jittery.

'So he's taking up smoking to leave us alone together?'

'He has a smoke on the odd occasion, but he's doing it now as an excuse to give us some time on our own.'

'The poor guy. He could be outside sucking in nicotine,

thinking you've met the girl of your dreams, when really you're trying to think of an exit strategy.'

'Are you fishing for a compliment?' he teases. 'Because I'm not looking for an exit strategy. Not just yet. So his smoke is worth it.'

'Ah, Mr Confident.'

There's a twinkle in his eyes. 'What do you mean?'

'How do you know *I'm* not looking for an exit strategy?'

He folds his arms across his chest and leans back, getting comfortable. 'Are you?'

I shrug. 'You're safe ... for now.'

He grins again and my body temperature increases.

'So what do you do?' I ask.

'I'm a graphic designer and filmmaker.'

'Wow,' I say, leaning back in my chair. Then I quickly sit upright, remembering it's more flattering. 'What kind of films?'

'The ones that don't make money.'

'Struggling artist, huh?'

'Something like that.' His smile widens.

'So tell me about some of the films you've made.'

'My first film was a horror flick. Very low budget. About an MP who goes around killing vocal constituents. Funnily enough, not blockbuster material.'

I laugh. 'Not a very subtle message.'

'No.' He grins. 'I've learnt a lot since then, though. It doesn't pay the bills, but that's what the graphic design work is for.'

I cock an eyebrow. 'Are you being modest and I'm

actually talking to a indie film sensation?'

'Not exactly,' he chuckles. 'But hey, I've had some death threats. I've got my critics. That's got to be some kind of claim to fame.'

As he talks I realise I can't wipe the grin off my face. 'Critics, hey? Why?'

'Some Muslims and Turks only want films that depict us in the best light. They don't like it when I make films about the Armenians, or homosexuality, for example. They're taboo subjects but, on the other hand, the middle classes in the West love them. They see me as some kind of insider who speaks with authority about my own culture. So fundraising for a film on the gay scene in Turkey was relatively easy and the critics loved it. But then when I tried to raise money for a film that explores the centre of power in Australia's corporate world, suddenly the wallets snapped shut. There was immediate hostility and suspicion.'

'You're seen as useful as long as you only expose your own culture, right?'

'Yes!' he says excitedly. 'Exactly! And that, Esma, pisses me off.' He grins at me. 'But I'm the kind of person who channels my anger into something positive. Instead of getting pissed off, I set out to piss off others. Because that's when you know you're shoving people out of their comfort zone and getting them to think.'

I regard him with wry amusement. 'Wouldn't it be less confronting if you *nudged* people out of their comfort zone? If you're aggressive with your message, won't you lose more people than you gain?'

There's a permanent smile on Aydin's face, an exuberance and energy that radiates from him, even as we're disagreeing. There's something sensual and exciting about his energy and passion.

'I'm not the kind of person to hint and imply,' he goes on. 'There's enough hypocrisy and stonewalling and politeness and I don't want a part of that. I want people to walk out of my films with a headache.'

I laugh hard. 'A headache? You're a sadist.'

'Yeah,' he says, laughing along. 'Instead of popcorn, bring in some paracetamol. No, seriously, I mean it literally: I want their minds to ache with a longing to change things. We need more mind explosions. How else are people going to feel compelled to act?'

My mum walks in then, offering us some drinks and cake. When she leaves, the conversation has turned to my job, hobbies, favourite movies and books. There are so many moments when we cry 'That's exactly how I feel!' or 'I know what you mean!' When our parents return, we're surprised that an hour and a half has passed without us noticing.

When they call it a night, and we're walking them to the front door, Aydin turns and, in a low voice, asks me if I'd mind giving him my number. I don't hesitate.

Thirty-Two

Our No Sex in the City catch-up has morphed into a dinner with Anil, his sister, Neela, and her husband, Sunil. Ruby, Lisa and I aren't terribly happy about this, but when I rang Nirvana to check her availability she said she was booked out with family stuff for the next three weekends. She and Anil were taking Neela out for her birthday so she suggested we join them for dinner. We agreed because we didn't want to miss out on seeing Nirvana.

Almost as soon as we've ordered entrées, I start to regret our decision. Sunil and Neela are clearly not on speaking terms, which is made all the more awkward because it's Neela's birthday. Sunil doesn't even try to create the illusion of a happy couple.

Anil is compensating by being animated and talkative, trying his best to draw Neela out, which puts added pressure on us to focus all our attention on her. It's a little strange, given that the tense atmosphere has been created by the sullen idiot beside her, and the fact that we don't really know her. But we're there for Nirvana's sake and that's enough to motivate us.

'So what do you do, Neela?' Ruby asks.

Neela hesitates for a moment, her eyes flicking to the side quickly as if she's assessing the impact of her words on Sunil. 'I'm a network administrator,' she says almost shamefully.

Sunil squirms in his seat as Neela answers.

'And what do you do, Sunil?' Ruby asks, a hint of self-satisfaction in her tone. I know she's trying really hard and is pleased with her effort to be inclusive of the hostile lump sitting beside us.

Anil clears his throat and starts fiddling with his phone. Nirvana distracts herself by refilling our water glasses.

'I don't have a job,' Sunil spits. 'Neela stole my job.' Then he laughs cheerlessly.

There's a pause, and an ominous silence descends over the table. Neela looks down at her lap. 'Don't be silly, Sunil,' she fumbles.

Sunil's lips curl up into a sarcastic half-smile. He gives her a quick squeeze of the shoulders and she seems to collapse into herself, trying hard to smile at us all and defuse what is clearly a difficult situation. 'Come on, Neela, I was only joking. You shouldn't take things so seriously.'

'Not a very funny joke,' Anil says. But he must regret his tone because he then lets out an awkward chuckle. 'Companies can be so brutal, hey?'

Sunil ignores him, turning to us instead. 'Neela and I worked for the same accounting firm – that's how we met. Six months ago I was made redundant and Neela had my duties added to hers. Cost cutting.'

'Happens every day,' Ruby says authoritatively. 'The employment law group at work act in those sorts of reshuffles all the time.'

'Yes,' Sunil says through gritted teeth.

'I never asked for it ...'

'Sure you didn't, *honey*,' Sunil says cheerily, patting her on the hand like a parent trying to placate a child.

Anil and Nirvana change the topic and Sunil tunes out.

I realise that the only person who hasn't spoken is Lisa. She's been quietly watching and listening, not contributing a word to the exchange. Neela excuses herself to have a smoke outside and Lisa goes with her.

Lisa doesn't smoke. But I know that's not why she's joining Neela. Lisa is a born listener.

When I get home I log on to Facebook and am pleasantly surprised to see an invite from Metin to be his friend. I accept. I have to wait for him to confirm before I can log on to his account and rummage around through his life, checking out his photographs and wall messages.

He called me last night. While he still hogs a lot of the talk time, at least his stories are interesting and he's trying to be more reciprocal.

Okay, who am I kidding? Sure, the European adventure stories and doctor-saves-the-day-in-Cambodian-camp stories are gripping and entertaining, but the main reason I'm attracted to Metin is because he oozes sex appeal.

But is that such a bad thing?

Even when we're talking about topics as ordinary as our

worst experiences on public transport, my mind wanders: standing on a crowded train ... It comes to a sudden halt as all good CityRail trains do. I'm thrown into Metin's strong, powerful arms ... Or maybe I faint and then he does CPR on me on the platform of Central Station in front of a cheer squad of winos and kids jigging school ...

It's ridiculous.

Maybe my overactive imagination has something to do with the fact that I'm twenty-eight years old and I've never felt the touch of a man's lips on mine. Never even held a man's hand, or leant against a man's chest, close enough to inhale his scent. I'm intelligent enough to know that because I've never experienced physical intimacy with a man, the intensity of sexual tension between me and Metin is clouding my judgement. Because the feelings Metin arouses in me are new and exciting, I'm too distracted to heed the tiny voice in my head that questions whether he's the right guy for me.

As for Aydin, he called me about half an hour after I'd hung up the phone with Metin.

Guilt has set in.

How can I lead on two guys in the one night? And, worse still, what does it say about me that I'm so good at it?

With Aydin the conversation is different. It's not just about the easy flirting, which is reciprocal and smart and sassy (with Metin I'm the giggling, blushing schoolgirl too overwhelmed to know how to respond). Aydin and I have an intellectual connection, which sounds wanky but is true. He cares about social justice, and it's not just lip service – he acts on it too. I love that he motivates and challenges me. We have more in common, too. We both grew up in Sydney. We love the same music. It all just clicks.

So why am I confused?

I feel there's potential with both of them. But it's too early to decide who's right. Or who's wrong. There's a big difference: I'd rather make a decision because I feel that one of them is the one, than have to make a decision because one of them isn't.

This morning Metin sends me a text message while I'm at work, asking me if I'm free for dinner and a movie on Saturday night. I say yes (and then instantly go into overdrive planning what I'm going to wear, how I'll do my hair; there's even more pressure to look good when you're out with someone who looks like a model). And then the fun begins, because Aydin calls me in the afternoon, while I'm driving to a pharmacy for a training session.

I put him on speaker phone and we chat for a while. One thing I've already noticed about Aydin: he's on full speed. He's a crusader for social justice but with the sense to be self-deprecating about it; he doesn't strike me as a zealot. There's nothing worse than being with somebody who tries to make you feel guilty for not living on two dollars a day.

When he asks me out for dinner on Friday night I don't hesitate to say yes.

Except I feel guilty. I'm two-timing. There's no way of sugar-coating it.

I need some advice, so I call Ruby. She's on her way back from court and, miraculously, has a moment to talk (getting her during the day is almost always impossible). I know if I call Nirvana she'll probably sympathise with Aydin and Metin and give me an answer I don't want to hear. Ruby's the kind of girl who can cut through the emotion.

'Don't you dare feel guilty,' she says briskly. 'You have to look out for yourself. Plus it's unfair to drop one of them without a good reason. You owe them both a proper chance. It's not your bloody fault they showed up at the same time. They're big boys. They can look after themselves. Got it?'

Thirty-Three

'If you knew something about somebody I was seeing that you thought was troubling, would you tell me? At the risk of me perhaps not sharing your point of view?'

Lisa, nervously waiting for my response, staples the document she's holding with even more vigour than usual. We're at the Sydney Refugee Centre tonight, putting together last-minute asylum applications.

'You mean as a warning? Careful, by the way. The staples aren't actually going to hurt Julia and Tony, even if you press down as hard as you can.'

The words go straight over her head. 'Not necessarily as a warning. Just for the sake of giving me as complete a picture as possible of the man I'm with. Here, pass that pile to me, your stapling is atrocious.'

'You've got standards for stapling too? My God, you have issues.'

'Just answer the question.'

I shuffle through the papers strewn all over the desk and start to sort them into piles. 'This pile for torture. This pile for rape as a weapon of war. This pile for religious persecution. Do you think the shock jocks and dog-whistle politicians might shut up for five minutes if we locked them up in a room and got them to read this stuff?'

Lisa nods. 'Maybe an all-expenses-paid holiday in a detention centre? We won't even ask for receipts.'

'I've never been good at hypotheticals. Just tell me what this is all about.'

'Well, what would you do if you knew something disturbing about a guy I was seeing?' She looks at me beseechingly. 'Would you tell me?'

'It would really depend on the gravity of the information. If I'd seen the guy shoplifting – then yes, I'd tell you. But if it was just a personality thing, I probably wouldn't because that's so subjective and I wouldn't want to risk losing you.'

She nods her head once, satisfied with my response.

'You can't stop there. Who's the hypothetical based on?' She looks at me grimly. 'I can't say.'

'Why not?'

'Confidential information.'

'Oh, come on. You can't use that card. Spill it.'

'I'm serious. It's work-related.'

I heave a disappointed sigh to indicate I understand her position but nonetheless disapprove.

Danny sticks his head into my office on Friday afternoon.

'Are you able to come in tomorrow for a couple of hours? Don't look at me like that,' he says, pouting. 'I know it's *horrible*, but we've got a stack of stuff to do on the business development plans and I'm going to be out of the office for half of next week. Mary's insisting we spend quality time together.' He sighs to convey the oppressiveness of such plans. '*Please?*'

'I have boot camp at eight,' I lie.

'We can start at ten.'

'For how long?'

'Two hours max. If we start at ten, we can be out by twelve. I'm going to ask Kylie and Veronica to come in too.'

It's not like I have much choice, so I agree and his face lights up.

Then, in a breezy voice, he says, 'Would you prefer we meet at a café rather than the office?'

'A *café*?' I struggle to disguise my contempt at his suggestion.

'Just to keep things relaxed,' he says. 'We can have a business brunch. My shout.'

Fat chance I'm going to say yes to a cosy weekend brunch.

'I think it's better if we stay in the office. All the files are here,' I argue. 'It makes sense to have them within reach.'

Oh great, now he's going all wounded on me. Not wanting to provoke him, I say, as sweetly as I can, 'How about we all bring something to share for the meeting? Muffins sound good?'

He grins and says, 'Sounds great. I'll bring in some champagne.' My jaw almost drops. 'Just kidding!' he laughs. 'It's a business meeting, after all. I've got to remember that, don't I?'

He laughs and leaves.

It's funny but sometimes you can get along with somebody, overlooking their sleaziness, or sloppiness, or any other annoying aspect of their personality, and then suddenly, at some random and inexplicable point, you just can't stand them. You can't stand the sight of them. You can't stand to be in the same room as them, and when they talk to you, their voice grates on your nerves. I realise, then, as I reflect on how excited Danny was at my agreement to work at the weekend, that I'll never go back to liking him as I did when I first started work, or even tolerating him as I have lately. I now can't stand him. It's as though the sum of all his interactions with me is now weighing down on my shoulders like a heavy brick. A brick I want to throw at his head.

I still haven't heard anything from the three recruiting agencies I've sent my résumé to, and decide I'll harass them by phone on my way home (no doubt annoying them as much as some candidates annoy me). But when I call I get a voicemail message for each one. I look at my watch. Five o'clock. *Slackers*, I think. *I'm going to be working on a Saturday. What's your excuse for leaving before five on a weekday?*

Thirty-Four

I love getting dressed up in winter. For my date with Aydin tonight I'm wearing a classic double-breasted white coat (a sauce-based pasta is clearly not going to be an option) and dark-blue skinny-leg jeans. I pull my favourite brown stiletto boots over them. I got the boots in Italy and I love them like they're a part of my family. I pull up half my hair with a clip and let the rest fall softly around my shoulders and down my back.

I meet Aydin at a McDonald's on Parramatta Road. We've agreed I'll leave my car here and we'll go into Darlinghurst in his car. I've avoided him picking me up from home because although my dad's relaxed the Rule of Six, he doesn't need to know I'm out following the Rule of Two.

Aydin's dressed well and smells amazing; he's exuding sexy confidence and making me go weak at the knees.

He's not catwalk good-looking, and although he's solid, he's not big and buff like Metin. Oh, and he's only slightly taller than me (I shouldn't have worn heels because we have a Tom and Nicole case on our hands).

But when he smiles, it's magnetic.

He opens the passenger door of his Mazda and I hop in. It's squeaky clean, with one of those small tissue boxes that fit neatly into the middle console, a DVD case in the door pocket and an Ambi Pur attached to the air vent. The rest of the car is empty. No tissues or empty food wrappers on the seats. No unopened bank letters, junk mail or books strewn across the back seat. No CDs without cases lying on the floor.

'You got it cleaned, didn't you?' I accuse him, a grin plastered on my face.

He laughs as we drive out of the car park. 'Of course. You think my car normally looks like this? I usually advise passengers to be immunised before they get in.' He picks up the tissue box. '*Floral?* I was in a rush in the shops and didn't realise!'

I'm sure Aydin must be able to hear my heart hammering away at my rib cage. My hands are folded in my lap, but I'm conscious of how close he is to me, one hand on the steering wheel, the other resting casually on his thigh. I know my parents would never approve of me being alone with a guy in his car. Judging from the chemistry between us, I can understand why.

As we drive to Oxford Street the best thing happens while we're stuck in a traffic jam near Hyde Park. The car beside us is packed with a bunch of young guys and the driver is checking me out, thank you very much. He looks my way and I'm sure I'm not imagining it but he winks, and his mates seem to be egging him on, grinning and pointing. He doesn't look a day over his driving test, but that doesn't matter. He's a hot-blooded male, isn't he?

Checking. Me. Out.

With Aydin beside me.

That's right, Aydin. Let your head swell up with pride. You're taking out one hottie tonight.

I turn to face Aydin, putting on my most nonchalant and innocent face, as though I'm so used to such attention that I don't even notice it happening any more. Aydin's oblivious, focused on trying to find a CD ('I knew exactly where they were when they were lying everywhere, but now they're organised in this stupid case, I can't find what I want!'). That's when I notice the car on the other side of us. A convertible. With the lid down. Five girls. Four practically standing up in their seats. Ten E-cup boobs. One metre of fabric between the lot of them.

I sink down into my chair to give the poor boys a better view.

Once we're seated at the restaurant we launch straight into the 'So how's your week been?' talk. After covering the usual ground, we momentarily hit a wall.

'Oh my God, quick!' he cries, crouching down towards the table and waving at me to do the same.

'What's wrong?' I say, copying him.

'An awkward silence! Duck for cover!'

I laugh.

'Quick! Let's use it as a cue to order. Hopefully the menu will stimulate some conversation.'

'Do Peking duck and dumplings normally inspire you to talk?'

'Maybe! Who knows? There are probably a lot of interesting stories about dumplings and sushi.'

Ordering turns into a riot, with Aydin making a joke about every selection I make. Luckily the waiter humours us. We must have 'first date' written all over us.

Once we've ordered, there's another silence, then Aydin shifts tone. 'Okay, Esma, jokes aside, tell me about the *real* you.'

'Hmm.' I drum my fingers on the table. 'What can I say without sounding cheesy?'

'Cheesy's fine.'

'Okay. Don't say I didn't warn you.' And it does sound cheesy too, when I talk about wanting to make a difference, about the Refugee Centre and all the ambiguous feelings that brings. But he doesn't sneer, or laugh, or look embarrassed. In fact he looks happy, as if he knows exactly what I'm talking about.

That gets us going again until the waiter brings out our food and Aydin raises his glass (sparkling water) to a toast. I raise mine (sparkling Coke), we clink glasses and he says, 'To sounding cheesy.'

I go to the bathroom and when I return I venture into the more personal. 'So what do you want in a woman?'

'That's easy. It starts with similar values and goals.'

I smile. 'Me too ... although ...'

He gives me a cautious look. 'Yes?'

'Do you sometimes think that you're not sure what your values and goals are? I mean, they'd have to be fluid, wouldn't they? I don't mean your moral code, or core beliefs. But it's hard to predict what kind of person you're going to be.'

'I guess it's all about trusting the laws of probability that the other person won't turn out to be a complete jerk.'

I smile in agreement. 'We sound so cynical.'

'It's a healthy dose. What about religion? Are you religious?'

'I'm pretty lax with the praying and fasting. But my faith is important to me. I think it'd be nice if the guy I ended up with woke me up at dawn to pray with him.'

'I'm not the most religious guy. I try to pray but I'm not very regular. I do fast in Ramadan, though.'

'Do you drink?' I ask.

He shakes his head. 'I used to. Gave it up last year. Would it make a difference if I did?'

I pause. 'Yes,' I say eventually. 'Having an alcohol-free house is a big deal to me. But I'm not going to impose that on anybody, it needs to come from them. I know I might not look like the religious type, but there are some things I try to maintain.'

'No such thing as *looking* religious. If a person's religious, they don't need to show it off, or prove it to anybody.'

I love how much we think alike.

'I think growing in faith as a couple is really important. It's definitely something I want too. God knows, I've mucked around and got up to my fair share of trouble. Gave my parents a lot of grey hairs.' He chuckles.

'Have you got *a past*?'

He laughs. 'I've been into the clubbing and bar scene,' he

says. 'Does that answer your "how far did he stray?" curiosity?' The grin on his face tells me he's having fun teasing me.

'For now.' I grin back. 'There's a lot of hypocrisy in our community, though,' I add.

'Wholeheartedly agree with you on that.'

'It's more acceptable for guys to go out and fool around. But if a girl does it, it's another story altogether.'

'Us guys get away with a hell of a lot more. Depends on the family, of course. I'm just as answerable to my parents as my sister is.'

I cock an eyebrow. 'You can't expect me to believe they'd be okay with her getting up to the stuff you have?'

He shrugs. 'That's probably true, but in our culture there are some mistakes parents don't want their children to make because they have such a stigma attached to them. Especially for girls. There's no room for learning from your mistakes if that mistake happens to involve sex before marriage. That's just the way it is.'

'For girls. Not for guys.'

'Yeah, well, there's the double standard.'

'If I ever have a son and a daughter, I'm going to give them the same rules. The same curfew. The same limits. And that includes no fooling around before marriage. For either!'

'And how would you enforce that rule?'

'My parents don't enforce their rules with me. I can do whatever I want – they're not with me every moment of the day. Ultimately, I'm the one who makes the choices about my life. They just raised me a certain way. I've embraced my traditions because I believe in them. That's how I would hope to raise my kids too. It's about trust.'

'I like that. And it's very true. My parents raised my sister and me like that. Only I broke their trust – I was always a sucker for a pretty girl. Still am actually.'

I smile shyly. His comment hangs in the air and it's like a warm glow over us.

The conversation eventually shifts away from serious talk to the more light-hearted, and it's that shift that I love the most about tonight. It's as though we're catching up on each other's lives, working out whether we have what it takes to be friends – best friends.

We talk for hours, through dinner, dessert and two rounds of coffee. And when I eventually get home and jump into bed, I spend the night tossing and turning, my brain about to explode, because something tells me Aydin is The One!

Thirty-Five

Or is he?

Because the next morning I wake to my mum jumping on my bed, shouting, 'Esma! Wake up! He sent you flowers!'

I leap out of bed. 'What?' I cry, still half-asleep. 'Who sent flowers?'

'The doctor. The tall one.'

Just in case I get him confused with the nonexistent short one.

She grabs a bouquet box of mixed flowers from the floor and presents them to me, grinning proudly. I know exactly what's going through her mind. She has *I told you so* written all over her face.

Sure enough, she says, 'I told you so. I told you to give him another chance. And look. He sends you flowers.'

'Yes, Mum,' I mutter. 'He's clearly perfect.'

Of course, I'm only playing the cynical card to stir her. Deep down I'm thrilled. Who isn't a sucker for flowers?

I grab the card and read it.

Dear Esma,
Looking forward to seeing you tonight. And asking you
lots of questions.
Metin

'Why did he type it?' my mum asks. 'Ahh, he's a doctor.
Their handwriting is always so messy. Well, isn't that
thoughtful of him.'

I give my mum an affectionate squeeze. 'Oh Mum, you'
really are adorable.'

I jump into the shower and then get ready for work,
which is utterly depressing given it's a Saturday. My mum's
standing outside the bathroom.

'Make sure you call him to say thank you. Or send him
a textual.'

'A what?' I yell out.

'A textual. Whatever that thing is called. You know what
I mean,' she ends in a huff.

'Of course I do, Mum. I just wanted to hear you say it again.'

I call Metin on my way to the office. He answers on the
second ring.

'Good morning,' he says cheerfully, in a deep voice that
sends shivers down ... I've got to get a grip.

'Thanks for such a beautiful start to my morning,' I say.

'It's a pleasure,' he says. 'Everything still okay for this
evening?'

'Yes. I'm looking forward to it.'

'Me too.'

I park near my office building and grab a box of muffins

and a takeaway coffee from a nearby bakery.

I rarely come in on a weekend and when I do I hate the desolation of the usually bustling city building. It's enough to wipe off the goofy grin that's been plastered on my face since Mum woke me up this morning.

I swipe my card at the entrance to our offices and turn on the lights. I'm the first to arrive. I go to my desk, flop into my chair and turn on my computer.

The last thing I feel like doing right now is working. All I can think about is how I'm stuck between two potentially great guys, not ready to choose between them and being unfair to both of them in the process. If the tables were turned, I know I'd be furious that a guy I was getting to know was taking out another girl as well.

I put on my headphones and hope Coldplay can drown out the confusing messages in my head.

'Hi, Esma!' Danny's cheery voice cuts through my thoughts.

'Hi, Danny.' I force myself to go for the small talk. 'Too quiet, isn't it?'

'Sure is,' he says. 'I brought some pastries. How about we set up in the boardroom?'

'Okay.' I follow him out of my office. 'I've got some muffins.' I place them on the boardroom table. 'What time are the others coming?'

He shrugs. 'I'm not sure. They should be here soon. How about we make a start? It's quarter past ten and I promised I wouldn't keep you long. They can join in the meeting when they arrive.'

I grab my notes and files from my office and return to the boardroom.

'Did you go to boot camp this morning?' he asks.

Oh. I forgot about that lie. 'Um, no, I slept in.'

'Oh, too bad. Well, it's obvious from your figure that you work out. Good for you.'

The muscles in my face tense.

'It's nice to see you out of a suit,' he says casually as he gets his papers in order on the table in front of him. 'You look just as good.'

I mumble something unintelligible, neither thanks nor rebuke, and make myself look busy with my files.

'So what did you have in mind for today?' I finally ask.

He looks at the clock. 'On second thoughts, maybe we should wait. Give them a bit of time to get here. Maybe they slept in. It's not ideal to talk about business development when there's only the two of us here.'

'In that case,' I say, standing up, 'I'll go do some work.'

'Ah, come on,' he says, motioning for me to sit back down. 'It's not even worth logging on to the intranet. We'll give them another fifteen minutes and we'll get started. What are you doing for the weekend?' he asks brightly, taking a pastry. 'Might as well dig in. Want one?'

I take a small croissant. 'I've got plans with my friends.'

'God, I miss being single. I know I give you a hard time about it, as a joke of course, but those really were the days. Now I'm stuck. And with Mary pregnant, there's no way out.'

'That's awful,' I say before I can stop myself. I don't want to be drawn into a conversation about his marriage.

I realise, then, that this has always been his tactic. Say something cruel about his wife and provoke a reaction from me. 'Anyway, it's your business. You should talk to your wife if you have issues.'

'Well, I am trying,' he says, grinning at me. 'As a matter of fact, I'm heading to the shops straight after our meeting to get her a present. She's been feeling so down about getting fat—'

'She's pregnant, Danny,' I snap. 'She's pregnant, *not* fat.' There I go again, falling straight into the trap.

He laughs, raising his hands in surrender. 'Sorry, I know, I know. Well, I want to get her something to cheer her up. Make her feel sexy again, because she's feeling so depressed about her body that she won't let me near her.' He pops a bite of a muffin into his mouth. 'A man has his needs,' he says. 'But you don't need to hear about that. Especially when you've never had a boyfriend.'

'Danny,' I say in a low growl. 'Don't go there.'

He pulls a face, failing to look contrite. 'I'm sorry. There's something about you that makes me forget myself. I'm clearly too comfortable with you. Let's just start the meeting.'

'I think we should call the girls to see where they are.'

He gives a firm nod. 'Of course. I'll do it right now. Give me a minute and I'll call them from my office.'

He leaves and I rest my forehead on the table and close my eyes. This is a nightmare. I'm going to harass the recruiters next week. Night and day until I get a job. Any job. I don't care any more. I can't go on like this, repressing every instinct in my body to stand up to him and tell him off. I feel ashamed ... compromised somehow. I've always been so assertive. Demanded that people, especially guys, show me respect.

He returns shortly afterwards, a disappointed look on his face. 'They're still asleep,' he sighs, throwing his hands in the air. 'There's not much point in them coming in now. I told them not to bother. They need an hour to get here and we want to be out of here in another hour and a half.'

My stomach plunges. I'm not going to hang around with this sleazeball all alone in the office. I stand up quickly. I don't care how I sound. 'Sorry, Danny, I can't stay.'

Disappointment washes over his face. 'Why not?'

'I just don't think there's any point. All of us need to be here.'

'But we can still get started,' he insists.

'Not without them. They have all the information on the new clients and amendments to the contracts. I'll meet them on your days off next week and we'll have something ready to show you when you get back.' I swipe my papers into a pile, grab them and turn to the door.

Danny steps towards me and puts a hand on my arm. 'Wait, *please,*' he says.

I yank my arm away from him. 'Don't touch me,' I say, looking him directly in the eye. 'I need to leave.'

I run out of the office without bothering to turn off my computer. It feels like the lift is taking ages and I keep pressing the button. I'm half-expecting Danny to race after me, but he doesn't. Finally the lift doors open. I practically jump into them and press hard on the close-doors button. And when the lift starts its descent I take a deep breath and struggle not to cry.

Thirty-Six

I call Nirvana. It's been a while. I've tried getting in touch with her several times in the past two weeks but she hasn't called me back. She messaged the other day to say she's been busy. It's not like her to let so many days pass between calls, but I give her the benefit of the doubt. I know her family commitments have escalated since her engagement to Anil.

So I try Ruby next. I start to tell her about what happened with Danny but almost before I can get the words out I suddenly find myself crying.

'Esma! Hon, what's wrong?'

Once I catch my breath I feel strong enough to talk without bawling again and I tell her everything. Except I can't bring myself to tell her about Dad's debt. It's not my shame that stops me. It's his. And there's something inside me that feels such a tender pity for him that I can't bear to expose him, especially when he sets such store on being respected by my friends. So of course Ruby's only getting half the story; she doesn't know what's preventing me from acting on what is blindingly obvious: that I need to get away from Danny.

'He can't get away with that kind of disgusting behaviour. Who does he think he is? Esma, financial security and being employed is never enough of an excuse for suffering through harassment. Report him and move on. Put your welfare first.'

I feel suffocated, but I don't say anything. Ruby's right. But right and wrong have no place when it comes to family loyalty.

I have the solution to the problem of renewable energy. Arrange for Metin to stand in front of me then hook me up to a generator.

Wait a second. Since when am I this superficial? Dinner with Aydin last night was amazing. But there's no question that I feel more physically attracted to Metin. Metin's got the wow factor. The 'I want to jump you' factor (in a religiously compliant way, of course). His eyes, his skin, his dimple (case closed), his body, his towering, manly height. I've always had a thing for tall guys and it's the kind of thing that goes against every feminist bone in my body. I feel protected in a helpless-heroine-engulfed-in-the-arms-of-a-strong-prince kind of way. Monumentally pathetic.

Metin and I are eating at a Mexican restaurant in the city. It's been an hour and the conversation is improving. Admittedly, it doesn't flow as it does with Aydin, but there's so much chemistry between us that I find myself forgetting to be annoyed by the fact that the talk is always about Metin. He's a flirt too. Holds my gaze. Winks a lot. Stirs me up. He has a story for everything, and maybe I'm becoming more tolerant of him dominating our conversations because his stories are so fascinating and I like imagining him rock climbing in Sweden (T-shirt off, of course) and swimming in Bosnia (Speedos? Six pack?). Or maybe I should just admit it's because he's so damn hot.

'So did you save anybody's life today in your boxer shorts?'

No. I don't ask him that. I want to, but I resist.

My phone beeps, alerting me to a message, and Metin urges me to read it. It's from MyNaseeb.com. At first I'm bewildered, but then I remember that this was one of the matrimonial websites I joined and realise that I must have forgotten to delete my profile. I quickly scan the message. In seconds, my shoulders are convulsing and Metin's staring at me with a questioning smile.

'What's the joke?'

I could make something up. After all, admitting that I've gone down this path is potentially humiliating. I don't care how common online dating is, as far as I'm concerned it's usually a last-resort option. And the last thing I want Metin to think is that I'm last-resort material.

But then it strikes me that Metin is easy-going and fun-loving and something like this will probably just make him smile, not think less of me. So I tell him how, in a moment of desperation after yet another failed matchmaking experience, I decided I'd venture into online dating.

He chuckles. 'I've been there too.'

'You have no idea what a relief it is to hear that,' I say. Then I read him the message. '*I'm looking for a Muslim* woman who adheres to the tenets of Islam and is able to assist me in all endeavours. She has to be attractive and beautiful with curves that excite my sacred minaret.'

We both double over in hysterics; the people seated at the table beside us flash disapproving looks in our direction, which only makes us laugh harder.

When we've finally recovered our breath, Metin asks how long ago I was online. I tell him it was only recently and his eyes narrow.

'Something wrong?' I ask.

'No,' he hurries to reassure me, but there's a tightness in his voice. 'So you deleted all the accounts?' he asks.

'Yep. Except I forgot to delete the one I just read to you.'

It takes me by surprise when Metin asks me whether I've ever been in love. He must notice me hesitate before I answer. 'Yes.'

'Really?'

'Why do you sound so surprised?'

'I'm not,' he says. 'So tell me about it. Who was he?' He puts his fork down and gives me his full attention.

'There was a guy in my last year of university,' I say. 'His name was Seyf. I met him at a Turkish ball, of all places. We got to know each other over several months, and I honestly thought he was the one. We never spoke openly about it, but it was implied. We both just knew that what we felt for each other was strong enough to last.' I shrug. 'And then one day it all came crashing down.'

'What happened?'

'His ex was pregnant. He didn't know until she was six

months into the pregnancy. She wanted to get back together with him and he felt he owed it to her and the baby to give it a try. And even though I understood and respected his decision, he broke my heart.'

He raises an eyebrow. 'Did they stay together?'

'Yes. They're married. The last I heard, they had three children.'

For a split second, a shadow crosses his face. Even his dark side is sexy, I think to myself. Then he asks whether I'm still in contact with Seyf.

'No. But we have mutual friends on Facebook. You know how it is. Everybody's life's on display.'

'Do you still have feelings for him?'

'No!' I say with a laugh. 'It's been five years. He's got his life now, and I've got mine. What about you? Have you been in love before?'

There's a long pause. 'I've been engaged,' he says.

'*Really?*' He nods. 'You never mentioned it,' I say, a hint of reproach in my tone.

I hope she was fat and ugly with acne on her back. Yep, I'm as immature as it gets.

'She was German. We met at university, too – she was studying medicine with me. At first my parents didn't approve, but when they knew I was serious about her, and I'd proposed and she'd accepted, they backed down.'

'They wanted you to marry a Turkish girl?'

'That was their preference. But once we were engaged, they actually became very fond of her. We had a lot in common. She was an enthusiastic rock climber too.' His eyes darken. 'And then disaster hit.'

Oh God, I think. Don't tell me she fell off a cliff and he's never really got over her. I can't compete with that kind of baggage.

'She cheated on me.'

Whoa. It's worse than I thought. 'While you were engaged?'

'She fell in love with my best friend. We often went away together with a group of friends. Apparently they were seeing each other for a couple of months and then, when she'd decided she had stronger feelings for him than me, she dumped me.'

I exhale. 'That's horrible.'

He clears his throat and then gives me a gentle smile. 'I'm over it.' Oh sure, I've heard that one before. 'I've learnt my lesson. It was partly my fault, losing Giselle. There was so much that I let pass and in the end I was betrayed.'

Giselle? A silence settles between us, and the change in mood is dispiriting.

Metin sets down his glass and smiles at me uncertainly. 'So,' he at last manages. 'I want to say something, but I don't want you to take it the wrong way.'

I let out a nervous giggle; clearly acting like a bimbo in such moments is the rational way to go.

'Promise me you won't be offended or take this badly?' he says nervously.

In other words, you are about to be offended and take this badly.

I frown. 'I can give you a false promise but there's no point. I have no idea what you're going to say.'

He leans forward and suddenly grabs hold of my hand. I inhale sharply. Is it possible not to melt at the touch of his hand? This is the first physical intimacy we've ever had. In fact, I've never gone further than holding a guy's hand. I think I hear the sound of several million bodies falling to the ground in shock.

'Look, I've never felt this way about anybody since Giselle,' he says.

(While he's still holding my hand.)

'So I don't want to blow it by not being honest.'

(He's still holding my hand.)

'We've got to go into this knowing each other, as much as we can.'

(Still with the hand.)

'Okay,' he says solemnly. 'I noticed ...' He stalls and then tries again. 'I noticed you have a lot of male friends on Facebook.'

HUH?

I instinctively pull my hand away from his. I hadn't expected such a ... weird statement.

'Do I?' I wonder aloud, frowning as I try to remember my list of friends. 'I hadn't noticed.' I let out a short laugh. 'Most people don't even know half of the friends they add. School, university, all the million things in between.'

He's clearly disappointed with my response. 'Do you just add anybody who sends you an invitation?'

'No!' I say, my voice trembling. 'That's not a very nice thing to say.'

He tries to backtrack. 'I didn't mean to upset you, Esma.

It's just that I'm very particular about who I add.'

I look at him dumbfounded. 'Look,' I say in a sharp tone, 'why is my Facebook profile suddenly an issue? We're adults, aren't we? The last thing I would have expected was to be discussing my list of Facebook friends.'

He looks at me. 'To be honest, I don't believe guys and girls can just be friends.'

'I think that's a bit of a generalisation,' I scoff.

'Well, I think my experience justifies the generalisation, Esma.' His tone is low and gentle. 'There's always going to be an element of attraction, so why put yourself in that kind of position? Why allow yourself to be tempted?'

'Tempted to do *what*? I know guys who I would never think twice about being with.'

'That's what you think now. But it's naive—'

'I'm not naive,' I shoot back.

'Love can come from friendship. It's often the best kind of love.'

'But if I'm in love with somebody else, I'm not going to allow myself to ever cross the line with a male friend. I wouldn't even think twice about it.'

'You can't know that,' he argues. 'That's the point. Everybody is vulnerable at some stage.'

'It comes down to two people being secure in themselves and their relationship.' I fiddle with my napkin.

Oh, Metin! Male model from Germany, doctor with potential for good future and gorgeous kids, don't tell me you have trust issues. Have a wart or hairy birthmark (but not too big), but not *trust* issues.

'You can always trust your partner,' he says, 'but how can you trust others? How do I know those male friends don't want something more from you? I just believe that if we're to be together we need to cut ourselves off from our past. From your male friends and from my female friends.'

'Metin,' I say gently. 'I know you've been betrayed, but you have to learn to trust me. We can't segregate ourselves from the opposite sex; that's not how the world works. Each of us is going to be thrown into situations where we're tested. Ultimately, it's about our character.'

Another long silence settles between us. I stare at the table as I fiddle with the salt and pepper shaker. And then, quite suddenly, he leans over and I almost pass out.

Because he takes my hand again and gently raises it to his mouth and then presses his lips once against my fingers. My insides go all funny. I'm practically paralysed, but obviously not totally because I'm so shocked by his move that my hand drops when he lets go.

Idiot, I think.

But then my conscience reminds me about my 'thou shalt not touch before the ink on the wedding certificate dries' rule and I accept it's probably a good thing that my hand has fallen into his tortilla.

'I'm so sorry!' I cry, mortified, and quickly grab a napkin.

He starts to laugh, a great hulking laugh that rises up from deep within him, until I've joined him and am laughing so hard that I nearly choke.

'I'm sorry,' he says when we've calmed down. 'I know I must sound paranoid.'

I cut him off. 'You have to learn to trust again. I'm telling you now, I can be trusted.'

But then the irony of my words hits me hard and my head begins to throb.

Metin walks me to my car. I'm aware of how close he is to me. I can tell he wants to hold my hand again, even put his arm around me, but I've folded my arms over my chest, not trusting myself. I've never been this close to a guy before. Even Seyf never crossed the line with me. But with Metin I feel there's so much sexual chemistry that it's muddling my thoughts.

When we say goodbye I hurry into my car, not daring to linger.

Every instinct in my body tells me he wants to kiss me goodnight, but if I let him kiss me, I know I won't want to stop. Isn't that the whole point of abstinence? That sexual desire is such a powerful, intoxicating force that one small kiss can lead to much much more. If the end of that journey is forbidden to me, then so is the start, because there is absolutely no doubt in my mind that if Metin were to start that journey, I wouldn't want him to stop.

I roll down my window and his eyes scan mine.

'I'm sorry, again,' he says, thrusting his hands in the pockets of his jacket. 'Let's just forget I ever mentioned anything. I know I'm overreacting.'

I give him a reassuring smile, even though I feel like I'm the one who needs reassurance.

Because this is the thing: people are not black or white. They can't be neatly defined: 'crazy jealous type', 'tight-arse', 'fanatic'. If they could, it'd be so much easier to dismiss them outright. But we're all a jumble of personality traits, some of which may surface only haphazardly, depending on our circumstances. In the end, I have to try to weigh up whether Metin's jealous streak is going to overshadow his generosity, his playfulness, the chemistry between us. The thing is, I can't tell yet.

Thirty-Seven

Nirvana, Lisa and I have planned to have lunch at Bondi and Nirvana has invited Anil to join us. Ruby's got something on at church with her parents.

We stroll through the Sunday markets on our way to an Italian restaurant. Lisa and Nirvana spot a jewellery stand and make a beeline for it. The last thing I need is temptation to spend money, given my tight finances. So I wait with Anil, enjoying the live music. Although the weather is cool and the sky a little melancholic, Bondi still draws a big weekend crowd and the place is bustling.

It's easy to chat with Anil. The more I talk to him, the more I realise my first impression of him as arrogant was wrong. Sure, he has expensive tastes and can afford to indulge them. Maybe there is a little bit of vanity in that, but I don't think he's aware of it, and it's not that he's shallow or shows off in a way that makes you feel like he's putting you down. Even though he's a bit too materialistic for my liking, at least it's balanced with the warmth of his personality. I ask him how the engagement plans are going.

'So far, so good,' he says. 'We've booked the hall and

photographer, and our outfits are just about ready. Or so Nirvana and my mum tell me. I'm not really involved in the organisation.' He smiles. 'Even if I wanted to be, I don't think I'd be allowed!'

'At least you avoid the stress that way,' I say.

'Exactly! See, I'm not stressed at all. Nirvana is, though. She's such a calm person, but when it comes to planning the engagement she's become a bit edgy. As for my mum, she's in a frenzy, ordering food and planning menus.

'At the end of the day, she's Indian and I'm her only son. That's a recipe for an emotional meltdown. There's nothing I can do about it except indulge her obsessive planning fits and look forward to the honeymoon.'

I burst out laughing. 'So the engagement is just something to be endured?'

'You bet,' he says. 'And God knows what the wedding planning will be like if the engagement party is causing so much drama.'

'Test of your relationship with Nirvana, hey?'

'The problem is that it's a test of a *lot* of relationships, not just mine and Nirvana's. One thing is for sure: we were both crazy to think my mum was going to go for anything low-key. That'd be like telling a kid who dreams of Disneyland that you'll take them to a local fair instead.' He shrugs his shoulders and, in a cheery tone, says, 'Some fights aren't worth having!'

The girls return and we head to the restaurant. While we're ordering our lunch Lisa gets up to take a call and doesn't return for a quarter of an hour. She sits down slowly.

'What's wrong?' I ask.

'One of my clients is in hospital,' she says. 'Her boy-friend beat her so badly they're saying she might lose the sight in one eye.'

We're all shocked and we sit in silence until Anil asks Lisa if this is the first time the woman had been beaten by her boyfriend.

'No, it's been happening for a couple of years,' she says distractedly, cradling her glass.

'Why didn't she go to the police?'

'We counselled her to report him. And to leave him. But it's not as easy as it sounds.'

'Does she have kids?' Nirvana asks.

'Yep. A one-year-old and a toddler.'

Anil frowns. 'But if it's been happening for a couple of years, why would she have a baby with him? It's wrong to bring a child into that.'

Lisa raises an eyebrow. 'Of course she should have left him. The second he raised his hand to her she should have walked out. Even before that probably, because of the mental abuse. But that's just armchair moralising. My job is to give her advice and listen to her, not to judge her. I just hope she has the strength and courage to do what we all know she needs to; in practice, though, it's very difficult.'

Anil crosses his arms. 'I sympathise with that, but I still don't get it. She's brought kids into the abusive situation.'

'She didn't want to terminate the pregnancy.'

'Of course not. That would be awful. Which is why women shouldn't get themselves into that kind of situation in the first place,' Anil says solemnly. 'If you're in an abusive relationship, you shouldn't allow yourself to fall pregnant.'

Lisa is momentarily speechless.

'Anil, you can't just make blanket statements like that,' I say. 'There are so many factors involved. And it's not all about the woman preventing pregnancy – you need a man in order to fall pregnant, remember.' I struggle not to groan. 'Don't forget what kind of relationships these women are in. There isn't a lot of self-determination in the first place. It's been beaten out of them.'

Anil remains unconvinced. 'Look, these guys should be strung up. But that's not going to happen, is it? They're going to keep getting away with it so long as their women let them.'

'You're blaming the victim,' Lisa says, her eyes flashing. 'I can't believe we're even having this conversation! There are layers and layers of complexities. And sometimes the presence of children actually makes it harder for the woman to leave.'

'I've delivered babies to women who are in abusive relationships,' Nirvana says. 'Some women hope that a baby will change a man.'

'I don't like to judge,' Anil says, 'but I think it's wrong that a woman would bring a new baby into an abusive relationship. If she does it knowingly, when she has plans to leave the relationship, then I think she's selfish. She needs to think twice about leaving at that point. It's just not fair to the child. Divorce is ugly and the child starts life on the back foot.'

Lisa tenses. 'So you think she should stay in the relationship for the child's sake, do you? Let's punish her and demand she be a martyr and cop the abuse for her kid's sake?'

'I'm not saying she should be punished. I just think there's a moral distinction between women who stay in abusive relationships because they care about how divorce will impact on their children, and women who leave when they've knowingly brought children into that situation. I feel sorry for both women, of course, but I just think there's a difference.'

'If you just focus on the victim and her response, aren't you taking attention away from the guy's actions?' I say.

Lisa stands up. 'I've got to go,' she says, grabbing her purse. 'I'm going to visit Lucy in the hospital.'

'Look, I'm sorry if I offended you.' Anil raises his hands in a conciliatory gesture. 'Maybe I'm out of touch. I mean, I get that you're in the thick of it and would know more. I'm just saying what I feel, my gut reaction. I've never been exposed to domestic violence. I don't know anybody who has. It just makes me so mad. No hard feelings, yeah?'

Lisa bites down on her lip. 'Yeah, we're cool.' She turns to Nirvana and me. 'I'll see you both soon.'

'I'll drive you,' I say. 'You don't have a car. You came with me, remember?'

'It's okay, I'll get the bus. You haven't even finished eating.'

'Don't be an idiot. I'll take you.'

'We come across that kind of self-righteous indignation

all the time,' she says as we drive. 'It makes me want to tear my hair out. It's sexist and arrogant and ignorant.'

'Everybody wants a one-size-fits-all solution,' I mutter.

'Exactly. I know how hard it is to comprehend that even the smartest, most sensible women can find it difficult to leave. Sometimes the first instinct is to try to fix what's broken, not throw it away. It can take a long time to realise that some things can *never* be fixed.'

While Lisa goes in to see her client, I take a seat in the waiting room. When she eventually comes out she tells me she needs a good strong coffee and we head across the road to the nearest café. We order and I'm talking when Lisa abruptly interrupts me.

'I know something. And it's in strict confidence. I'm torn about whether I should talk, but this affects somebody we both know.'

'Can you tell me, or is that a breach of professional confidence?'

She hesitates. 'I can tell you some parts, but you have to keep the conversation between us, okay?'

I assure her of my silence and she takes a deep breath.

'Neela confided in me. That day at the birthday party, when we were outside and she was smoking.'

'Yes. I remember. I noticed you go outside with her.'

'She's having some serious problems with Sunil. I don't think that's any surprise to you. Nirvana's already told us that much. I've given her some advice. But if Nirvana finds out it was me who advised her, I don't know how that will affect her relationship with Anil. It shouldn't, but it might.'

'Did you give her this advice directly? Is she your client?'

'No. I figured that would be a conflict of interest. I referred her to somebody else.'

'Then there shouldn't be a problem. If Neela needs help, Nirvana would probably think you would be the best person to talk to.'

Lisa anxiously taps her fingers on the table. 'I'm not so sure about that.'

Thirty-Eight

I have a couple of days' reprieve from Danny. On Monday morning I'm almost skipping to the office, I'm so glad that he's away. The first thing I do is approach Kylie and Veronica and ask them what happened on Saturday.

'We didn't have a clue what he was on about when he called,' Kylie says. 'Then this morning we saw the email from him about the meeting. He sent it at nine o'clock on Friday night. Who's going to be around to see their emails at that time?'

'But ...' I stop. I don't want to tell them he approached me directly on Friday afternoon.

'He apologised. Said he thought we had remote access to our emails from home,' Kylie scoffs. 'He knows we don't, though. Remember, he didn't approve it for security reasons?'

My face collapses and I quickly turn away. I never imagined Danny would be so conniving. If I had any doubts about his intentions, Kylie's words crush them for good.

Because there's a bank statement waiting for me at home showing me how little I have to my name despite my income, and because there's talk that the Reserve Bank is likely to raise interest rates this week, I go a teeny weeny bit mental when Senem and Farouk are over tonight and announce they've booked a ten-day holiday in Hawaii.

'You did WHAT? Whatever happened to saving for a deposit? Isn't that the whole reason you're moving in? To save? What's the point of moving in if you're going to blow your money on holidays?'

The horrified silence is evidence enough that I have crossed a line.

When Senem was a sister and daughter, and not a *married* sister and a *married* daughter, I might have got away with this kind of reprimand. But by virtue of her marriage to Farouk, I am supposed to accord her a certain respect, otherwise it will look as though I am being disrespectful to Farouk too.

I can tell Senem is trying very hard to remain composed. 'Esma, can I talk to you alone please?' she hisses.

Meanwhile, my dad is so uncomfortable that he shuffles to the couch, closes his eyes and stares up at the ceiling. My mother, mortified, laughs nervously and asks Farouk if he can help her fix the remote control for the satellite television.

Senem storms upstairs, expecting me to follow her, which I do.

It takes every atom of self-control to resist the temptation to blurt the truth out to her. The truth equals redemption and understanding and sympathy. It means liberation. It means we all share the burden of digging Dad out of the quicksand.

But I'm the dutiful daughter. So I trudge up the stairs into the spare bedroom where Senem is pacing angrily.

'What's going on?' she snaps. 'Since when do you have a say in our finances?'

Since I'm helping pay for the house you're going to move into.

'I don't have a say,' I say defensively. 'I'm just surprised that after complaining about how far behind you are in saving for a deposit, you'd book an overseas holiday.'

'But what business is it of yours, Esma? How do you think it looks in front of Farouk for you to say that? For his sister-in-law to lecture him about money.'

'Okay, so I lost my temper. I just think it's unfair to expect Mum and Dad to put you up you while you go and spend the money you're supposed to be saving.'

'I already told you that we're going to insist on helping out with the bills. The holiday won't be expensive. And Mum and Dad paid the house off years ago, so I can't see what the big deal is!'

I bite my lip. Dig my nails into my skin. Muster every ounce of control to stop myself from responding. But it's no good.

'I CAN'T TAKE THIS ANY MORE!' I burst out of the room, run down the stairs, grab my keys and bag from the hall table, rush past my dad who launches towards me in an effort to calm me down, hurl the door open, rush out, slam it in his face, get into my car and speed away.

I drive to a nearby park. I sit in my car. And I cry.

Text message from Senem that night:

I don't know what's going on with you. I could never have imagined my own sister wouldn't welcome us home. Whatever's upsetting you, talk to me. Farouk is talking about us renting again. He doesn't want to get into your space or hurt you, he says. You know we can't afford that though. Not if we're going to buy.

And because we can never stay mad at each other for long, and because I have no choice but to try to fix things, I text her back.

Tell Farouk I'm sorry and I'll never speak to him again if he doesn't move in because of me. Sorry for the tantrum. Bad day at work. I heard the shopping in Hawaii is amazing. I'll give you my wish list when you go.

'Esma, are you awake, darling? Can we talk?'

My dad is at my door. I pretend to be asleep. He sighs heavily and walks away.

Thirty-Nine

Aydin is teasing me because I locked my keys in my car and therefore arrived an hour late to our dinner date. He called me out of the blue this morning to see if I was free to catch up for dinner after work.

When we sit down in the café he's still going on about it.

'So let me get this straight: you locked your car, opened the boot to get something, threw the keys in the boot, rummaged around in the boot, forgot the keys were in there and closed the boot on them?'

'Yep,' I say casually, extending my hand and examining my nails.

'See, I would have thought the logical thing to do is never put your keys in the boot.' He grins. 'Like, put them in your pocket.'

'No pockets with this dress.'

'In your bag?'

'The keys *were* in my bag.'

'Oh! So you locked your bag in the boot too?'

I hold my hands up. 'As you can see, I'm bagless.'

He shakes his head slowly, in a 'what am I going to do

with you?' way.

'Look,' I say, smiling cheekily at him. 'I need one flaw. It's hard being this perfect, so, you know, being a little careless ... it's all part of the bigger picture.'

'Hmm ... And what *bigger picture* is that?'

'I don't want you to feel so bad, you know? If I'm flawless it's just going to stress you out. So I left my keys in the car to make you feel better about yourself. If I've got *a* fault, you don't have to feel so insecure about your faults. Note the plural.'

'Oh *really*? Plural, hey?'

'Yeah,' I say with a wave of my hand. 'But don't beat yourself up about it. You're male, so you're already born imperfect.'

We continue with the banter, interrupted by Aydin's phone ringing. He declines the call.

'Tell me about your family,' I say, changing the topic. 'You haven't mentioned if you have any brothers. You said you have one sister.'

'I've got an older brother and a younger sister. Have you been to Turkey before? I've been meaning to ask you. I was there last month with some friends.'

'Wow, I've seen subject changes before, but that one was on speed! Tell me about them.'

'My best friend, Tony—'

'I mean, tell me about your brother and sister.'

'There's nothing to tell.'

'Oh, come on, of course there is. I've told you all about Senem. Family means a lot.' I smile.

'I'd rather talk about you.'

'But I want to know,' I say with a pout. 'What are they like? What do they do?'

He sighs and looks uncomfortable. 'Ayshe is an optician. She's a sweet girl with a big mouth, always got a comeback … Kind of like you, actually.'

'Smart girl, hey?' I say.

He gives me a half-smile. 'I don't know about that. I mean, you did manage to lock your keys in your car. And you weren't all that surprised either. Happens quite often then?'

I smile confidently. 'So, you have a brother too?'

'Yep. He's not working at the moment.' He picks up the menu. 'I feel like cake. They do a great lemon tart here. Do you like lemon tart?'

'Yeah, sure, sounds nice. What's the age difference between you and your brother?'

'He's two years older.'

'Are you close to him?'

'No … Or maybe some gelato?'

'Are you very different from each other?'

'You could say that.'

'Senem and I are very different. Opposite in almost every way, actually.'

'Mmm. Do you get along?'

'We have our moments. That's part of the sibling deal, isn't it? Are you close with Ayshe?'

'Yes.'

'But not your brother?'

'No.'

'A case of opposites too?'

'Esma, don't you get it?' he says, calmly placing the menu down on the table. 'I'd rather not talk about my brother.'

'Oh ... sorry.'

But as I apologise I wonder why I should have to. Aydin's the one who said we needed to be upfront and honest. He's the one who said he's seen too many of his friends hook up with their wives based on both people pretending. Acting out a part before marriage, only to let the truth of their personalities surface when it was too late.

But for now I decide to let it go. I'm not here to play therapist.

Not to mention, I've got a skeleton in my closet too. A part of me realises that if I'm going to be responsible for helping Dad with the debt, the person I end up with has the right to know.

So I don't press him.

'I called him yesterday.'

'Ruby! Nooo!'

She puts her head in her hands and lets out a muffled moan. 'I'm an idiot.' She looks up at me, a tortured expression on her face. 'I need to have the last word. That's just the way I am.'

'I know,' I say, nodding sympathetically. 'I get it.'

'We had an amazing connection at the wedding. He texted me the next day. And then, suddenly, the first class after the wedding, he shuts down. You saw it.' I nod. 'It's crazy! Men are crazy! They call *us* moody?'

'If they called us that to our face, they'd do it at their own risk.'

'I caved. I called him. Because curiosity trumped my self-respect. I hate that.' In one quick move she sweeps her hair up into a high bun. 'He didn't answer. I left a message and he called me back six hours later. It was *so* awkward.' She cringes.

'Was he acting like a jerk?'

'No. That's the thing. He was nice and cheerful, but formal. No, worse! He was *professional*.'

We each pull a face.

'I was back to being a client. The thing is, it felt like an act. Like he's trying to deny there's something between us, or he's had second thoughts.'

'Except he doesn't have the balls to be direct about it.'

'Exactly. It was so embarrassing, Esma. I had to pretend I was calling to ask for the bank details so I could pay the ticket for the party.' She shudders. 'So even if I wasn't going to go, now I have to.'

'He doesn't deserve you.'

She waves her hand dismissively. 'Yes, yes, I know all that. I'm better off. I can do better. Save your breath. It's not as though I was about to buy a dodgy car and avoided a bad deal.'

I nod slowly. 'I know, Ruby. It hurts.'

'Yes,' she says grimly.

Forty

At five-thirty I exit the lift in my building, flanked by Veronica, Kylie and Danny, and am astonished to see Metin in the lobby, leaning against one of the guest couches, waiting for me. He smiles, raises his hand and gives a small wave.

Wearing jeans, a black leather jacket and sporting a bit of sexy stubble, he looks sensational, and Veronica sucks in her breath and hisses, '*Who* is that?'

Kylie giggles. 'Esma,' she says in a low growl, 'have you got a boyfriend?'

'No,' I say, blushing. 'He's just a friend.'

Mercifully, Metin has the sense not to approach us and is waiting patiently for me. Although I'm annoyed that he's come to my workplace without telling me, I also can't help but feel the boost to my ego that comes with the girls' reaction to him.

Then I remember Danny's beside me. 'What a little hypocrite you are,' he says, giving me a malicious grin. 'Not so innocent after all.' He tut-tuts. 'Aren't you going to introduce us?'

I give him a filthy look. 'This has nothing to do with you,' I say through gritted teeth.

Veronica scolds Danny. 'Come on, leave her alone.'

'Fine,' Danny says in an unconvincing show of nonchalance. 'You're right. Esma's sex life is her own business. Have fun, Esma.' And with that he walks out of the building.

Veronica and Kylie shake their heads. 'He can be so immature,' Veronica says. 'Just ignore him. See you tomorrow, Esma.' They pat me on the arm and leave.

I feel like somebody's punched me in the guts. My eyes sting and it takes every ounce of self-control to stop myself from crying. I walk slowly over to Metin and he grins.

'I thought I'd surprise you. Take you out for dinner and maybe a movie, if you're up to it ... Um, are you okay?'

'Y-yes,' I stammer. 'I'm fine.'

He looks concerned. 'Was this a bad move? Have I made you uncomfortable?'

'No, no ...' It's not his fault, I remind myself. He's just trying to be romantic. Don't let Danny ruin everything. Forget about him! I make the effort to give Metin a big smile. 'I was just distracted by some annoying colleagues. Dinner sounds lovely. I don't have anything on tonight.'

'You look great in a suit, by the way,' he says. 'And I love your hair up like that.'

There's nothing sleazy about Metin, even when he's checking me out. That's part of his appeal. I feel my face burn and he laughs. 'You can't take a compliment, can you?'

'Come on, let's get out of here,' I say, laughing back.

We opt for eating takeaway in Hyde Park. I don't know what's in the air tonight, but Metin seems to be even more forward than usual. His timing isn't the best, though: I'm eating noodles (a bad choice for a picnic meal, in hindsight) when he asks me if I've ever been kissed.

I quickly slurp up the noodle dangling from my fork. 'No. And what kind of a question is that anyway? Out of the blue, while I'm eating noodles too.'

He takes a napkin and, before I know what's happening, quickly dabs the corner of my mouth and then throws the napkin in the bag beside us.

'Soy sauce,' he says, grinning at me.

Mortified, I wipe my mouth. 'So, how was your day?' I say, trying desperately to change the subject.

'Ah, you're not getting off that easily. You said I'm not inquisitive enough. So now I'm asking questions and you're trying to avoid them.'

'I didn't mean questions as personal as that,' I say.

'You can't have it all your way. So. Have you ever wanted to be kissed?'

'Metin,' I scold, 'I'm not having this conversation with you.'

'Why not? We're only talking about kissing. There's no crime in that. It's not as though I'm kissing you. Although you do have very kissable lips.'

Okay, so where do I go from that? My insides go all tingly and I feel my face getting hotter with each second.

He notices and, to his credit, says, 'I'm sorry. I've gone too far and made you uncomfortable. You're the first girl

I've gone out with who is so ... how can I say? ... conservative. It's intriguing.'

Relief washes over me. If Metin had said frigid or uptight I would have taken that as a cue to leave. But conservative I can wear as a badge of honour (the irony of this is not lost on me when I notice we're sitting near a billboard displaying a women's magazine with the headline *You Voted: The Best One-Night Stand Story of the Year*). Oh, how proud Mum and Dad would be if they knew I'd taken being labelled conservative as a compliment. It would seem Turkish weekend school paid off after all.

I could never have imagined somebody as good-looking, confident and eligible as Metin would take an interest in me. I've got very little experience with men, and yet here I am, apparently possessing the kind of sexual allure that attracts somebody like Metin. He's 'the catch'. A sexy European doctor. Let's face it, marrying him would make a lot of girls I know green with envy.

And as much as I feel guilty that I'm leading two guys on at the same time, a part of me is also enjoying the attention.

So while it's difficult to make a decision because they're both great guys, it's even harder when my ego is enjoying being in the limelight too.

When the subject of family comes up again while we're talking on the phone later in the week, once more Aydin shuts down.

'Esma, I'll talk to you about anything. But like I said,

there's nothing to say about my brother. We're not close. End of story.'

'So you want us to be honest with each other, but talking about your family is off limits?'

His silence is answer enough.

'Don't you trust me?'

'I've known you for a couple of weeks but, honestly, I feel like I've known you for years. I trust you. But this has nothing to do with trust. I'm just ... not ready to talk about him.'

I can't help but feel hurt. And I know I'm being a hypocrite, keeping my own family secret from Aydin. From my sister. From my own mother. But I can't help how I feel. My gut tells me there's something wrong here.

I'm not getting to know Aydin for some casual affair. We both know why we're here; what our expectations are. In fact, he's pushing this faster than me, calling me a lot, flirting with me and making me feel like the centre of his universe. So why is he shutting me out of something so important? We've both had it drilled into us that you 'marry a family, not a person' – God, I've heard that line often enough to last me a lifetime. It's not as though I'm asking him about some distant uncle. It's his brother. I can't understand what the big deal is.

As I have this argument in my head I realise what an idiot I am. I'm trapped in my own hypocrisy. Something has to change.

I email Lisa.

Is it weird that Aydin won't open up to me about his family? About his brother?

Lisa: It depends. If his brother's a serial killer, then yes, you have the right to know. If his brother's an arsehole who he hasn't spoken to in years and who has nothing to do with his life, then leave the poor guy alone. He wants to put it in the past and move on.

'Ruby, Aydin seems to have some baggage when it comes to his brother. But he won't tell me about it. Should I be—'

Oops. Wrong person. I've forgotten Ruby broke up with her ex because his parents were overbearing.

Hysterics ensue. 'Make him tell you, or dump him! Honesty is everything! There's no such thing as putting the past in a vault! You have the RIGHT TO THAT KEY!'

'You can't put family in the past!' Nirvana says, slightly more hysterically than Ruby. 'That past is part of him! You're not here to get to know him for his present and future only! You need to be honest with each other. Anil has to be UPFRONT WITH YOU! YOU MARRY A FAMILY, NOT A PERSON!'

Oh dear.

I call Metin. Just for a dose of masochism.

'So, Metin, tell me more about your family.'

'I've got two brothers and a sister. They're all spread out. Germany, Norway and London. I'm closest with ...'

And on and on he goes. Uninhibited. Open. Metin never holds back. He's a walking autobiography, with absolutely no hesitation in telling me about his life, his relationships, his past. Metin's family is in Europe. They're relatively irrelevant. But Aydin's family is in the next suburb. There's no question of us not spending an overdose of time together. The ritual weekly dinner; birthdays, Eid festivals, a midweek coffee drop-in, picnics, shopping expeditions, house renovations – and that's before children come into the picture. Then it's all of the above plus children's birthdays, daily midweek drop-in sessions to see the kids, Friday night visits, Saturday night dinners, Sunday lunches. So if Aydin's family is going to be in my face, and my family in his, we have the right to know about the family we're going to be spending so much time with.

Forty-One

'Do you still want to go?' I ask Ruby. We've skipped an extra boot-camp session tonight for wedges with sour cream at a local café. The boot-camp party is this Saturday.

'Of course! I'm not going to let him stop me having fun with the others. I can't wait to see what everybody looks like all dressed up.'

'Look your best.'

Her eyes flash. 'Don't worry, I intend to.'

I make up my mind. It is as if I am powerless to hold back any longer. I call my dad and ask him to meet me at a café near our house.

I get there early and sit at an outdoor table, knowing my dad will want to smoke. I order a strong coffee. I'm halfway through it when my dad arrives. I see him before he sees me. He walks slowly over the pedestrian crossing. He looks so thin and defeated. A pang of love for him hits me hard, as I imagine the cloud of guilt that hangs over him. It is hard to reconcile this defeated man with the reliable, proud father I've always known.

He catches my eye, raises his hand in a half-wave and walks to my table. We order him a coffee and he immediately lights a cigarette. We suffer through some small talk. It doesn't last very long. We're under no illusions as to why we're meeting.

'How are you coping?' he asks gently.

'Dad. I'm not.'

He flicks ash into the ashtray. 'I know ...'

'No, Dad, you don't. I can't continue with these lies. I'm getting to know people, Dad. What if it works out? How do I start my life with this debt on my shoulders? How can I expect the guy I commit to to accept that?'

When I finish talking, my dad takes a long deep breath. 'I don't know what to do.'

'You need to tell Mum.'

His eyes widen in panic.

'It has to be done, Dad! You can't drag this out any longer.'

'Just give me some time,' he pleads.

'I don't have time. I can't demand honesty from some-body else when I'm lying.'

'I understand. Let me talk to the banks. Look at my options. Okay? Please, darling, give me a couple more weeks.'

I give in. 'Fine,' I mutter.

On Friday I'm on Gmail chat with Metin while at work when Aydin sends me a message at the same time. Which is to say I am in for one confusing chat session.

Metin: I was thinking of you today at work.

Me: Oh really? Well I *am* hard to forget.

Metin: Come to think of it, I was removing wax from an old man's ear at the time.

Me: That's lovely! Now I feel really special.

Metin: It's not my fault I can't stop thinking about you and that most of my day is spent doing disgusting things to the human body.

Me: My God, that must be the most romantic compliment I've ever received.

Aydin: Hey Esma ☺ Clearly you're a bludger too, hey?

Me: Well hello there ☺ It's not bludging. It's called multitasking.

ARGHHHHH!!! How did I get myself into this situation? This has got to stop.

My fingers hover over the keyboard. The question is, who to get rid of from the conversation first?

Before I have a chance to decide, Metin messages again.

Metin: So when can I see you? How about tomorrow?

Me: I can't. I'm going to a party.

Metin: What party?

Me: You'll laugh.

Aydin: Are you free to go out for lunch on Sunday?

Me: Our boot-camp instructor's hosting a party to celebrate us surviving the programme.

Me: Sure, this Sunday's good for me. What did you have in mind?

Metin: Where is she holding the party?

Me: *He* holds it at different venues. This time it's at a Greek restaurant in Leichhardt.

Metin: Rhodes?

Me: Yep.

Metin: I hate that place.

Me: I'm not a fan either. But Ruby and I missed the last party. Alex really wants us to be there.

Metin: And Alex is a guy?

Me: Yes. The instructor. Who, by the way, I have zero interest in. He treats us all like one big family. It means a lot to him for us to celebrate with him. And we've made some good friends. That's what group pain sessions do.

Metin: What's the point of you going? You don't drink. That place is known to be a pick-up joint.

Aydin: How about lunch under the bridge at Kirribilli?

Me: Relax. I know how to take care of myself. I'm a big girl, remember. Survived twenty-eight years without a problem so far.

Aydin: Sorry, lost in translation there. Is Kirribilli a problem for you?

&*(@&)(@&#)(@#)@()@#&) !!!!!

Me: Sorry Aydin! I was just chatting with another friend.

Aydin: I'm not stimulating enough for you?

Me: No! No! You're very stimulating.

Aydin: Wow. I've never impressed a girl so much with such little effort ☺

Suffice to say, I end up making plans to see Aydin for lunch and Metin for dinner, both on Sunday.

I log off and rest my head against my desk, thoroughly exhausted.

Forty-Two

Dad calls me as I arrive at the Sydney Refugee Centre.

'I spoke to some real estate agents,' he says. 'If we sold this house and paid the bank, we could buy a flat or small town house.'

My ears prick up. This is progress. 'Okay. I'm listening.'

'But not in this suburb. It would need to be out west, where it's much cheaper. Do you think your mother would consider living in a flat? I won't need to tell her the real reason for selling. I'll try to convince her that something smaller is easier on us. Not mowing the lawn, less housework.'

I throw my bag under a desk, sit down, put my head in my hands and sigh deeply.

'Esma, are you there?'

'Yes, Dad. I'm here.' I sit up. 'Even assuming this is an option, how will you explain the bank taking a chunk out of the sale proceeds? Don't you think Mum would notice that? She has to sign the papers, you know. Her name is on the house too.' I am struggling very hard to avoid sarcasm.

'Oh, I can probably explain something about fees or capital gains tax.'

'You wouldn't be subject to tax as it's not an investment property.'

'But she doesn't know that.'

I snap, 'Dad! Can you hear yourself? You're worried about her discovering what you did because she'll feel betrayed, and yet you're considering lying again! Mum is not a child, you know. Sheez!'

'Esma, I'm doing this because I love her. I want to protect her. Please understand, I'm only doing this to save our marriage.'

'I can't deal with this now, Dad. There are some kids here who have real problems.'

Silence on the other end of the line. I've gone too far. My stomach lurches.

'I'm sorry, Dad. I didn't mean that,' I say quietly.

'It's okay, darling,' he says sadly. 'You're twenty-eight with the problems of a fifty-three-year-old.'

Something inside me twists, and guilt at pushing my father like this sets in.

We're writing poetry in class today. Christina raises her hand. 'I met American soldier one time. His first time leaving his country is war in Iraq. He know nothing about me or my people. I am trying to writing what I feeling in my poem. I am writing something about the boat I come on. It being a wooden whale. We being like Jonah. But we inside the whale more than three days. I was inside two month.'

Christina's too shy to read the poem aloud and I don't

push her. Sonny volunteers instead. He stands and throws his shoulders back confidently.

I come in boat
To a new country
My family waving goodbye but hearts breaking like bones
  of friends soldiers broke
When will I become a refugee, not boatperson?
When will I become a human being, not a refugee?
When will this country becoming home, not refuge?'

He grins at me. 'You like? I think it very good, yes?'

I smile fondly at him. 'Yes, it is, Sonny.'

I turn to face the whole class. 'When we get the digital-storytelling training, you can perform your poems to the camera. Tell your story on the screen.'

They nod and we spend the rest of the class working on their poems.

Later, I step outside to do some photocopying when Lisa pops her head out of her cubicle and asks me if I've heard from Nirvana.

'Heard from her about what?'

'How she is?'

'I spoke to her a couple of days ago. Nothing new. Engagement party preparations. She helped deliver triplets on Tuesday. Crazy mother-in-law. Why?' I eyeball her.

'I've just been so busy ... I've been meaning to call her but haven't had a chance.'

I study her face and give her a quizzical look. 'Honest?'

She waves her hand airily. 'Everything's fine.' She looks

behind me, through the window at the students, hard at work. 'You better get back to class.'

I'm up late tonight talking to Aydin when the conversation turns towards our past. The dating kind. Given that I don't have much of one, he's the one in the confessional.

'So have you been in love before?' I ask.

Okay, so it's the same question Metin asked me, but I'm pretty sure I'm not going to have the same reaction.

'Yes. But then life got a bit complicated and my girl-friend couldn't handle it.'

I twirl my hair around my finger. 'What do you mean, complicated? What happened?'

'Just stuff,' he says.

'Ah, Mr Mysterious, hey?'

'Why is my past important anyway?' he asks cheerfully. 'I'm a different person now. I'm looking ahead, not behind. All those girls are irrelevant. Does that reassure you?'

'I'm not asking you because I feel threatened or insecure. I'm just curious because the past shapes us all.'

'Yeah, the past sure does shape us,' he says dryly.

'You said life got complicated ... I just wanted to know what you meant by that.'

'I won't be hostage to my past,' he says. 'Some things you want to keep out of the present.'

'Aydin, I have no idea what you're talking about,' I say impatiently.

'Give me some time, Esma,' he says. 'There's plenty of time to focus on the past. Let's just enjoy now.'

I pluck at my pillow. You know what? I don't need Aydin's confessions, I don't need to know everything about him. If information is power, then there must be a power in withdrawing any interest in that information.

So I change the subject.

Ruby and I are getting ready for the boot-camp party. Ruby is all boobs and long legs tonight, in a short white Grecian dress and killer heels. Her hair looks magnificent, spiralling down her back, highlights dancing off each curl. She'd stop traffic.

'I'm cheering for Aydin,' she says as she runs the hair straightener through my hair. I've been filling her in on what's been happening. 'There are some things you just can't put up with in a guy. Being a tight-arse, for example. Being a mummy's boy. And being the jealous type.'

I sigh heavily. 'Yes, I know, Ruby,' I say. 'But I don't think Metin's the psycho-jealous type.'

'There are no acceptable degrees of jealousy. You either trust or you don't.'

I nod slowly. 'But ...'

'But what?'

'But I honestly think he's just reacting to what happened to him and once he feels secure with me he'll relax.'

Ruby rests the straightener on the dressing table and rolls her eyes. 'Esma,' she thunders, 'he's got some serious emotional baggage. And you're still in interview mode, on your best behaviour, but Metin's already got two strikes against him. Cut it off now before it starts to get messy.'

I stand up and rub some serum in my hair. 'Yeah, I know, I know,' I say wearily. 'I'm meeting Aydin for lunch tomorrow afternoon, then I'm having dinner with Metin in the evening.' I put my face in my hands. 'Ruby! This is shocking! My mum's to blame. It's all her fault: "What if you miss out on your *kismet*?"' I say, mimicking my mother's voice. 'I feel like an absolute bitch!'

'So it's time to make a decision and ignore all that fairy-tale destiny talk.'

I groan loudly. 'I'm going to make a decision tomorrow night.'

'Good girl.'

Don't think the irony isn't lost on me. I'm getting to know two guys at the same time and possibly rejecting one because I think he has an unreasonable paranoia about being betrayed. I need to make a decision and take a risk. It's only fair. Not to mention that, under the circumstances, I feel like a major hypocrite trying to convince Metin to trust me.

When we're finally on our way to the party, I ask Ruby how she's going to play it tonight.

'I'm sick of childish games,' she says. 'I'm not some cheap distraction. As far as I'm concerned, tonight is about having fun and making him regret sending me mixed signals.'

'Good. Because nobody has time for childish games.'

Alex has booked out half of Rhodes in Leichhardt. We arrive fashionably late. It's strange seeing everybody dressed up when we're used to seeing each other in gym clothes. As we walk in, I notice we're being checked out by the guys and girls standing around the entrance and near the bar (it's always scarier when girls size you up). The latest dance music is blaring through the speakers and the room is buzzing with energy. Ruby suddenly grabs my arm.

'There he is,' she hisses. 'The bastard looks good too.'

Alex is standing in a huddle of guys and girls across the room. He's animated and enthusiastic as usual, talking and waving his arms around. And then he catches sight of us and his face lights up. He grins, excuses himself from the group and heads straight towards us.

'You're kidding,' Ruby says. 'My God, I hope he's bipolar because this is getting ridiculous.'

'Quick, let's go to the bar,' I hiss back. 'If he's giving you mixed signals, give him a mixed response. He's going to have to work hard tonight.'

We turn around and head straight to the bar. I order a lemon squash and Ruby orders a Red Bull and vodka. Pina, Theresa and two guys, Adam and Bradley, join us. Ruby's in her element. She looks fabulous and is making us all laugh. I can tell we're turning heads. I watch her. Not once does she so much as throw a glance in Alex's direction. It's as though he doesn't exist.

We use an eventual lull in the conversation as an excuse to work the room and catch up with some of our other new friends. We spot Kalinda and Mo. As we walk towards them, Alex steps into our path.

'Hey, it's great to see youse could make it,' he says warmly. He seems slightly nervous, which is a good thing.

Even though his words are addressed to us both, his eyes are on Ruby.

'Mmm,' Ruby says distractedly, looking around the room.

'Can I get youse a drink?' he asks.

'No. Thanks,' Ruby says bluntly.

'I'm fine, too, thanks,' I say, a little more graciously.

'So, um, Ruby, I've got to announce some awards and make a speech now, but can we talk later?'

She turns her head slowly to him and says casually, 'Sure. If I'm still around.' Then she walks off to the bar to get herself a drink.

I don't even bother to wipe the grin off my face. Alex is standing still, watching Ruby.

'You stuffed up.' The words come out before I can stop them.

He looks at me and sighs. 'It's complicated.'

I give him a knowing look. 'It's *complicated*, is it? How original, Alex.'

He looks so wounded that for a moment I feel sorry for him.

'Yeah, I know,' he mutters. 'I want a chance to explain things to her. Am I too late?'

'Too late for what, Alex? You're too late to mess her about again, but if you want to apologise and explain, well, I'd say Ruby's bigger than *too late*.'

By the time the awards and speeches are finished, most people are drunk. It's a fairly boring sight when you're sober, and way past my cue to leave. Ruby's had a fair few drinks too and is tipsy. I go to the bathroom and when I return I ask her if she's ready to leave.

'I've agreed to hear Alex out,' she says with a shrug. 'But don't worry, I know what I'm doing.'

'I know,' I say. 'I'll wait for you. Pina's trying to tell me a story about her trip to Europe, except she's so drunk she keeps getting it confused with her trip to Thailand.'

'It's okay,' she says gently. 'I spoke to Pina and we're going to share a cab home. She lives around the corner from me. I know you've been hanging around here longer than you wanted.'

'No way,' I say. 'What if things don't go well with Alex? I can't just leave you.'

'Oh Esma,' she says affectionately. 'It's fine. Don't go all protective chaperone on me.' She hugs me tight. 'Love you! Now get out of here.'

When I get in my car I check my phone. I've missed five calls from Nirvana. It's very late so I send Nirvana a text, asking her if she's awake. Within seconds, she calls.

'What are you doing up so late?' I ask as I reverse out of the car park.

'I broke off the engagement,' she says and then bursts into tears.

Forty-Three

I drive straight to Nirvana's house. I call my parents on the way and let them know not to wait up for me.

Nirvana is a mess. We sit on her bed, my arm around her shoulder as she tries to compose herself enough to talk. Her bed is strewn with empty chocolate wrappers and packets of crisps.

'I can't do this,' Nirvana says with a sob. Then she takes a bite out of her Kit Kat. 'We're not even married yet and she's trying to take control. She's so jealous of me. I'm sick of her nonstop comments about *losing* her son. I'm sick of fighting about whose family we spend more time with, like it's a competition. She's seriously freaking out that Anil will be closer to my parents. As if that's somehow going to make him love her less. He adores his mum! And I've got no problem with that. But he has to stand up to her. He can't keep making excuses. She's not a kid. She knows *exactly* what she's doing.'

She blows her nose and then looks up sharply, as though she's remembered something. 'Lately things have been really tense at their place because Neela and Sunil keep fighting. I don't know the full story and Anil doesn't say much about it. But I think his mum is trying to compensate for Neela's bad marriage by making this massive deal about our marriage plans. And I think Neela resents all the fuss and attention over our engagement when she's going through rough times with Sunil. And if all that wasn't bad enough, his mum wants the wedding in India.'

'*India?* Why?'

'Because most of Anil's family is there and they can put on a bigger wedding there because of all the connections they have. She wants it in all the newspapers.' Nirvana moans. 'To think we wanted something intimate and low-key. Now she's talking about getting stamps with our photos on it, and a helicopter entrance to the engagement party.' I snort and she looks up from her tissue and manages a smile. 'It's so corny and it's just not me. But I could handle that if it meant we had the wedding here, as we planned. How can I expect all my friends and family to fly to India for my wedding?'

'What does Anil think?'

She winces but doesn't say anything for a moment, plucking at a loose thread on her quilt. 'That's just it,' she says eventually, a slight tremor in her voice. 'I think he's caved in to the pressure. At first he tried to convince her to have the wedding here, but she started the emotional blackmail. "Just give me this one last gift before I lose you to Nirvana and her family. Who knows what will become of Neela and Sunil – give me some happiness." I was there, Esma. She didn't hold back.'

'Do you have any family in India?'

'Some. But most of them are here. It's only convenient for her side. How can I expect my friends and family to fork out the money to go to India? My aunts and uncles here have three or four kids each. With the flights and accommodation, it would cost them a fortune. My parents are pretty angry, too. They haven't got the money to keep up with her plans, but they can't say that without losing face. It's enough that they're paying the dowry and buying gold for each member of his family. A Rolex for Sunil, for God's sake! I can't stand him as it is.'

'Do you have to, though? Can't you put your foot down?'

She grabs a bag of chips and opens it. 'Yes. I would have. I refuse to do something just to save face or keep the gossip factory busy. I made that clear to Anil. I never want to be a hostage to my culture.'

'I'm with you on that one,' I say. 'So what happened with Anil? How did you break it off?'

She wipes her eyes with a fresh tissue. 'We were at his mum's house this afternoon when she started on about the wedding again. She was talking as though a decision had been made! And Anil wasn't correcting her, even though he'd promised me the night before that he'd talk her out of the idea. But she was so fixated. I couldn't stand it any more.'

'You lost it, huh?'

A smile spreads slowly up to her eyes. 'Totally,' she says guiltily.

'What happened?'

'I went a teeny-weeny bit overboard and started yelling at her. Anil was shocked and tried to calm me down. But she was yelling back, saying that I was twisting her words, deliberately assuming she had bad intentions when all she cared about was our happiness.'

I raise an eyebrow but don't interrupt.

'And then she did what all clever mother-in-laws do, which is turn on the waterworks and pretend to have an anxiety attack.'

'You've got to be kidding me.'

'Anil panicked, which only made her more hysterical. I tried to calm her, give her some water and get her to lie down, but she wouldn't stop crying. So I left. He didn't run after me. He stayed with his mum. I think it's pretty obvious that he's chosen her over me. So I called it off. I'm meeting him tomorrow to return the ring.'

There's nothing else to say. I pop an éclair into my mouth. And then I wedge a corn chip between two chocolate biscuits and hand it to her. She gives me a grateful smile and rests her head against my shoulder.

I leave Nirvana's house at two in the morning and am woken at seven by the sound of Mum clearing the cupboards in Senem's old bedroom. She's got it in her head to start spring-cleaning in preparation for Senem and Farouk moving in.

Needless to say I'm not in the mood for meeting Aydin or Metin today. I know that's unfair on them, but I'm drained. To their credit, they both understand and are happy to reschedule: Metin on Wednesday night, and Aydin on Thursday night.

I'm making a decision by then. I'm not going to drag this out any longer. If I end up losing both, so be it. That's my destiny (vomit).

I spend Sunday evening hanging out at Senem's place. Farouk is out fishing with a friend. Senem and I are watching a rom-com starring Jennifer Aniston and pigging out on junk food (me) and carrot sticks and rice crackers (her).

'She's got no hope,' I mumble as I stare at the TV screen. 'If you start with Brad Pitt, it's all downhill from there.'

My phone beeps. A text message from Ruby: *Can't talk, call you back tomorrow.*

I've been calling and texting her all day to find out what happened with Alex but until now she hasn't responded. I send her a text back: *That's evil! I'm dying to know what happened. Have you been over to Nirvana's yet? She told me she'd spoken to you.*

I figure Ruby must be busy because she doesn't reply.

'Hey, there's something important you're forgetting,' Senem says in a muffled voice, her mouth filled with rice crackers.

'What's that?' I ask, popping a Malteser and some popcorn in my mouth.

'Make sure you talk about your faults.'

I give her a bewildered look. 'Huh?'

'It's in all the relationship books,' she says authoritatively. 'Have you and Aydin and Metin—' She laughs, 'You sound like such a tease – have you discussed your faults?'

'Senem!' I cry, hitting her with a cushion. 'Is there a checklist of topics we need to get through?'

'Of course. You're in fast-forward mode, remember? That's how it is with arranged dates.'

'I'm so confused,' I groan. 'I'm two-timing.'

'I know! Let's draw up a list for each of them!'

'Senem!' I growl. 'I'm twenty-eight, not eighteen.'

'Sor*ry*,' she mutters.

I raise my eyes to the ceiling and sigh. 'I didn't mean to snap. I just don't want to talk about it.'

'I only want you to be happy.'

'I know,' I say.

We're silent for a few minutes, watching the movie.

Then Senem, to my surprise, changes the topic. 'Do you think Mum and Dad are happy?'

At first I'm too startled to respond. Worrying about Mum and Dad? That's my territory. I fumble for an answer. 'Why?'

'You can't answer a question with a question.'

'Says who?'

It would be the perfect time to confide in Senem. I don't, though. Because I'd be asking her to lie to Farouk, and I don't think she would do that, even for the sake of family. I trust Farouk, but if Dad doesn't want him to know, then it's not for me to disrespect his wishes.

'I think they're happy enough,' I say. 'Well, I guess they don't seem *unhappy*.'

She snorts. 'That's something to aspire to. Dad's been a stress-head even more than usual lately.'

'Oh, you've, um, noticed?'

She plays with a strand of her hair, staring at the TV screen. 'Yep. Stressed out and on edge. When I see him, that is. He's always working. I don't understand why he doesn't retire. He's old enough. He's got to stop being such a workaholic. It's not fair on Mum.'

I start to choke on the corn chip I've just put in my mouth. I splutter and cough, and once I've gulped down some water, Senem looks at me with wry amusement.

'What's wrong with you?'

'Nothing,' I say. 'Let's just watch the movie.'

'Is everything okay, Esma?' she says hesitantly. 'You've been so distracted lately.'

'Everything's fine.'

She's clearly not convinced but, mercifully, she doesn't probe. Instead, she looks at me tenderly, then leans in close and snuggles up to me.

Forty-Four

I don't hear from Ruby until the next day, as I'm waiting to order my ritual morning coffee.

'Where have you been?' I shout when I answer my phone.

'Meet me for lunch,' she says soberly. 'At the statue in front of the Queen Victoria Building. Twelve-thirty okay for you?'

'Is everything okay? What happened?'

'Nothing, I'm fine. How's Nirvana?'

'Terrible. Have you spoken with her?'

'Let's talk at lunch. See you then.' She hangs up and I'm left looking down at my phone, a little puzzled by her abrupt tone.

I'm used to seeing Ruby in control. So when I see her pale face and puffy eyes I immediately know something's wrong.

'What happened?' I ask as I hug her hello.

She leads me to the nearest café. We sit at an outdoor table and the waiter zooms over to take our order.

'Sticky date pudding and an iced chocolate,' Ruby says.

I turn to the waiter. 'Make that two heart attacks, thanks.'

'With or without cream?'

'With,' Ruby orders.

When the waiter leaves I fix my eyes on her. 'Out with it,' I say. 'What's wrong?'

'All men are bastards,' she says matter-of-factly. She's looking everywhere except at my face, trying so hard to remain composed.

'What happened, Ruby?' I ask gently.

Her face crumples and she starts to cry. I jump up and sit beside her, putting my arm around her. My instinct is to protect her from people's gazes. I know how much it pains Ruby to lose face. Her pride is deep. I've rarely seen her break down and I'm suddenly assailed by a deep sense of rage at Alex.

'Take your time,' I say softly, offering her some tissues.

She blows her nose and blots her eyes, trying to compose herself.

When she's ready to talk she lets out a bark of laughter. 'He made me cry. The bastard.'

'What happened?'

'I'm so embarrassed.'

Not wanting to push her, I wait for her to continue.

'You left before things got crazy. The party was just starting and everybody wanted a piece of Alex. That made it easier for me to avoid him. But he was looking at me all night. Every time I glanced his way, I caught him staring at me. But each time he made it to me it was impossible to talk. Nobody would leave him alone. So he asked me if he could take me home. At least that way we could talk. And I said yes.' She clears her throat.

'Did he drive?'

'No, we got a cab. He'd been drinking too. That was it, really. We were in a cab and it's just not the place to have a serious conversation. And he couldn't exactly ask the cab driver to sit outside my place while we spoke. Don't ask me how it happened, but we ended up back at his apartment ... Oh, I don't know if I can even tell you.' She pauses, fixing her gaze on a spot on the table.

I'm suddenly angry with her. 'Oh for God's sake, Ruby, stop treating me like I'm some kind of judgemental prude! Since when have I *ever* imposed my beliefs on you? I'm one of your best friends!' She looks up at me. 'Ruby,' I say, 'after all these years if you don't know me on *this*, you don't know me at all. Don't hurt me like that.'

'I know, I know.' She draws in a deep breath. 'We slept together.'

'Okay. So what happened?'

'We got to his place. We were going to talk. I swear until that point I wasn't going to back down. I was staying strong. He knew I was hurt and angry and deserved an explanation. I know alcohol isn't an excuse either. It had something to do with it, but to be honest it was a combination of things. Just this heat and tension and ... I don't know, before I knew what was happening he was kissing me and we couldn't stop. I didn't want to.'

'Okay, but why is he a bastard? ... Oh my God, he didn't hurt you, did he?' My mind, corrupted by one too many episodes of *Law & Order: SVU*, goes into overdrive.

'No! Nothing like that.'

'But he's a bastard?'

'Because he has a girlfriend, only they're kind of on a break. Well, were on a break. Oh God, who knows!' She moans.

'What do you mean, he has a girlfriend?'

'I wasn't imagining things between us. He was interested. After that night at the wedding, though, the guilt hit him, and that's why he pulled back.'

'So he was leading you on, even though he was in a relationship?'

'He's saying it wasn't really a relationship because they were on a break.'

'Oh Ruby.' I squeeze her hand.

'He's begged me to stay. He says he's fallen for me.' She snorts. 'Do you know what's so funny about the whole thing? He says that he can't believe I fell for *him*. That he thought I might have feelings for him but he convinced himself that I couldn't really like him. He didn't think a "big-shot lawyer" like me would think twice about a high school drop-out like him. Apparently his ex is an engineer and her parents got in her ear about being with someone on the *same level*, so they took a break to allow her time to think things through.'

'But why did he only feel guilty halfway through?'

'You mean, why did things between us go from the Sahara to Antarctica?'

I nod.

'Because after that night at the wedding, when things were moving so fast between us, he says he didn't want to get involved with me until he'd ended it properly with his ex. So instead of being upfront with me, he pretended nothing had happened.'

'That's just ... just ...'

'Mental! I know. I'm in denial, Esma. I feel like I'm in some kind of bad soap opera. How could I stuff things up like this? I've only been intimate with one other guy, and we were together for four years. I don't do one-night stands.' She tears at her napkin, throwing tiny bits into the empty ashtray.

'So let me get this straight. He's on a break with this engineer chick who's decided she's too good for him and has dumped him on the basis that he'll just wait around for her to decide whether or not he's worth being with, *and* he's agreed to this?'

She nods.

I scrunch up my face. 'No comment.'

She shrugs. 'Love makes people idiots. He thought he loved her and at one stage he was willing to wait for her. I think it was a matter of her having to convince her parents that he's good enough, rather than her feeling he's not.'

'Is she Greek too?'

'Nope. Eastern European.'

'Okay, so where are the two of you at now?'

'He told me he's ending it with her. He says he wants to be with me, that meeting me has given him back his self-confidence. Her family made him feel like nothing. Which makes things all the more complicated, given my family will probably be just as bad. But even putting that aside, how can I trust him?'

'What's worrying you the most?' I ask. 'That he'll go back to his ex?'

'No, it's not that at all ... I really doubt he's going to wait around for her to make a decision. It's pretty demeaning for him. I just feel betrayed. It's not as though his ex is in his past. She's still part of his present. Even if he tells her he never wants to see her again, I had the right to know all this before we slept together! I mean, what if being with me had made him realise he wanted his ex *back*?'

I cock an eyebrow at her. 'I really doubt that, Ruby.'

'It's possible,' she argues. 'Then he would have been using me to test his feelings. I don't need to be sucked into some kind of love triangle. I deserve better than that.'

'Of course you do. What does he say in his defence? Has he tried talking to you since you walked out?'

'He keeps calling and sending me text messages. I've ignored him.'

The waiter brings us our order and Ruby thrusts her fork into the sticky date pudding (no doubt visualising Alex's body parts, and *not* the upper variety either) but then pushes the plate aside.

'I don't know why I bothered ordering. I've lost my appetite.' She taps the fork on the side of her glass.

'Ruby?'

'Mmm?'

'Do you still have feelings for him?'

'Yes.' Her voice is soft.

'He backed off because he felt guilty two-timing. Okay, so it was dumb of him not to talk to you before you ended up in bed, but it does sound as though things were pretty steamy between you. He could be the worst mistake of your life. Or the best. Maybe you should give him a chance to explain. Talk to him and find out if he's willing to earn your forgiveness and start all over again.'

Forty-Five

'Lisa,' I groan on the phone in the afternoon. 'I need some escapism.'

'One sec, Esma. Yes, those applications *must* be lodged before five or the tribunal won't accept them. And don't forget the Vsediah appeal! Sorry, Esma, it's crazy here. As usual.'

'I'll let you go then.'

'I'm sorry. What's up?'

'Can I come over this afternoon to help out?'

'Are you kidding? Of course you can! See you after five.'

Oh, the irony of it all. Working on asylum seeker applications is going to be my form of escapism. But I need to forget a world of confused relationships and agonising family dynamics, of stupid guys and broken hearts; I need to feel that there's something bigger than that, something more important.

It's not that I feel inconvenienced by Ruby's and Nirvana's problems. It's because I'm aching for them, feeling their pain. I've had many friends over the years, but Nirvana, Ruby and Lisa are the ones who've marked me. They're part of me now. And when they're hurting, I'm hurting too.

I once read an anonymous quote posted on somebody's Facebook wall that said: *A friend is someone who is there for you when they'd rather be anywhere else.* It sounds horrible, but God, how true it is this week. That's how it is when Nirvana calls me on my way home from the Sydney Refugee Centre. I really just want to go home to bed, but I can't ignore the quaver in her voice. She lives only ten minutes from my house so I swing by to see her.

'He's begging me to reconsider,' she says when we're ensconced on the couch drinking steaming cups of hot chocolate and demolishing a packet of ginger biscuits. 'I gave him back the ring and he cried, Esma. And I was so tempted to take it all back. But if I don't have courage now, I'll never have it.'

'Does he admit that his mum's a problem?'

'Yes. But he still defends her. He thinks I need to learn how to deal with her and that I should be more sympathetic to her point of view.' She slumps further down into the couch. 'I told him I'm emotionally drained. We haven't even had the engagement party yet, let alone started our married life. I told him that I'm not supposed to feel so unhappy. If it's like this now, imagine how it'll be later.'

'Is he fighting for you?'

She nods slowly. 'He says he's talked to her, but she just cries and thinks I'm misunderstanding her. She says she's trying to give me the best and I'm rejecting her efforts.'

'Oh boy.'

'I know a lot's happening in their family at the moment. Neela and Sunil are really going through a crisis. The last thing Anil's mother wants is a divorced daughter, not after what she's been through. So if we have the perfect engagement and wedding, she thinks it will deflect from the shame of what's going on in Neela's life.'

I cringe. 'That makes me so mad. The poor thing is in a bad marriage. She needs her mum's support, not her emotional baggage.'

'She is seriously out of touch, fulfilling some old-fashioned Bollywood script. Hardly anybody acts like she does any more.'

Nirvana's mother, Mina, enters the room then. I get up and give her a kiss and a hug.

'I've been cooped up in the study correcting essays.' Mina is a high school English teacher. 'Can I get you something to drink?'

I hold up my mug of chocolate. 'Thanks, aunty, but I've got one already.'

'So what do you think about the whole business?' Mina's tone is filled with uncertainty and confusion. She sits on the armrest of the chair beside us.

'I think Nirvana's one of the bravest people I know. It can't be easy to call off an engagement. I'm sure many people have had their doubts and problems but got married anyway, out of a sense of duty.'

'I know,' she says. 'I'm proud of Nirvana, and I'm furious with Anil's mother. It's all so silly. Nirvana's grandmother has lived with us since I got married, and it's been difficult at times, especially in the beginning. But she never behaved like this. And she belongs to a different generation where such antics were far more common.'

'Mum, the problem isn't so much Anil's mum. The real problem is that Anil won't stand up to her.'

Mina raises her eyes to the ceiling. 'I really like Anil, and I don't doubt that he adores Nirvana, but there are some men who simply never cut the apron strings. When Nirvana told us she was breaking it off, she was nervous about how we'd react. But her father and I didn't hesitate. I would rather my daughter were happily single than miserably married. And that's the honest truth.'

'Thanks, Mum,' Nirvana says. 'Now can I have my best friend to myself, please?'

Mina laughs. 'Fine. I have a couple more essays to mark anyway.'

Once she's left I ask Nirvana if she still loves Anil.

'Yes,' she answers emphatically. 'But so what? Since when is love enough? I didn't ask for this, but the reality is that if he really loves me, he has to hurt his mother. If I push him to stand up to her, and in the end he does, it won't matter, I'll still lose.'

I call Ruby before I go to sleep. She doesn't answer but sends me a text.

Sorry. Can't be bothered talking. Big day. Was @ Redfern legal centre 2day str8 after work.

That's cool. Have you spoken to Alex?

Not yet. I told him I need time to think. He broke up with her tho. Officially.

That's progress.

Yep.

Made a decision yet?

No.

Still angry?

Yes.

Crazy for him?

That too.

Forty-Six

On Tuesday afternoon Danny calls me into his office 'for a talk'. Great, what now? Advice on which condom brand to use? An invitation to dinner?

It's even worse.

'Esma,' he starts, adopting the formal tone he uses when he wants to play boss, 'we need to talk about your promotion.'

'Okay,' I say.

'I'm afraid I've got some bad news. While your application was fantastic, there were some areas I feel you need to develop further before I can offer you a team-leader role.'

'Really?' I snap. 'And which areas were they, Danny? As I recall, you were more than satisfied with my performance, and clients have been raving.'

He leans back in his chair and puts his hands behind his head. 'Although you're making budget, on closer reflection I think I need to see you going beyond your budget to justify the pay increase and greater responsibility.'

He pauses, expecting me to respond. But I don't. I stare stonily at him. I'm not going to say a word. I'll just sit here and silently wish him a lifetime of painful urination and infected mosquito bites.

For a second my silence ruffles his composure, but he quickly gathers his momentum again and says, 'Let's see how you go in the next quarter. I'm not saying we need to put this off for another financial year. I'm still very keen on seeing you rise up the ranks of the agency and I'm here to support you to do that. How about you send me a proposal of strategies that will assist you to be even more productive? An outline of things we can do as a team to help you go beyond your targets and KPIs?'

'Sure,' I say coolly. I stand up and he flashes me a triumphant smile.

You prick, I think. *That's it. Game over.*

I flash him an insincere smile, thank him for his time, promise to get the document to him as soon as possible, turn on my heel and storm back to my office.

Metin calls me on my way home from work. 'So how was the party?' he asks, a hint of hesitation in his normally confident voice.

I've been waiting for him to ask. When I spoke to him on Sunday he was obviously dying to know. At least he was sensitive enough to drop the subject when I told him about Nirvana. But it's clearly been bothering him because before I have a chance to answer he quickly adds, 'Was it a late night?'

'It was a very late night,' I say, all narky, 'given the situation with Nirvana. But to answer your questions, the party was great and I left before eleven. Does that satisfy you? Do you want to check with my dad what time I got home?'

'I'm sorry,' he says. 'I'm really giving you the wrong impression of me. I'm not trying to control you.'

'Really?' I ask doubtfully. 'Because it doesn't sound that way, Metin. I'm used to answering to my parents, but even they stopped questioning my movements years ago.'

'Look, I can't help it if I'm protective. You're a beautiful, attractive girl. I think of you at Rhodes and I want to smash my fist through a wall, imagining all those sleazebags drooling over you.'

Oh God. Should I be worried? Or flattered?

'I appreciate the concern, Metin, but trust me, the guys there weren't distracted by my presence.'

He doesn't need to know about the guys from the stag party next door who tried their pick-up lines on me ('Do you put out?').

'I highly doubt that,' he mumbles. 'You're too modest. They'd be crazy not to notice you.'

I feel my cheeks flush. A part of me knows that Metin is dangerously close to being unreasonably overprotective, but another part of me is enjoying the attention and compliments. And it's that other half that seems to be winning out.

Forty-Seven

'Mum, do you think there are some things that can't be forgiven between a couple?'

Mum looks up from her book. 'It depends on the couple,' she says after a long pause.

'What would you consider unforgivable?'

'Why?' she asks suspiciously.

'No particular reason.' I rack my brain for a plausible excuse. 'Just that Nirvana's having some problems with her fiancé. Well, ex-fiancé.'

'Oh. That's sad to hear. But what I might forgive, someone else might think unforgivable.' She closes her book and looks at me. 'The truth is, I've never had to think about it. Your father and I have always had such a good relationship.'

I swallow the lump in my throat. 'But you must have thought about what you wouldn't put up with in your marriage. There's no perfect relationship.'

She laughs. 'I didn't say that. Our marriage is far from perfect. We're happy because it's possible to be happy and flawed. That doesn't mean we haven't had hard times,

Esma.' She smiles. 'I remember I would sit up with you and Senem when you were little, while your dad was at work. I would have cooked and cleaned and picked you up from preschool. And sometimes you'd refuse to eat or sleep. I remember I used to think that marriages needed a reset button.'

'What do you mean?'

'A chance to reinvent yourself every three or five years. So you could start all over again, go back to when there was some mystery to the person you were getting involved with. Back to when you couldn't possibly believe your life would be one endless routine.'

I smile at her.

'But,' she says, suddenly animated, 'if you press reset, you lose all the shared experiences, the tenderness that comes with familiarity. It would be like learning a language and then suddenly forgetting it, having to start from scratch again.'

'Hmm, that's true as well.'

'So?'

I look up at her, surprised.

'So ask me what conclusion I drew from all this.'

'Oh,' I say with a laugh. 'What did you decide?'

She winks at me. 'I decided to let you and Senem sleep in the same bed so you'd fall asleep together and give me a much-needed break!' I laugh. 'That bought me some time to myself. It's easier to stay in love when you look after your mind and body.'

'So were there times you fell out of love with Dad?'

She ponders my questions. 'No. Love can exist, even if it's wilted and dehydrated. It's not ideal, but that's life. Love is the hardest thing in the world to keep in bloom. It needs attention every day. Some days I tried. Some days your dad tried. But that's okay. Because we both knew we'd never both give up trying.'

Forty-Eight

I'm not up to facing Danny today. I call in sick. The good news is that I get a call from a recruiter offering a job interview. I'm thrilled.

I'm meeting Metin tonight, which means I have the perfect excuse to buy a new outfit. I spend most of the day defying the theory that retail is suffering from a lack of consumer confidence. I'm pretty sure I've made several retailers happy today.

To my credit, I don't indulge in any designer brands. Instead of buying one good quality item for a heap of money, I buy twenty bad-quality items for the same heap of money.

I'm in one of those cheap accessories chain stores trying hard not to lose control at the sight of rows and rows of earrings and necklaces in every colour. It's too late. I see rose-petal earrings in white, red and green and it's all over.

As I walk to the food court to grab a coffee, I call Nirvana. She's at work.

'Seventeen-hour labour,' she says, her voice sapped of energy. 'And the poor girl had to get a C-section in the end.'

'Yikes.' I shudder. 'Have you finished your shift?'

'No. I'm just on a break and having a coffee.'

'How are you doing?'

'He asked me out for dinner tonight. I said no. He's so upset, Esma. He says he's going to talk to his mum. He's just waiting for the right moment because things are so bad with Neela and Sunil.'

'I don't know, Nirvana. I don't think something this important should wait.'

'That's what I think. But this is the first time he's acknowledged that it's up to him to deal with this.'

'Well, that's a big step. For him, I mean.'

My phone vibrates, indicating I have a message.

'Nirvana, hang on a sec.' I check who the message is from. It's Ruby: *CHECK YOUR FACEBOOK NOW!*

'Nirvana, I've got to go.'

'No problem. I've got to help sew a woman up anyway.'

'Too much information,' I say queasily.

I log on to Facebook and scroll down my wall.

I can't help it. I yell out, 'The mother-fucker!'

A woman standing beside me asks me to watch my language in front of her child.

'I'm so sorry,' I fumble, utterly horrified. 'But,' I plead defensively, 'he's posted Madonna's "Like a Virgin" clip on my wall with the message, *I thought you might appreciate this.*'

'How dare you say such a thing in front of my child!' She gives me a disgusted look – a look that implies she thinks I was raised by drug addicts who made me sniff petrol – and scurries off, dragging her young son behind her. I want to yell out, *You're wrong! I was raised by uptight conservative Muslims who didn't let me watch* Neighbours *because they thought it would corrupt me.*

My head begins to throb. Because under Danny's post are twenty-four messages. Some samples:

> Hey Esma, some things are better left unsaid.
> Are you getting married?
> Are you getting divorced?
> Appreciate what? Virginity, or losing it?
> Virginity is overrated.
> No. I disagree. It's underrated.

Who are these 'friends' posting such inane comments on my wall? I have absolutely no recollection of adding them. I can only guess I accepted their invites by accident, or as an act of charity.

I won't respond. I'll ignore it. I'll pretend I haven't seen it. New messages will be posted on other walls and this will be forgotten by tomorrow.

But not by me.

On the drive home from the shops I almost don't hear my phone. I've got the music blaring loudly and I'm singing at the top of my lungs. I eventually feel a vibration and pick up my phone.

'Hi, Esma.'

'Hi, Metin.'

'It's been a really rough day.'

I try to forget about Danny. I take a deep breath and exhale slowly. 'Everything okay?' I ask.

'Well, Esma, actually, no, it's not.'

'Did you lose a patient?'

'I beg your pardon?'

'Did one of your patients die?'

He laughs awkwardly. 'No, Esma. Nobody died. Don't forget I'm a GP, not a surgeon.'

'Well, common colds can be quite deadly if you're old.'

'Are *you* okay?'

'Not really,' I say with a melodramatic sigh. 'I wish it was the nineties.'

'The *nineties*?'

'Yes. When a social networking site was a café and sexual harassment was restricted to the workplace. God, they had it easier then.'

'I'm not following you at all.'

'Never mind,' I say. 'Just forget it. What's wrong?'

He clears his throat. 'Well, Esma,' he says soberly, 'I saw something that really concerned me today. On your Facebook wall.'

I wince.

'Who's Danny? And what was that post all about?'

'Danny's my boss.'

'Your *boss*? And he's mucking around like that?'

'Yes. He unfortunately belongs to the segment of the male population that thinks misogyny is endearing.'

'So this isn't the first time he's humiliated you like this?'

I let out a bitter laugh. 'Nope.'

'How can you allow yourself to be treated like that?' he snaps.

A wave of fury floods through me. *Oh no*, I think, bristling. *I don't give a damn how hot you are, you are not blaming me for this.*

'For your information, it's not as easy as me walking into his office and telling him to stop. Because I've done that and it hasn't worked. These things are complicated.'

'They're not complicated,' he says with deadly calmness. 'It's about nipping things in the bud. This is exactly what I was talking about. If you let them cross the line, just once, it's all over. You can't trust guys. There's always an underlying motive. If you'd put a stop to things from the beginning, I guarantee it wouldn't have continued. Joking around, innocent flirting – the way we behave gives people permission to treat us in certain ways—'

'*Excuse me?*'

'Sorry?'

'What did you just say?'

'I said how we behave gives people permission to treat us in certain ways.'

A sudden sense of liberation washes over me. 'Thanks for making this so easy, Metin.'

'You agree? What a relief! Because, Esma—'

'I've got self-respect. And I won't let you take that away from me, Metin.'

'What do you—'

'It was nice getting to know you, Metin, but I don't see a future for us.'

'But—'

'I'm sorry your ex broke you.'

'Huh?'

'I'm sure there's a girl out there willing to put the pieces back together. But that girl's not going to be me. Good luck finding her. Goodbye.'

I know for a fact that there are people out there – many of them my mother's friends – who would think my decision was wrong. *Rejecting a doctor! Just because he's the jealous type! She should be flattered he cares.*

I also know for a fact that there are girls my age for whom my decision would be equally shocking. *You don't want to end up lonely, Esma. Don't be so fussy.*

But I also know this: I'm whole, whether I'm single or married, in love or out of love. And I'm determined to be my own person no matter what.

I let myself be seduced, swept off my feet. Well, my feet are back on the ground now. And it feels good to have my balance back.

Forty-Nine

Aydin calls me to ask if we can postpone dinner to Sunday night. He's been offered tickets to a film festival in Melbourne and he wants to meet a visiting director from the UK and pitch an idea to him. I tell him it's fine.

'You'll like the new doco I'm working on,' he says. 'I want it to be about a group of asylum seekers and refugees.'

I squeal with excitement. 'Do you have a group yet?'

'Not yet. I'm looking around.'

'Meet my students! They're wonderful!'

He laughs. 'Backtrack a bit.'

I start to gush. 'You'll love Sonny – he's funny and unapologetic and brutally honest. Miriam is young but *so* mature for her age. Ahmed is shy but has these incredible moments when he forgets to care about what people think of him and this defiant spirit just bursts out of him. And then there's Christina who's so thoughtful and perceptive – oh, and Faraj who just wants to get on with life.' I pause to take a breath and he laughs quietly.

'Have they been in front of a camera before?'

I explain my digital storytelling plans to him. 'I want

them to have a chance to be more than refugees. I want them to have a voice. I want them – no, *they* want people to treat them as more than just victims of war. And they're all so eager to tell their stories.'

I feel an electric charge through the line. Something special is happening and the pause on the other end tells me Aydin is feeling it too.

I clear my throat. 'Do you think you could come by and talk to them about digital storytelling? You don't have to. And they don't have to be in the documentary, not unless you feel they're the right fit ...' I bite down on my bottom lip, anxiously waiting for his response.

'I'd love to,' he says.

I call the girls and organise a last-minute No Sex in the City dinner. I don't expect they'll all be free, but surprisingly they are. Ruby's left work on time for once, Nirvana isn't rostered tonight and Lisa's had an in-service and finished work early.

It's a beautiful night. I step out of the house and an un-expectedly warm breeze embraces me. My mood instantly lifts.

Our catch-up is at a restaurant in Surry Hills, and we drive in together (I'm the designated driver). The mood is subdued but we've been friends long enough to feel comfortable in our silences. Nirvana, who's in the back, is staring out the window. Ruby is beside her, glued to her phone. Lisa's in the passenger seat, quietly humming to the music and also on her phone, responding to messages and work emails.

We arrive, miraculously find a good parking spot, and are seated at an outdoor table at our favourite Italian restaurant.

'My boss is sexually harassing me.' The words fall out of my mouth before I have time to think.

'Still?' Ruby asks, shocked.

'What do you mean, *still*?' Lisa says. 'Did you know about this?'

'Just a few details,' she explains, probably not wanting Lisa to feel excluded.

Nirvana and Lisa gape at me.

'It's true,' I say, my voice tight. 'I'm an official sexual harassment statistic.'

'Don't say that,' Lisa reprimands me.

I fiddle with the sugar sachets on the table and start to tell them the whole story, minus the dilemma of staying on because of Dad's debt. It's in situations like these that you realise how unreliable language can be. As I speak I realise that all the words in my vocabulary still can't begin to convey my feelings over the course of the last year. Words will only get me so far. The girls' capacity to empathise will take me a little further. But there's still a gap filled with a complexity and incongruity of emotions that I can't verbalise. How do I articulate that I've felt both confused and flattered? Ashamed and sexually empowered? Enraged and self-pitying?

And looming over all of this is that my experience makes no sense without the context of the debt. Just as I expected, they're incredulous as to why I've stayed on this long.

I can't betray my father, though, even to my best friends. It's not that they would judge him. It's just that it would be like stripping him naked when he's trying so desperately to remain clothed. A tear rolls down my face.

'I can't believe you've been going through this alone,' Nirvana says, a bewildered expression on her face. 'You should have told us. You've been there for us. We should have been there for you. You should have *let* us be there for you.'

Ruby looks devastated. 'Here we are venting about our problems and you've been going through this by yourself.' She suddenly hits me. 'You idiot, what were you thinking, not telling us?'

I wipe my nose. 'I didn't want to tell you guys because I was too ashamed.'

'Esma!' Lisa scolds.

Ruby folds her arms and huffs indignantly. 'I can't believe you would put this back on yourself!' She hits me again.

'Ouch!' I rub my arm. 'Keep your hands to yourself, will you?'

Then Nirvana and Lisa start hitting me and we all succumb to giggles.

'I *know* it's ridiculous,' I say eventually. 'I *know* it's his fault and I have nothing to be ashamed of. But sometimes I felt that I might have let the lines blur ... or that I didn't speak out soon enough. And I know that blaming the victim is wrong, but I find it so demeaning to even *be* the victim.'

Lisa frowns. 'If you start to doubt yourself, he wins. The fact is that you should never be in a situation where you have to remind a colleague, let alone your boss, what behaviour is acceptable and what isn't. If you're put in that situation, then they've already crossed the line.'

'Threaten to sue him,' Ruby says angrily. 'I'll help you draft a letter of demand, and if he doesn't settle we'll take it all the way. And start looking for another job in the meantime.'

The beginning of a hopeful smile stirs the corners of my mouth. 'I've already started sending out applications.'

'Good,' Ruby declares. 'But we're going after him too. You're not leaving without compensation.'

'You could easily find something just as good,' Lisa says, her voice soothing. 'I've seen enough people who have been harassed and bullied to know it can turn you into an emotional wreck. Don't let it get to that point, Esma.'

'Yes, I know. I'm dealing with it. Trying to work out what I'm going to do.'

'If it's this bad,' Nirvana says, 'and you're going to work feeling sick every morning, shouldn't you just quit?'

'I ... I can't quit ... I've got a big personal loan ...'

'No, don't quit yet!' Ruby cries, her eyes flashing. 'You shouldn't be a cent out of pocket. Wait until we give him the letter of demand.' Her thoughts wander for a second. 'What loan have you got?' she asks. 'Your car's a shitbomb.'

'Um ...' I search for a plausible answer. 'I helped my parents out with the renovations.'

'Oh, okay.' She accepts my answer and we're soon sidetracked when the waiter interrupts to take our order. After we order I can sense Lisa quietly observing me and when I catch her eye she offers me a reassuring and gentle smile. Nirvana, the most tactile in the group, offers solidarity by squeezing my hand. Ruby is on her phone, looking up fact sheets on sexual harassment laws, letting out the occasional 'uh-huh' and 'hmm' as she reads.

I put my face in my hands. 'I hate all this sympathy and pity.'

Ruby has two words for me: 'Shut up.'

Then Nirvana's phone begins to vibrate on the table. Anil's name flashes on the screen and Nirvana winces.

'I think the moment of truth is approaching. He was going to talk to his mum.'

We mouth 'Good luck' as she takes the call. The music is too loud and she's struggling to hear Anil. She walks around the corner and doesn't return for another fifteen minutes. When she does, and we see her face, we panic.

'What's wrong?'

'What happened?'

'Anil's sister is in hospital. Suicide attempt. She overdosed.'

Lisa jumps up. 'Oh my God! Is she okay?'

'Yes ... She's under observation now. They managed to pump the pills out ...' Nirvana falls into her seat and Lisa sits back down, a stunned expression on her face.

'Sunil came home and found her unconscious,' Nirvana explains. 'She left a note.'

'What did the note say?' Lisa asks grimly. I look at her weirdly, not quite understanding the intensity of her reaction. Her stricken face is so pale it's almost translucent. Her blue eyes are dilated and gripped with fear. We're all shocked by the news, but Lisa seems to be taking it very hard.

'I don't know every detail, but Anil said that the letter explained that she had an abortion last month. She was three months pregnant. Nobody knew. I had no idea. It's so hard to believe.'

'Why did she have an abortion?' Ruby asks.

'The letter didn't say but they've spoken to her now. Apparently she didn't want to bring a baby into a marriage she wanted to leave.'

'Did Sunil know she was pregnant?' I ask.

She shakes her head. 'Anil says he had no idea. Nobody knew. She just went off to a clinic for advice. But then Sunil came home just a couple of days after the abortion. He had a job offer. Suddenly, he was sorry. He was going to quit drinking. He swore he'd make it up to her.'

'And she believed him?' Ruby and I both say. We're unabashedly cynical.

'Well, apparently she was willing to forgive him. But then she felt so guilty about the abortion, especially when he started talking about trying to have a child. Her letter says she couldn't live with herself.'

Lisa whimpers and puts her head in her hands. 'Oh my God,' she says.

'What's wrong?' I ask.

She doesn't respond for some moments. Finally she calms down and turns to face Nirvana. 'I have something to tell you.'

Nirvana's eyes search Lisa's. 'What?'

'Neela came to me for help. She didn't know where to turn, and after we met at the birthday party and she found out what I do, she contacted me. She wanted to know her options. She was adamant that the baby had to go. She'd fallen pregnant by accident. She was sick of Sunil's moods, his nastiness, his drinking. She said she'd had enough and was going to leave him.'

My head begins to hurt. I steal a glance at Ruby, who's frowning, absorbing what Lisa's saying. Nirvana is still and dangerously silent.

'She didn't want to bring a child into an unhappy marriage,' Lisa continues. 'She wanted to know what her options were. I explained that I couldn't advise her because of our friendship, but I gave her the names of some abortion clinics and women's counselling services.'

Nirvana finally speaks. 'How could you?' she hisses.

'How could I what?'

'She had an abortion because of you!'

Lisa's face contracts. 'Are you kidding me, Nirvana?'

'Oh come on, Nirvana,' Ruby scolds. 'That's unfair.'

'No, it's not!'

'Nirvana,' I say, 'it's pretty clear Lisa went out of her way not to advise Neela either way. She just referred her.'

'Isn't it her choice anyway?' Lisa snaps. 'I wasn't there to persuade her either way. I was just sending her in the direction of people who could offer her advice on her options. That was where it ended. I didn't advise her or see her afterwards. She messaged me the day before she was booked for the procedure to tell me about her decision. That's all.'

'That's fair enough,' I say, naively thinking Nirvana will agree.

'You kept it from me!'

'Nirvana, please,' Lisa pleads. 'It was her choice. I didn't interfere and I didn't allow the lines to blur. I referred her and that was it.'

'You could have told me.'

Ruby speaks before Lisa has a chance to defend herself. 'Nirvana, if it's over between you and Anil, what difference does it make anyway?'

'That's cruel, Ruby,' Nirvana says quietly. Then, her voice rising, she says, 'I was still engaged when all of this happened. This is about Lisa knowing something I had the right to know. This was the family I was marrying into!'

'But I would have been breaching Neela's confidence,' Lisa argues. 'And I would have put you in a difficult situation too. If I'd told you not to mention anything to Anil, you'd have had to lie to him. I couldn't ask you to do that. And if you had told him, I'd have been responsible for what would have happened between Neela and her family. I'm a counsellor, Nirvana. It's my job to keep confidences. That's what I do and I won't make exceptions, no matter how much I love you as a friend.'

'This was different! All those times I told you guys about

her and Sunil, you knew what was going on. You could have hinted. Some small warning.'

'Hinted?' Lisa explodes. 'Hinted that Neela was pregnant? Or that she was going to leave Sunil? Or that she wanted an abortion but was terrified of how her family would respond? That she couldn't turn to her brother because she was scared he would judge her? You heard him the other week at Bondi. He was unsympathetic to women who knowingly have a child with a violent partner. He seemed to be saying they should accept the situation for the child's sake. And Sunil was never violent towards Neela. So if Anil thinks you should grin and bear physical abuse for the sake of the kids, can you imagine how he'd view Neela for wanting to leave because of Sunil's *emotional* abuse? I bet that wouldn't even count as a legitimate complaint to Anil. Neela was convinced he'd advise her to keep the baby and stay with Sunil. Tell me, Nirvana, apart from my professional integrity, how could I tell you that your fiancé, the guy you were madly in love with, would rather save face than see his sister happy?'

Nirvana sucks in a deep breath. 'You're wrong,' she whispers. 'He told me himself that he couldn't stand Sunil and wished she'd just leave him before they had a child.'

Ruby clears her throat.

'Well, there you go,' Lisa says coolly. 'You said it, not me. *Before* they had a child. A child came into the picture, Nirvana, and Neela knew that her family wouldn't support her decision to leave after she and Sunil had a child.'

'That's not their decision to make,' I say.

'I need to leave.' Nirvana stands up quickly. 'Can we please just leave?'

Lisa places a hand on Nirvana's arm. 'Look, Nirvana, this is not about you and me. If you make this about you and me, then I seriously wonder what kind of friendship we had in the first place.'

'How about a friendship based on trust?'

Lisa stands up, her face grim and tense. 'Exactly. If only you'd see it that way.'

We walk to the car in silence. And we drive to Lisa's home in silence. After we drop her off, Ruby and I try to reason with Nirvana, but she stops us almost as soon as we start to talk. She's not in the mood for talking, she says, and barely manages an audible goodbye when we reach her house.

'Was Lisa wrong not to say something?' Ruby asks me now that we're alone.

'Absolutely not,' I say. 'I can see Nirvana's point of view, but if Neela came to see Lisa in confidence, there's no way in the world she could betray that confidence. Neela's decision was hers alone, and it was up to her whether she wanted her family to know about it.'

'Nirvana will come round. It must be the shock of what's happened.'

We drive to Ruby's house in silence.

'What about you?' I say as we approach her driveway.

'What about me?'

'Have you come round yet?'

'As a matter of fact, yes.'

'And?'

'I'm meeting him after work tomorrow. He's called every day, sent me texts.'

'And the other girl?'

'He says it's over. And I believe him.'

I smile at her. 'You're positive you're making the right decision?'

She gives me a firm nod. 'I think he deserves a second chance. I understand why he didn't tell me about his girlfriend. He tried to do the right thing and back off, but that night of the party, things were pretty hot between us. I could have held back, shown some self-control, but I didn't. He told me the truth, and then broke it off with his girlfriend. So he made a mistake, but he's fixed it, and I think that's all we can ask of each other, don't you?'

I drive. And I can't explain how it happens but I find myself driving to my dad's work. As I enter the car park I realise the time has come to take charge of my life, no matter the consequences. Mum and Dad will have to face up to selling the house and buying out west where it's cheaper.

He's delighted to see me, but then goes into panic mode. 'Is everything okay? What's wrong?'

He tells the other guy he's working with to cover him for half an hour and we walk over the road to a park and sit down. He immediately lights a cigarette.

'Tell me what's wrong,' he pleads.

'I'm so sorry, Dad, but I'm going to quit my job.'

The colour drains from his face. 'Quit? Do you have a new job?'

I shake my head. 'No ... I'm looking and I have an inter-view soon.'

'But, Esma, why would you quit without securing another job first? How, Esma? How can we pay the mortgage? We'll default.' His face contorts in pain and confusion. 'I could manage one month, maybe. But not more than that. Without your contribution, the bank will sell ...'

'Dad, listen to me.'

And I tell him all about Danny. It's humiliating, but I can no longer be a plaster over a wound he has created.

He shrinks further and further into the bench as I talk, but he doesn't interrupt. When I'm finished, there's a long pause before he speaks. And then he says, 'You're right. We can no longer carry this alone, darling. It's time I told her.'

Fifty

On Friday night I sleep over at Senem's to give my dad the space and privacy to speak to Mum. After dinner, Farouk retreats to the study and Senem and I are left alone in the family room, the latest inane reality TV programme flickering on the screen. I switch it off with the remote and turn to face Senem.

'Hey,' she says. 'It was just getting tacky enough to enjoy.'

'We need to talk.'

'Are you going to tell Farouk?' I ask her, breaking the silence that descends once I've told her the whole story. 'Dad will understand.'

Senem shakes her head. 'Do you all have such little faith in Farouk? Do you think he'd go and blurt it out to his family? Try to score points against us?'

'Actually, no, I don't,' I say curtly. 'I never did, in fact. That's been Dad's fear, not mine.'

She picks at a loose thread on a cushion. 'Sorry ... I didn't mean to snap at you.'

'It's okay.'

'I can say with absolute certainty that not only would Farouk not breathe a word of this to anybody, he'll try his best to help Mum and Dad find a way through this.'

'Do you think there will be a Mum and Dad after to-night? Once Dad's confessed?'

'Whatever they decide, we'll be there for them.' Senem moves so she's sitting close beside me and looks me in the eye. 'You've carried this with you for so long and I've been such a spoilt brat ... I can't even begin to imagine the stress you've been under.'

She hugs me, and although we're both crying, I can't remember a time this year that I've felt so free.

Some families don't speak about their grievances; their misery and hurt is hidden by silence or sly digs, so when you walk into their house the tension is palpable. But my family's never been like that. Before the debt, we were the type of family to scream and shout and rant one minute, and forget and laugh and joke the next. We always let the poison out. No matter how much it hurt, we knew that keeping it in would eventually kill us.

That's part of the reason why keeping Dad's secret has been so unbearable. When I walk into the house with Senem beside me (we thought it best that Farouk stay home for our first visit after Dad's confession), I trust that our capacity to vent will ultimately be what saves us.

When we open the door Senem and I can hear Mum yelling.

'I woke up this morning and realised it wasn't my

imagination. It's real. How could you, Mehmet? How could you sink so low? And with our security? All these years we've dedicated to our family, to the girls, to our home, and you threw it all away! Down a machine!'

My mum's voice is shrill and hysterical. Senem and I rush to the kitchen where Mum is standing over the work-top, weeping.

My dad is standing at the other end of the worktop. 'Please forgive me,' he says, over and over again.

'What will we do now? We'll lose the house. Where will we go? Will you have us move in with our son-in-law and daughter? To think they were going to move in with us! They were going to depend on us for help, not the other way round!'

She starts to cry again and I walk over to her and put my arms around her. 'Calm down, Mum. It'll work itself out. Dad's been trying so hard to make it up. Working two jobs. It's all he's thought about. You have to know how sorry he is. That's why he couldn't bear to tell you.'

'He dragged you into this. He had no business! You hear, Mehmet! You had no business doing that. Let her have her own future, not have it snatched away by her own father!'

My mum's words sting and my dad walks backwards, slumping into a chair at the dinner table. He sits silently, not responding to the torrent of words pouring out of Mum.

'Mum,' Senem says gently, 'you'll get through this. Forgive him.'

Mum doesn't reply straight away. When the silence becomes too much to bear, I open my mouth to speak, but

Mum beats me to it.

'There is forgiveness. And then there is the matter of what is to be done. I'm going back to bed.'

'It'll take time,' I tell Dad once Mum has left. 'She's trusted you all these years. The least she deserves is some space.'

Dad looks up at Senem and me. 'Yes, but what if she decides she no longer wants me in that space?'

Later I call Lisa.

'Have you spoken with Nirvana?' I ask.

'I called but she texted me to say she needed time to think things through. She said she was sorry for flipping out but she didn't want to talk about it yet.'

'She's going through a lot.'

'Esma, I know. You don't need to tell me, I get it. But I won't apologise for what I did. I'm only sorry she thinks I betrayed her, sorry that she'd have such a low opinion of me. She has to understand, my job is my life. I love what I do. I believe in it. I believe in trust and confidence and choice and freedom. Breaching somebody's trust runs counter to everything I believe in. And I just hope that Nirvana gets that. Because what's left between us if she doesn't?'

Fifty-One

Aydin calls me at eight-thirty on Saturday night. 'I just got in from Melbourne. Do you want to go for a walk?'

'What, *now*?'

He chuckles. 'Yes.'

'Are you kidding? It's freezing outside.'

'It's okay, I'll keep you warm,' he says boldly.

'Oh yes, I'm sure you will. But we both know that's not going to happen.'

'Okay, I'll keep my hands to myself and you can wear a million layers. Come on, I'll pick you up in half. I'm on my way back from the airport.'

I laugh. 'Sure, I'll just tell my dad I'm going for a romantic walk out in the park with you after dark. Although he's come a long way since the Rule of Six, he's never going to accept you arriving on our doorstep to take me out on a date.'

'But he knows we're getting to know each other, right?'

'Yes. That is the official terminology.' I chuckle. 'Mum keeps him in the loop. He doesn't talk about it directly with me, though. We've never had that kind of relationship.'

'Really traditional, hey?'

'Actually, really shy.'

'Okay, so then meet me at the park round the corner from your place.'

'Just drop everything to see you?' I laugh again.

'You're killing me here, Esma. Come on,' he pleads. 'I want to see you.'

'Okay,' I say, pretending that I'm giving in reluctantly, although secretly I can't wait to see him.

'The other week you asked me about my brother. And I told you I didn't want to talk about it.'

We're sitting in Aydin's car in the car park next to the park, looking out onto the oval where several games of football are taking place.

He gives me a half-smile. 'I'm sensing you were annoyed about that.'

'Annoyed?' I give him a look of mock indignation. 'Not at all. I was overjoyed when you pressed control–alt–delete right in the middle of our conversation.'

He laughs. 'Okay, I get it.'

'I'm only joking,' I say. 'To be honest, I was a little hurt at first. But you know what, Aydin? I don't care about your past. If you don't want to tell me about it, then I trust it's for a good reason. Besides, I've got my own secrets.'

He smiles. 'Okay. So confessions?'

I smile back. 'Yes. Confessions. You first.'

'My parents would be mortified if they knew I was telling you. I think they'd prefer that you knew much later on.'

'I'm in exactly the same situation. If I can't trust you won't judge my family poorly, then there's no point in continuing to get to know each other.'

'Exactly.'

'Our parents' generation is all about saving face. But things have changed. People our age tolerate and accept a lot more.'

He turns to look me in the eye. 'Can you accept that I have a brother who will be in jail for another eight years for manslaughter?'

I take a moment to process what he's said before answering. 'It's not for me to accept,' I say, trying to contain my shock. I don't want him to interpret my shock as judgement. I'm the last person to hold others to account for something they weren't responsible for.

'He was a drug addict.' He sighs deeply. 'He dropped out in Year Ten, promising my dad he'd go into a trade. Dad got him a zillion jobs through friends – plumber, electrician, labourer. He'd stay for a week or two, get into a fight with somebody, then quit or get the sack. When he hit about twenty he started going to rave parties. He'd smoked pot up until then, but he started on the harder stuff. Mum and Dad bailed him out of trouble so many times. Ayshe and I did too. We covered for him, paid off debts, gave him money for all the times he'd leave home to live with his friends, which we knew meant bumming it with other druggies. And then a couple of years ago he was off his face at a party and he got into a fight and punched some other guy. The guy fell and hit the pavement. Cracked his

354

head open.' My stomach turns. 'Karem got ten years.' Aydin lowers his head, staring at his lap.

'Hey,' I say. 'There's nothing to be ashamed about.'

He laughs bitterly. 'Esma, I'm not ashamed. I'm furious with him. He's put my family through so much and he's not remorseful. He still insists the guy had it coming. Sure, he's devastated that he died, but he still defends his actions. He's cocky, walks around thinking the world owes him. He hasn't learnt a thing. He's in Silverwater, another eight years ahead of him. He picks fights all the time.' He throws a glance my way. 'You must think I'm an arsehole talking about my own brother like this.'

'No, I don't,' I say. 'I get it. I *really* do.'

He shakes his head. 'No. You can't get it, Esma, because even I don't get it. I know blood is thicker than water, but there are times I hate my brother. I hate the burden of caring for such a son of a bitch.' His voice falters then and he stops himself, opens the window and breathes in the crisp night air. '*That's* why my ex broke up with me. She couldn't handle the stigma.'

'That's awful.'

'Well, not really.' A smile spreads to his eyes. 'I wouldn't be here if she hadn't.'

I smile back shyly.

'Family does count,' he says. 'And this is my family. Are you comfortable getting to know me with that scandal in my family? You don't have to answer me now. And I totally understand if it's a problem for you because—'

'Aydin,' I say gently, 'I'm not like that. Your brother is his own person and he made his decisions. That shouldn't be something you have to pay the price for.'

'What about your parents, though? There's no way they'd see it like that too.'

I shrug. 'It shouldn't matter. I don't think it will.'

He puts his hands behind his head. 'Well, that's a weight off my shoulders. Your turn.'

I gulp, take a long calming breath and, in a low voice, tell him about Dad's debt.

When I finish I look up. He's smiling.

'Why are you smiling?'

'I'm smiling because you have nothing to be ashamed of either. Your dad's situation isn't unique. I know so many families going through similar problems. I would never expect the woman I'm with to turn her back on her parents, especially when they depend on her.'

He stops, because to continue means articulating something we both haven't expressed yet. There's silence, but it's not uncomfortable. I'm just enjoying the feeling of weightlessness that confessions can bring. I turn to face him and can see desire in his eyes.

'You're really beautiful,' he says softly.

I blush.

He shakes his head and grins. 'It's really hard to keep this kind of distance.'

'Not used to self-control, hey?' I tease.

'You know something, Esma? ... Actually, I wonder if I should tell you. Nah. I better not.'

'Nobody who starts a sentence like that gets away with

nondisclosure. It's plain cruel!'

'So is sitting here with you in a car in the moonlight and having to think about tax bills and work to keep myself under control.'

I burst out laughing. 'Sorry about that. Nothing I can do about it, though. This is who I am.'

'We were talking about hypocrisy the other day.'

I nod and he continues.

'I get the feeling you think I was some kind of player.'

'I don't know,' I say with a shrug. 'Were you?'

He folds his arms across his chest. 'Well ... hmm ... how should I say this? I wasn't as rebellious as you might think.'

I give him a quizzical look. 'Meaning?'

He leans closer and motions to me to lean in. 'I've never gone all the way,' he whispers.

'You're a virgin!' I cry.

'Thanks, Esma,' he says dryly. 'The entire football oval is going to take that home with them now.'

I laugh.

'Oh, and laugh while you're at it too.'

That only makes me laugh harder.

'What's so funny?' he says, although he's smiling.

'I don't know,' I say. 'You said you had girlfriends and mucked around.'

'I may be a virgin, but I'm still a big hypocrite. I mean, I'm not exactly innocent here. I just never went *all* the way. Something always stopped me. Guilt. Shame. A feeling that I was selling out to a double standard, wanting to settle down with a girl who would be with me for her first time but applying different rules to myself.'

'Oh,' I say, too stunned and touched to offer more.

'So are you relieved? Disappointed?' he asks eventually. 'What are you thinking?'

A smile. A long pause.

What am I thinking? I'm thinking this guy has character. I'm thinking that I don't care what the movies or magazines or society says, sex is a big deal and being with someone who 'saved' himself for me is exciting and terrifying and thrilling all at once.

But I'm not about to tell him that. Instead, I look at him, smile and say, 'I'm thinking I'm happy. That's all ... What are you thinking?'

'Exactly the same thing, actually.'

Fifty-Two

My parents call a family meeting on Sunday morning. Senem and I exchange an anxious look as she walks through the front door, Farouk behind her.

'Hey, Esma,' he says softly. 'It'll be okay.'

I nod and give him a grateful smile.

We all sit down in the family room. Mum and Dad sit beside each other on the couch. I try to interpret their body language, but they're not giving anything away.

Dad speaks first. He clears his throat and fixes his gaze on a spot on the coffee table. My mum is picking at the tassels on the cushion.

'We've decided to sell this house.' His voice is composed, if a little choked. 'I'm sorry, but there's no choice. I can't expect Esma to sacrifice her life because of my mistakes. I've spoken with the bank and there'll be enough left after we sell to buy something small.'

'Where will you buy?' Senem asks.

'It won't be in this area,' my mum says bluntly. 'There's nothing we can afford here. It will be something small. Probably a flat. Maybe a small town house. We'll look at the options.'

Dad clears his throat again. 'Senem and Farouk, I'm so sorry but we can't offer you a place to stay while you save.' Dad looks down at his lap and swallows hard. His guilt is palpable, and I can feel the weight of it around my heart.

'It's fine, Dad,' Senem says breezily. 'Don't worry about me and Farouk. We're both working. We'll get there eventually. Just think of setting yourselves up.'

'I want you girls to know that I've forgiven your father,' Mum says, a slight tremble in her voice. 'But I want you all to know this too: I haven't forgiven him for your sake, or for his. Don't any of you ever again assume you can predict how I'll react. Of everything that has happened, being kept in the dark has hurt me the most. I'm not a child. Do you hear me?'

We all nod, and Senem and I start to cry softly.

Mum's crying too but she still manages to talk. 'Yes, I've made sacrifices for the sake of my family, but I didn't do anything I didn't want to do. I will not be thought of as a woman who lives only for her husband and children. I live for myself too. I never want to be protected from the truth in the name of love. That is not love. That is a lack of trust. So. That is the last I will say of it. We have to move on from this.'

My dad speaks next. He wants to acknowledge how much of a burden he imposed on me, what an amazing woman Mum is for allowing him to rebuild all he's broken, how he hopes we can all forgive him for what he's done – and my mum is looking at him with what appears to be a new sense of confidence. It's as though she's taken the terrible facts of what Dad has done and used them as a chance to prove her strength and character – not to my dad or to us, but to herself.

We all misjudged Mum, including me. I'm ashamed of how patronising I was towards her. How little credit I gave her.

Mum asks Senem and me to keep her company that night. I can't refuse. I call Aydin and start to apologise, but he won't let me.

'It doesn't need any explanation or apology, Esma,' he says. 'Be there for her, simple as that.'

So our dinner plans are cancelled. The good news is that he's free to come to the Sydney Refugee Centre this week to meet my class and do a screen test for his documentary, as well as start on some digital storytelling training. I can hardly wait.

Fifty-Three

The group is nervously waiting for Aydin. They've all come to class dressed in their best outfits. Ahmed's drowning in his aftershave and sits at his desk, tugging at his shirt. The girls share a compact mirror as they fuss over their hair and make-up. I keep catching Sonny looking at his reflection in the window, and Faraj is sitting silently, jiggling his foot up and down. When I ask him what he's thinking about, he says he's practising his sentences. I feel so close to them at this moment. Proud and humbled and happy for them.

When Aydin walks in with his filming equipment, my heart skips a beat. I'm excited for the group, and thrilled to see him, and conscious of not allowing my feelings to be obvious. I feel my face flush, so I busy myself with some random task to deflect any attention.

I introduce Aydin to the group and then let him talk to them about his documentary. Within a couple of minutes I can tell he's made a connection with the class. He's funny and warm and self-deprecating and, most importantly, he's making it clear that this is about empowering *them*. I sense the group sit up taller.

'You can talk about whatever you want. It doesn't have to be about the trauma you've gone through, all the suffering you've seen. Maybe you're sick of talking about that. Or maybe you don't feel you've talked about it enough.' He smiles warmly at them. 'The point is, nothing's off limits.'

Aydin's enthusiasm and energy are infectious, and soon the kids are clamouring for a turn in front of the camera. Some of them talk about life in the camps, and the horrors of their journey to Australia by boat. Sonny, however, is more interested in talking about the need for extra buses and trains in the outer suburbs of Sydney.

'How we expecting to integrating when there not enough buses and trains? If I could drive, I no affording a car anyway. We needing transport to be better. You showing the government my video and maybe they do something, yes?'

When everybody's left, and Aydin and I are alone packing up, I start to thank him and he laughs it off. 'Oh come on, I should be thanking *you*. They're amazing.'

'I know,' I say cheekily. 'I was just being polite.'

He takes a step towards me and there's a sudden intensity between us. I'm sure he can hear my heart hammering away at my rib cage because he quickly steps back and starts to chatter cheerily as he finishes packing up his bags.

As we leave the building, a familiar figure suddenly appears before us.

'Metin!' I feel dizzy, as though I've been punched in the guts. 'What are you doing here?'

It's as if he doesn't see Aydin, even though he's standing right beside me.

'You can't just break up with me like that,' he says, a tormented look on his face. 'Without a proper explanation. I didn't mean to offend you. I'm—'

'What's going on?' Aydin asks, looking at me in confusion. 'Who is this guy? What's he talking about?'

Oh my God, I'm in a soap opera. This can't be happening. I feel sick. 'Metin, just go, please.'

Metin looks anguished. 'But I thought it was going well.'

'What was going well?' Aydin asks, crossing his arms.

There's nothing I can say to him. And even if there is, I'm not going to say it here. I feel the colour draining from my face.

I turn to Metin. 'I told you I don't want to see you again. You have no right to come here. I never made you any promises. We were just getting to know each other and I decided you weren't the guy for me. I'm sorry. Now please leave me alone.'

But Metin can't take no for an answer. He tries to plead with me until Aydin tells him to back off and get out of here.

'She's asked you to leave her alone. It's not a hint.'

Metin's taller and bigger, but that doesn't seem to perturb Aydin. *This is so humiliating*, I think to myself.

'Who the hell are you?' Metin demands, puffing up his chest.

I forget to breathe, waiting for Aydin's reply. For all he knows, Metin and I could have been seeing each other last year. I might get away with it. As the thought runs through my mind, I realise I've reached the heights of hypocrisy.

'That's none of your business,' Aydin says, and I breathe a sigh of relief.

Metin stares at me one last time. There's anguish and disappointment in his eyes. As controlling and jealous as he is, I know he doesn't deserve this. I do not have the moral high ground here. I feel so small.

He takes one last desperate look at me, mutters something and storms off. I stare after him stupidly and then heave an exhausted sigh.

'Wow. What on earth was that about?' Aydin asks me. And what hurts so badly is that there isn't the slightest suspicion in his eyes. I can't let things start on a foundation of betrayal. If I've learnt anything these past weeks, it's that lying is never the better path.

'Can we talk?'

He searches my eyes. 'Sure. Come back to my car. It's cold outside.'

When we're sitting in his car he says lightly, 'The past rears its ugly head, hey?'

I tuck my hair behind my ear and take a deep breath. 'Aydin, Metin wasn't in my past ... He came to my house with his parents a couple of weeks before you did. I didn't want to say no to meeting you because I didn't know if I might be turning away the right person ...' I don't look at him as I talk. My eyes stay fixed on the dashboard. 'I never, *ever* thought it would drag on for as long as it did ... I was confused ...

'I ended it with Metin last week,' I continue. 'Not only because he seemed pretty controlling, but because ...' my voice cracks and I try to clear my throat, 'I fell for you ...'

I look up at him and feel a contraction of fear around my heart. The muscles in his jawline are tense as he stares stonily ahead. Tears sting my eyes, but I don't want to cry. I want to retain some semblance of dignity at the end of all this.

'I'm so sorry, Aydin. I'm not saying that because I got caught. I honestly am ashamed of how things turned out. If only you knew me ... really knew me ...'

'It just doesn't make any sense,' he says after a long silence. 'We sat in my car. We spoke about honesty, we confessed our secrets. And you didn't bother to mention Metin.' He shakes his head in disbelief. 'I get that you needed time to decide between us. I just wish you'd told me.'

My heart ruptures. I've lost him.

'I can't offer you anything except sorry,' I say. I know I'm about to cry, so I quickly open the door, get out and walk to my car. It feels like the longest walk of my life.

Then I hear a car door open behind me.

'Esma.' Aydin's voice is low but firm. I turn around and before I know what's happening he's in front of me, kissing me long and hard on the lips. He pulls back, gently holding my face in his hands. There's tenderness and forgiveness in his eyes. 'I understand you didn't do this deliberately to hurt me or lead me on. And I can't imagine the situation has been easy for you. You have too much integrity not to have taken this seriously. I'd be a hypocrite and an idiot to let you go.'

I look at him and smile and he wraps me in his arms.

Oh, I think. *So this is what* kismet *feels like.*

Fifty-Four

On Monday morning I send an email to reception: *Sick again. I'll be in tomorrow.*

Within half an hour I've got three missed calls from Danny. I ignore them. Then a text message from him: *What's going on? Are you okay?*

I reply: *I'll see you tomorrow. Bright and early.*

He shoots back: *Excellent! The office is so dull without you. Let's meet to talk about the promotion again. We'll go through the proposal plan. Maybe over lunch?*

I don't reply. Instead I get dressed in my best power suit for my job interview today. Then I send Ruby a text, arranging a meeting at her office at one.

I turn on the charm and wit for the interview. The job doesn't pay as well but I'm beyond caring about money. The position itself is almost identical to what I'm doing, with the added incentive of working in a bigger office with more opportunities and, importantly for me, more accountability and structure. I walk out feeling confident I've made a good impression. I'll be disappointed if I don't get the job. But if that happens, I'm feeling philosophical enough to accept the experience as a good practice run.

After the interview I walk the few blocks up to Ruby's building. She ushers me into her office and takes a seat at her enormous desk, piled high with folders and files. I walk over to the massive window with a view of the Harbour Bridge and Opera House. I cross my arms and stare out, captivated by the view.

'How do you get any work done?' I say breathlessly.

'I don't have time to appreciate the view,' she says matter-of-factly. 'That's why my back faces the window.'

I don't respond, just stare out in silence. Ruby doesn't press me. She just sits quietly, waiting for me to speak.

I turn around and face her. 'Okay,' I say grimly, 'let's write that letter of demand.'

She grins at me. 'I thought you'd never ask.'

The next morning I arrive at work groomed to within an inch of my life. My make-up is dramatic, my hair voluminous and ready to be tossed and flicked at whim. I walk through reception confidently. I do trip over a slight hitch in the carpet, but that's entirely beside the point.

'Good morning, Shae,' I say with exaggerated cheerfulness.

'Esma! Welcome back! How are you feeling?'

'Great. Is Danny in?'

'Yes, he's in his office. He's been a bloody tyrant while you've been off sick. Thank God you're back. You're the only one who knows how to deal with him.' She starts to fill me in on the office gossip, but I cut her off.

'How about we chat later this morning? I've got work to catch up on.'

I storm straight towards Danny's office, knock once and barge in. 'Good morning, Danny!' I cry buoyantly.

His face positively lights up when he sees me. He jumps up. 'Esma! You're back! How are you feeling?'

'Fine thanks, Danny,' I say, falling into a chair, crossing my legs and fixing him with a dazzling smile. 'I've finished the proposal you wanted me to do.'

The idiot seems to have forgotten. 'Proposal? What proposal?'

'The proposal you asked me to prepare after you withdrew your offer of promotion.' I flash him an insincere smile.

'Oh, come on, Esma,' he says jovially, 'don't be like that. It wasn't an official offer. And it wasn't an official withdrawal, either.'

A look from me silences him. He sits back down in his chair, loosens his tie.

'Well, here it is,' I say grimly, throwing a manilla folder down in front of him. 'Please read through it now.'

'Okay,' he says warily. He opens up the folder and starts to read aloud, looking queasier and paler with every second.

Dear Mr Blagojevic,

You recently informed me in writing that I would be promoted and receive a pay increase prior to the end of this financial year. But then, for no apparent reason, the offer of promotion was withdrawn. Despite having previously praised my performance, you have now asked me to effectively make a case as to why I deserve a promotion, and how I can go beyond my KPIs.

Accordingly, here are my thoughts.

1. It's very difficult to concentrate on work when I am experiencing a constant feeling of slight anxiety. Will you, my boss, pay me an inappropriate compliment today? Will you discuss your private life? Confide in me about your wife's ovulation cycle? Ask my opinion about what kind of lingerie to buy for her? Or concoct fake weekend work meetings to get me into the office to spend some time alone with you?

2. Although this office has state-of-the-art IT systems, I assume Facebook was never meant to be part of our online work communications. I would appreciate you explaining to me why you feel you have the right to pose inappropriate and suggestive messages on my Facebook wall.

3. Furthermore, while I have provided my mobile telephone number for work purposes, I am equally confused as to why you feel the need to send me text messages.

Given your fondness for communicating via Facebook, I am posting these thoughts onto your wall, hoping you will be able to respond.

Kind regards, Esma

'What the fuck?'

'What's wrong, Danny?' I ask innocently.

He launches at his keyboard and starts typing frantically. 'The fuck you put this on Facebook!'

I fold my arms across my chest and stare at him with a smug expression on my face.

'My wife will see. Everybody will see! What the fuck do

you think— It's not there? When did you post it? Where the fuck is it?' He furiously jabs at the keyboard. Beads of sweat have formed on his forehead and his eyes are bulging.

'Relax,' I say coolly. 'It's not there ... yet.'

He snaps his head up.

'I haven't posted it yet.'

He sinks back into his chair and lets out a long, slow breath. 'Thank fucking hell.'

'I've got something else for you, Danny,' I say, standing up. I take out an envelope.

'What the hell is this?' he demands, ripping it open. He unfolds the letter inside, printed on Ruby's law firm's letterhead.

'That's a letter of demand. I've been putting up with your sexual harassment for too long. I've got two words for you, Danny: constructive dismissal. Because I'm hereby giving you notice. I refuse to spend one more day as a victim of sexual harassment.'

'You have got to be kidding me,' he says with a bitter laugh. 'What kind of perverted twist on things is this?'

'I've got emails, text messages, Facebook wall posts, diary entries – I've got a mass of evidence that will sink you if I take you to court. And take you to court I will if you don't comply with my lawyer's demands. I want a payout to compensate me for the crap you've put me through.'

'Like hell I'll pay you this!'

'You're getting off lightly, believe me. Call your lawyer and see how much you'll be paying me if I take you to court. I'll fight you, Danny. All the way.'

'And you expect me to believe you'd go to court with this? Don't you think I've got stuff on you?'

I laugh out loud. 'Stuff on *me*? What on earth could you have on me, Danny? All you've ever done is lament how *innocent* and *naive* and *pure* I am. The only reason you've taunted me is because you never *had* anything on me.'

He gives me a look of such pure rage that for a second I'm worried he's going to hit me.

'Who knows about this?' he eventually asks in a tight voice.

'My lawyer. And me.'

'If I pay you this, I'll be ruined.'

'Do you think I'm an idiot? This company is raking it in. I'm letting you walk away from all this unscathed. Don't you get it? You've broken the law. Sexual harassment is illegal. I don't come to work to hear jokes about my sexuality, or to be asked advice about underwear, or to discuss your sex life. I come to do my work and I expect to be treated with respect and dignity.'

I throw my resignation letter onto his desk. 'Here, read this too. I'm officially resigning. So pick up the phone and speak to my lawyer, because I never want to have to speak to you again.'

I turn on my heel, wrench open the door and storm out of his office. Breathing out, I instantly feel ten kilos lighter. I'm too pumped to wait for the lift so I rush down the fire-exit stairs.

When I'm finally outside the building my legs are wobbly and I'm shaking. I call Ruby.

'I did it!' I shout.

She screams.

'It was exhilarating!' I start to laugh hysterically, and put my hand up against the wall of the building to balance myself.

'Are you still in the office?' she asks.

'No! I got out of there fast. I bet my life he'll be on the phone to you soon.' I have another giggling fit. 'As of this moment I don't have a job,' I gasp. 'And I've essentially just blackmailed my boss!'

'You've done him a favour. He would be a stinking carcass at the end of a court case, believe me. I'm so proud of you.'

'You should have seen his face when he started reading!' I calm down a little and say, 'Ruby, thank you.'

'Esma, if you ever get into trouble again and don't tell us, I'll whip your arse. I'm a boot-camp graduate, remember? Don't say I didn't warn you.'

It's the sum total of all the little things that have kept us together as friends. The thing about the four of us is that we've got history. We did our first European adventure together. I remember when Lisa and I were trapped in Madame Tussauds after closing time and had to scream to be let out. I remember the time we were all in Amsterdam. It was snowing. A junkie walked into Ruby, accused her of bumping him and making him drop his cocaine into the snow, and then demanded money. Nirvana, Lisa and I were freaking out, but Ruby barked back at him that cocaine on snow was a convenient story and that she'd fight him rather than give him money. Scared, he ran away. I remember Nirvana and I had a crush on a guy who went to university with us. We used to swap information about his movements on campus; find out the spare periods in his timetable so we could stalk him together. Pretty pathetic when you come to think of it, but we had lots of fun doing it.

That we're all opinionated and passionate has meant we've argued and fought. There were times during our trip overseas when we'd have to split for a couple of hours just to get some time apart before we killed each other (Nirvana and Ruby would always clash over the sightseeing itinerary). But we've never argued for long, which is why I take it upon myself to declare another No Sex in the City get-together tonight at a fabulous restaurant in Paddington that Ruby recommends, having been there the night before with Alex.

Ruby and I arrive together first, then Nirvana, followed moments later by Lisa. At first Nirvana and Lisa are teeth-jarringly nice to one another and it's so nauseating to watch that I bang my fork on the table and bellow, 'For crying out loud, would you both stop being so immature!'

'What are you talking about?' Lisa says.

'All this – this politeness!' I wave my hand as though I'm swatting a fly.

Nirvana half-laughs. 'Since when is being polite imma-ture?'

'That's more like it!' I declare.

'Esma, what on *earth* are you going on about?' Nirvana says.

'There's obviously tension between you both. So just sort it out and move on.'

Lisa lets out a sigh. 'You know something? You're insufferable when you're being a do-gooder.'

'Thanks,' I say, grinning madly at her.

Ruby stretches her arms in the air. 'Esma's right. Just get it over and done with, will you? I'll start you off. Nirvana, you overreacted and completely misinterpreted Lisa's intentions. After years of friendship, you should know better.' Ruby smacks her hands together and turns to Lisa. 'As for you, Lisa, we get that you acted ethically, but you have to appreciate that Nirvana felt hurt by your silence. Now, it's time to kiss and make up because I swear to God I'm not going to allow two of the most intelligent and amazing women I know to fight over a guy.' Ruby shudders at the prospect.

'It was never about a guy,' Nirvana says curtly. She twists her body to face Lisa. 'The fact is, you knew something pretty significant about my future sister-in-law but didn't tell me. I get that you have a *code of ethics*.' She struggles not to roll her eyes. 'But what hurts is that Neela wasn't some random person in the street, she was part of the family I was marrying into, and you still treated the whole situation so objectively.'

'I agonised over telling you,' Lisa says. 'It's not as though it was an easy decision—'

'I would have thought our friendship made it easy.'

'Would you have told Anil about Neela? Or kept it to yourself?'

Nirvana can't answer that question.

'The thing is,' Lisa says softly, 'I couldn't be sure that Neela wasn't wrong about how Anil would react. I also didn't want to risk bad-mouthing him to you in case it was an overreaction on her part. You were in love. How could I risk everything because of what Neela told me?'

'Well, what did she tell you?'

'She said she thought that if he knew about the baby he'd try to persuade her to stay in a bad marriage for the sake of the baby and so as not to lose face by being a single mum.'

Nirvana sucks in her breath and sits in silence, mulling over Lisa's words.

'From my point of view,' Lisa says, 'that was troubling on many levels, *if* it was true. But I didn't know if it was true.'

'It probably was true,' Nirvana says quietly. 'The last I heard, Neela went back to Sunil. Anil was so glad. I can't be certain but I got the impression he was more pleased that she'd avoided scandal than concerned about whether it was the right decision.'

'I'm sorry again,' Lisa says gently, placing her hand tentatively on Nirvana's arm. 'Hurting you was the last thing on my mind.'

'I know.' Nirvana sighs. 'Anyway, it's all over between me and Anil. It doesn't matter.'

'He didn't speak to his mum?' I ask.

'He did. But it was a half-hearted effort. I'm just not prepared to take the risk.' She draws in a deep breath and smiles bravely. 'I'm devastated, but I know I've made the right decision. Anil isn't worth fighting for. Plus, with everything that's happened with Neela, I don't know if I want to be a part of a family that's so obsessed with how other people see them. There's no breathing space in that kind of life. I don't think it has anything to do with Indian culture. I think it's Anil's family, particularly his mum, who sees life as a competition.'

'You deserve better than that,' Lisa says.

Nirvana lets out a laugh. 'Well, it looks like I'm back in the singles club again. You're the only one flying the *I'm in Love* banner now, Ruby.'

Ruby raises her eyebrows. 'Actually, I think Esma has some news to share.'

I grin at them and Lisa grabs my arm. 'You made a decision?'

'Aydin.'

Lisa punches her fist in the air. 'Yes!'

'We want the full story,' Nirvana says.

I tell them about Danny's Facebook message and Metin's reaction. And then I start to tell them about Aydin, but as I speak, it occurs to me that I'm gushing, and I suddenly feel guilty for Nirvana's sake. I cut my long story short, but Nirvana's not a fool.

'Don't you dare,' she warns me. 'I know what you're doing and you better get it out of your head.'

'I know, I know ... but it's still so raw for you.'

'Esma, please shut up.'

'Wow, Nirvana,' Ruby says gleefully. 'We've had sarcasm

and rudeness in the same evening. This is wonderful progress.'

Nirvana ignores Ruby. 'I can't believe I even have to say this, but I'm going to say it once and once only: if any of you ever thinks I'd begrudge you happiness because of what happened with Anil, then you can forget knowing me. Got it?'

'Loud and clear,' I say.

'That's not a problem for me,' Ruby says, raising her glass. 'I love you to bits but I'll be gushing about Alex until you tell me to shut up.'

'As for me,' Lisa says, 'I'm happy to hold the fort in defence of singledom for a long time to come, so don't worry.'

We stuff our faces with dinner and a decadent dessert. At Nirvana's insistence, we confess to her our first impressions of Anil, and she laughs so hard that she has to get up and run to the bathroom to pee. At the end of the night, we stumble out of the restaurant, drunk on an evening of memories and laughter.

'We can never split up,' I say as we walk to our cars, arms linked. 'I won't let it happen. Because if we do we'll lose one of the best things about us – our punchline!'

'What are you talking about, Esma?' Ruby asks.

I grin at them. 'A Christian, a Muslim, a Jew and a Hindu walk into a café ...'

Epilogue

Ruby and Alex are seeing each other, despite her family initially resisting the idea that Ruby, first-class honours in law, rising star at her law firm, should fall for a guy who, in her dad's words, 'runs around a playground screaming at people to do push-ups'. Ruby gave them one week to grieve the loss of their rich Greek lawyer/pharmacist/brain surgeon fantasy, and after that it was zero tolerance.

I don't think I've ever seen Ruby so happy. Not every relationship has to make sense from the outside. Sometimes the most seemingly incompatible couples are the ones who, years on, still giggle under the sheets, read each other's moods from across a crowded room, effortlessly manage small acts of kindness.

Nirvana, got the fairy-tale ending because she had the sense to realise Anil wasn't going to give it to her. While there are nights she calls me in the middle of an emotional eating binge, begging me for an honest answer as to whether she's made the right decision, by morning she's back to her senses, relieved that she had the courage to end it when she did.

As for Lisa, well, she's still happily single and isn't the slightest bit interested in changing that unless somebody truly amazing comes along. Until that happens, she'll continue resisting her mother's matchmaking attempts and enjoy the life she's making for herself.

What about me?

My parents put our house on the market and received an offer that's allowed them to pay off the loan to the bank and buy a two-bedroom town house in a cheaper suburb on the other side of Sydney. They move in a month and are in the process of packing now.

It's not going to be easy adjusting to a new neighbourhood and community. Moving into a place that's half the size of our house. Leaving the home in which they've spent most of their married life. But on the bright side, it means Dad can work less and my parents can spend more time together. Everything that's happened to them has taught me that marriages can fail over and over again, but it's not so much the failing as the trying that counts.

Danny paid me out. And I have it on good authority from Veronica that he doesn't so much as make sustained eye contact with female staff any more. Danny and his wife separated. Oh, and apparently the baby isn't his. It's Marco's.

I have a new job in a large recruiting firm and my boss is everything a boss should be: professional and courteous – and he only comes undone when it's budget time, not when I'm wearing a skirt or high heels.

And what happened with Aydin?

Oh, nothing much. It's not like I'm happy almost every moment I'm with him.

It's not like he proposed to me.

Well, okay, he did. And I am.

But hang on. Don't get too excited. There was no sparkling sapphire buried in a baked pudding. No getting down on one knee on a twilight ferry on the harbour. No ring presented in a hot-air balloon.

For one thing, how would my parents fit in the hot-air balloon with us? Not to mention that my mother is terrified of heights and not that fond of ferries either.

So Aydin's options were a little limited. He ended up coming to my house (with his parents) to officially propose to me (and my parents).

Also present were Senem and Farouk. And Aydin's sister, maternal aunt and uncle. And their two sons. And Aydin's best friend. And his business partner, who is also his cousin. And my cousin who, although three times removed on my father's side, had to be invited if my parents were to avoid a massive family feud. Plus my grandmother in Turkey, who watched (and commented loudly) via Skype ('It's about time! I thought I was going to die before seeing Esma engaged! Hurry up and set a wedding date. I've got one foot in the grave!').

And that small party was simply in honour of Aydin making an official promise to marry me. With such a big audience to propose to, Dad's Rule of Six seemed quite modest in comparison.

Before he proposed, and in deference to the stock-standard 'you marry a family' kind of talk, I thought I should warn my parents about Aydin's brother. I wanted to get their objections over and done with as quickly as possible. Once again, I misjudged them. As it turns out, the friend who had recommended Aydin to my parents had already told my mother.

The wedding is in six months. That's because Aydin's sick of taking a cold shower after every date given we're *both* sticking to our 'No Sex in the City' rule until we're married (oh, and to be really cruel, I haven't let him kiss me again. I don't trust myself if he does).

The wedding plans are enormous fun – if you enjoy family arguments over seating arrangements and the propriety of a bridal registry. But Aydin and I grin and bear it. It's not so bad because, to Aydin's relief, most of the work has already been done, seeing as I've been planning this for years.

My class at the Refugee Centre are all excited too – so much so that the documentary they're working on with Aydin is in danger of becoming a film about weddings.

All the failed matches and arranged dates have been for a reason. Because waiting for me at the end of that long line was Aydin. The One. Mr Right. My soulmate.

And the wait was worth it.

Acknowledgements

I'd like to first confess that I probably had too much fun using the horror matchmaking stories of family and friends when writing this book. To protect their dignity, I will avoid surnames and thank them for sharing their humiliations with me by using their first name only: Nada, Abear, Jenny, Heba, Nahla, Reham, Vanessa, Gada, Omima, Monica and Sally. Having access to their experiences and anecdotes made this book even more fun to write. I'd also like to thank Heba's dad for inventing the Rule of Six, because the comedic potential in that rule far outweighs any humiliation Heba suffered as a result of it being imposed on her.

Thanks also to Maha for the Tool/mosh-pit story.

I'd also like to take this opportunity to confirm that no, this is *not* my autobiography, and no, there is absolutely nothing about Esma's life or family that is remotely close to mine. Or Nirvana's, Lisa's or Ruby's lives for that matter. Or Esma's married friends. Okay, scandal averted.

Sincere thanks are due to my family for their unending support.

Thank you to my agent, Sheila Drummond, for being so caring and for *always* looking after me. And thank you to my publisher, Claire Craig, and editor Julia Stiles, both of whose intelligence, wisdom and piercing insight always help me in doing justice to my early drafts. Thanks also to Catherine Day and Clara Finlay.